HOLY GHOST

ALSO BY JOHN SANDFORD

Rules of Prey
Shadow Prey
Eyes of Prey
Silent Prey
Winter Prey
Night Prey
Mind Prey
Sudden Prey
Secret Prey
Certain Prey
Easy Prey
Chosen Prey
Mortal Prey
Naked Prey
Hidden Prey
Broken Prey
Invisible Prey
Phantom Prey
Wicked Prey
Storm Prey
Buried Prey
Stolen Prey
Silken Prey
Field of Prey
Gathering Prey
Extreme Prey
Golden Prey
Twisted Prey

KIDD NOVELS

The Fool's Run
The Empress File
The Devil's Code
The Hanged Man's Song

VIRGIL FLOWERS NOVELS

Dark of the Moon
Heat Lightning
Rough Country
Bad Blood
Shock Wave
Mad River
Storm Front
Deadline
Escape Clause
Deep Freeze

STAND-ALONE NOVELS

Saturn Run
The Night Crew
Dead Watch

BY JOHN SANDFORD AND MICHELE COOK

Uncaged
Outrage
Rampage

JOHN SANDFORD

HOLY GHOST

SIMON &
SCHUSTER

London · New York · Sydney · Toronto · New Delhi

A CBS COMPANY

First published in the United States by G.P. Putnam's Sons, 2018

First published in Great Britain by Simon & Schuster UK Ltd, 2018
A CBS COMPANY

3 5 7 9 10 8 6 4 2

Simon & Schuster UK Ltd
1st Floor
222 Gray's Inn Road
London WC1X 8HB

Simon & Schuster Australia, Sydney
Simon & Schuster India, New Delhi

www.simonandschuster.co.uk
www.simonandschuster.com.au
www.simonandschuster.co.in

A CIP catalogue record for this book
is available from the British Library

ISBN: 978 1 4711 7487 2
Trade Paperback ISBN: 978 1 4711 7488 9
Ebook ISBN: 978 1 4711 7489 6

Printed and bound by CPI Group (UK) Ltd, Croydon, CR0 4YY

For Mickey

HOLY GHOST

1

Wardell Holland, the mayor of Wheatfield, Minnesota, was sitting in the double-wide he rented from his mother, a Daisy Match Grade pellet rifle in his hands, shooting flies. His mother suspected he let the flies in on purpose so he could shoot at them. He denied it, but he was lying.

He was tracking a bull-sized bluebottle when the doorbell croaked. Like most other things in the place, there was something not quite right with it, but not quite wrong enough to fix. In this case, the bell probably indicated that the beer had arrived. The kid had taken his own sweet time about it; school had been out for an hour.

"Come in," Holland shouted.

The fly tracked out of the bedroom and lazily circled through the living room and toward the kitchen. He picked it up with the sight, and the kid outside yelled, "Don't go shooting—"

POP! A clear miss. The fly juked as the pellet whipped past, then circled around the sink and out of sight. The pellet ricocheted once and stuck in the fiberboard closet door by the entrance.

"Hey! Hey! You crazy fuckin' pillhead, you're gonna put my eye out."

Holland shouted, "He's gone, you can come in."

John Jacob Skinner edged through the door, keeping an eye on Holland, who was sprawled on the couch, his prosthetic foot propped up on the arm, the rifle lying across his stomach. Skinner, who was seventeen, said, "Goddamnit, Wardell . . ."

"I won't shoot, even if I see him . . . though he is a trophy-sized beast."

Skinner eased into the room, carrying a six-pack of Coors Light. "You want one now or you want it in the refrigerator? They're cold."

"Now, of course. I shoot better with a little alcohol in me."

"Right." Skinner pulled loose two cans, tossed one to Holland, put four in the refrigerator, popped the top on the last one, and took a drink.

Skinner resembled his name: he was six foot three, skinny, with long red hair that never seemed overly clean, a razor-thin face, prominent Adam's apple, and bony shoulders and hips. He had about a billion freckles.

He'd shown a minor talent for basketball in junior high but had quit the game when he'd went to high school. He'd told friends that he needed nonschool time to think since it was impossible to think when he was actually in school.

The coach had asked, "Now, what in the Sam Hill do you want to think for, Skinner? Where's that gonna get you?"

He didn't know the answer to that question, but he did know that being the second man on the lowest level, the 1-A Border Conference would get him nowhere at all. He'd thought at least that far ahead.

"One of these days," Skinner said to Holland, "you're gonna catch a ricochet in the dick. Then what? Army gonna give you a wooden cock?"

"Shut up," Holland said.

Holland had been elected mayor as a gag played by the voters of Wheatfield on the town's stuffed shirts. What made it even funnier was that after an unsuccessful first term, Holland was reelected in a landslide. He'd run for office on a variety of slogans his minions had spray-painted on walls around town: "No More Bullshit: We're Fucked," "Beer Sales on Sunday," "I'll Do What I Can."

All of which outshone his opponent's "A Bright Future for Wheatfield," and "Happy Days Are Here Again."

This, in a town whose population had fallen from 829 in 2000 to 721 in the last census, and now probably hovered around 650, leaving behind twenty or thirty empty houses and a bunch of empty apartments over the downtown stores. Half the stores were themselves shuttered, and some had been simply abandoned by their owners, eventually—and pointlessly—taken by the county due to lack of property tax payments.

This, in a town where fifteen years earlier the city council had purchased in a corrupt deal from the then mayor a forty-acre tract on the edge of town. The town had run water and an electric cable out to it, and advertised it on a lonely I-90 billboard as the "Wheatfield Industrial Park." In fifteen years, it had not attracted a single business, and, in the estimation of voters, never would.

Therefore, Holland.

Holland, a former first lieutenant in the Army, had lost a foot in Afghanistan and lived on a military disability pension, which, in

Wheatfield, was good enough. He'd refused the thirty-dollars-per-meeting mayor's salary, and had rented out the industrial park to a local corn farmer, so the forty acres was finally producing a bit of money. Sixty-eight hundred dollars a year, to be exact.

When he was feeling industrious, Holland would limp around town with a Weedwacker, trimming grass and brush from around stop signs, fire hydrants, and drainage ditches. Once a month or so, he'd run the town's riding lawn mower around the local park and Little League ball field, which was more than any other mayor had done. None of that took too long in a metropolis of 650 souls.

Skinner asked Holland, "Remember how you said you were gonna do what you can for the town? When you were elected?"

"I was deeply sincere," Holland said, insincerely.

"I know."

Skinner dragged a chair around from the breakfast bar, straddled it backwards, facing Holland on the couch, and said, "I was walking by the Catholic church last night."

"Good," Holland said. And, "Why don't you open the door and let a couple more flies in? I'm running out of game, and that big bastard's hiding."

"There was some Mexicans coming out of the church," Skinner continued. "They're meeting there on Wednesday nights. Praying and shit."

"I know that," Holland said. He was distracted as the bull bluebottle hove into view. He lifted the rifle.

Skinner said, "Honest to God, Holland, you shoot that rifle, I'm gonna take this fuckin' can of beer and I'm gonna sink it in your fuckin' forehead. Put that rifle down and listen to what I'm saying."

The fly reversed itself and disappeared, and Holland took the rifle down. "You were walking by the Catholic church . . ."

The church had been all but abandoned by the archdiocese. Not enough Catholics to keep it going and not enough local hippies to buy it as a dance studio or enough prostitutes to buy it as a massage parlor. There was a packing plant forty miles down the Interstate, though, with lots of Mexican workers, and the housing was cheap enough in Wheatfield that it had lately attracted two dozen of the larger Mexican families.

The diocese had given a key to the church to a representative of the Wheatfield Mexicans, who were doing a bit to maintain it and to pay the liability insurance. Every once in a while, a Spanish-speaking priest from Minneapolis would drop by to say a Mass.

Skinner: "I got to thinking . . ."

"Man, that always makes me nervous," Holland said. "Know what I'm saying?"

"What I thought of was, how to make Wheatfield the busiest town on the prairie. Big money for everybody. For a long time. We could get a cut ourselves, if we could buy out Henry Morganstat. Could we get a mortgage, you think?"

Holland sighed. "I got no idea how a seventeen-year-old high school kid could be so full of shit as you are. A hundred and sixty pounds of shit in a twelve-pound bag. So tell me, then finish your beer and go away and leave me with my fly."

Skinner told him.

Holland had nothing to say for a long time. He just stared across the space between them. Then he finally said, "Jesus Christ, that could work, J.J. You say it'd cost six hundred dollars? I mean, I got six hundred dollars. I'd have to look some stuff up on the internet. And that thing about buying out Henry . . . I think he'd take twenty grand for the place. I got the GI Bill and my mother would probably loan me enough for the rest—at nine percent, the miserable bitch—but . . . Jesus Christ . . ."

"I'd want a piece of the action," Skinner said.

"Well, of course. You came up with the idea, I'll come up with the money. We go fifty-fifty," Holland said.

"That's good. I'd hate to get everything in place and then have to blackmail you for my share," Skinner said.

Holland's eyes narrowed: "We gotta talk to some guys . . ."

Skinner said, "We can't talk to *any* guys. This is you and me . . . If we . . ." He realized that Holland's eyes were tracking past him and he turned and saw the fly headed back to the kitchen. "Goddamnit, Holland, look at me. We're talking here about saving the town. Making big money, too."

Holland said, "We'll have to tell at least one more person. We need a woman."

Skinner scratched his nose. "Yeah, I thought of that. There's Jennie. She can keep her mouth shut."

"You still nailin' her?"

"From time to time, yeah, when Larry isn't around."

"You know, you're gonna knock her up sooner or later," Holland said. "She's ripe as a plum, and I'd guess her baby clock is about to go off. What is she anyway, thirty-three? When that red-haired bun pops outta the oven, you best be on a Greyhound to Hawaii."

"Yeah, yeah, maybe, but she'd do this, and she'd be perfect. Who else would we get anyway?"

"I dunno, I . . ."

The fly tracked around the room again, and Holland said, "Shhhh . . . he's gonna land." He lifted the rifle and pointed it over

Skinner's shoulder toward the sink. Skinner lurched forward onto the floor to get down and out of the way as Holland pulled the trigger.

The fly disappeared in a puff of guts and broken wings.

Holland looked down at Skinner and whispered, "Got him. It's like . . . It's like some kinda sign."

2

Five months later, Mayor Wardell Holland told Virgil Flowers that there weren't any available motel rooms in Wheatfield, and not even over in Blue Earth, down I-90. He'd checked. "Your best bet is Mankato. It's an hour away."

"I *live* in Mankato," Virgil said. "That's my best shot?"

"Well, we've only got one operating motel, the Tarweveld Inn. It's booked solid five months out, with a waiting list. There's a Motel 6 coming online in a couple of months, but that won't help. You need to get down here. And, I mean, right now. Today!"

"I didn't know things were that tight," Virgil said. "I can do it, but it'll be a pain in the ass driving back and forth every day."

"Okay, had a thought," Holland said. "Let me make a call—gimme ten minutes."

Virgil hung up, dropped the phone in his pocket, dragged a spoon through the pot of Cream of Wheat on the stove, and shouted, "It's ready." At his knee, Honus, the yellow dog, looked up anxiously, always worried that he wouldn't get his fair share, although he always did.

A moment later, Frankie Nobles eased into the kitchen, barefoot, wearing a pink quilted housecoat straight out of Target. She was a short, blond woman, busty, with a slender waist, and normally rosy-cheeked. On this morning, her face was a greenish white, and she had one hand on her stomach. "Why don't I remember these parts? Five kids, and I never remember."

Morning sickness. She burped, grimaced.

"Bad?"

She thought for a second, said, "About a four on a scale of one to ten. That's not too bad. When I get to a seven, you'll know it."

Virgil was spooning the Cream of Wheat into a bowl. "Tell me when."

"Keep going," she said, "I'm starving. At least I can keep that stuff down."

All three of them—Virgil, Frankie, and Honus the yellow dog—were eating Cream of Wheat, and two of them were reading different pieces of the *Free Press,* when Holland called back. "Okay, I got you a place. Mother-in-law apartment, the local hairdresser and her husband. Nice folks. Separate entrance, and you get a refrigerator and a microwave. Fifty bucks a day. Extra ten for housekeeping, if you want it."

"Aw, jeez, I dunno," Virgil said. "What happened to the mother-in-law?"

"Dead. Choked to death on one of those vegan fake-meat burgers. That was a few years back. And listen, this place isn't exactly what you might think—it's not a dump in the basement. They fixed it up nice, been renting it out to pilgrims. I've seen it. The only reason it's available is, Roy's picky about who they rent it to."

"All right, I'll take it," Virgil said. "I'll be there by noon. Where will I find you?"

"I run the local store," the mayor said. "We're a block north of downtown, across from the Catholic church. Skinner and Holland, Eats and Souvenirs. You can't miss it."

When will you be back?" Frankie asked when Virgil got off the phone.

"Any time you need me—it's only an hour from here," Virgil said. "With lights and siren, fifty minutes max."

"I'll be out at the farm, the boys can take care of me," she said. They were sitting in Virgil's kitchen, the May sunlight streaming through the window over the sink, a pretty Sunday morning in Mankato.

Less than a month away from summer and the longest day of the year, the spring so far had been cool and generously wet without being offensive, and through the window they could see the pink blossoms on the neighbor's apple tree. "It'll be a nice drive down there. You be careful. I always worry when you're dealing with a nut."

"We don't know he's a nut," Virgil said. "Or she. Could be a woman."

"Not likely. When was the last time you heard of a random sniper who was female?"

"Don't even know he's a sniper," Virgil said. "There might be a motive that ties the two shootings together. That would make him a shooter but not a random sniper."

"You just said 'he' and 'him,'" Frankie pointed out.

"That's because you're right," Virgil said. "It's a guy."

Frankie went to shower and get dressed while Virgil got his traveling gear together, which, as usual, bummed out Honus. Honus was a dog of no specific breed, although there had to be some Labrador DNA in the mix: he loved to go out to the swimming hole. That wouldn't happen for another few weeks, as the water coming out of the spring uphill from the hole was essentially liquid ice.

Virgil gave him a scratch, then roughed up his head. He was getting neurotic about the dog, which the dog took advantage of. Frankie never made him feel bad about going out on a case, and she loved to hear about them afterwards. Honus, on the other hand, always acted like this was it: Virgil was ditching him, never to play baseball again. The dog could chase down grounders forever.

Virgil was a tall man, thin, athletic, with longish blond hair and an easy smile. He was wearing a "got mule?" T-shirt, purchased in the parking lot at a Gov't Mule show a year earlier in Des Moines, an inky-blue corduroy sport coat, and bootcut blue jeans over cordovan cowboy boots.

As an agent of the Bureau of Criminal Apprehension, he should have been wearing a suit with a blue or white oxford cloth shirt, a dull but coordinated nylon necktie, and high-polished black wingtips. What the BCA didn't know, he figured, couldn't hurt him.

Since he'd be close to home, he packed only one extra pair of jeans, with five days' worth of everything else. To the clothing, he added a pump shotgun and a box of shells. A Glock 9mm semiautomatic pistol went in his Tahoe's gun safe with two extra magazines. If he needed more than fifty-one shots at somebody, he deserved to die.

When he was packed, he considered the boat. He rarely went anywhere in Minnesota without towing the boat in case an emergency fishing opportunity should jump out in front of him. This time, though, he decided to leave it. There wasn't fishable water anywhere near Wheatfield, unless you liked carp and bullheads. And he was only an hour from home, so, if he needed to, he could always come and get the boat.

Frankie reappeared to kiss him good-bye and give him a few more minutes of essential advice: "Don't get shot. With your rug rat chewing on my ankles, I'm gonna need your help."

"I'll be back for the ultrasound, even if I haven't gotten anywhere on the shooting."

"Better be," she said. The ultrasound was scheduled for the following week.

Virgil rubbed his chin on Honus the yellow dog's forehead and then he was on his way, turning south down Highway 169 and out of town.

Virgil had passed through Wheatfield a couple of times but had never stopped. He knew little about the place, other than what he'd read in the newspaper stories, of which there had been many in the past few months. It had been settled by Dutch pioneers in the nineteenth century, who gave the town the name Tarweveld, which means "wheatfield." The Dutch were followed by a bunch of Bavarians, then finally the Irish, few of whom could pronounce the town's name. By 1900, even the Americanized inhabitants were stumbling over it, and, in 1902, the name was officially changed to Wheatfield. But the Dutch influence remained: just about every other lawn had a miniature windmill on it, the product of a manic carpenter who loved building them and insisted on doing it.

Like a lot of prairie towns, Wheatfield had been dying. Minnesota and the surrounding states had plenty of jobs—Minnesota's unemployment rate was three percent, and Iowa's was even lower, down in the two's. The problem was, the jobs were in the larger towns, the smaller towns having less and less to offer their residents, especially the younger ones.

Wheatfield had reached its peak population of 1,500 as a farm service center after World War II. The Interstate had severely damaged its businesses—it was too easy to get to the larger towns—and a regional Walmart had pretty much finished them off. There was still a cafe and a gas station and a hardware store, and a couple of other businesses, but they'd been moribund as well.

Not anymore, thanks be to God.

The previous winter, on a Wednesday night between Thanksgiving and Christmas, the Virgin Mary had appeared at St. Mary's Catholic Church before a congregation of mostly Mexican worshippers, with a few devout Anglos mixed in. Unlike other Marian apparitions, as her appearances were called, this one had been documented by numerous cell phone cameras.

The night after the first apparition, the church had been jammed with worshippers and the simply curious, as word of the miracle spread. There had not yet been a priest in attendance, so a deacon was presiding when the Virgin appeared the second time, floating in the air behind the altar.

The Virgin spoke. According to television commentators on Telemundo, she said, *"Bienaventurados los mansos, porque ellos heredaran la tierra,"* or, "Blessed are the meek, for they shall inherit the earth." The same commentators said the Virgin didn't have a very good accent in any dialect of Spanish that they knew of, but somebody quickly pointed out that she couldn't be expected to since her native language would have been Aramaic; or, perhaps, she was speaking what would have been closer to Latin. A few skeptics suggested a local accent, more of a oodala-oodala-oodala Minnesota version of Spanish.

A panel of experts convened by CNN agreed that the Virgin's appearance could cost Donald Trump three to four percentage points in the next presidential election by encouraging meek female voters who wished to inherit the earth. A similar panel on Fox argued her appearance would certainly increase the vote for Donald Trump, possibly by as much as five percentage points, by encouraging the religious right.

A television reporter from the Twin Cities had been interviewing people outside the church when the second apparition occurred, and when worshippers began screaming, she rushed inside. Her cameraman tripped and fell going up the stairs, was nearly trampled by people fighting to get past him. He managed to get video of only the very end of the apparition as the figure of the Virgin faded away.

But he got *something.*

The reporter herself had seen and heard the Virgin.

At the end of her report, she had tearfully confessed, "I came to St. Mary's as a nonbeliever, but now . . ." She fell to her knees: "I believe. I BELIEVE!"

She went worldwide, and a week later was offered a job as a weather girl on an L.A. television station, an offer she accepted.

As Virgil rolled past a million acres of newly sprouted cornfields on the way to Wheatfield, he realized that there were damn few wheatfields around anymore. Everything had gone to beans and corn. A patch of oats might pop up here or there, recognizable by the bluish tint, and there were spotty plots of commercial vegetables—cucumbers, string beans—but that was about it.

On the animal side, there were pigs and cows and some riding horses.

One interesting thing about spring, Virgil thought, especially a wet one, was how you could identify the livestock without ever seeing them. Cow shit was a definite stink, but a tolerable one. Pig shit, on the other hand, wasn't tolerable: it had a hard ammonia overtone that made the nostrils seize up. Chicken shit had an unpleasant edge, like when damp pinfeathers were scorched off a roaster's carcass; horse shit, on the other hand, was almost sweet, if not actually cheerful.

He thought about it as the car rolled through a swampy smell and decided he might have been working out in the countryside a tad too long, now that he had begun comparing and contrasting the different varieties of livestock odors.

He switched to contemplating the appearance of the Blessed Virgin. Virgil's father was a Lutheran minister, and Virgil had gone to church almost every Sunday and Wednesday from the time he'd been born until he'd gone to the University of Minnesota. At the university, he'd lost his faith in churches as bureaucratic organizations, but hadn't entirely lost his faith in God: if you spent time immersed in nature, in his opinion, you simply saw too many wonders to casually dismiss the possibility of a deity. Think about a solar eclipse for a while . . .

About the Virgin Mary, he was agnostic. The Lutheran Church, in the years he'd spent in it, seemed confused on the subject of Mary. But if Mary was actually out there somewhere, as a spirit, it didn't seem completely unreasonable that she might decide to appear from time to time.

On the other hand, most Marian apparitions—he'd looked it up on the Wiki—seemed to present themselves to children or deeply religious folk whose testimony was accepted on the basis of faith rather than hard evidence. Skeptics might ascribe these apparitions to religion-based psychological phenomena or even a type of hysteria, if not outright fraud.

Wheatfield was a whole new kind of apparition: the crowd was large, not uniformly religious, and armed with cell phone cameras.

Virgil crossed I-90 and ten minutes later entered Wheatfield. Most similar small prairie towns resembled the main street in the movie *High Noon* before the shooting started—a line of ramshackle stores on an empty street. Wheatfield had all the ramshackle you could hope for but was busy. Even six blocks out, he could see people crossing Main Street and walking along the sidewalks, cars lining the block-long business district.

St. Mary's was located at one end of a block with another church at the other end, a flat green lawn between them. A wooden windmill squatted in the middle of the lawn, looking a lot like a two-story red-white-and-blue fire hydrant, with ten-foot-long vanes that rotated slowly in the breeze. There were no parking spaces on the street, so Virgil drove around the corner, past the Immanuel

Reformed Church. Both churches had parking lots in back; Virgil squeezed into the one behind St. Mary's, along with fifteen other vehicles.

He got out, looked around to orient himself, walked past the church and spotted Skinner & Holland, Eats & Souvenirs, across the street. He let a couple of cars go past, hurried across, and went inside. The place was packed: two women were looking at a rack of three-dimensional postcards of the apparition, several other people were buying soft drinks and snacks and ice-cream cones. A tall, thin, freckled kid was manning the cash register, keeping up a steady sales patter with the customers. Virgil took a Diet Coke out of a cooler, got in line, and, when his turn came, gave the kid a five-dollar bill, and said, "I'm looking for Wardell Holland. I'm with the BCA."

The kid nodded, and turned and shouted, "Wardell! The cop is here."

Virgil said, mildly and in the spirit of educating the young, "Not all cops like to be called cops."

"I heard that," the kid said, handing Virgil his change. "I figure they got bigger problems to deal with than me calling them cops. I'm Skinner, by the way."

Holland pushed through a curtain that closed off the back of the store, looked toward Virgil, and asked, "Virgil?"

"That's me," Virgil said. They shook hands, and Holland said, "Come on back. I'd have given you a free Coke, but Skinner . . ."

Virgil looked back at the kid. "He doesn't like cops?"

"When we had a town cop—that was a few years ago—he'd give Skinner a hard time every time he saw him."

"For what? Dope?"

"No. Skinner would be out driving his girlfriends around, and the guy would pull him over. Every time. He'd yank him out of the car and yell at him," Holland said. "Embarrass him. Skinner hasn't had much time for cops ever since."

"I don't blame him," Virgil said, as he followed Holland through the curtain into the back room. Virgil had had some problems with cops himself as a kid. "The cop sounds like a jerk."

"Well, Skinner usually had an open beer or something . . . and he was twelve at the time."

"Ah."

Holland was Virgil's height, heavier in the chest and shoulders, clean-shaven, with reddish brown hair; he was wearing a blue work shirt and jeans and one boot; his other foot having been replaced with a flexible, sickle-shaped piece of black metal. He waved Virgil at a well-used green easy chair and took a matching chair on the other side of a battered round coffee table. The back room was mostly used for storage, stacks of cardboard cartons full of chips and soft drinks and beer, and smelled exactly like that: cardboard and beer, with an undertone of pizza. In addition to the easy chairs, four more chairs, no two alike, were arranged around a card table, with a microwave on a shelf over a sink on the back wall. The room was apparently used for employee breaks.

"Sheriff will be here in five minutes," Holland said. "We're seriously worried. Right on the edge of desperate. The sheriff says you're the man for the job."

"Nice of him," Virgil said. "I heard about the first shooting, but nobody called us."

"We thought it might be accidental. Lots of hunters around

here, and nobody heard the shot or had any idea where it came from. Could have come from a mile away," Holland said. "The guy who got shot—his name was Harvey Coates, and he and his wife were here from Dubuque—wasn't hurt all that bad. I mean, bad enough, but he won't be crippled, or anything. Dimples on his thigh, is all, after he heals up. Two inches lower and he would have lost a knee. Anyway, we didn't have a slug, didn't have any clues . . . Not much we could do. And, besides, like I said, we thought it might be an accident. We asked the shooter to come forward but nobody did. That's now starting to look . . . idiotic. We should have called you guys."

"Huh. Then yesterday . . ."

"Same deal," Holland said. "Even the exact same time, four-fifteen, or a minute or two after that, just before the first evening service at St. Mary's. The second time, the shooter—whoever he is—took out a woman. She got hit in the hip, the shot went all the way through. She won't die, either, but she's in a lot worse shape than Coates. Busted the ball in her hip joint; she's got bone splinters all through her pelvic area. She's gonna need a full hip replacement before she can walk again. She's over at the Mayo."

"You say there's no bullet?"

"Nothing. No idea of where it ended up," Holland said. "Both times, the people were waiting at the corner and they were all talking with each other and turning this way and that. We know where the slugs entered and exited, but since we don't know their positions, exactly how they were standing, we don't have a good idea of where the bullet came from. The deputies talked to both of the victims and they themselves don't know where they were standing. I believe—"

From outside, Skinner shouted, "Wardell! 'Nother cop!"

"Gotta be the sheriff," Holland said. He heaved himself out of the chair and went to the curtain, and called, "Karl. Back here."

Karl Zimmer came through the curtain, spotted Virgil, and said, "It's that fuckin' Flowers. Nice to see you, Virgie."

"Karl," Virgil said, as they shook hands. "I heard you sank your boat."

"That's not a happy subject," Zimmer said. He was a tall man with a gray crewcut and gold-rimmed glasses, wearing a tan Carhartt canvas jacket with a badge sewn on the left side. He looked around, picked a kitchen chair as Holland sank back into his easy chair. "My kid was over on the Cedar, hit a snag, ripped a hole in the hull. Instead of beaching it, he tried to run back to the ramp. Sank it with the engine running full bore, which didn't do it a hell of a lot of good."

"Insurance?" Virgil asked.

"Well, we're arguing about the engine," Zimmer said. "The Farmers guy said hitting the snag and putting a hole in the boat was an accident but wrecking the motor was negligence. We'll get something, but I don't think we'll get it all. Two-year-old Yamaha V MAX 175."

"Ouch," Virgil said.

"Yeah. But, you know, shit happens . . . Did Wardell tell you all about the shootings?"

"He's started to fill me in," Virgil said.

The woman who'd been shot the day before was named Betty Rice and she'd been in town for two days, going to all the church services at St. Mary's, hoping for an apparition. "She was over from Sioux Falls with her sister and a friend," Zimmer said. "Never been here before; none of them had. Same with the fellow who got shot last week."

"You didn't call for a crime scene team?"

"What'd be the point?" Zimmer asked. "We don't know where the shooter was, we don't know where the bullet went."

"Crime scene might've been able to tell where the bullet came from by looking at the blood spatter," Virgil said.

Zimmer shook his head. "We thought about that. The fact is, after she got hit, everybody went running, and, when nobody else got shot, they all came running back. It happened on the grass over there. Everybody was calling for doctors and police, and by the time things got sorted out the whole area had been trampled over for an hour and they'd moved the woman around a couple of times and she was bleeding bad . . . Virgil, I'm saying we had a bloody mudhole, and you couldn't tell anything in there."

Virgil nodded. "Okay."

Holland said, "I think the shot came down from the business district. Maybe from a two-story building on the east side of the street. There are only a dozen of those, but most of the top-floor rooms are still empty. Some of them are being rehabbed to rent, and the walls are open for the construction work. Guy could get up there and have a pretty nice sniper's nest. I borrowed one of Karl's deputies, and we walked up and down over there, never found anything—no shells, nothing. Judging from the wounds, I suspect both people were shot with a .223. Small entry, bigger exit, but not all that big. About as big around as your middle finger, and clean on the edges. So: powerful, small-caliber full metal jacket slug. Maybe military ammo or target stuff."

"You seem to know a lot about it," Virgil said.

Holland lifted his prosthetic foot. "Infantry, Afghanistan. I've seen wounds like it."

"Why do you think it was from a second story?" Virgil asked.

"Clear sight line. Had to be on the east side because on the west side the guy would have to lean way out the window to get the shot off. At that time of day, there are people on the sidewalks and on the street, crossing . . . lots of movement. I think the guy's picking out people who are headed for the church but are standing still, waiting for traffic, when he pulls the trigger. And it occurred to me last night that maybe he isn't trying to kill them."

"Or maybe he's so far out there that he's shooting center of mass and hitting low," Zimmer suggested. "Maybe he's five hundred yards out, doesn't have the elevation on his scope quite right. Maybe on that first shot he was holding on Coates's chest and hit his leg instead. Adjusted the scope to hit higher but didn't know what he was doing, gave it two or three clicks instead of five or six, was holding on Rice's chest but still hit her in the hip. With a woman like Miz Rice, there aren't more than about eight to ten inches between a ball joint shot and a heart shot."

"Lot of maybes in there," Holland said. "I keep thinking psycho in a sniper's nest."

"'Cause you were in the Army," Zimmer said. "Say he's on the second floor—you're saying that he climbs down from there after shooting and carries his rifle to his car and drives away, and nobody sees him?"

Holland scratched his chin. "I can tell you he didn't leave the gun behind or any brass. Me and Don . . ." He turned to Virgil. "Don's the deputy I was working with . . . Anyway, me and Don went over those open places inch by inch, and there aren't any guns hidden up there. Then we got all the store owners to open up the closed places, and there wasn't anything there, either. We even stomped around looking for loose floorboards, and so on, where something might have been hidden. The only hidden thing we found was a porno magazine from 1952. The kind where the guy wears black socks."

"Are there any witnesses still around?" Virgil asked.

Holland nodded toward the curtain. "Skinner was coming across the street to work when Rice got hit. He was one of the first to get to her. When Coates got hit, Father Brice was standing on the church steps, looking right at him. Brice's been coming down once or twice a week from St. Paul; he'll be here tomorrow."

"I'll want to talk to them," Virgil said. To Zimmer: "Suppose Wardell's right—a .223, a long way out. But when he looked, he didn't find any brass. If the guy was in a hurry to leave his spot, he wouldn't want to be fumbling around, looking for the shells. I'm thinking it might not be a semiauto. He could be shooting a bolt-action, which would be more accurate than most semiautos, and would be quite a bit more rare. Maybe you could check gun stores for bolt-action .223s? And maybe for suppressors?"

Zimmer nodded. "We'll start right now. Probably not more than a dozen places between the Cities and here, not more than another dozen between here and Des Moines."

"If he's shooting from a car, he wouldn't have to worry about any of that," Holland said. "He could be shooting anything from anywhere, and shooting from inside a car would muffle the shot."

"Like those Washington, D.C., snipers," Virgil said.

"I was thinking about those guys, but they were travelers . . . I believe this is gonna be a local guy," Holland said. "Somebody who knows his way around downtown, somebody people know, somebody who wouldn't be out of place if he was seen."

"If we get him, it's because we'll have figured out one thing," Virgil said. "That's why—why is he doing it?"

"Unless he's nuts," Zimmer said. "Then there's no 'why' that you can figure out."

"That's the nightmare," Virgil said. "We don't want to go there yet."

3

Virgil, Holland, and Zimmer talked a while longer—Virgil asked whether there were any known anti-Catholic bigots around town, but neither one of them knew of any. Zimmer mentioned that a couple of Nazis lived out in the countryside and were known to have .223 black rifles, but Zimmer said, "They're, basically, play Nazis. I've known both of them since they were born, and they're a couple of dumbasses."

"Doesn't take a real smart guy to pull a trigger," Virgil said.

"No, but they have to get away after they pull it," Zimmer said. "Neither one of those guys could elude his way out of a cocktail lounge."

"If nothing else comes up, I'll take a look at them," Virgil said.

"Call before you do that, and I'll have a deputy go along. They do have those guns," Zimmer said.

As they were leaving the back room, Holland said, "I'll introduce you to Skinner before you leave. He saw Miz Rice get shot."

"This was the kid who was driving around town with his girlfriends and an open beer when he was twelve?"

"You gotta make some allowances for Skinner," Holland said. "He's sort of . . . a genius."

"A genius who runs a cash register?"

"He's a high school senior, part owner of the store, and he's pulling down eighteen hundred dollars a week working weekends only. He generally goes to school during the week," Holland said. "How much were you making when you were seventeen and going to school?"

"Shoot, I'm not making that much now," Virgil said.

Holland said that Skinner was the only child of the town hippie. The identity of Skinner's father was not precisely known; his mother, Caroline, admitted that there were several possible candidates.

"Tough for the kid," Virgil said.

"Yeah, but growing up here, in Wheatfield, who you are is more important than who your old man was. Everybody knows Skinner and that he's a good guy."

"Except your former cop," Virgil said.

"Yeah, well, I believe he was excessively focused on . . ." He glanced at Virgil as he trailed off.

"The law?" Virgil suggested.

"Don't get all stuffy about it," Holland said.

Holland took over the cash register, and Skinner trailed Virgil outside.

The kid pointed up the street. "She was standing at the corner, waiting to cross to the church. Wearing a green jacket and black pants. I was walking up to the store when I saw her get hit. I don't know, maybe because that Coates guy got shot, and I had it in my mind, but as soon as I saw it, I knew she was shot. She jerked sideways, and then she made this noise, not a scream, more like she was calling out to somebody, and then she fell over, and tried to crawl . . ."

"You didn't hear the shot?"

"Nope, not a thing. Anyway, I ran up to her, and she was bleeding bad, and she said, 'Somebody shot me . . . Somebody shot me . . .' I had a newspaper under my arm, and me and another guy pressed some folded paper over the holes in her hips. And I saw this guy I knew, and told him to call the hospital at Fairmont, to get an ambulance down here. They took her to Fairmont, and then Fairmont called the Mayo in Rochester, and they flew her there on the Mayo chopper."

A good-looking, forty-something woman walked by and winked at Skinner, who said, "Hey, Madison."

She said, "Skinner . . . Don't be a stranger."

Virgil looked at her for a second as she walked away, then checked out Skinner's face, which was a picture of innocence, before wrenching himself back to the original topic. "Do you remember which way Rice was facing when she got hit?"

"Yeah, I talked about that with Wardell. She was looking across the street at the church, but I couldn't tell you if her hips were square to the street or she was square to the church—that's a big difference in terms of where the bullet would've come from and where it wound up."

"All right."

"Then me and Wardell were talking about whether the shooter was up high or level with her," Skinner continued. "The thing is, if she had a little more weight on one leg than the other, it would have cocked her hip one way or the other—so you can't tell where the shooter was. I can tell you that the bullet hit the ball of her joint on the entry side but not on the exit side. On the exit side, it was lower."

"You seem to have thought about it quite a bit," Virgil said.

Skinner nodded. "I don't ever see people getting shot. I'll remember it for the rest of my life. It's got me worried, Virgil. The town's got a good thing going, and I'd hate to see some nutball mess us up. One or two more shootings and we're toast."

"Why'd you stick newspaper in the wounds?"

"Untouched by human hands, or any other hands, or even germs," Skinner said. "That newsprint pulp comes out of a big vat and gets ironed out flat and rolled up on a reel, and then it's printed on, so the inside of a newspaper is about as sterile as a bandage."

"How do you know that?"

"Went on a tour of a paper plant when I was at Scout camp. The guide told us."

"So, tell me about the Nazis."

"Aw, don't waste your time on them. It's two guys and their girlfriends, and they don't have a pot to piss in or a window to throw it out of," Skinner said. "They decided they wanted to be somebody, get somebody to pay attention to them, so they signed up to be Nazis and got themselves a couple of pit bulls. They're not exactly harmless, but bar fights are really more their style. The Nazis, not the pit bulls."

"Then they're seriously stupid."

"Yeah, they are that. They used to work over at the elevator, but after they signed up to be Nazis they got fired. Now they all live on welfare. They didn't shoot anyone, though. The shooter is somebody smarter."

"Got any ideas?"

Skinner scraped his lower lip with his upper teeth, then said, "No. It could be somebody who doesn't like what's happened to the town since the apparitions, but I can't think who that would be. If maybe there are a couple of people like that, none of them would be crazy enough to go around shooting people. You have to understand—I know every single person who lives here. Not counting the visitors."

"You think it's a visitor?"

"Could be. When I lie in bed and try to think of a person I know, who could be doing this, I come up with a total blank. We got our assholes, we've got a couple of goofs, some people angry from watching Fox News . . . but it seems to me that it has to be something more than a goof."

"Like what?" Virgil asked.

"Don't know. It's like an oxymoron: random shootings for a reason," Skinner said. "Gonna have to think more about it. The two people who got shot, Rice and Coates, don't have any connections. Nothing at all. Didn't know each other, didn't come from the same place, Coates isn't even a Catholic. The only thing they have in common is the fact that they were shot and where they were shot. That could mean the shooter has a particular spot he likes to go to and is maybe sighted in at a specific range."

"I told Wardell and the sheriff that we need to figure out why people were shot . . ."

"That's exactly right, Virgil," Skinner said. "If you can figure that out, we'll know who's doing it. Unless he's some outsider religious nut and he really is crazy. But how would he know the town well enough to find a spot and not be seen or even caught? People here notice if you drop your Sno Ball wrapper on the ground. That he can get away with shooting people . . ."

Skinner shook his head.

"I'll tell you something, Skinner. Anybody who snipes innocent people is seriously unbalanced even if he believes he has a reason," Virgil said. "Most people won't even shoplift for fear of getting caught. Shooting people? You're dealing with a nut even if there's a payoff somewhere."

Skinner nodded. "I'll think about that, too."

Virgil walked Skinner up to the corner where Rice was shot and then down the street where Coates was hit. They talked about possible angles, but if you made the simplest assumption, that both were square to the street, then the shots would have come from the general area of the business district. If their hips were turned one way or the other, the shots could have come from behind any business on either side of Main Street or from a residential area farther back.

"I need to look at a satellite photo," Virgil said, "to try to narrow things down. Will you be around?"

"Until five, at the store. We got a girl that comes in and takes it to eight o'clock, when we close. I'll give you my cell number. If you need anything, call me."

They exchanged cell phone numbers—Virgil gave Skinner his direct number on the off chance that Skinner actually might think of something—and then Virgil went out to his truck and got his iPad. A Google Earth satellite photo gave him a solid overhead shot of the town. It had been taken in the winter, with no leaves on the trees, so he had an unobstructed view of the street layout.

Assuming that both victims had either been standing more or less square to the street or turned slightly one way or the other, Virgil configured a slice of pie extending from the points where the victims were standing down to the business district.

Only a half dozen houses fell within the pie slice, as well as a number of auto- or farm-related shops and services. One section of the slice that included Rice didn't include Coates. Virgil thought that probably eliminated that area. If the sniper successfully got away from his first position, why wouldn't he go there again?

Time for a walk-around.

Virgil spent two hours working his way up and down the Main Street shopping area. There were twenty storefronts on the block-long business district. All of them had apartments or storage on the second floor, and a half dozen of them were being rehabbed as short-term housing for visiting pilgrims. The carpenters and other construction workers quit at 4 o'clock, according to one store owner, which made Virgil think that might have restricted the time that the sniper had to shoot—it had to be after 4.

Virgil climbed the stairs to two of the units being renovated. The entire length of Main Street stretched out below him, and he could easily see both ends of town, fading into newly plowed rolling black prairie, and the church steeples, which were the highest points in Wheatfield. He could clearly see where the two victims had been standing. There were several solid positions—windowsills, framing for walls—where a rifle could have been supported. There hadn't been much wind the day before—at least, not in Mankato—and a quiet day would help with accuracy.

The building owner had climbed the stairs with him to the

second apartment, watched him calculate the distances and angles. "Even on a quiet day, it'd take some good shooting," Virgil told the owner, whose name was Curt Lane.

Lane said, "Hang here one second," and he turned and ran down the stairs; he was back a minute later with a golf range finder. He handed it to Virgil, and said, "Put the crosshairs on the spot they got shot and push the button on top."

Virgil did and got two hundred and forty yards for Rice and two hundred and seventy for Coates. "Good shooting," he said. "Our guy might not be just a regular nut, he might also be a gun nut. Know anybody like that?"

"There are a lot of gun guys in town, there not being a lot else to do," Lane said. "You go out to the old quarry and shoot you some soda bottles, or there's a sportsman's club a few miles farther out. Most all the guys hunt, and quite a few of the gals."

Virgil nodded, then looked up and down the street. Two-thirds of the parking spaces were taken, and he could see perhaps twenty people out walking. "If the shooter was up here, you'd think somebody would have heard the shot."

"I would have," Lane said. "I'm right downstairs. You say the guy was shooting a .223? I hunt up north, where rifles are legal, and I know what a .223 sounds like. Guys up there deer hunting let go a half dozen shots—*POP-POP-POP-POP-POP-POP!*—most likely a .223 or an AK. They're loud. Not a big boom like a .30–06, but you'd hear them for a few blocks anyway."

"As far as I can find out, nobody heard anything," Virgil said.

"Don't know what to tell you, except maybe he was a lot farther out," Lane said.

"I hope so," Virgil said. "If he's local and he's shooting from a thousand yards, or something, we'll spot him pretty quick. Not many people are that good, and the ones who are are known."

When he'd worked his way down one side of Main Street and up the other, Virgil walked around behind the buildings, first on the east side, then on the west. The east side was bricked in with commercial buildings: a Goodwill store, housed in an unpainted metal hobby barn, Burden's Tractor & Implement, a car wash, the brick Fraternal Order of the Eagles, which was mostly a bar with a rooftop that might have provided a sniper's nest, and STM Wine & Spirits. The Eagles club wasn't open, but Virgil saw somebody walking around inside and banged on the door until Goran Bilbija pulled it open an inch, and said, "We're closed."

Virgil identified himself, and Bilbija let him in and pointed to a stairway that led to a second-floor office and storage room. Virgil looked in both, but neither had a window that a sniper could have shot out of. A ladder, bolted to the wall, led to the roof, with a hatch held in place by heavy hooks, the kind seen on barn doors.

"I don't know the last time that was opened, but it's been a while. When we retarred the roof—that was, mmm, five years ago?—we did it with ladders from the outside," Bilbija said.

Virgil climbed the ladder anyway, got the hooks loose, and when he pushed up on the hatch a double handful of dust rained down on his hair and shoulders.

He managed to heave the hatch up onto the roof and climbed outside. When he looked at the hatch, he decided Bilbija was right: the thing hadn't been opened in years, and part of the problem with pushing it open was that it had been tarred shut.

On the other hand, the roof had good sight lines to the places where the shooting victims had been standing. When Virgil walked around the roof, he found the second floor was built over half the structure, with the back half dropping to a single story. If someone had a short ladder—not even a stepladder but one of the three-step stools used to reach high cupboards—he could have climbed onto the back roof, then used the stool to climb to the top. Getting down would be even faster, if it had become necessary to flee. He could have gone from roof to roof with no more than a three-foot drop.

If the shooter climbed up and down the back of the building, between the wall and the dumpster by the kitchen door, he might even do it unseen.

Virgil put it down as a possibility. The roof didn't show any footprints, discarded DNA-laden cigarette butts, a book of matches from a sleazy nightclub, an accidentally dropped driver's license, or any other fictional possibilities, so he went back down the hatch and pulled it shut.

"Find anything?" Bilbija asked.

"A nice view, but . . . no."

"Didn't think you would," Bilbija said. "Say, you want a beer or a quick shot to keep you going? I got a nice rye."

Virgil declined the offer and worked his way back up Main Street, this time behind the stores on the west side, and found a more complicated situation, a mix of mostly ramshackle prewar houses and small businesses, some of them in converted houses. The ProNails place had a dusty, handwritten "Out of Business" sign in a window, but Auto Heaven, Buster's Better Quality Meats, and Trudy's Hi-Life Consignment were still operating; nobody had heard a shot fired.

Because of the way the houses and businesses were mixed, there were multiple spaces and slots between hedges and behind fences where a rifleman could have hidden. Virgil was lining up a theoretical shot down toward the churches when a man's voice called, "Hold it right there! I got a gun on you!"

Virgil raised his hands: "I'm a cop. Don't shoot."

A heavyset man in a blue T-shirt and a ragged pair of Dickies coveralls stepped out from behind a garage twenty feet away. He was maybe fifty, balding, with a wind-eroded face. He was aiming an ancient twelve-gauge double-barreled shotgun at Virgil's stomach. "Cop, my ass."

"Call the sheriff, ask him. Call the mayor. My name is Flowers, I'm with the state Bureau of Criminal Apprehension." Virgil was talking fast and trying to keep his voice from shaking, not entirely successfully.

The guy looked less certain in his resolve but didn't drop the muzzle of the gun; from Virgil's point of view, the twin bores of the shotgun looked about the size of apples. Instead, the man half turned his head and shouted, "Laura! Call down to the store and ask somebody if they know a cop named Flowers." To Virgil he said, "Keep your hands up."

Virgil kept his hands up, and said, "Point the gun somewhere else."

"Bullshit."

"You pull that trigger and you're gonna spend the rest of your life in Stillwater prison for killing a cop," Virgil said. "I've identified myself, and if you don't point the gun somewhere else, I'm gonna bust you for aggravated assault, and that's a minimum of five years. Now, point the fuckin' gun somewhere else."

The muzzle moved a foot to the left, and Virgil took a breath. They stood there like that, and then, a moment later, Laura yelled, "Wardell says he's a state police officer."

The guy considered that, then lifted the muzzle, pointing it at the sky. "I thought you were maybe that sniper guy," he said, "a stranger sneaking around like that."

Virgil walked up to him. The guy was holding the gun in one hand, and Virgil snatched it away from him, then turned and kicked the guy in the ass—hard. "You fuckhead, you could have killed me. Jesus Christ, I oughta beat the crap out of you. I mean . . . Jesus, going around pointing a shotgun."

"I thought . . ." the guy moaned, squeezing his ass with one hand.

"You think you see the sniper, call the cops," Virgil shouted. He was still furious. He broke open the gun's action and ejected two shells that looked as old as the gun itself.

A woman came out from behind the garage and asked the heavyset man, "Now what have you done, Bram?"

Virgil, shaking his head, shouted at him again, "You fuckin' moron . . ."

Bram said, "There aren't any cops. You know how long it takes a cop to get here? A half hour, if you're lucky. If you live in this town, you take care of yourself."

Virgil looked at him for another few seconds, then tossed the gun back to him. He kept the shells. "You point this fuckin' gun at anyone else, I swear to God I'll stick it so far up your ass you'll blow your head off if you sneeze."

"I thought you was the sniper . . ."

Virgil shook his head again. "Man!"

Virgil turned to the woman. "Thank you for helping out. I apologize for the language, but he scared me to death."

"He didn't mean no harm," she said, anxiously twisting her hands together. She was also heavyset and also windburned; they had to be husband and wife, Virgil realized.

"Doesn't make any difference if he meant no harm," Virgil said, his voice softening. "If he'd jiggled that trigger, he'd have cut me in half."

Bram and Laura Smit—"Not Smith, Smit, ending with the 't'"—disagreed about the sniper's gunshots. They'd been home when the two shootings took place, and Laura Smit hadn't heard anything that might have been a gunshot. Bram thought he might have, but was uncertain.

Laura said, "That was your tinnitus, honey."

Bram shook his head. "I'll tell you why I know I heard it. Because with the second one, I called it before we knew anybody was shot."

"That's true," Laura admitted.

Now Virgil was interested. "What did it sound like, exactly? Was it close by?"

"Couldn't tell where it came from, how close it was, or anything, but it didn't sound like a gun," he said. "It sounded like when you're downstairs and somebody upstairs drops a boot. More like a thump than a bang. Not too loud. With the first one, I went to see if Laura had fallen or something, but she hadn't, so I almost forgot about it. Then, later that day, we heard about the shooting down by the church, and I wondered if I might have heard the shot."

"You tell anyone?"

"Well, no, because I really didn't think I had," Smit said.

"But the second shot . . ."

"Yesterday afternoon, I had my head in the refrigerator and I heard that sound again. I went and found Laura, and said, 'I heard it again,' and she thought I was imagining it. Then we found out somebody had been shot again."

"Did you tell anyone about that?"

"I talked him out of it," Laura confessed. "I didn't think, you know, it was any of our business . . . if there's somebody around shooting people. Bram got his gun out . . . I mean, there aren't any police around here, Virgil. Not since Wally left, and that was three years ago. We're on our own, and I don't want to go poking a stick in a hornet's nest."

Virgil walked around the garage with them, into their house, which smelled like cookies because Laura had been baking. Virgil accepted a peanut butter cookie and looked out some of the windows; from nowhere in the house could he see the place where either of the victims had been standing when they were shot.

They went out in the yard, and he looked at the other houses in the neighborhood. As far as he could see, none of them had clear sight lines to the shooting scenes, but, then, the shooter wouldn't need much of an opening. A .223 slug was about the thickness of an ordinary number 2 pencil—if the shooter could find an opening the size of a soup can, he'd be able to use a scope and have a clear line between the muzzle and the target. In other words, he could shoot right through most solid-looking trees, just as you can see blue skies through most trees if you look around a little.

He accepted a second cookie, and said to Bram, "I'm sorry I kinda lost it there, but I've had too many guns pointed at me lately.

I'm going to give you a card, and if you think of anything I might need to know, or if you hear the sound again, give me a call."

Smit nodded. "I will. We're not Catholics, but that church saved the town. Everybody knows that. This crazy man could send us back to the poorhouse."

Virgil spent another half hour wandering around the area on the back side of Main Street but didn't see anything that made him want to look closer.

He went back to Main Street, got an exceptionally bad cheeseburger and even worse fries at Mom's Cafe, the only restaurant he could find, then headed back to Skinner & Holland. Skinner was behind the cash register, and Virgil picked up a package of cinnamon gum to get the taste of the burger out of his mouth, paid most of a dollar for it, and dropped the change in a jar that said "Tips. Help the Deserving."

"You the deserving?" Virgil asked Skinner.

"Maybe," he said.

"How come this place is called Skinner and Holland, Eats and Souvenirs, and the only eats you've got are Sno Balls and Cheetos and fake-cheese crackers?" Virgil asked.

"There're some frozen entrées in the freezer, and you're welcome to use the microwave," Skinner said. "That's what me'n Wardell mostly eat. We're talking about starting a diner, but we haven't found the right venue. And Holland's mom would get pissed. She owns Mom's Cafe."

"She sure doesn't need the competition," Virgil said. "I ate the worst cheeseburger of my life there about five minutes ago."

Skinner winced, and said, "I wouldn't wander too far from a

toilet. They got three cooks there; we call them Hepatitis A, B, and C. That burger's gonna hit the bottom of the bucket in one piece, if you know what I mean."

"I do," Virgil said. "Maybe I ought to start a cafe if you're afraid to piss off Holland's mom."

Holland had come up behind him, and now he said, "Who's gonna piss off Mom?"

Skinner said, "Virgil got a cheeseburger down at the cafe."

"That'll teach you," Holland said. "God knows where the meat comes from. Probably from a veterinarian's." Then, "Figure anything out?"

"Found a guy who thinks he might have heard the shots; I need to check some sight lines." A couple of customers had edged up to listen in. Virgil said, "We can talk about it later."

"That's more than anybody else has gotten," Holland said.

"If you could prove that it's Holland's mom who did the shooting, it'd benefit everybody," Skinner said.

"Except Mom," Holland added. To Virgil: "You had a hepatitis shot?"

"Already heard that joke," Virgil said.

Skinner and Holland looked at each other, and then Skinner said, "That wasn't a joke."

"Ah, Jesus," Virgil said.

Virgil left Skinner & Holland, chewing his way through the pack of gum, walked around to his truck, opened his camera case and took out his Nikon and a long lens. He hung the camera on a shoulder and got a pair of image-stabilizing Canon binoculars out of the gear box in the back. After locking the truck, he trudged over to where the shooting victims were hit and glassed the west side of the business district, picking out spots where a shot might have come from.

There were several. He took a series of photos that he could later review on his iPad.

On his way back to the truck, he saw Skinner leaving the store.

"Solved the restaurant problem," Skinner said.

"Yeah?"

"Taco truck," Skinner said. "Who doesn't like tacos? On top of the tourists, we got a whole bunch of Mexicans in town, so that'd add to the market. Bet there's a truck up in the Cities that we could buy—I'm gonna look at it this week. Get it going. Maybe we could find a Mexican lady to run it. I know there are some in town who make damn good tacos 'cause I've eaten them."

"Why don't you start a corporation?" Virgil said.

"Where would that get us?" Skinner asked.

"It'd give me an opportunity to buy some of your stock."

"Ah," Skinner said. "Hmm. Let me think about that."

4

Virgil downloaded the photos to his iPad and walked back to the business district, checking the photographs for holes in the foliage or any other place where the shots might have come from. He discovered that the photos were a lot less help than he'd imagined they'd be. If the shot had come from that area, it could have come from anywhere.

When he finished, it was late in the afternoon. He heard the bells from St. Mary's, saw a rush of people cross the street to the church for the first Mass. Nobody had been shot, so he went back to his car, found the address where Holland had arranged a room, and drove over.

An older Ford F-150 was parked nose in at the front door; a bumper sticker said "I dream of an America where a chicken can cross the road without having its motives questioned."

Maybe the Vissers had a sense of humor; or maybe they were sincere and deeply into fowl. He climbed the stoop and knocked. A woman opened the inner door, looked through the screen, and said, "You'd be Virgil. You desperately need a decent haircut, and, fortunately, I'm the gal to give it to you. You don't need it a lot shorter, but it does need to be cleaned up. Get rid of those split ends."

Virgil asked, "Miz Visser?"

"Yup, as in 'real pisser,' as my husband would say, if he were here," she said. "Walk around back, I'll go through the house and open the door for you. You can park your truck at the side, on the gravel."

Virgil parked on a gravel strip, got his bag, flipped the switch on what he believed was the loudest car alarm in the world, locked the truck, and walked around to the back door, where Visser was waiting. Virgil got a better look at her without the screen between them: a Netherlander blonde with pale blue eyes and nearly invisible eyebrows, she might have been a workout queen on a free cable channel. She was wearing a tight mock turtleneck, black yoga pants, and flats. She was pretty, in an earnest, small-town way.

"We don't serve food, but you've got a microwave, and a comfortable bed."

"It's fine," Virgil said, looking around the room. A compact bathroom, straight out of Home Depot, opened off the back wall, with a toilet, sink, and shower. The room smelled of pine-scented deodorizer.

"Fifty dollars a day, and we take it any way you roll it—cash, check, or Visa. But if it's credit card, you have to go charge it at Skinner and Holland, and it'll be fifty-five, because the store adds a ten percent service charge."

"Of course they do," Virgil said. "I'll pay cash."

"Great. Now, about the haircut—that'll be forty, and again, if you charge it at Skinner and Holland . . ."

"Listen, Danielle—it's Danielle, right?—I'm not sure I need . . ."

"Virgil, you do need one," she said. "In a position like yours, you have to look professional or people won't respect you."

In the end, Virgil caved. He'd never liked his Mankato barber especially, because in his heart the guy wanted to give Virgil a military buzz cut. Danielle guided him back through the house and into the front parlor, which had been set up as a hairdresser's shop, with a chair, hair dryers, an oval mirror, and bottles of hair stuff.

She pushed him into the chair, and Virgil said, "Not too much off, right? Neaten it up, that's all I want."

"Correct," she said, as she threw a nylon cape over his chest and pinned it tight around his neck. "Now, let me tell you what's going on with these shootings, okay? We've got a lot of smart women in this town and they all sit right here, and we talk. I can boil down what they told me."

"I'd appreciate it."

She turned Virgil away from the mirror and started talking and cutting. The women of Wheatfield rejected all suspicion of outside interference. "Somebody we know is doing this. You know why?"

"If I knew why, I could break the case," Virgil said.

"Then I'll tell you why." She leaned close to his ear, and said, "Money. One way or another, it's money. Specifically, it's going to be money that somebody isn't getting that they think they should get."

"It's a theory," Virgil said.

One of Visser's breasts gave his right ear a brief massage, but the hair snipping never slowed. "You're dismissing me. You shouldn't. This whole town was doomed until we got the Marian apparitions. Not only was the town doomed, all of us residents were, too. Except for a couple of government people and teachers, we were all poor. Or getting that way. Now, all of a sudden, everything has changed. But . . . But . . ." She leaned close again. "Some people have been left out. They're still poor. They're still doomed. They hate that."

He got the ear massage again, as though for emphasis. He said, "That's an interesting idea. Somebody who's been left out but still owns a good, accurate rifle."

"Piffle," she said. "Everybody in town owns a good, accurate rifle. Roy has a .308 that could knock the testicles off a chickadee at a hundred yards."

As she said it, the front door banged open and then banged shut again. She shouted, "Isn't that right, honey?"

Roy walked in. He looked like a Special Forces sergeant, arms like small tree trunks, a neck that went out to his ears, small waist. He was dressed in a gray work shirt and gray slacks with oil splotches.

"Isn't what right?" He came over to get a kiss and then sat down in a customer chair at the side of the room. The odor of 10W-40 wafted through the room.

"This is Virgil. I told him you had a .308 that could knock the testicles off a chickadee at a hundred yards."

"Only if it was bendin' over," Roy Visser said. He added, "You gotta stop this craziness, Virgil. It's ruinin' the town."

Virgil asked for names of people who'd been left out of the gold rush and who might own a highly accurate .223.

"You know, not many people around here have .223s, because they're pretty useless. All you can do with them is play army. I understand the Nazis got a couple, and they play army, and they're left out and poor. I don't know who else would. You could talk to Glen Andorra about that."

"Who's he?"

"Farmer. He's got some rough land out west of here. He didn't know what to do with it, and then he came up with the idea of starting a sportsman's club. You know, rifle range, trap, skeet, sporting clays, pistols, archery. I believe the rifle range goes out to six hundred yards. He might have some ideas."

"Does he live out there?"

"Yeah, he does. Hard to explain how to find his place, but I could show you on the computer," Visser said. And, "Jeez, Danny, get your tit out of his ear."

"He doesn't mind," Danielle said. "Do you, Virgil?"

"I'll let you guys work it out," Virgil said. Although it did feel good, and was beginning to have an effect.

When she was done cutting his hair, Danielle said, as she was putting her scissors away, "You sit right there, we're not quite done yet. You're entitled to a shoulder massage."

"I don't . . ."

"Take it," Roy said.

Virgil took it. The massage lasted five minutes, and he could have used another five. He also decided not to tell Frankie about it. Danielle took the cape off and spun the chair around. Virgil checked himself, and said, "All right, I'll drive down here for haircuts from now on. That's the best one I've had in . . . maybe forever."

"Got some hair down your neck, though," Danielle said. "You might want to jump in the shower before you head out to Glen's place."

The day was working out, Virgil thought, as he showered. He had some ideas of where the bullets were coming from, a lead to a guy who might know about local shooters—Roy had shown him on a Google satellite photo of the gun range and the house where Glen Andorra lived—and he'd gotten an excellent haircut.

He left the Vissers' house at 5 o'clock, still with more than three hours until sunset. At five-twenty, he pulled up to the gate that blocked the dirt track to the sportsman's club. The gate needed a key card for entry, which he didn't have. He climbed out of the truck to see what he could see, which wasn't much because the range was behind a low ridge that began just beyond the gate.

He could hear the boom-boom of a heavy rifle being fired slowly. Aimed shots. He was about to turn around and go out to the main road and down to Andorra's house when a pickup topped the ridge and rolled down toward him. He got back in his truck and, when the gate opened, drove through to the other side and flagged down the pickup.

The driver ran his window down, and asked, "Forget your card?"

"Don't have one," Virgil said. "I'm with the state police. I'm looking for Glen Andorra."

"Haven't seen him, he's not out here. Maybe check his house."

"I'll do that," Virgil said.

Before going to Andorra's, he drove over the ridge and down to the shooting area, which was a series of ranges based around a parking lot in the middle of a deep bowl, with a creek oxbowing at the bottom of the lot. The ranges weren't fancy, mostly defined by a row of picnic-style tables and benches, with a roof overhead for shelter. The rifle range was in the deeper part of the bowl, and shooters fired at a series of bulldozer-built berms. To Virgil's eye, the berms appeared to have been set at fifty, one hundred, one hundred and fifty, and two hundred yards, and then four more berms out to six hundred yards. A narrow dirt two-track ran down the length of the range, so shooters could drive down to check out their targets.

The shooting end of the range featured four benches with picnic table seats and a flagpole atop which a red flag fluttered in the breeze to make newcomers aware that shooting was going on.

Two men were sitting at one of the benches, one of them with a rifle snuggled on top of Army-green sandbags, the other looking downrange through a scope, his rifle lying on a case off to the side. The aimed rifle went boom, the shooter jerked with the recoil, and the scope man said something to him. Virgil got out of the truck, and called to them: "Hey! Excuse me."

They were both wearing electronic earmuffs, which cut the sound of a muzzle blast but allowed them to hear normal speech. They both turned to look, and Virgil walked down and identified himself.

"I'm looking at the shootings up in Wheatfield," he said. "I'd be interested in anyone shooting a .223 at longer ranges—four hundred to five hundred yards, or so—maybe with a scoped bolt-action."

The two men looked at each other and then simultaneously shook their heads. The shooter said, "There are a couple of Nazis on the county line over toward Blue Earth, they got .223s, but Glen kicked them out when they announced they were Nazis. Only one of them had a card anyway; he'd bring the other one in with him."

"Is that common?" Virgil asked.

"Hell, no," the man said. "Membership costs fifty bucks a year. Me'n Bill are shooting up a box of .300 Winchester Magnums, goes for forty bucks a box. A year out here costs less than a box and a half of ammo. A heck of a bargain, and they wouldn't even pay that. Pissed some of us off even before they were Nazis."

The scope man said, "It wasn't the Nazis that shot those people in town, though. They had about the cheapest guns that would actually work and thirty-dollar scopes. They had trouble keeping their shots on the paper at a hundred yards, never mind for four or five blocks."

"All right," Virgil said. "Have you seen Glen Andorra around today?"

"Haven't seen him for a while," the shooter said. "But I'm not out here that much. Can't afford it."

"That's where a .223 would be good, if you could get a bolt-action," the scope man said to the shooter. "Get more practice with centerfires, don't get banged up by the recoil. Then, shoot the mag enough to be sure its hittin' where you want, and don't go burnin' whole boxes of million-dollar ammo."

"What are you usin' the mag for anyway?" Virgil asked.

"Brother's got a place out in Colorado with elk on it. Me'n Bill drive out every year," the shooter said.

"Good deal," Virgil said.

They talked guns and hunting for a few minutes, and Virgil mentioned his sideline as an outdoors writer. The shooter said, "You oughta do an article on supercheap elk hunts. Everyone thinks they're superexpensive, but they don't have to be. You get somebody with a piece of land out in Wyoming or Colorado, bunk on their kitchen floor, you're only spending three hundred bucks for gas. Plus, you gotta pay for the tags. That's another six hundred. We shot a big cow elk out there, we took a hundred and eighty pounds of boned meat off her—that's five bucks a pound for better than anything you'd get out of a supermarket. Don't have all them chemicals, and so on."

"Not a bad idea," Virgil admitted. He took their names, and said, "I might call you about that."

As Virgil was walking away, another pickup rolled down into the shooting bowl and turned off toward the pistol range. Virgil stopped to talk as the couple in the truck were getting their weapons out of the back of the camper, but the woman said, "We don't pay much attention to the rifle people. We shoot handguns at seven yards."

They hadn't seen Andorra for a couple of weeks, and the man said they came out to shoot most evenings.

No card was needed to get out of the range. The gate slid sideways as Virgil approached it, and he took the dirt road out to the highway and turned left. Andorra lived in a typical early-twentieth-century Minnesota farmhouse, a white four-square clapboard, with a front porch, a side entrance off the driveway, and triangular attic dormers.

The place was neatly kept, without having been modernized. There was still a clothesline, on the side of the property opposite the driveway, with a rug hanging on it; the lawn needed to be cut, if you were a serious lawn guy. Virgil couldn't see any cars, but they could be in the garage in back. He got out, sniffed the country air—cows, he thought, but not too nearby—went to the side door, and rang the bell. And rang again. No movement inside.

He walked down the driveway to the garage and looked in the windows. He could see a newer Mustang 5.0 parked next to a Bob-Cat.

He said, "Huh," scratched his head, and glanced back at the house. He was getting a bad feeling about this. He called Wardell Holland. Holland answered on the second ring, and Virgil asked, "Do you know Glen Andorra?"

"Sort of. I nod at him," Holland said. "He doesn't live in town."

"Yeah, I know. I'm out at his place. Do you know anyone who would know him well enough to have his phone number?"

"Yeah. Try Doug Cooper. Let me get Doug's cell number for you . . . He farms out there."

Virgil called Cooper, who didn't have Andorra's phone number. "Why are you looking for him?"

Virgil explained, and Cooper said, "Tell you what, I thought about checking on him. I drive by his place every day—I'm about two miles down the road—and there's been this rug hanging on his clothesline for a couple of weeks now. That's not like Glen. He's a fussy guy, and we've had some rain coming through, but the rug never moved, so . . . I thought about checking on him."

"I'll check, I guess," Virgil said. "There's a Mustang in his garage . . ."

"Well, that's his only car. Since you're the law, I'd go look inside, if I were you."

Virgil walked all the way around the house and wound up climbing the six steps of the front porch and peering through the hand-sized cut-glass windows in the door and the big window on the porch itself.

The only thing he saw that might be useful was a double-hung window on the far side of the house that appeared to be cracked open at the bottom. He walked around to check it, but the window was up eight feet. He went to the garage, found the door unlocked, borrowed a stepladder, walked it around to the side of the house, set it under the window, climbed up, looked inside.

The window was open, but only two or three inches. Virgil stared into what was once a dining room but was now being used as a place to watch television. The wide-screen was tuned to a game show, the cheery quizmaster joking with a group of D-list Hollywood celebrities. A man whom he assumed was Glen Andorra was lying back in an easy chair, and he had the withered, rotted look of a genuine zombie.

And Virgil could smell him in the air that wafted out through the window.

"Ah, jeez," he said aloud. He got on the phone to the sheriff's office, and Zimmer said he'd send a bunch of cars. "Does it look natural?"

"Hard to tell . . . He might have been sitting there for two weeks," Virgil said. "There's warm air coming out—I think the furnace is turned on."

"Oh, boy. Sit right there, Virgie, I'll have you two cars in ten minutes, and I'll be out in twenty."

Virgil went to his Tahoe, got a couple of vinyl gloves out of his equipment box, and tried the front and two side doors. The rearmost of the two rattled in its frame, and Virgil went back to his truck, got a butter knife out of his equipment box—stolen from the Holiday Inn for this very purpose—fit it into the space between the door and the jamb, and pushed back the century-old bolt on the door.

He found himself in a mudroom, as he expected. The door opened on the kitchen, and it was unlocked. When he stepped inside, the odor of decomposition was overwhelming. He went back outside, got his jar of Vicks VapoRub from the equipment box, and jelled up his nostrils.

Back inside, he stepped carefully through the kitchen. A door to the right would lead to a stairway that would go three or four steps down to a landing, then out the other side door and down into the basement. He knew this because most old farmhouses were built like that.

Straight ahead was a narrow door that would lead to the living room; and, to his left, a two-panel door that would lead to the dining room, where Andorra lay back in his chair. A couple of Persian-style carpets were rolled up next to the basement door, and with the carpet hung from the clothesline, it suggested that Andorra may have been doing spring cleaning.

Virgil, watching every footstep, moved into the dining room. Andorra's face was a combination of dark gray and purple skin, hanging loose. His eyelids, thankfully, hung down over whatever was left of his eyes, which Virgil didn't want to think about.

Virgil decided that the death was not a natural one, the chief indicator being the large-caliber bullet hole at the side of Andorra's head. An older-looking 1911 .45 semiautomatic pistol lay on the floor by the side of the chair.

The Vicks was doing its job, but Virgil gagged and stepped away, into the kitchen, got himself together again breathing through his mouth. If he blew his guts all over the place, the crime scene crew would be distinctly unhappy.

As he stood there, head down, he heard movement, and all the hair on the back of his neck stood straight up. He backed away into the mudroom, then jumped off the stoop and jogged to his truck, got his Glock out of the gun safe.

The sound he'd heard had been quiet but distinct, with the

feeling of some weight. But despite a mildly superstitious nature, he didn't believe that Andorra was about to lurch out of the dining room. There was somebody else here.

He called Zimmer.

"I'm in my car, on the way," Zimmer said.

"There might be somebody else in the house," Virgil said. "Something's moving, didn't sound like a rat. Something bigger."

"Oh, boy . . ."

"I wanted you to know. I'm gonna check . . . Talk to the cops coming out, tell them to take care."

"Wait 'til they get there."

"Ah . . . I'm too curious. I'm going to take a look."

"Take your gun with you, Virgil."

"Got it."

Virgil rang off and walked back to the stoop, then up into the mudroom. He stopped to listen, heard nothing at all. He moved slowly through the kitchen, listening. The house had three floors, but the noise had felt closer, and not above him.

He was coming up to the dining room door when he heard it again, off to his right. Behind the basement door.

A chill ran up his spine, and he called out, "I'm going to open the door and I've got a gun . . . Don't move." He turned to his right, and said loud enough to be heard through the door, "Jim, line up on the door with your shotgun, but stay behind that wall. Be ready . . ."

He stepped quietly past the basement door, listened, heard nothing, reached way back, grabbed the doorknob, and yanked the door open.

No gunfire.

He peeked around the door, saw nothing but the empty landing in front of the exterior door.

He decided to wait for the deputies, but as he stepped back from the door, heard a whimper. Dog? Kid?

Whatever it was, it sounded hurt rather than dangerous. He swallowed, pushed the Glock out in front of him, hit the basement light switch, and stepped slowly down to the landing. Two more steps down was another landing, at the top of the stairway that led down into the basement. He listened, then stepped down and peeked around the corner into the basement.

From where he stood, he could smell dog poop, even through the Vicks and the background odor of decomposition. At the bottom of the stairs, he saw a shredded yellow sack and, beyond that, a dog. A big dog, lying on his stomach. The dog lifted his head and whimpered.

"Easy, there," Virgil said.

He eased down the stairs, into the stench of the poop. The basement was damp but not wet. At the bottom of the stairs, in the glare of the bare lightbulb, he saw that the shredded bag had once contained twenty pounds of dry dog food. The food was gone, and part of the bag had been chewed off by the dog.

The dog, a yellow-and-white collie, was watching him but not moving. Virgil stepped past him and looked around: the dog had had food, but he saw no water, though there must have been some if the animal had been locked in the basement for two weeks.

He moved slowly through the basement. The dog whimpered again, and Virgil saw a hole next to a wall going down through the concrete floor: a sump.

The sump was damp, but with no standing water. Normally,

there'd be a little water in it, but the dog must have drunk it, which answered that question. Virgil remembered . . . a bowl? Up on the landing?

He went back to the stairs, saw a stainless steel bowl that he'd ignored on his way down the basement. He picked it up, ran back down the stairs, went to a laundry sink, filled the bowl with cold water, and carried it to the dog.

The dog whimpered again and edged toward the bowl and drank. And drank. And drank. And then edged away from the bowl and lay down again, his head stretched out in front of him between his paws, his eyes rolling up to Virgil.

A man shouted, and Virgil almost jumped out of his skin.

"Virgil! Virgil Flowers!"

Virgil shouted back, "Down in the basement."

"Holy cow, it stinks in here . . ."

A deputy appeared on the landing, one hand pinching his nose. "What's that?"

"Collie," Virgil said. "He's alive, but not by much. I got him some water."

"Ah, man . . . I gotta get out of here."

"Go back out through the mudroom," Virgil said. He touched the collie on the head: his hair was matted and felt almost like plastic broom bristles. "We'll be back, boy," he said.

Outside, the deputy said, "Another guy'll be here in a minute. I don't know if I can go back in there until we air it out."

"Let me give you some Vicks," Virgil said.

5

Zimmer stood in the kitchen, his nostrils slick with Vicks, and looked at Andorra's body with disgust: "He was a good ol' boy, and that's no way to end up, all rotten and falling apart."

"I talked to my boss, and he's sending down the crime scene crew, so we gotta stay out of there," Virgil said. All the deputies had wanted a look. "They probably won't be here until late."

Zimmer nodded, and said, "I'll keep a couple of cars in the yard until they finish up and we move the body. You think he killed himself? Or somebody did it for him?"

"Looks like suicide, but if he wasn't murdered, it'd be a hell of a coincidence," Virgil said. "I wanted to ask him about long-range shooters."

Behind them, two deputies came up the stairs, carrying the collie in a blanket they'd stripped off a second-floor bed. They'd folded it like a hammock, with the dog slung inside. One of the cops had a sack of dog treats in his car and he fed peanut butter–flavored cookies to the collie, who ate them slowly, but wanted another. And another.

"Motherfucker who'd lock a live dog down in the basement,"

Zimmer said. "I don't think Glen would do that if he decided to kill himself. He'd at least let the dog outside. If Glen was murdered . . . Well, I can understand shooting somebody, but why would you do that to a dog?"

"If it's the Wheatfield shooter, we already know he's an asshole," Virgil said. "I don't think a dog would mean much to him."

Zimmer looked back at Andorra's body, waved toward it, and asked, "Suppose he was murdered. This tell you anything? The whole . . . you know . . ."

"The shooter probably came out to the range regularly enough that Glen knew what he was shooting. I'll say in passing that the Nazis used to come out here until Glen kicked them out, though that doesn't prove anything," Virgil said. "I think the gun on the floor will turn out to be the weapon that killed him."

"In my experience, people who like military stuff are attracted to 1911 .45s. Nazi people."

"Still not proof," Virgil said. "Besides, they might be more attracted to Lugers or something German. You also have to consider that Glen didn't like those guys—but he let the killer come right into his TV room. Working backwards from that, I'd say that the shooter was somebody he knew fairly well and who shot him because he knew that Glen had seen him sighting a .223. Or knew he was a good shot with a .223. Also, the guy had a big handgun, which means he's not a casual target shooter. He likes guns, and he probably has several."

"There are fourteen thousand people in Lamy County, half of them women. And of the other half, half of them are too young or too old and feeble to pull this off. That leaves about thirty-five hundred male suspects, and we can eliminate most of them by reading through the phone book and saying no," Zimmer said. "That ought to get us down to a few hundred."

"I'd bet that one of your deputies knows the shooter personally and knows that he has some guns," Virgil said. "Ask them. Ask who they think it could be."

Zimmer nodded. "I'll do that. And I gotta find Glen's son. My wife thinks he lives up in the Cities somewhere."

"Glen didn't have a wife?"

"Divorced. My wife thinks his ex lives in Seattle."

"Maybe I should be talking to your wife," Virgil said.

"I don't think you're ready for that," Zimmer says. "You'd need several years of preparation."

Virgil's boss, Jon Duncan, called to say that the crime scene crew was loading up, but it'd be 7:30 before they made it down. Virgil locked the doors of the house with a key he found in a kitchen cupboard, turned the scene over to the deputies, telling them that he'd be back at 8, and warned them not to go inside.

The dog was gone, loaded into one of the sheriff's SUVs and taken to a shelter. "Hope he's not too far gone. You let a dog go too long without water and it kills his kidneys," Zimmer said. "That's a good mutt. I'd take him myself if I didn't already have three."

Virgil caught Willie Nelson singing "Stardust" on the satellite radio on his way back to town; listened and thought about how far the song was from the afternoon's death scene. He needed something to eat before what would be a long night but stopped at the Vissers' to take a shower and change clothes to get the stink of the dead man off him. As he was parking, a battered Jeep pulled up to the front of the house, and Wardell Holland got out.

"I heard," he said. "Must've been ugly."

"Still is," Virgil said. "You know anybody who can operate a .45?"

Holland rolled his eyes up, thinking, then said, "Nope. Haven't had them in the Army for quite a long time, but they were always a popular gun, so I'm sure there are some around. Bob Martin—he lives over on Walnut—does some gunsmithing, he might know."

Roy Visser came out, slapped hands with Holland, said to Virgil, "We were in the Army at the same time. He was a hero; I fixed trucks."

"Trucks were more important than lieutenants," Holland said.

"That's true," Visser said. To Virgil: "Did you talk to Glen?"

"Glen's dead," Virgil said.

Visser's mouth literally dropped open, and Virgil scratched him off any possible list of suspects.

"Shot? Somebody shot him?"

Virgil nodded. "Sometime back. Probably more than a week, maybe even two."

"Holy cow . . . What about his dog?"

Virgil shook his head. "Locked in the basement. There was a sack of dog food on the landing, he had ripped it open, but he was hurting for water. Still alive, last time I saw him. Got some water in him."

"Oh, man. That's Pat. Pat the dog. World's best dog. Where is he?"

"Took him to the shelter," Virgil said.

"I'll go out and take a look," Visser said. "We lost our Lucky a year ago; it's about time we got another one."

Virgil said, "Do that. I'll call Zimmer and fix it. I need to get something to eat and get back out to Andorra's place."

"Hell, Danny'll fix you something," Visser said. "C'mon. And you kinda stink, so throw your stuff in the washer. I'll go see about Pat, later on . . ."

"Gonna need a vet," Virgil said. "He was locked down there for days."

"I got a vet," Visser said. "You c'mon, eat. And, Wardell, you need something to eat, too. You can't eat any more of that shit from the store."

"I resemble that remark," Holland said.

Visser herded them inside. Virgil went to take a shower and change clothes; Danielle got his clothes and carried them away while he was still in the shower. He wasn't particularly body shy, and she apparently wasn't easily impressed, so that's what happened, and without unnecessary commentary. When Virgil made it back to the kitchen, she'd warmed up leftover meat loaf and nuked a bag of frozen french fries.

"I'm going out to the shelter with Roy," she told Virgil. "I know Pat."

The food wasn't great, but it was hot, and tolerable when covered with ketchup, and Holland rambled on about the Marian apparitions being a mixed blessing: "If they hadn't happened, Glen would probably still be alive."

"Maybe, but the town would be dead," Roy Visser said, "And you'd still be sitting in that double-wide shooting flies." To Virgil: "I suspect he shoots them sitting, but he claims he wing-shoots them."

"I'd never shoot a sitting fly," Holland said.

"That's not what Skinner told me," Danielle said.

Roy Visser's eyes narrowed, and he asked, "You been talking to Skinner?"

"Shut up, Roy. He's a nice boy."

"He's screwed half the women and girls in town, and I don't want him messing around in my territory," Roy Visser said. "But I would like to know what that boy's magic is."

"You don't need to know," Danielle Visser said. "You already got me."

"And the answer's simple," Holland said.

They all waited.

"He likes women," Holland said.

Roy Visser and Virgil looked at each other, then Virgil said, "We all like women."

"Yeah, but Skinner really likes women. Not just sex. He likes women. Young women, old women. I've seen him bullshitting ninety-year-olds. Making them laugh, too. Getting a twinkle from them."

Roy Visser said, "Whoa! That's kinda nasty."

"I didn't say he was screwing them. He likes them and they know it. That's his whole secret."

They contemplated that, then Danielle Visser said to her husband, "Let's go get Pat. All you men can think about is Skinner liking women and what you might learn from it."

When they finished dinner, Virgil drove back to Andorra's house. Bea Sawyer was standing on the mudroom stoop when he got there, a 3M mask hanging under her chin. In addition to the crime scene van, there were two sheriff's cars in the yard, with the deputies leaning on fenders and chatting with each other.

The chances that Sawyer, the crime scene crew chief, would let a deputy into her crime scene were nonexistent.

Virgil walked over, and asked, "Suicide?"

"Don't believe so. The way the slug went through his head, he was leaning away from it, but the shot came in level. We found the bullet hole in the wall, hit a stud. We can dig it out."

"Brass?"

"One shell. Like you'd get in a suicide."

"But no note, or anything?"

"Eh, I wouldn't say not anything. Andorra was divorced, as I understand it, and his ex-wife lives a long way from here. But, he was still sexually active. There's a box of condoms in the top drawer of his bedroom dresser, a Trojan Super Value Pleasure Pack, hundred-count. Looks like there are about sixty of them left . . . so forty or so were used for protection, unless he was sponsoring a balloon festival."

"How about the sheets?"

"The sheets are absolutely fresh and unmarked. In my opinion, too fresh and unmarked. It looks like the last thing he did before blowing his brains out, or getting his brains blown out, is that he changed the sheets."

"Which you normally wouldn't do before eating a bullet."

"Can't tell. Maybe he was naturally neat. Some suicides get all dressed up for the act because they don't want their bodies to be disrespected."

Don Baldwin, Sawyer's partner, stuck his head out the door, and said, "I thought I heard you, Virgil. Another interesting one, huh?"

"I've been hearing about it from Bea," Virgil said. "How you doin', Don?"

"Got something to add. I should probably tell Beatrice first, you know, so everything stays in the proper bureaucratic channels."

"Oh, for God's sakes, Don, what is it?" Sawyer asked. Before he could answer, Sawyer told Virgil, "I've got him finishing the scan of the house."

"Down in the basement, there's a workbench with a canvas bag full of gun-cleaning tools, earmuffs, and a partial pack of handgun targets," Baldwin said. "There are four boxes of .45 shells in the bag, two partially used. There's also a gun safe. I opened it, and there's a custom slot for a handgun that isn't there but which would fit a .45 perfectly."

"Then that's probably his own gun on the floor," Virgil said.

Sawyer said, "If that is the case and it's not a suicide, it brings up the question of how the killer got hold of the gun."

"Could have just come back from the range with the killer," Virgil said.

Baldwin said, "There also appears to be a missing rifle. There are two shotguns on one side of the safe, one with a two-power scope, probably a slug gun for deer hunting, the other a twelve-gauge pheasant gun. There's a .30–06 on the other side, and then an empty slot that looks used, but the barrel would be too slender to be a shotgun. Did I mention that there's a box of .223 FMJ shells in that range bag?"

"Ah, shit," Virgil said. "The .223 we're looking for belonged to Andorra. The guy came here, killed Andorra, and took the rifle." Everything that Virgil had imagined about the shooter sighting the gun on the range and killing Andorra because Andorra had seen him doing it went out the window.

"Andorra must've known him pretty well, then," Sawyer said. "But how did the range bag end up down in the basement while the gun came back up with the killer?"

Virgil considered the question, shook his head, and said, "I can think of eight different ways that could happen—and there's no way to know which one to pick."

"Give me one," Sawyer said.

Virgil shrugged. "They came in with their guns, Andorra leaves the bag on the kitchen counter, they go into the dining room to chat, the guy goes back out to the kitchen like he's getting a drink of water, gets the .45, comes back, and shoots Andorra. Then he's smart enough to try to confuse us—he takes the bag downstairs so it looks like Andorra had to go down to get it and bring the gun back up."

"Nobody's that smart," Baldwin said.

"Well, who the fuck knows," Virgil snapped. "Besides, we'll never figure it out, so why worry about it?"

"'Cause I like mysteries," Baldwin said. He added, "I'm going back down there."

"Tell him what you said about the rubbers," Bea said.

Baldwin said, "Oh, yeah. They suggest that he's seeing a woman of child-bearing age, and since forty-two of them are missing, he's seeing her with some frequency. You wouldn't buy a box of a hundred if you were using one a month."

"Could also be seeing an older woman with an STD, but I'm siding with Don on this one," Bea said.

"No sign of a name for her? Cards, notes . . . ?"

"Not that we've found so far," Sawyer said.

Baldwin turned to go back down to the basement, and Virgil shouted after him, "Hey, Don!"

Baldwin shouted, "What?"

"Were any of those targets used?"

"No. No used targets."

Sawyer asked, "Is that important?"

"Well, the range is a homemade one. There are a couple of trash barrels down there that I suspect Andorra emptied. Right now, they're almost full, like they haven't been emptied in a while," Virgil said. "People throw used targets into them. I wonder if there'd be any .45 targets in there?"

"I got some nice thick rubber gloves, if you want to go look," she said.

"I probably should," Virgil said. "Have you gotten to his wallet yet?"

"Yeah. Nothing there of interest."

"Was there a magnetic key card?"

"A plain blue one. Do you know what it's for?"

"Probably for the gate to the shooting club. Let me borrow it . . ."

Virgil got the key card and the rubber gloves and drove back out to the range. The sun's disk was sitting right on the tree line: he wouldn't have much time. He drove through the gate and over the top of the rise and found that he was alone.

He drove to the pistol range, found what appeared to be new targets sitting at the top of the nearly full trash barrel. The targets had been gathered in a stack and then folded over before they were dropped in the barrel. Each target showed more than a dozen shots, grouped in a smaller-than-palm-sized space near the center. The occasional target showed individual holes that suggested the shooters had been using 9mm, or .38 caliber and .22 caliber, handguns. Virgil thought the targets may have been used by the couple he'd seen. Not bad shooting, if they were doing rapid-fire self-defense work.

He started digging through the trash, pulling it out and dropping it on the ground. There were used targets, water and soft-drink bottles and cans, empty ammo boxes, a couple of pizza boxes, sandwich wrappers from Subway, and two black plastic bags of the kind used to pick up dog poop. The deeper he got, the soggier he found the contents, from the intermittent rainstorms.

Some of the targets had names on them; most did not. He was nearly to the bottom of the can when he pulled out three that he would bet had been shot with a .45. There were other possibilities—a .40 caliber would make a hole only slightly smaller, and a .44 would be almost indistinguishable from a .45—but the .45 was by far the most common, and they knew that Andorra had one.

He set the targets carefully aside for processing by the crime scene people. There had been a couple of layers of cans and bottles above the .45s, but there were six targets that had been above those with the .45 holes.

They were soggy, but he could see that they were shot full of 9mm or .38 holes, and on one of them he could make out the initials "BD."

Whoever BD was, Virgil thought, may have been shooting around the time the .45 holes got punched.

If God were on his side anyway.

The range had fallen into twilight by the time he left. He drove back to Andorra's house, gave the targets to Sawyer and Baldwin for analysis. "Doubt that we'll get much, but you can never tell," Sawyer said. They both agreed that the initials on the target were "BD."

Sawyer and Baldwin still had work to do around the body and wouldn't be moving it to the medical examiner until later; an ME investigator was on his way with a van and would do the actual removal.

"I'm going back to town," Virgil said. "If anything amazing comes up, call me."

When he got back to Wheatfield, the place was closed: a few people lingered in the park between the two downtown churches, but the last service at St. Mary's had ended an hour earlier, and none of the stores, not even Skinner & Holland, were open. He was tempted to drive back to Frankie's farm, a little more than an hour away, to spend the night in a familiar bed, but, in the end, he drove back to the Vissers'.

On the way down Main Street, he saw a couple standing on the sidewalk, and the woman was poking the man in the chest. Virgil couldn't see the man's foot in the bad light, but he thought it might be Holland.

At the Vissers', he parked at the side of the house, took his weapons out of the truck, walked around to the rear entrance, and, as he was stowing the guns under the bed, Danielle Visser knocked on the interior door, and called, "Virgil?"

Virgil opened the door, and she said, "I thought you might like to know that we're going to take Pat. He's weak, but the vet said he should be okay when he's all rehydrated and everything. His kidneys are still working okay, that was the big threat."

"Good," Virgil said. "Listen, do you know if Glen Andorra had a girlfriend?"

"No, I didn't know. Does he?"

"There are some indications."

Visser turned, and shouted, "Hey, Roy! Did Glen have a squeeze?"

Roy walked down the hall, and said, "Not that I know of. We got a mystery woman now? Cool beans."

"Anything else happened since dinner?" Danielle asked. "Anything I can put in the town blog?"

"The town has a blog?"

"Sure. I'm the editor."

Virgil shook his head. "Probably not anything significant. I'll be looking for a guy whose initials are 'BD' and who goes out to the gun range and shoots a nine-millimeter or .38 caliber handgun. I'd also like to talk to the woman who was involved with Andorra."

"So would I!" Danielle Visser said. "That'd pump up the traffic on the old website. No idea who she is?"

"I don't even know it's a she," Virgil said.

"C'mon. Nothing queer about old Glen," Roy Visser said.

"Minnesota's full of Norwegian bachelor farmers," Virgil said. "Not because none of them can find women."

"Maybe, but not Glen," Roy said. "He'd come here twice a year for a haircut, and about the time Danny got finished working over his ear, we had firm indications that he was a straight shooter, if you get my meaning."

"You were checking him out? I find that interesting," Danielle Visser told her husband, who was not even slightly embarrassed. Back to Virgil: "Now, about this BD? Is he a suspect?"

"Not at all," Virgil said. "There's a chance he might have been the last person to talk to Glen, but even that's a little unlikely."

"I'll put up a request for information," Danielle Visser said. "Most everybody in town reads me, now that we got so much going on."

"Do that," Virgil said. "Ask for email replies to my official address. I'll give you that. Don't pass on my phone number. The nuts would drive me nuts."

The Vissers went to post the request for information, and Virgil turned on the small television and clicked around until he found a Minnesota Twins game, turned down the volume, and got on the phone to Frankie.

"I thought about coming home tonight, but . . . I need to push," he said.

"We're fine . . . It was windy here today. All the apple blossoms blew off the trees. They looked kind of neat on the ground, like a quilt."

They talked for an hour and a half about stuff that nobody else would be interested in.

The Twins lost.

6

Janet Fischer's great-great-great-grandfather had arrived in Wheatfield in the last half of the nineteenth century and, though Fischer didn't know it, had given her the same oval face, yellow-blond hair, and bright blue eyes as he had.

She'd inherited her figure directly from her mother, a woman of French-Canadian descent who could still turn heads after sixty-two years and five children. Janet had been considered a Wheatfield natural resource since high school.

Not a totally untapped resource. She'd been engaged to marry Larry Van Den Berg for nine years and was known to be growing impatient. She'd heard the phrase "If he's already gettin' the milk, why would he buy the cow?" at least fifty times too many, but still had some faith that Van Den Berg would take her to the altar.

Van Den Berg was an over-the-road truck driver, working out of Albert Lea, making regular runs in a refrigerated rig to supermarkets on the West Coast. Fresh sausage, mostly. As a driver, he was gone for days at a time, and Janet—Jennie—found somewhat guilty solace in the arms of John Jacob Skinner.

Fischer worked afternoons at Skinner & Holland, except on weekends, when Skinner covered the store, and she was exceptionally well paid for a cashier. That afternoon, she'd washed her car and spent some time texting with girlfriends; but at 5 o'clock she'd taken a phone call from Van Den Berg and had immediately called Holland. She told him they all needed to meet at her house as soon as it got dark, that it was urgent, and that she didn't want to talk about it on the phone.

At 9 o'clock, Skinner and Holland snuck between two Concord grape arbors in her backyard and into the house through the back door. The door led into a short hallway that went past her bedroom and into the living room. When they were in the living room behind drawn curtains, safe from the eyes of passersby, Holland asked, "What's going on?"

Before Fischer could answer, Skinner asked, "Where's Larry?"

"He's parked off I-80 outside of Cheyenne, Wyoming, conveniently close to Diamond Jim's Gentleman's Club, all-nude entertainment twenty-four/seven, free parking for trucks," Fischer said.

Holland: "How do you know that?"

"I put a tracking app on his cell phone," Fischer said. "There are times"—she glanced at Skinner—"when I wouldn't want to be surprised about where he is."

"Okay. So what's the big crisis?" Holland asked. "He find out about you and J.J.?"

"Worse," she said. "He might suspect that I'm the Virgin Mary. It's my fault."

"Oh, no," Holland said. He ran both hands through his hair. "That's bad."

"You didn't tell him?" Skinner asked.

"No. He doesn't know for sure. When the first postcards came out, he said something about how it looked like me. He never said anything more about it. But then after I got the job down at the store, I opened up a new checking account at First Bank over in Blue Earth. My regular account is at Wells Fargo, and that's where Larry's is, too. Anyway, I got a new Visa card through First Bank, and Larry was sort of snooping around the house while I was in the shower and he found a statement. I'd bought some clothes . . ."

"How much?" Skinner asked.

"Four thousand . . . at Nordstrom's, up at the Mall of America," Fischer said. "I'm usually at Old Navy. I told him I needed new clothes for the job. He seemed to buy it, but he called an hour ago and said to tell you that he wanted a cut. I asked him, 'A cut of what?' He said, 'You know what cut.' I said, 'No, I don't.' And he said, 'Yes, you do. You ain't that good a virgin.' I said, 'Fuck you, Larry, I don't know what you're talking about.' He said, 'Tell Wardell,' and hung up. I think he must've been sitting there in the driver's seat, all the way out to the West Coast and halfway back, wondering where I got the money, and thinking about how you guys got the store going right away after the apparitions, and he figured it out."

"Oh, boy," Holland said.

"He's got no proof," Skinner said.

"He doesn't need proof. All he needs to do is start running his mouth, and we're in trouble," Holland said.

They all looked at one another, and Fischer said, "Well, we can't just shoot him."

"Of course not," Holland said.

They looked at one another some more, and Skinner said, "We really can't."

"I know we can't," Holland said. "But we gotta do something."

"When's he get back?" Skinner asked.

"He makes the Des Moines terminal tomorrow night. He could try to sneak home and fake his logbook later, but he's been caught doing that before. I expect he'll stay there overnight."

"We've got some time," Skinner said. "Let me think about it."

Ten minutes later, Holland snuck out the back door. As he was leaving, he said to Skinner, "I got one word for you."

"Yeah?"

"'Blackmail.' Larry's always been a little sleazy. See if Jennie knows what he's been sleazy about."

An hour later, with Fischer's head in the hollow between his chest and shoulder, Skinner said, "I don't know Larry all that well. I kinda stayed away from him, because, you know . . . Is he a straight guy? Has he ever been in trouble on anything?"

She couldn't meet his eyes—she was about to betray her fiancé. She said, "He was investigated last year. By Iowa."

"Yeah?"

"Somebody stole a trailer full of Legos at the terminal down in Des Moines," Fischer said. "The Iowa cops were up here to talk to him because they knew his tractor unit was down there at the time. He denied it all, but one night, later on, he hinted that he knew where the Legos were. I think he's still got a lot of them."

"At his house?"

"Oh, I don't think at his house," Fischer said. "We're talking about thirty-eight hundred cubic feet of Legos. That's the size of the inside of a fifty-three-foot trailer. I don't believe his house is that big."

"Huh. You know a lot about it," Skinner said. "Trailer sizes."

"Well, he tells me about it, even though it's pretty boring. His idea of pillow talk," she said. "Something else: he knows a lot about eBay. I'm pretty sure he has, like, a bunch of different accounts there. I think he sells the Legos under fake names."

"Huh."

"You think you could . . . use that?" she asked.

"Blackmail might be the only way to shut him up," Skinner said. "But first, you gotta have something to blackmail him with."

"Are we turning into criminals, Skinner?" She was twisting her hands. She'd been worried about events in the town since the appearance of the Virgin in December; and even more since the shootings.

"No. If he stole those Legos, he's a criminal. If we could find them, all we'd be doing is . . . Well, we're not cops," Skinner said. "We don't have to investigate somebody to see if he committed a serious crime. I mean, if he knew that we knew, if he knew that we had evidence . . . then he might not want to piss us off."

"Okay. But we're not criminals because of the Virgin Mary thing, are we?"

"Who have we hurt?" Skinner asked. "Nobody. All we've done is saved a town and made a lot of people happy."

"Okay." She shivered. "I think we should have some more sex to take our minds off all of this."

"Fine, but before we do that . . . do you have a key to Larry's place?"

"Of course."

"I need to borrow it," Skinner said. "I need to investigate him myself. I'm probably smarter than the Iowa cops."

"I'll get it for you. After this, I think I'm going to stop sleeping with him."

"Good idea," Skinner said. "There are other fish in the sea. Larry just isn't that much of a catch, you know? Besides, he hangs out at gentleman's clubs."

"That's true," she said. She sighed, and said, "Speaking of more sex, you think we should get the toys out?"

At 3 o'clock in the morning, Fischer led Skinner through Van Den Berg's backyard, unlocked the door, and took him through the kitchen and down to the basement, where Van Den Berg had built his man cave.

Fischer hadn't wanted to go along, but Skinner patiently explained that if neighbors saw lights and knew that Van Den Berg was on the road, they might call a deputy. If the deputy found Fischer there alone, it'd be okay, because everybody in the county knew her and Van Den Berg were engaged.

"I'm still a little nervous," she said, as she showed him around. "I don't lie so good."

"You're not lying. You're his fiancée. You have a key, you're over here all the time. You check the house for him," Skinner said.

"At three o'clock in the morning?"

"If somebody knocks, run upstairs and mess up a bed," Skinner said. "You were sleeping over because you missed him."

"Oh. Okay. If somebody knocks, I will."

"If you hear his tractor pull in, for God's sakes warn me."

The man cave was decorated with mixed martial arts and Vikings posters, plus the centerpiece, a sixty-five-inch LG television that had fallen off a truck in North Platte, Nebraska, where Van Den Berg had been lucky enough to catch it.

To one side, next to a urine-scented half bath, were a beer refrigerator, plus two filing cabinets, as well as a homemade desk, constructed of two sheets of three-quarter-inch plywood cut in half lengthwise, glued back-to-back to make a thick, two-foot-wide plank, then painted black and screwed down to two carpenter's sawhorses as legs. Sitting on top of the desk was an older Macintosh Pro computer with two screens and an ancient dot matrix black-and-white printer.

"Didn't know Larry was into computers," Skinner said.

"Well, he was going to be one of those day traders," Fischer said. "He got some how-to CDs on day trading and he played them in his truck until he had them memorized. He borrowed five thousand dollars from me that I'd saved up for the wedding, and then he had another five thousand in savings and he put that in. He spent half of it on computer equipment and lost the other half five years ago. Lost it in two months."

"Surprised it lasted that long," Skinner said.

"Yeah, well—he was actually up, like, fifteen thousand dollars for a week," Fischer said. "Then he got a letter from the brokerage he was using that said he owed a bunch of taxes. So, you know, he put it all on red and lost. He was getting letters from the IRS for three years."

"That sounds like the Larry we know and love," Skinner said.

He was probing around the homemade desk. "He might have figured out how to day-trade, but he didn't know anything about security."

He reached out and tapped a piece of paper taped to the wall behind the desk.

"What's that?" Fischer asked.

"All his passwords." Skinner peered at them, and said, "Mostly porn sites. Plus, eBay."

"Porn?"

"Let me get this thing up . . ." Skinner brought the computer up, dug through it, and brought up Van Den Berg's emails. He spent fifteen minutes scanning through them. Fischer got him a beer, and one for herself, and finally she said, "I'm going upstairs to mess up the bed, but I want to see this so-called porn when I get back."

When she came back, Van Den Berg's cheap printer was grunting out a stack of paper. Skinner asked, "Who is Ralph Van Den Berg?"

"Larry's brother. He lives down by Armstrong. Why?"

"Because Larry's taking orders for something, which I think are Legos, and he talks to Ralph about shipping them out through UPS. Larry keeps telling Ralph to go to different UPS stores to make the shipments. Ralph's running all over southern Minnesota and northern Iowa."

"I bet that's where the Legos are, down at Ralph's," Fischer said. "Those brothers are tight. Ralph lives on this acreage down there; he's got a woodlot, which would be like the perfect place to hide a trailer. It's already full of junked farm machinery and cars."

"I'll go over and take a look tomorrow," Skinner said. "In the meantime . . . this printer is gonna take an hour to print out all these emails. I'd put them on a thumb drive, but I can't find one. I mean, everybody's got a thumb drive."

"Show me one of these porn channels he's signed up for," Fischer said. "That jerk. He told me once that he never looks at porn because it's tacky. I thought I was his main sexual connection. I tell you, Skinner, this explains a lot about his attitudes."

"You actually don't need to go out to the porn sites. He's got his own collection on the machine, and it's hooked up to the TV." He pointed to a cable snaking along the wall and up behind the TV. "That's an HDMI cable."

"Then let me see one."

Fischer settled on a video called *Last Tango in Chatsworth*, and Skinner fired it up for her, then began sorting through the paper chugging out of what must have been a fifteen-year-old dot matrix printer. "Got a fuckin' parallel port," he muttered, as he worked. "I didn't even know you could find parallel ports anymore . . ."

Behind him, Fischer said, "Oh my God. OH MY GOD!"

Skinner turned to look, said, "Well, that's not something you see every day. Wonder how they did that? You'd think they'd get stuck."

The printer and the video ended simultaneously, and Skinner stacked up the paper, and said, "We gotta get out of here before it gets light."

"You gotta get out of here. I'm going to look at every one of these filthy things. I want to know what kind of man I've been engaged to," Fischer said. "Show me how that computer thingy works."

"Okay, but I don't want to walk all the way home. How about if I crash at your place?"

"Whatever," she said, waving a hand at him, as *The Gang Goes Bang!* came up on the TV.

Skinner kissed her good-bye, left her on the couch, and crept out the back door. Dark as a coal sack outside, except for the stars, which were bright and plentiful. With the incriminating pack of paper under his arm, he went back to Fischer's house, snuck in again, and lay in her bed until dawn, reading the emails.

By first light, he was convinced that the Van Den Bergs were up to something illegal, sending shipments of illegal somethings all over the country. Had to be the Legos. Could have been drugs, the way they talked in code, but they weren't making enough money to be drug dealers.

It occurred to him that if a legitimate seller of Lego kits could find an off-the-books source that only cost, say, half of the normal wholesale price, he could make a killing. Wouldn't even have to pay taxes on the profit. The Lego company would supply the advertising, and if you bought even a small number of kits from the company . . . you'd have the perfect cover.

"Sweet," Skinner said. "Crooked but sweet."

Shortly after dawn, he heard the back door rattle and was seized by the sudden fear that Larry had come home unexpectedly; but then Fischer called out, "Skinner? You still here?"

"Back in the bedroom," he called.

She appeared in the bedroom doorway and posed there, one hand on the jamb. She had, he thought, a weird glow in her eyes.

7

Three people shot, one of them dead, all possibly tied to the Marian apparitions.

As Skinner and Fischer were sneaking into Van Den Berg's house, Virgil was in bed; he'd spent a few minutes thinking about God and His religions and wondered why religions were so often tied to violence. When he was in college, years earlier, during the usual late-night weed-fired discussions of sex, politics, and religion, he'd decided that religions and political parties were quite alike, except that religions dealt with morality, primarily, while political parties dealt with economics.

In other words, they were both dealing with people's deepest feelings about how the world should work. Differences could escalate to physical clashes, as they might have even in the late-night weed-fired college discussions, except, of course, for the weed: "You're so full of shit, dude. Pass the joint."

Now, lying in bed all these years later, he still wondered why religions, since they dealt with morality, shouldn't shun any form of violence to others? Then again, he thought, maybe they did. Maybe the connection between religion and violence was Fake News.

His mind got caught in a loop speculating about it, and he finally got out of bed and opened up his laptop and looked up the most religious states and the most violent states. Turns out the six most religious states, as determined in one major study, were also among the ten states with the highest murder rates. The six least religious states were among the ten with the lowest.

He found that depressing, turned off the computer, and lay awake thinking about other demographic characteristics that could account for the overlap. Perhaps the most religious people lived in the parts of the country that were also the poorest and that accounted for the crime rather than religiosity? But, then, was religiosity related to poverty or were the two unrelated?

What would happen if the most religious places legalized weed?

He was still speculating about that when he drifted off.

When he woke the next morning, he had a text from Bea Sawyer that said "We were at the scene until 2 a.m. Got a motel room in Albert Lea. Not much new. Don't call early."

Virgil got up, shaved and showered, contemplated his store of T-shirts and picked a white "Larkin Poe" shirt that showed a snake wrapped around an apple. After dressing, he walked over to Mom's Cafe, where he had two of the worst pancakes of his entire life, which made him wonder how, exactly, a cook could screw up something so simple. The pancakes tasted as though the flour had been cut with sawdust, while the syrup had the consistency of tap water.

Done with breakfast, he walked down to Skinner & Holland, where he found a tall, rugged-looking Catholic priest, in a black suit and clerical collar, standing on the sidewalk, eating an ice-cream cone, and talking with Holland.

When Holland saw Virgil coming, he said to the priest, "Here he is."

Virgil walked up, and Holland introduced him to the priest, George Brice, who said, "I think we have a mutual friend."

He mentioned a St. Paul priest that Virgil had met through his father, and they talked for a moment about one of Virgil's earlier cases that had involved a Lutheran minister who was an international criminal, a fake but politically explosive archaeological find, a variety of gunmen from the Middle East, and a secret American intelligence organization that Virgil wasn't even supposed to dream about but occasionally did anyway.

"There's been a murder now. Wardell tells me you think it's related to the two church shootings," Brice said, bringing the conversation back to the present. "Is that correct?"

"Yes, but I'm not a hundred percent on that," Virgil said. "We found out that Glen Andorra was having a sexual relationship with somebody, but we don't know who. Sex can be a powerful motivator for homicide. If his death was murder and not a suicide, it might not have anything to do with these church shootings. Even if it doesn't, though, I believe the gun used in the church shootings came from Andorra. And since we're talking about murder, whoever killed Andorra is probably the church shooter. It's just not a hundred percent."

"He was shot up close, and in cold blood, before anyone was shot here," Holland said. "I don't see how a lover would have done both things unless killing Andorra unhinged her."

"Ah, it's not his girlfriend, it's a madman," Brice said, as he finished the ice-cream cone. He stepped over to a trash can and dumped the cone's paper wrapper.

"I believe you're right," Holland said. "But is that all he is?"

I need to talk to you about what you saw when Harvey Coates was shot," Virgil said to Brice.

"C'mon in the back room," Holland said.

Virgil and Brice followed him through the store, where a dozen people were lined up at the cash register. "Still going gangbusters," Brice said.

"I'd cross myself, but you might think I was joking," Holland said. "I wouldn't be."

As they went through the store, several of the customers reached out to the priest:

"Hola, padre."

"God bless you, Father."

"God bless . . ."

They settled into the three chairs in the back room, and Virgil asked Brice, "So, what did you see?"

"I was standing on the church steps looking right at him, at Coates. I saw him jerk like somebody had slapped his back, and then he . . . croaked . . . and looked around . . . and fell over. I thought maybe he'd had a stroke or a heart attack, but then people started screaming, but nobody else fell. I ran across the street, and a couple of other men were trying to get him, and themselves, behind an old concrete planter over there in case there was another shot. There wasn't. One of the other men was from here in Wheatfield, and he had the sheriff's department on speed dial and he called them and got an ambulance going. Then we just sat there and held some towels against the wounds to keep him from bleeding out. His wife was with him; she's a nurse, she knew what to do but was pretty panicky and crying . . ."

"Didn't hear a shot, or anything?"

"Nothing like that," Brice said, shaking his head.

"Did you notice exactly how he was standing? Whether he was turned one way or the other?"

"No, I didn't notice. Wardell was curious about that, too, but I didn't notice."

"I called Coates himself after Miz Rice was shot, and he didn't know exactly how he was standing, either," Holland said. "He thought he was more or less square to the street. He wasn't sure, though."

They talked for a while longer, but Brice had nothing to add about the shooting. He knew more about the wound. "Went right through his thigh, from one side to the other. I noticed that the exit wasn't much larger than the entry, which I think probably means he was shot with a military-style non-expanding bullet," he said.

"You know about bullets? Wardell told me the same thing about Miz Rice."

"I was a chaplain at the Balad military hospital in the early days in Iraq," Brice said. "I saw a lot of wounds. Most were shrapnel from roadside bombs, but some were bullets."

When they were done, Virgil and Holland followed the priest through the store to the front exit, and Virgil asked, as they stepped outside, "What about the apparition? What do you think?"

Brice half smiled, and asked, "What do you mean, what do I think?"

"Was it real or did somebody . . . fake something? Or what?"

Brice squinted across the street at the church. "Something happened. We know that for sure because we have photographs. Lots of photographs, quickly converted to postcards. We even have some partial voice recordings, which is more than we've ever had at any of the other apparitions. So something happened. And happened before one of the sincerest Catholic congregations in Minnesota. Or anywhere else, for that matter."

"You sound the tiniest bit skeptical," Virgil said.

"I believe in the possibility of Marian apparitions," Brice said. "That doesn't astonish me. What astonishes me are the other miracles in Wheatfield. It's inevitable to wonder if they're related."

Holland and Virgil looked at each other, and Holland shrugged. Virgil asked, "What other miracles?"

"The miracle of Skinner and Holland, among others," Brice said, gesturing at the store. "The town could barely support a gas station and yet this store appeared, like magic, barely minutes after the first apparition."

"C'mon, George. You know the story," Holland said. He turned to Virgil. "Right after the first apparition, Skinner came running to me and told me what was going to happen. I knew he was right, and we went to work. There was nothing magic about it: this store is the result of several people working like dogs for weeks."

"I will admit that Skinner is an unusual young man," Brice said. "Perceptive. In this case, perhaps even . . . clairvoyant." He shook his shoulders, brushed off some nonexistent dandruff, tugged at his coat sleeves, and said, "I better get over to the church. The management committee is meeting in a few minutes."

Brice started toward the corner to cross the street, and when he was out of earshot, Holland said to Virgil, "You see, that's the kind of thing we have to deal with—skepticism, even from the Church. Or maybe he played a little too much football."

"Yeah?"

"Notre Dame. Linebacker. Had a lot of head-to-head collisions," Holland said.

"A university devoted to the Virgin Mary—interesting," Virgil said. "I think he's probably trying to protect the Church. Its credibility," Virgil said. "If the apparitions turn out to be a fraud of some kind, they don't want to be out front vouching for their authenticity. Gettin' punked."

"Who would do that? Who could be cynical enough to defraud the public using the Blessed Virgin Mary?" Holland asked.

Virgil stepped out to the edge of the sidewalk and looked up at the storefront sign, "Skinner & Holland, Eats & Souvenirs," and said, "I have no idea. Nice sign, Wardell."

"Hey!"

Virgil said, "See ya," caught a break in the traffic, jaywalked across the street, and called to Brice before the priest entered the church. "Father Brice! . . . George!"

Brice stopped on the steps leading to the church's portal, and Virgil caught up with him. "If there are no services going on, you think it'd be okay if I looked around the church?"

"Sure. Let me know if you see anything that . . . I should be aware of."

"I'll do that," Virgil said.

Across the street, Holland shook his head and disappeared into the store.

Virgil had been in a lot of churches, most of them Lutheran, but a few Catholic or other Protestant types, as well as a few temples, both Jewish and Buddhist. He'd been in one of them as a result of his job, two more as the result of his relationships with hippie women, but most he'd been dragged into as a result of his father's ecumenical interests.

As a result, he knew something of traditional church layouts, and, though small, St. Mary's was traditional, built on the plan of a Christian cross.

Immediately inside the front doors—the portal—there was a vestibule called a narthex. Through the narthex door, he entered the main part of the church, called the nave, which consisted of a clutch of pews with kneelers and was suffused with the odor of melting candle wax. The pews were divided by a wide center aisle like the upright of a cross, with narrower aisles running along the sides. Above these side aisles were colored plaster reliefs denoting the Stations of the Cross, and at the end of each aisle was a rack of red votive candles, about half of them burning.

A transept—an aisle like the crossbar of a cross—divided the pews from the altar and pulpit. There was a bell tower directly above the transept. From the inside, the tower revealed a domed ceiling, also made of painted plaster, with faded angels playing ten-foot-long Renaissance-style trumpets. At the left end of the transept was another rack of candles, this one with white tapers, most of them showing bright, flickering flame.

The Marian apparition had appeared over the altar, which was at the far opposite end of the church when seen from the entry.

Five or six men and three women had gathered at the right side of the transept, where a table and chairs had been set up for the management meeting.

As they walked toward it, Brice said quietly, "We have to have our meetings in the church. There used to be a rectory right outside, where the little park is, but it burned down thirty years ago.

Never replaced." He added, "Probably shouldn't go wandering around the altar, but you can see the back parts of the church if you take the stairs over there."

He pointed out the left side of the transept as he turned right, toward the men around the table. Virgil went left, out a door at the end of the transept, where he found a closet containing threadbare vestments and church paraphernalia, a tiny kitchen, two restrooms, a room full of new-looking cleaning gear—push brooms, mops, buckets—and a back door. The door opened to the parking lot. He went back inside.

Everything about the structure was old and not recently repaired, but originally had been well built and well fitted with brick and oak, and now it was very clean, as if every inch had been scrubbed by hand. Virgil realized that being the scene of a miracle, it probably had been.

A door that must have been directly behind the altar, which was on the other side of the wall, opened to a narrow winding stairway. Virgil took it up to the top of the tower. There was still a bell there, but both it and its clapper had been tied off with heavy blue nylon ropes that appeared to be years old, if not decades.

Openings to the street were covered with louvers. There were four newer-looking 4×12 Marshall speaker cabinets perched on metal racks so that they faced up and down Main Street, with two amplifier heads connected to a central control unit connected to a CD player. Three CD cases sat next to the player: three identical copies of the *Bells of Notre-Dame*.

Nothing to see up there, Virgil thought. He went back down the stairs; partway down, there was a small maintenance door in the wall. Virgil tried to open it, but it was locked.

He listened for the sound of anyone nearby, then took out his pocketknife and went to work on the simple lock; opening it only took a few seconds. The door was less than half height and opened on a crawl space that was behind the altar but within the wall that separated the altar from the back rooms. The space went in both directions and apparently was used to service the lights that illuminated the altar.

He crawled a few feet to his left, to a small door in the wall. When he opened it, he found himself looking at a floodlight. The door wouldn't be visible from below, and he couldn't see down, only the back of the light fixture. He closed the door and crawled back out. He noticed that while the walls of the crawl space were made of aging plaster, everything was remarkably clean and dust-free.

Also, he thought, evidence-free.

Virgil walked back down the stairs and into the church, looked up at the half dome that framed the altar. The light fixtures were two-thirds the way up, shelf-like affairs of painted plaster that concealed both the lightbulbs and the service door.

As he headed down a side aisle to the front of the church, Brice called out, "Virgil—hang on." Brice said something to the men and women gathered around the meeting table, then hurried over to Virgil, and asked, "Was that you rattling around above the altar?"

"Yeah, it was. I didn't mean to disturb you."

"What disturbed us was the possibility that it was raccoons or a skunk," Brice said. "Law enforcement officers are a lot easier to get rid of."

Virgil laughed, and Brice asked, "Did you find anything interesting?"

"Actually, no." Virgil scratched his neck and looked up at the altar. "It's just that . . ."

"You're looking for a scam, a cheat," Brice said. "You're not buying into a miracle."

"I'm not there yet," Virgil admitted.

"Neither am I," Brice said. "If you find that there's something . . . awkward . . . going on, it probably won't be directly related to the shootings. In other words, not a crime that would be of professional interest to you. I hope you'd alert me before any announcement."

Virgil nodded. "I'm not in the business of making announcements even when there is a crime," he said. "I let other people do that. If I see something . . . awkward . . . I'll let you know."

Brice said, "Thank you," and clapped him on the arm.

As Virgil was leaving, he realized that whatever the origin of the apparition, it probably had nothing to do—and everything to do—with the shootings. He suspected that there would have been no shootings without the apparitions, but the immediate cause of the shootings was something else. As Danielle Visser had suggested, money could be one cause, although a twisted religious fanaticism could be another.

Think of the devil and she shows up: Danielle Visser almost ran over the toes of Virgil's cowboy boots as he was starting to cross the street and she was pulling over. The window on the passenger side of her truck rolled down, and she leaned across the seat, and said, "Virgil. We got a reply on the BD initials at the shooting range. Bud Dexter called and said he shoots out at

Andorra's from time to time, and when he's shooting with someone else, he'll initial his targets."

Virgil leaned in the window, and asked, "Did he say when he was last out there?"

"I asked him that exact same question, and he said it was a couple of weeks ago," Visser said.

"How do I get in touch?"

"He works over at the Spam Museum in Austin. He gets off at three, he'll be home around four or a little before. He'll hook up with you at Skinner and Holland."

"Excellent," Virgil said. "I guess you got nothing on Andorra's girlfriend or you would have mentioned that first."

"That's correct. I gotta tell you, not knowing is killing me. I've been matchmaking in my head all morning."

He fished a notebook out of his pocket, flipped it open, and said, "Somebody mentioned a gunsmith, Bob Martin. Know where I could find him?"

She patted the truck seat. "Hop right in here, and I'll run you over. Six blocks, and he's retired, so he's usually around."

He hopped in, and she drove him over to Martin's house. Frankie drove a truck, and Virgil thought about how there was something about truck-driving women that made them even more attractive than they naturally were; even the Eagles sang about it.

Visser was chattering along about nothing, the sun reflecting off the downy hair on her forearms and her near-invisible eyebrows, and if she'd had a little J.J. Cale on the radio, Virgil could have ridden around like that for all eternity, but they got to Martin's house in three minutes.

She waited on the street while he rang Martin's doorbell, and when he saw an elderly man making his way onto the porch, he waved at her and she drove away.

Martin was a burly man, probably in his late seventies, unshaven, wearing rimless glasses thick enough to burn ants with. He had a spot of what looked like dried egg yolk on his chin. He peered through the porch's screen door, and asked, "What?"

Virgil identified himself, and said, "I need to talk to you about what local people might have which guns."

"I wondered if there might be a cop coming around," Martin grunted. He pushed the door open, and said, "Come on back. I heard somebody went and shot Glen Andorra."

"Yeah, but we're not exactly sure of the circumstances. He was apparently shot with a .45 while he was sitting in his easy chair, and there was a .45 on the floor."

"A 1911?"

"Yes."

"Probably his," Martin said. "I reload for him. Did you find the bullet that killed him?"

"Yes, but I don't know what it is yet," Virgil said.

"Check and see if it's a 230-grain plated roundnose. If it's plated, not jacketed, it's one of mine. He supplies the brass, I supply the bullet and powder. I can sell them to him for thirty cents a round and make a dime apiece. I guess that's gone now," Martin said. His house smelled like a soft-boiled egg, confirming the yellow spot on his chin. "They'd cost forty cents each if you bought them at a store, so he saves a dime apiece. He probably shoots a thousand rounds a year . . . Saved himself a hundred bucks."

"Do you know if he had a .223?" Virgil asked, as Martin led him into a dining room that had been converted into a gun-repair shop and pointed him toward one of two leather easy chairs.

"Yeah, he did. Bought it up to Cabelas," Martin said, as he dropped into one of the leather chairs. "A CZ 527 Varmint with a Leupold variable-power scope. Is that what those people got shot with downtown?"

"I think so. Mr. Andorra's been dead a couple of weeks, so he didn't do it. There's an empty spot in his gun safe."

"You're saying it probably wasn't a suicide, then," Martin said.

"You could think of ways that it could be . . . He shoots himself, a friend drops in and finds him dead, decides he might as well do a little shopping down in the basement."

Martin shook his head. "This is a small town. If a guy was going to steal a gun, it wouldn't be something like that—it'd get spotted in a minute. Got this big, fat bull barrel on it, for one thing."

"Okay."

"Anyway, Glen wouldn't commit suicide. He was tough, one of those guys who can live through hell and who'll still go every last inch before he gives up the ghost. I don't believe it would occur to him to shoot himself. Of course, it could have been an accident . . ."

"But the missing .223 wouldn't be and the people downtown weren't shot by accident," Virgil said.

"That's true," Martin conceded. "I've been thinking about those shootings. One hit in the leg, the next in the hip. That's either good shooting or bad shooting. Can't tell until he shoots one more. With that scope and a decent rest, a good shot could keep five rounds inside a playing card at four hundred yards. He either meant to shoot them where he did or he doesn't know how to use that scope. It's a real good scope."

Virgil said, "Huh." He peered out the room's side window, letting the silence drag on.

Martin: "You figuring something out?"

"Nobody at the shooting scene heard the shot," Virgil said. "It just occurred to me that we don't know that he shot just once. He could have missed, and nobody noticed."

Martin said, "Somebody should have heard the shots."

"Can't find them if they did," Virgil said.

"You're sure they were shot with a .223?"

"Seems most likely. Why?"

"A .243 might do a similar amount of damage if it was a solid point. I know a guy in town who could shoot a two-inch group at four hundred yards, half minute of angle, but his go-to gun is a Remington 700 in .243. He does have a .223, and I believe more than one. Nice enough guy. The only thing that brings him to mind is, he's a little gun nuts."

"Nuts, how?"

"You know that big-titted girl that shoots the bow and arrow in that movie?" Martin asked.

Virgil thought he did.

"This guy would rather play with his guns than play motorboat with that girl," Martin said.

"Okay, I'm gonna need his name," Virgil said. And, "You're a dirty old man."

"Yeah, well, at my age, that's what I got," Martin said. His tongue flicked out and picked up the egg on his chin. He said, "Mmm."

8

The gun nut's name was Clay Ford. A tall, too-thin man with silvery eyes who appeared to be in his early forties, he was wearing a cowboy hat inside his house; otherwise, he was dressed like Virgil: T-shirt, jeans, and cowboy boots. He lived three blocks over from Martin, and when he saw Virgil standing on his porch, he said, "I didn't do it. If I had done it, I'd have done it better."

"Well, you don't know that," Virgil said through the screen door. "'Cause if you didn't do it, you probably don't know what he was doing. He shot two people and he did it under the pressure of shooting another human being and then having to get away with it. And he probably did it from four or five hundred yards away. Maybe farther, because nobody heard the shots."

Ford scratched his chin, and said, "Everybody in town knows that Glen Andorra's been killed and that you think it goes together with the people shot downtown. Why would he murder Glen and then shoot two people to wound? Why not murder them, too? Won't make any difference if he's caught. And if he's trying for a public relations disaster, murder is better than dinging somebody up."

Virgil said, "Maybe because he had to kill Glen to get the gun, but he didn't have to kill the others, so he didn't?"

"That's a goddamn generous way of looking at it," Ford said. "If he'd killed Glen, I don't think he'd much care about the others, especially if they were out-of-towners. I could be wrong." He pushed the door open. "You better come in. I'll show you my guns."

"You obviously know who I am," Virgil said, as he followed him inside.

"Everybody in town knows who you are," Ford said over his shoulder. "Danny Visser put up a story on the town blog and links to some newpaper stories about you. I liked the one where all those school board members were arrested for murder. You ought to arrest more government people, IMHO." He said the letters as words: "Eye Em Aich Oh."

Virgil was mildly annoyed that Visser had put up newspaper stories about him but said nothing as he followed Ford through his neatly kept house to what once had been the master bedroom. Ford had covered the windows with slabs of heavy sheet plywood, "to defeat possible burglaries," he said. "I don't want to arm any criminals."

He had a gun workbench against one wall and eight high-end gun safes, which he said were anchored to the house's concrete slab. He used a magnetic card to open the safes; he had forty guns.

"I divide them into three groups," he said, pointing at them as he read them off. "My carry guns, all pistols, nine-millimeter or

.45. And my rifles: .22, .223, .243, .308. And if that won't do it, one Barrett .50 cal."

"Why so many?" Virgil asked.

"There's a day coming in this country when you're gonna need a gun to survive," Ford said. "That's why I'm living here in Wheatfield. It'll take the dictator's men a while to get here, and that'll give us time to organize."

He was completely unself-conscious about it. Virgil said, "Okay."

Ford was just getting warmed up. He waved an arm at the gun safes, and said, "That's why I have all these different calibers. What do you notice about them?"

Virgil shrugged. "I don't know . . . Maybe they're all pretty accurate?"

"Of course they're that. They're my guns, and I won't have an inaccurate gun in the house," Ford said. "But they're common, that's the main thing. Every one of them, except the .50. There's no more common pistol ammo than nine-millimeter or .45 ACP, except maybe .22, which would be worthless as an anti-personnel round in a SHTF situation." He pronounced the letters individually again: "Ess Aich Tee Eff." "The grid goes down, people can't get food or gasoline, transportation falls apart . . . You won't fight off the incoming with a .22. The only thing a .22 will be good for is hunting. I got ten thousand rounds, which is a lot of rabbit. Along with thousands of square miles of corn, to eat and feed the animals with, we got a chance of making it. I got fifteen semiauto .223s in there, and I got fifteen thousand rounds of ammo—enough to set up my own platoon, to defend us. I got six .308s for sniper teams, along with the Barrett. Of course, to use them right, we'd have to have time to train. Nobody wants to train. They think I'm goofy."

Virgil understood "SHTF" to mean a "Shit Hits The Fan" situation.

"Interesting," he said. He bobbed his head, and said, in his best gun nut voice, "I would have put in a couple of twelve-gauge shotguns. They're good threat guns when you don't want to shoot anyone but might have to. They'd also be good for pheasant, in a SHTF case."

Ford regarded him levelly for five seconds or so, then said, "Now you're fuckin' with me. You think I'm goofy, too. I admit, it could turn out that way. New generation—could be all sweetness and light. That's not the way I see it, though. A rising tide of mean little fascist rats, is what I see."

Virgil swerved away from the argument: "Who do you think might have done the shooting in town?"

Ford tilted his head back, his eyes going to the ceiling. "I don't have a candidate right now. If you'd asked me before yesterday who was the best shot in town, I wouldn't have hesitated: me. But now you bring up some interesting points . . . If he shot them from far enough away that nobody heard the shots, and he wasn't shooting to kill, then he's got to be good. On the other hand, I suspect he hadn't figured out the drop over the distance he was shooting and underestimated it. He hits that first man in the leg, then the woman up higher. Next one will get it in the heart. If that's what happens, we'll all know he was using live targets to sight his rifle. Seems like he might be a guy who knows how to hold on target but has only shot some other rifle before, like a little .22, and doesn't know about ballistics. About the sound thing—nobody hearing the shot—that could mean he's got a suppressor."

"He's maybe using a CZ .223 Varmint that he took from Glen Andorra," Virgil said. "Did Andorra have a suppressor?"

"Not that I ever saw," Ford said. "I was out there a lot, too. I even shot that particular gun a couple of times, if it's the same one the killer is using. It's decent; if you gave it to me, I'd want to tune it, but it's decent as is. It wasn't threaded for a suppressor, or, at least, it wasn't when I fired it, which was probably a year ago or more. Didn't have a muzzle brake, either. You need a muzzle brake if you go the quick-attach route for your suppressor. If he bought a suppressor on his own, he had to get a federal permit for it. You could check that."

Like most hunters, Virgil liked to talk guns from time to time, but he was out of his depth with Ford. "You don't know anybody who can shoot up to your standard?"

"Not in town. There are some good shots, by any regular standard, guys who can keep it inside a minute of angle, as long as they've got the time and are shooting with a support. You can see them every day out at Glen's. I've never seen Wardell Holland shoot, but he was infantry in Afghanistan, or Iraq, so he's probably an okay shot . . . I kinda asked around about him, and he was in his store, with people talking to him, when the shootings happened, so he's out. Old Man Martin, he's a local gunsmith; his eyes are so bad, he couldn't hit the side of a barn from the inside. Glen was a hunter-level rifle shot, and a better pistol shot, bordering on good, with his .45, but, of course, he's dead. No, I can't think of anyone in town who'd be good enough to make those shots from way out on purpose. You gotta consider the possibility that the placement of the shots was accidental."

"Where were you when those people got shot, if you don't mind my asking?"

"Surprised it took you this long to ask," Ford said, with a thin grin. He'd taken a .223 black rifle from one of the safes and was handling it, turning it, as easily as a drum major twirling a baton. "I got my own business doing computer maintenance and WiFi installations, and also solar panel sales; I got an associate who does the installation on the solar panels. With that first shooting, I was at the Creighton house over in Fairmont. It's new construction, big house, they want WiFi in every room and solar on the roof. George and Elizabeth Creighton—they were both there the whole time I was. The second shooting, I was sitting in Elmer's Tap, off the Interstate, eating a hamburger and watching some guys shoot pool. I can give you names and all."

Virgil took a card from his pocket, wrote his BCA email address on the back, and said, "I believe you, but this is murder, so I gotta check. Email me the names."

"I'll do that soon as you're out the door," Ford said.

"What about the Nazis?"

Ford made a farting sound with his mouth. "Those guys are an embarrassment to the whole county. When the SHTF, they'll probably get eaten first." He hesitated, then added, "I'll tell you, though, they got one little woman out there, name of Rose, if she wanted to move in with me . . . I'd say yes in a New York minute. She's got a sense of humor, and she's not a bad shot, either. She's a little wild, but maybe you need somebody like that when the SHTF."

"Speaking of women, if you read Danny Visser's blog today, you'll know that we're looking for a woman who might have been having a relationship with Glen Andorra," Virgil said. "Any idea of who that might be?"

"Nope. But I suspected something was going on. I even kidded

Glen about it. I was over there once, and there were some dirty dishes on the kitchen table, set for two. I even kinda thought the woman might still be in the house because I could smell something feminine—perfume, or deodorant, something that sure wasn't Glen. He got kinda flustered, and pushed me right out the door. I'd stopped by to give him a check for my range dues, and he didn't even want me to take the time to write it out. Said he'd get it later. That was not like Glen. Not a bad guy, but he did like his cash money."

"No idea who she might have been?"

"No, because—you know what?—she wanted it kept a secret, which made me think she might be married."

"Yeah? Why?"

"There was no car in the driveway. If she was still there, either her car was in the garage or Glen picked her up somewhere," Ford said. "Why hide it if she wasn't married? If she was single, nobody would care. In fact, everybody would have thought Glen getting together with a woman, that'd be great. He'd been divorced for quite a while."

"Huh." Virgil thought about that, then grinned at Ford, and asked, "So, you like guns a lot. If you had to give up guns or women, which would you do?"

Ford peered at Virgil, then said, "Fake question. You wouldn't have to give up women unless they all died off, and that ain't gonna happen. On the other hand, when the government starts kicking in the repressive measures—and that's just a matter of time—IMHO, you're gonna need the guns. I'd say, sure, women are important, but guns are fundamental. You know, our Constitution doesn't even mention women, but it does mention our right to bear arms."

"Okay. Well, I'll be going out there to visit the Nazis," Virgil said. "I'll tell Rose you could be interested."

Ford actually blushed and rubbed his nose, and said, "Well . . ." And a few seconds later, "She's got dark hair. There are two dark-haired ones out there. She's the one who doesn't have swastikas tattooed on her earlobes."

"One of them has swastikas tattooed on her earlobes?"

"Saw it myself," Ford said. "The whole bunch of them were down at Skinner and Holland's."

Virgil said, "Fuckin' Nazis."

"You know what? They don't know anything about being Nazis. They don't know anything about history, about Jews and all of that. In fact, they don't know shit about shit," Ford said. "What they know is, Nazis are badasses who get on TV. That's it. They want people to think that they're badasses and they want to get on TV."

Virgil said, "Terrific . . . Listen, if you don't mind, I'm going to come back and talk to you if I need more information about guns. I hunt, but I'm not a gun guy like you are."

"Happy to do it. That's one fella we need to get off the streets, and in a hurry. I'm living here because of the food and water supply, because we're big enough that we'd be a tough nut to crack for armed refugees from the Cities but small enough to be obscure. Can't even see us from the Interstate," Ford said. "We do need to start providing our own electrical service, and I'm trying to talk the city into buying some solar panels, but they never had the money. Now, if housing values go up, they might. I'd get the panels at cost; I'd even set the solar field up for them, no charge. But they're dragging their feet. In the meantime, I've already got panels on my roof. You might have noticed."

"I'll take a look on my way out," Virgil said.

Virgil took a look at the solar panels, but they resembled all the other solar panels he'd seen in his life so he didn't linger more than three seconds. He was five or six blocks from the Vissers', where he'd left his car, and was walking out toward the street when Ford stepped outside and called to him.

"I thought of something," Ford said. "As everybody knows, that CZ has a twist rate of one in nine, which is not what you'd want for the best accuracy with a solid boattail bullet like you'd use in the military or with a target. That gun's made for shooting varmints with light, high-speed bullets. If you're shooting that big boattail at longer distances, you'd want a faster twist—you'd want a 1:8, or even a 1:6, to stabilize the bullet, especially if there's any crosswind at all."

"But how many people know as much about it as you do? I mean, he steals the gun, sees a box that says 'Bullets,' they fit the gun, and that's it. He doesn't know about boattails and twist rates," Virgil said. "He's shooting what Glen Andorra shot."

Ford considered, then nodded. "I give you that one. But it baffles me. Guns are some of the most common tools in America, and most people don't know any more about them than point and shoot."

"They manage to kill their wives and kids at a pretty ferocious rate," Virgil said.

"That's unfair, but I won't argue with you. Maybe we'll get a beer someday. In the meantime, I'm gonna go by the church and take a look. There are all those trees along Main, he's gotta be shooting through them or under them . . . It's an interesting problem, shooting-wise."

"Do that. I'll tell Skinner or Holland to go with you so people won't wonder why the best shot in town is lining up positions at the church," Virgil said.

Ford nodded again, and said, "I'll talk to Wardell. And if you see Rose . . . I saw her win a women's turkey shoot up at Madelia."

Virgil said, "Got it."

The Vissers' place wasn't far, but a detour over to Skinner & Holland would only take five minutes. Virgil thought about the ice-cream cone that the priest, George Brice, had been eating that morning, realized he was hungry, and decided to stop.

On the way over, he called Sheriff Zimmer and told him he was going to visit the Nazis. "I ought to be there about one o'clock," Virgil said.

"You know your way around out there?" Zimmer asked.

"More or less."

"More or less won't work—they're back in the sticks," Zimmer said. "I'll have a guy out at the Wheatfield interchange on I-90 at one. You can follow him out."

"Excellent."

When he got to the store, a heavyset, sixtyish woman who had a strawberry beret perched atop her iron-gray hair was shouting at Skinner and Holland, who were standing behind the cash register. Three embarrassed patrons, including a nun in a black habit, were standing behind her at the counter, holding individual serving sacks of fried crap. As Virgil walked in, one of them wandered off, apparently to hide at the back of the store.

The woman turned away from Skinner and Holland, stormed toward the exit, where Virgil was standing. She snapped, "Out of the way, bum," and steamed on past. Holland gave her the finger, which she didn't see.

"What the heck was that?" Virgil asked Skinner.

"Holland's mom," Skinner said. "She told all her friends that they could come in and shoplift, and Wardell started asking them if they could pay for the stuff. A sack of Fritos here, a sack of Cheetos there—it adds up."

"She told them they could shoplift?"

"Not exactly," Holland said over Skinner's shoulder. "She told them that her friends could eat free and that it was all right with me. It isn't. She thinks it's all right because she loaned us the money to buy the store."

"Okay. Not saying I agree with her, but I can see her thinking," Virgil said. "She does you a favor, you do her a favor."

"She got us for nine percent interest," Skinner said.

"Nine percent. So, basically, fuck her," Holland said. His eyes flicked over to the nun. "Excuse the language, Sister."

The nun said, "I can forgive the language. I'm not sure I can forgive your making an obscene gesture at your mother."

"Ya gotta know her," Holland said. "If you knew her, you'd give her the finger, too. Let me get those Fritos for you."

As the nun's Fritos were being rung up, Virgil asked, "If I buy a chicken potpie, can I use your microwave to heat it up?"

"Sure, go ahead," Skinner said.

The nun, looking at her Fritos, said, "You're lucky."

Virgil got the chicken potpie from the freezer, paid for it, went in the back room, popped it in the microwave, and was waiting for it to heat up, when Holland came in. "Plastic forks and spoons in the drawer under the sink. You figure anything out?"

"Not much, except that your mom's cafe sells sugar water as syrup."

"She puts sugar in it now?"

"Okay, I couldn't go to court and swear to it." Virgil told him that Ford might drop by and ask for an escort down to the church, and Holland said he'd do it or get Skinner on the case.

"What's next?" Holland asked.

"Nazis," Virgil said.

9

The deputy was sitting in his patrol car, reading a John Connolly novel, *Every Dead Thing*, when Virgil pulled in beside him. Darren Bakker got out of the car, carrying the book, and said, "Good thing we're going to talk to heavily armed Nazis 'cause now I can quit reading this book. It's scaring the hell out of me."

"That's a good one. I gotta say, reading it in a patrol car is the right way to do it," Virgil said, as they shook hands. "You don't want to read them at night in bed."

Bakker was a tall, thick man, with rosy cheeks, a blond brush mustache, close-cropped blond hair, and small blue eyes. He had a U-shaped scar on one cheekbone about the size and shape of a pull tab on a beer can. He was wearing a radio with a shoulder mic.

Virgil had gotten the impression that there were only two Nazis, plus spouses or girlfriends, but Bakker said that there might be three. "Which is a problem," he said. "The third one is a guy named Woody Garrett, and there are a couple of warrants out for him for assault and ag assault. Beating up his wife and daughter. He used a two-by-two on his daughter, told his friends he spanked her because she'd snuck out at night, but he managed to bust her pelvis. He's got a substantial track record, too."

"Charming guy," Virgil said. "Why's he hanging out with the Nazis?"

"He's a cousin to one of them. We don't know that he's there for sure, but a farmer called in this morning and said he saw him in Jim Button's yard last night, in the rhubarb patch. Button's the cousin. And a Nazi. The other Nazi is Raleigh Good."

"Raleigh? It's not pronounced 'Really'?"

"Nothing really good about Raleigh Good," Bakker said. "He is an asshole of major dimension, believe me."

"Hate assholes," Virgil said. "You can't even put them in jail for that."

"That's pretty hateful. I sometimes think we'd be better off if we put the assholes in jail and let the criminals go," Bakker said. "Now, Jim and Raleigh are mean guys. Mean! They like to start fights in bars with guys they know they can beat up. They made a mistake with one old boy a couple of years ago; he just about beat Raleigh to death, and was starting in on Jim Button, when some people pulled him off. Jim and Raleigh—they usually know their limits, though. Black eyes and bloody noses. I don't think they'd kill anybody, not on purpose anyway. The whole idea of prison scares them. The 'Don't drop the soap in the shower' thing."

"Glad to hear it. Too many guys look on it as free health care," Virgil said. "You want to lead the way?"

Virgil followed Bakker down eight miles of blacktop highway, three miles of blacktop side road, and a half mile down a dead-end gravel road. Jim Button lived in a decrepit clapboard farmhouse that a Midwestern cartoonist might have drawn: it appeared to be taller than it was wide or deep, like an inhabited silo, and it had all gone crooked, as if the two floors had rotated in different directions. Virgil could see eight windows, none of them matching. The last flakes of paint were peeling off the boards, and the front steps had collapsed into the weeds beneath the porch. The only new-looking thing anywhere was a silver propane tank next to a stand-alone machine shed.

A too-heavy blond woman was in the backyard, hanging clothes, and a red-and-black Nazi flag, on a clothesline. She stopped to look at them, and instead of running for the house, she took a cell phone out of her pocket and made a call.

Virgil parked beside Bakker, who had gotten out of his car and was talking into his shoulder microphone. When Virgil came up, he said, "I let the boys in the office know that we got here alive."

As he said it, a man in a black wifebeater shirt came out a side door, looked them over, called something back inside, and started toward them. Behind him, another man and two women came out of the house and trotted after him to catch up.

Bakker nodded at the leader—a thin, muscular man, with a fuzzy black beard and mustache—who displayed a variety of Nordic symbols tattooed on his arms, but nothing that would have impressed the average NBA player. Bakker said, "How you doin', Jim? . . . Virgil, this is Jim Button."

"What's up, Darren?"

As the others came up, Bakker said Virgil was a BCA agent, and Virgil said, "You heard about those people in town getting shot, right? Apparently with a .223, and we've been told that you folks have a bunch of .223s, and a grudge against the town. I'm checking to see if you can tell me where you were on Saturday around four-fifteen, and about the same time the Saturday before that."

"Wouldn't you fuckin' know it?" Jim Button asked the air. "Somebody gets shot, so who're you gonna blame? The National Socialists." He turned to his friends. "Can you believe this?"

Both the women who'd come out of the house had dark hair, but only one had swastikas on her earlobes. The other was prettier and had a dime-sized black rose tattooed on one side of her neck. She said, "I can tell you where I was the day before yesterday. I was at work, from three 'til nine, over in Austin. Raleigh dropped me off at three, and then he hung around for a while, bullshitting with my boss."

"Trying to get a cleaning job over there, after closing," Raleigh Good said. "You can call up Bob and ask him."

"So what time did you leave there?" Virgil asked.

"About four."

"You were bullshitting with the boss for an hour?" Bakker asked. "That's a lot of bullshit."

"Wasn't all bullshit," Good said. "We were talking about how I wouldn't be an employee, I'd be my own business, and I'd have to provide my own equipment and supplies; we also talked about what needed to be cleaned every day and what needed it once or twice a week. There was a lot of bullshit, but it wasn't bullshitting, if you see what I mean."

"About four o'clock, then."

"At least. No way to get back to Wheatfield and set up and shoot somebody. And I didn't have a gun with me—ask Rose."

"He didn't have a gun," Rose said. "They got two of them, and I saw both of them, in the rack, before we left."

Raleigh said, "See?"

Virgil asked Rose, "Where do you work?"

"Bob's Spinners and Bells," she said. "It's a gym. I'm a spinning instructor."

Button said, "I was at an assembly plant over in Albert Lea, looking for work."

"On a Saturday?"

"Weekend work. You can call and ask."

The clothesline lady said, "They had both cars. Me'n Marie stay home when they're all gone."

Virgil asked, "Do you have WiFi out here?"

Good, a short, wide man who seemed to consist mostly of tangled black hair and who undoubtedly had a broken-down Harley somewhere, snorted. "We're lucky we got runnin' water out here."

"You don't like it, you could always move," Button snapped.

"We got WiFi at the gym," Rose said. "Why?"

"Because you're all talking about reasonable alibis, but I need to check. If you could email the names of people who saw you around those places, who you'd talk to, I'd appreciate it. If everybody backs you up, then we got no problem."

The five of them eye-checked one another, and then Button said, "Sounds okay. We'd appreciate it if you could skip over the National Socialist stuff when you talk to them. Hard to find jobs, with all the bigots out there."

Virgil nodded. "I can do that. Though I gotta say, this being Minnesota, you'd have been better off to pick Communism. If you know what I'm saying."

"Got that, all right," said the unidentified, clothes-hanging blond woman. "I'm thinking about switching over."

Bakker gave Virgil a tap in the ribs with an elbow, and said, "Give me a minute, Virgil." He walked a dozen steps away, and when Virgil came over, he whispered, "If you look behind the machine shed, you'll see the back end of a black Chevy Camaro. Woody Garrett drives a black Camaro."

Virgil nodded, and said, "You want me to lead or you?"

"You got a gun on you?"

"As a matter fact, I do, at my back," Virgil said. "You know, heavily armed Nazis."

"Right. I don't think these guys are dangerous, but Garrett could be a problem."

They walked back to the group, and Virgil said, "Could you ask Woody to come out here?"

Button did an astonishingly bad imitation of a confused man. "Woody who?" He scratched his head and looked at the others. Rose rolled her eyes.

"Woody Garrett, who drives that black Camaro parked over there behind the machine shed," Virgil said, nodding toward the shed.

The group all turned to look, and Rose said, "Oh, *that* Woody Garrett. Jim thought you meant some other Woody."

Virgil was getting the impression that the group lacked cohesiveness. "Could you ask him to come out?"

"What'd he do?" the clothes hanger asked.

"Beat the heck out of his wife and daughter," Bakker said. "Busted the daughter up real bad, using a two-by-two the size of a baseball bat. Broke her pelvis."

"What! He beat up Anna? She's nine years old!" Rose turned to Button. "You said he had an argument with Sandy and needed a place to sleep for a couple of days."

Button said, "Well . . . he did. He didn't mention the beating-up part."

"You dumbass," Rose said. To Virgil: "He was sleeping in the back bedroom, first floor, when you showed up. He was drunk last night, so I believe he's still asleep."

"Are we invited in?" Bakker asked.

"No," said Button.

"Harboring a fugitive from the law is a felony," Virgil said.

"Like I said, you're welcome to come in," Button said. "Don't go shooting the place up."

"Yeah, we don't need any home improvements," Rose said.

The entire group moved to the house, but Button, Good, Rose, and the others waited in the kitchen, after pointing Virgil and Bakker to a door at the back of the house. Rose whispered, "The lock's broken."

Virgil tiptoed across a worn carpet, with Bakker a couple of feet behind, and tried the doorknob. It creaked, and Virgil gave it a fast twist and pushed the door open. The room contained an empty, two-tier bunk bed, a dresser supported on one side by a two-by-four that was replacing a broken leg, and an open window whose curtain was blowing gently into the room.

"He's run off," Bakker said, and he turned to sprint to the front door. As he took his first step, Virgil hooked his arm, put a finger to his own lips, and pointed beneath the lower bunk. Bakker stooped and looked under the bed; he could see two jean-clad knees.

"What do you want to do?" Bakker asked.

"Ask him to come out of there. Be careful, though, he could have a gun." Virgil stooped, and said, "We can see your knees, Woody. Don't make us drag you out."

A couple of beats later, "Fuck you."

Rose had walked up behind them. "What a dimwit," she said. "Woody, did you beat Anna with a board?"

"Fuck you, Rose. Did you tell them I was here?"

"No, dumbass. Your car was sticking out from behind the shed," Rose said.

"You got a gun?" Virgil asked.

"Fuck you."

"You go shooting at a cop, you're gonna die right here," Bakker said. "Keep that in mind."

"Fuck you."

Virgil walked to the end of the bed, noticed that it was bolted to the wall, and peeked under the lower bunk. He could see the soles of a pair of cowboy boots a couple of feet back. "I'm going to pull him out," Virgil muttered to Bakker. "Get your gun. If the motherfucker shoots at me, kill him."

"Happy to do it," Bakker said.

"Fuck both of you," Garrett said.

Virgil reached deep under the bed, grabbed one of the boots, and began pulling. Garrett kicked at him, and Bakker shouted, "Okay, there's another felony—assault on a police officer."

The boot came off, and Virgil fell back on his butt. The boot stank, and he threw it in a corner. "Come out of there."

"Fuck you."

Virgil reached back under and grabbed Garrett's sock-covered foot and pulled. He could get Garrett stretched out, but couldn't move him. Bakker peered under the bed, and said, "He's holding on to the inside leg, over in the corner . . . Give me some room."

Bakker knelt and grabbed Garrett's leg just above where Virgil had him by the foot, and they both pulled. Garrett kicked at them with his other, booted foot, hit Bakker's forearm, and Bakker fell back, and said, "Goddamn, that hurt."

Rose, in the doorway, said, "This is better than clowns at the circus."

Virgil said to Bakker, "Keep him stretched out. I'll be right back."

Virgil got up and jogged into the kitchen, where he'd seen an aging gas stove. Sitting on a shelf above the stove was the usual box of wooden kitchen matches. He carried the box back to the bedroom, broke one of the matches in half, said to Bakker, "Hold him tight," and then jammed the match through the sock between Garrett's big and second toes.

"What the fuck you doing?" Garrett demanded.

"I stuck a match between two of your toes," Virgil said. "I figure that when I fire that mother up, you'll let go of that bed."

"That's gonna hurt," Bakker contributed. "Only got a hotfoot one time, in high school. If I had a choice between getting my nose broken again or a hotfoot, I'd take the nose every time."

"Hold him tight, here we go," Virgil said. He scratched a match on the ignition strip on the side of the box and it fired up with a puff of smoke. Virgil blew a little of the smoke under the bed.

"Wait, wait, wait—I'm coming out," Garrett said. He let go of the bed's leg, and Virgil and Bakker dragged him out from under the bunk. Then Virgil tossed Garrett his boot.

"I'll put him in my car," Bakker said. To Button he said, "I'll be sending somebody to tow that Camaro. Don't go putting it on Craigslist."

Garrett to Button: "Better not fuck with my machine . . ."

The group followed behind Bakker and Garrett, who now had his hands cuffed at his back, out to the driveway. Virgil said to Rose, "Your friend's got swastikas tattooed on her earlobes."

"Yeah, well, she thought it was the thing to do at the time," she said. "We were up in the jug at Shakopee, and this chick offered to do it for free . . . I said no. Shirley decided to go with it."

"Bad life choice."

"No kiddin'. She went to one of those tattoo doctors to get it erased, but they can't do it. The doctor suggested she get her lobes cut off. He said trying to laser them would hurt worse than getting her tit caught in a wringer."

"Ouch. A doctor said that?"

"Yeah. Not that much of a doctor, though. We're still not sure what he was a doctor of."

"How come you guys were in Shakopee?"

"We borrowed some cars," she said.

"A lot of them? They don't usually send you to Shakopee for car theft."

"Two or three, and the people got them back. Not a scratch on them. But, the last one we borrowed belonged to a judge. We didn't know that. A new Corvette. Red. We drove it over to Sioux Falls and back. The judge wasn't the one who sent us to Shakopee, but judges hang together, you know?"

Virgil nodded. "I do."

"Sad story, huh?"

"Shouldn't borrow cars, Rose. At least, not from judges. By the way, do you know a guy named Clay Ford? Over in Wheatfield?"

"I know who he is."

"He kinda likes your looks," Virgil said.

Rose stopped and turned toward him. "Where'd you hear that?"

"From Clay. He's consulting with me—guns, these shootings. Kind of a shy guy, though. I don't think he'd come right out and hit on you."

"He's a great shot . . ." She thought it over. "Not a bad-looking guy, either, I gotta say. You're sure he was talking about me?"

"He said Rose, a dark-haired woman who won a turkey shoot up at Madelia, living out here with the Nazis."

"That's me, all right," Rose said. "Huh. I'm gonna look into this. These fuckers . . ." She waved toward Button and Good. "They were lame to start with, and they're getting lamer by the minute, but I needed a free place to stay after I got out of Shakopee."

Bakker put Garrett in the back of the patrol car, and he came over to Virgil, and said, "Good bust. That'll keep old Zimmer off my back for a couple of weeks. He's always talking about 'quality arrests.' . . . Can you find your way out?"

"Right, left, right."

"That's correct. Take it easy, Virgil," Bakker said, and he got in his car and rolled away.

Virgil turned back to the group, and said, "Okay. I'm willing to believe that none of you are involved in these shootings if you send me those names of people who can confirm your alibis. If any of you do know something, you better get in touch with me. If I bust you for being an accessory . . . You know, being a Nazi in front of a Minnesota jury isn't exactly a place you want to be . . . Email me those alibis. Names and dates."

They all nodded, and Rose followed him down to his truck, and, when they got there, Virgil said, "Get a cup of coffee with Clay. He's a little goofy about guns, but he's got a decent job and seems . . . calm."

She gave him a thumbs-up, and he backed out of the driveway.

10

As Virgil was driving to Wheatfield, Bea Sawyer called to say that she and Baldwin were on their way back to St. Paul with all the evidence collected at Andorra's farmhouse.

"We have a curiosity," she said. "Andorra's prints are on file with the feds. I know that because when we were looking at the .45, I could see a partial on the trigger, and I called and got a pdf of his prints. I can't be sure, because I was eyeballing it, but I'm fairly sure that the print is his. I can see an odd, interrupted whorl."

"Don't tell me you're now thinking suicide," Virgil said.

"No, not yet. I talked with the ME, told him what we'd found. He's going to have a real close look at the wound, checking all the angles and powder printing and all. But . . . if the shooter pulled on a pair of gloves before he pulled the trigger, then Andorra's prints could still be on the trigger. That would mean there was nothing spontaneous about the killing. It was planned and prepared for."

Bud Dexter—the BD of the target Virgil found in the trash can—was a semiretired farmer who lived in town while his son ran the farm. He was waiting for Virgil at the Skinner & Holland store, chatting with Holland and a woman working behind the counter. Skinner, Holland said, was probably at school, although not necessarily.

"He only goes about half-time, which is okay with the teachers," Holland said. "He can be a wiseass in class, but he aces all the tests." Holland nodded to Dexter. "Virgil, meet Bud Dexter . . . Bud, this is Virgil Flowers."

"Let's go in the back," Virgil said.

Holland: "Am I invited?"

"Of course," Virgil said.

They settled around the card table in the back room, and Holland poured some corn chips into a wooden bowl. Dexter took some chips, and said, "I'll tell you right from the start, I can't help much. The last time I was out there shooting, Glen was there, and we talked for a few minutes, but we were shooting pistols in separate bays. I had my nine, and Glen had his .45. Wardell says the guy shooting people here in town is using a rifle. There were some guys over at the rifle range when I was there with Glen, but I can't remember who they were—if I ever knew. You can't see the rifle range from the pistol range."

Virgil didn't mention it, but he was more interested in Dexter than the rifle shooters because Andorra had been shot with a pistol, and the rifle was probably stolen later. "Did Glen seem depressed or confused? Any reason to think he might have killed himself?"

"Nah. He was cheerful enough. He said he was going to run

over to Blue Earth when he was done shooting and pick up a showerhead. He said he had a leaky head that was really annoying."

"You think he went?" Virgil asked.

"I dunno," Dexter said. "He left before I did. The thing is, he was almost done shooting when I showed up. He probably left ten or fifteen minutes later; I was there for another hour. You know what I'd do?"

"What?"

"I'd check to see if there's a new showerhead. If there isn't . . . then . . ."

"Got it," Virgil said.

Virgil opened his mouth to ask another question, but there was a commotion out in the store, and then the young woman who'd been behind the cash register burst in and shouted, "They shot somebody! They shot—"

Virgil nearly knocked her down as he ran out the door. He saw people looking down toward the church, and a body in the street, and a woman shrieking, then people running away. He twisted around wildly, as though he were winding himself up, looking for somebody also running, but alone, or a car or van speeding away. There were at least a couple of dozen people on the street, but they were in clusters, nobody who looked like a possible shooter.

He ran to the body—an older woman, arms sprawled out on the street—stooped over her, and knew immediately that she was dead. He could see both the entrance and exit wounds; she'd been shot though the rib cage, behind her arm on one side, with the bullet exiting in front of her biceps on the other, probably passing directly through her heart.

Holland had run up behind him, a horrified look on his face, and Virgil shouted, "Keep everybody back—way back—and call the sheriff," and then he sprinted down toward the business district, as best he could in cowboy boots, looking for anything that seemed wrong.

There were people on the street, coming out of Mom's Cafe and the few open businesses, some now looking down toward the church and pointing, cluttering up his line of sight, and a few shouting or running back into the stores. The shot hadn't come from there, he thought, or the people would all be running, or milling around, looking for the shooter . . . so it must have come from behind the business buildings. But from which side?

He could go left or right; he glanced back and realized that one side was as good a possibility as the other. He went right because the yards and houses on that side were more of a jumble, with more foliage for concealment, than on the left side, and because the Smits' house was on that side. He was breathing hard now. He still had his pistol with him, since he'd been carrying it when he visited the Nazis, and he slipped it out of its holster and ran behind the first of the businesses.

Nothing was moving back there. He kept running, looking for movement, three hundred yards out, crossed a street and saw only two people, to his left, standing on Main Street, and they were looking down toward the shooting. It wouldn't be two people, he thought, and not in the middle of the street. The shooter had to be a singleton.

Five hundred yards and another street, nobody to his left on Main, but, a block down to the right, a woman getting in a car. He ran that way, shouting at her, and when he got close, she saw the gun and put up her hands, and he shouted, "Police," and, "Did you hear a shot? Did you see anyone running?"

She was twenty feet away, and she said, "No, no, I came out of my house . . . I just came out, I didn't hear anything . . . Has there been another one?"

Virgil turned away and ran back to the street behind the businesses, and ran even farther out . . . He thought he must be six or seven hundred yards from the scene, and there was nothing moving.

He ran toward the scene of the shooting, swerved when he came to the house where the old man with the shotgun lived, kicked open the gate, and banged on the back door.

Laura Smit looked at him from well back in the house, then hurried to the door and pulled it open.

"Did you hear a shot? Is Bram here? Did either of you—"

"I didn't hear a thing; I was using the vacuum," she said. "Bram isn't here, he went to the SuperValu over in Blue Earth."

"Goddamnit," Virgil said, and he spun around and ran out to Main Street, where people were still looking down toward the church. Virgil hurried over to the largest group, and said, "I'm an agent with the Bureau of Criminal Apprehension. Did anyone hear a shot a few minutes ago?"

Nobody heard anything, everybody had questions, which Virgil ignored, and he ran farther up Main, away from the shooting, asking everyone in the street. He couldn't find anyone who'd heard the shot.

Next, he crossed to the other side of Main, behind the storefronts. Nothing at the Eagles Club; the door was locked. He ran in widening circles and still found nothing. For the next fifteen minutes, he visited one store after another—there were only seven still open—asking if anyone had seen a man hurrying away in a long coat that a rifle could have been hidden beneath or with anything a rifle could have been concealed in. No luck.

He finally jogged back to the scene, where a single sheriff's car was now parked. The deputy had pushed the now thin crowd well back, and Holland was standing at the edge of the circle of onlookers.

In the middle of the circle, George Brice was kneeling over the body, apparently administering the last rites, although Virgil had understood that could only be done with the living—but, then, he didn't really know.

Holland grabbed Virgil by the arm, and said, "Not an out-of-towner this time. That's Marge Osborne. She lives here in town. Nice lady. I don't know who in the hell would want to do this to her . . ." A couple of tears trickled down his cheeks, and he wiped them away with the back of his hand. "Find anything?"

"Nothing, and nobody heard anything," Virgil said. He was breathing hard, his heart thumping, the blood pounding in his ears. He looked at the deputy. "You got anything in the car that we can use to cover the body? When the priest is done?"

The deputy said, "Yeah," and jogged over to the car and popped the trunk.

A man standing in the crowd called, "Hey! Hey!" Virgil looked his way. "Are you a cop?"

Virgil nodded, realized he still had his pistol in his hand, slipped it back in its holster. The man called, "Hey! I don't think she was shot from up there, where you ran."

Virgil went that way, and asked the man, "What do you mean?"

He pointed down the sidewalk. "I was walking up here, and when she was shot, she sort of . . . jerked. She was talking to somebody . . ."

A woman was sitting on the street, with a couple of other people, and she called, "Me . . . She was talking to me . . ."

The first man said, "So she was turned, and the bullet must have come from that way . . ."

He pointed down a street that ran at a right angle to Main.

The woman sitting on the street said, "I don't think so. I think it came from over there." She pointed to the business district.

The deputy was rolling a blue plastic tarp over the body, and Virgil called to him, and when he came over Virgil said, "I need to talk to these two people some more, so keep them close. And ask around and see if you can find more eyewitnesses. People who actually saw her get hit."

"Where are you going?"

"One guy thinks the shot came from down there," Virgil said, pointing. "I'm going to run down there, see if I can find anyone who saw anything. Get on your radio and tell Zimmer we need more people, we have to comb the neighborhood."

"Already got people on the way," the deputy said. He looked up the street. "Here comes one now."

Virgil looked that way and saw a sheriff's car coming, in a hurry, from the direction of the Interstate.

"When he gets here, send him down after me," Virgil said. "Make sure the witnesses stay close."

He ran down the street in the new direction, looking for somebody to talk to; after four hundred yards, he came to a cornfield, but the streets around him were empty, and the cornfield, with its ankle-high crop, looked like it stretched all the way to the Pacific Ocean. The second deputy jogged up to him, and asked, "What do you want to do?"

Virgil shook his head. "I dunno. I really don't."

Zimmer had arrived at the scene of the shooting, and the first thing he said to Virgil was, "Margery Osborne. I've known her my entire life. A nicer, more harmless lady you never met. When you find this sonofabitch, Virgil, I want you to kill him."

They both looked at the puddle of blue plastic tarp in the street, and Virgil said, "Get somebody to move her out of there. Crime scene won't have anything to work with. Get some photos and move her."

"One of my deputies knows her son. I'll have him do the notification. You see anything down the street?"

"Not a goddamn thing," Virgil said. "There's no place to hide down there, either. If that corn was two feet higher . . . But it's not."

"Could be a swale in the field," Zimmer said.

"Could be, but he'd have to stand up, sooner or later, and then he'd be as obvious as a scarecrow in winter. And if we went in there, he'd have no way to get away. He's smarter than that. The other possibility is, the witness is wrong. Or maybe he's right but misinterpreted what he saw. Maybe the shot came from exactly the other direction."

They both looked that way, down another long street, which also dead-ended at a cornfield.

"Fuck me," Zimmer said. "I'm going to send a couple of guys into that cornfield anyway. To look." He did just that, but they found no sign of anyone walking through the field.

Zimmer and his deputies had been talking to the witnesses before Virgil got back, and none of them had heard a gunshot. Virgil had never fired a gun with a suppressor, but he'd been involved in a couple of cases where they'd been used and had heard them fired—and they were loud. Nothing like in the movies, where they were a nearly silent *PHUT!*

More important than the loudness, though, was the quality of the suppressed sound. From a distance, unless you knew what you were hearing, they didn't sound like a gunshot. The sound was fuller, more that of a muffled bass drum than that of a snare drum.

The question became, did you hear an unusual sound? Did you hear that distant bass drum? He couldn't find anyone who would say he had. He wasn't even sure a suppressor was being used—Clay Ford, the gun nut, had said the rifle barrel wasn't threaded for one.

George Brice stayed with the body until it was moved to an ambulance. The deputies pushed the crowd back, and a volunteer fire department tanker truck washed away the puddle of blood. And then Brice walked over to Virgil, and said, "I'm going to close the church until you find the killer. There'll be some complaints, but we can't keep doing this."

Virgil nodded. "Good idea. I'll have the guy in a week. He's here, somewhere, and there aren't that many candidates."

Brice said, drily, "I admire your confidence."

"Yeah, well . . . that's about all I got. Did you know the dead woman?"

"Yes, I did. She was on the parish council. She was devout and levelheaded; she was even taking a computer course in Spanish. And she was the main source of funding for the repairs and cleanup. Oh, bother, we're going to miss her."

Virgil was thinking "Oh, bother" was something that he hadn't heard since a maiden aunt had said it years ago, and Brice looked nothing like her. Clay Ford jaywalked toward them, trailed by Rose, the woman who'd been living with the Nazis. Ford nodded at Brice, and said to Virgil, "I heard about Margery. I told you something about Glen's rifle that was wrong."

"Yeah?"

Ford said, "It's equipped with a suppressor. For sure. Rose was downtown when Margery got shot, and she ran and told me. She didn't hear a shot, and nobody else did, either. I couldn't figure that out, but I'd handled that rifle and there was no suppressor, and no way to mount one. Then, I thought, it's got a heavy varmint barrel, and it *could* be threaded for a suppressor, so I asked myself, where would Glen get that done? The answer was, over at Mark Ermand's machine shop in Fairmont. I called Mark, and, sure enough, Glen got it threaded a couple of months ago, which probably means the suppressor was on its way. It takes most of a year to get one, to get all the paperwork done, but if he was threading the barrel . . . he probably had it or was about to get it. I never saw it."

"Thank you," Virgil said. "That somewhat answers the question about nobody hearing any shots."

"Interesting shooting, though," Ford said.

The priest said, "I suppose," with a certain tone.

"Not what I meant," Ford said. "What I meant was, this guy shot two strangers, one in the leg and the other in the hip. Now he's getting zeroed in. I suspect he knows how to shoot, but he hasn't been able to practice. He's been afraid to take it out and shoot it. Maybe because people would recognize him. And maybe the gun, too, if they saw it."

"Hints at what we thought: he's from here," Holland said.

"And he might have been aiming to kill Miz Osborne all along," Ford said. "First two strangers are shot, like practice for the main event. Then, when he can be confident with the gun, when he knows the gun and scope, who does he kill? Miz Osborne. Why would you kill somebody like her? There are enough assholes—sorry, Father—hanging around the church, you'd think he'd shoot somebody that nobody liked. But he didn't. He's got a reason for shooting her."

"Madman," Brice said. "We're not talking about somebody operating on the common wavelength."

Skinner had walked up while Ford was talking, said to Virgil, "I heard," and to Ford, "You're making some good arguments."

"He's local, for sure," Ford insisted. "Glen wouldn't have gotten shot by a stranger, would he? How would the guy know what kind of guns he'd get? Maybe the guy wasn't exactly from Wheatfield, but he's from somewhere around here, and he probably knew Glen well enough that he knew about the suppressor."

Virgil: "I don't know."

Holland came up. "What are you going to do?"

"Gotta think about it," Virgil said. "I know a lot of stuff, but I haven't had a chance to sort it out."

"Thinking is good," Skinner said. To Holland: "I found us a taco truck, but we might not need it. Marge getting killed, that could kill the town as dead as she is."

Osborne lived at the other end of town, a two-minute drive, and Virgil and Zimmer talked about whether they needed to get a search warrant to enter her house. Neither of them knew.

"The problem is, she lives with her son—his name is Barry—and so we'd be going into his house, too," Zimmer said. The son was with his mother's body, Zimmer added, which was on its way to a funeral home in Blue Earth, for transfer later in the day to the medical examiner's office in St. Paul.

"We better call him," Virgil said. "I don't want him in the house before we have a chance to look at it."

"Seems unlikely that there'd be anything there . . . if this was another random shooting," Zimmer said.

"We don't know it was 'random.' It's different, because she was killed," Virgil said. "I gotta check her stuff."

"Better get a warrant, then," Zimmer said. "I got a judge who could have one here in an hour. I'll call him. And I'll have somebody talk to Barry."

While they were waiting on the warrant, Zimmer sent six deputies to knock on doors, asking about anyone seen on the streets at the time of the shooting. They got seven names. All but one of them were elderly, only one of them had anything that looked like a rifle, and that might have been a cane or a crutch, and none of them were in a place where they could see the shooting outside the church.

When Virgil heard that one man had something that could have been a gun, he went to talk to the witness. She'd seen a neighbor with something that might have been a cane, but she reported it because it was gunlike. Virgil went to talk to the man, who showed him the cane, and said, "I've had it for five years. Who told you it looked like a gun? Was it Wilson? That old bat never liked me."

As they walked away from the house, Virgil said to the deputy, "One guess."

"He didn't do it."

"You got it. And Wilson is an old bat."

They were operating on the basis of what eyewitnesses had seen, or thought they'd seen. Virgil kept in mind that of all the kinds of witnesses to crime, eyewitnesses were often the least reliable. They had two at the scene who actually saw Osborne get hit—and they thought the shots came from very different directions. Did either have a good idea of where the shooter had been? On reflection, Virgil thought it was about eighty for to twenty against.

"Goddamnit," Virgil muttered.

The deputy said, "Exactly."

They were standing at an intersection directly west of the business district. Virgil could see a dozen houses from where he stood, and perhaps eight of them were occupied. If he didn't get the shooter, give it five years and only four would be.

The deputy was like an earworm: lots of questions, none of them helpful.

"Now what?" he asked, as if he expected Virgil to pull a solution out of his ass.

Virgil didn't. He started back toward Main Street, and said, "I dunno."

A sheriff's deputy was taking statements, and he followed Virgil into the Skinner & Holland back room, where Virgil dictated a statement into the deputy's digital recorder. When that was done, Virgil called his nominal boss, Jon Duncan, in St. Paul, and told him about the killing.

"I need a little more intensity down here than I've got," he said. "Could you free up Jenkins and Shrake?"

"I can have them down there tomorrow," Duncan said.

"I'll see if I can get them a motel room."

They were two hours beyond the shooting when Zimmer retrieved Osborne's purse from a deputy, got her keys, and, when the warrant arrived, he and Virgil drove down to Osborne's house. "One of my guys spotted Barry Osborne coming out of the funeral home. Said he's pretty screwed up, but he said he'd come back this way. If he's not at the house now, he'll be there soon."

When they pulled up in front of the Osborne house, an older white Econoline van was sitting in the driveway, and Zimmer said, "I guess he's here." The van said "Steam Punk" on the side, in peeling vinyl letters, along with an image of a carpet steamer.

When they knocked on the front door, they heard a man croak, "Come in," and they went through door and found Barry Osborne sitting in the front room in a fifties leather chair, his feet up on a nonmatching ottoman. His eyes were red from crying and rubbing, and when he saw Zimmer, he said, "This is awful."

"I know, Barry. You have any idea who'd do this?"

Osborne was in his forties or early fifties, a fleshy, pink-faced man whose hair was going white; he wore a gray golf shirt and jeans and gym shoes with white ripple soles. "I don't," he said. "I don't know who'd do a crazy thing like this. Everybody loved Mom. They *loved* her."

"How often was she down at the church?" Virgil asked.

"Every day," Osborne said. "She went every day, and stayed

until they closed up. She was down in Florida when the Virgin appeared. She hates the cold up here, but she came back and went every night, hoping to see her. Every night. She believed the Virgin was coming back. She believed the church in Wheatfield had been chosen for a special mission."

He pushed himself out of his chair; his golf shirt had pulled out of his pants, and he shoved it back in with one hand, then wandered over to the front window and looked out, and said, "I gotta get out of this place. I walked in the door and saw her sitting there, in her chair by the TV, five minutes ago. I jumped, and she was gone."

"That happens," Virgil said. "It's a pretty well-known psychological phenomenon, after a tragedy like this."

"Really? She's not a ghost, is she? She turned to look at me." Tears started running down his face.

Virgil: "She's not a ghost. You'll see her image when you glance at a place where you're used to seeing her, and you're off guard. Like looking at her chair when you first come into a room. It happens to a lot of people."

Osborne said, "Okay," and wiped the tears away with the heels of his hands, and asked, "You guys need to see something?"

"I don't know . . . If she left something that might indicate that she thought she might be in danger . . ."

"She was scared about the shootings. She was there when that guy got shot. What's-his-name, from Iowa. She talked about it all the time, but she didn't think anyone would ever shoot her. She still kept going to church. I told her maybe she shouldn't, but she wasn't going to miss it, the Virgin appearing again."

"Did she do emails or Facebook, or that kind of thing?" Virgil asked.

"Oh, sure. I can show you," Osborne said. "You gotta get this guy. You gotta get him."

Margery Osborne had her own Facebook page, and Barry Osborne had her sign-on information. She had written a hundred posts, at least, about the Marian apparitions, and had saved reactions from her forty-six hundred followers. Zimmer, looking over Virgil's shoulders, asked, "You think one of them . . . I mean, Facebook is sort of known for crazies . . ."

"I don't know, but I'll scan it all tonight," Virgil said. "It's hard to believe that somebody from Idaho or Ohio would drive out here to shoot her."

Zimmer turned to Osborne, and asked, "When the Iowa guy was shot . . . how close did the shot come to your mom? Did she say where she was in the crowd?"

Osborne scratched his cheekbone, and then, "Well, I know she was close. Right there. But if you're asking six feet or ten feet or one foot, I don't know. Maybe some of the other people who were there could tell you."

Zimmer to Virgil: "What if this guy wasn't all that good a shot at all, that the first two tries were accidents? What if he was going for Marge and missed her and hit that Coates fellow?"

"It's a thought," Virgil said. "But what about the second shot?"

"Mrs. Rice . . . she sort of looked like Margery," Zimmer said. "I mean, not her face so much, but her general build. They were both pretty average height and a little heavy."

"Mom kept trying to lose weight," Osborne said. "I think maybe she . . . fantasized about finding another man. My dad died years ago, so it's been a while since she had a real companion."

Virgil asked Osborne, "We'd like to look through your mom's bedroom a bit, and around where she worked."

"Sure. The whole first floor. I've got the second floor. She spent most of her time on Facebook and doing emails, and then she watched television. She did cook, but, lately, mostly microwave stuff. She was down at the church every evening."

There was a pro forma aspect to their search: Virgil didn't expect to find anything meaningful, and they didn't. The first floor was what you'd expect if somebody had just walked out, locked the door, and then died. An unwashed coffee cup on a kitchen table, a slender glass vase with three bluebells next to the cup. The bedroom revealed an adjustable bed, raised to a semi-sitting position and neatly made. A television faced two chairs, one looking like it was used every day, another looking as though it hadn't been used for years. A basket with knitting needles and yarn in it sat next to the used chair.

"She was making another scarf for me. I've got about a hundred of them, they're the only thing she knew how to knit," Osborne said, and he began crying again.

A cat came out of a back room and looked at them.

An hour after they arrived, they were back in the street.

Zimmer said, looking at the house, "What a fuckin' mess."

Virgil stopped back at the Vissers' to use the bathroom and then sat on the bed and called the Tarweveld Inn to see if they had any available rooms for Jenkins and Shrake. They did. When Brice had closed the church, a dozen people had checked out, and whoever answered the phone at the inn seemed both surprised and grateful that somebody might want to check in. He almost signed up for a third room for himself but decided to stay with the Vissers. Not only were they friendly, they were a source of local information.

Night was coming down. Virgil had decided he needed something real to eat, so he drove down I-90 to Blue Earth and got some decent barbecue and California sweet corn.

Back at his room, he got out a legal pad and drew circles on it for a while, trying to figure out a rationale for shooting two out-of-towners, and then a well-known and well-liked local.

He could think of only one: the calculated killing of Glen Andorra to get the tool he needed—the rifle—and then two more to establish a pattern that would appear random, and then Osborne, to accomplish some unknown task while appearing to be the third in a random sequence. If that were the case, the shooter might take down one more to draw attention away from Osborne, the real target.

Of course, there might not be a rationale if the shooter were simply nuts. Maybe he'd been drawn to shooting at people at the church simply because that's where a crowd could be found; or maybe he hated the idea of something miraculous happening there that hadn't reached him.

He'd have to dig around, disturb the community, if he were going to flush out a crazy man. If the shootings had a solid motive, he had one question to ask:

Who benefits?

Though it was late, he pulled up the emails sent by Clay Ford and the Nazis, lists of people who could support their alibis. With a bit of luck, he got through to all of them. And both Ford and the Nazis were cleared. It wasn't absolutely definitive, but unless something else pointed to them, Virgil was willing to accept their alibis.

Before he went to sleep, Virgil contemplated God and His ways, an effort to make sense out of the chaos that cops regularly encounter. Sometimes, the act of rigorous contemplation led to new paths of investigation. But not on this night.

Instead, he spent some time thinking about Margery Osborne and what her son had said about her. She'd been born during World War II; her father was a veteran of the Pacific Theater and hadn't seen his daughter until she was three years old. He'd suffered from every disease the Pacific had to offer, frightening her with his random onsets of malaria. She'd been in junior high school before the farm got reliable television reception—she'd missed the advent of Elvis Presley but was there for the Beatles. She lived through the Vietnam era as the wife of a small farmer who, like her father, was a war veteran. She'd had two children, one of whom died shortly after he was born. She and her husband had struggled with a noneconomic farm, and she'd gone to work as a health care aide in Fairmont, seen the farm sold, and her husband die . . .

A world of experience and memories, all gone in an instant. For what? Money? What else could it be except the product of insanity?

But he wasn't getting that feeling, that edge of craziness.

Margery Osborne, he thought, had probably been sent into the final darkness for nothing more than the God Almighty Dollar.

11

Larry Van Den Berg rolled into Wheatfield at midmorning, parked his truck beside his house, went inside, made himself a pimento loaf with mustard and onion sandwich, got a beer from the refrigerator, and checked his secret email account for messages from his brother. Lego sales were holding up, though they hadn't gotten rid of them as fast as they'd hoped. But, then, there were a lot of them.

The last note said "This week, $1,400."

Nice.

He thought about the other iron he had in the fire: could he have been the only one to see the remarkable resemblance between Janet Fischer and the Virgin Mary? He'd give her a call. She didn't go to work down at Skinner & Holland until later in the afternoon. Even if she didn't confess, he might have time to rip off a piece of ass before she went to work.

She answered her phone on the first ring. "I'm not talking to you anymore, after what you said."

"I don't think you got any choice. Besides, you know you still love me," Van Den Berg said. "Tell you what. You at home? I'll come over, and we'll talk about it. Maybe snuggle a little."

"Well, you can come over anyway," she said, and she hung up.

Van Den Berg looked at the phone. Not the first time she'd hung up on him, although lately it had been happening more often. Still, he was the confident sort. He jumped in the shower, hit his pits and crotch with some 212 Sexy Men deodorant, in orange mandarin scent, got dressed, smiled at himself in the bathroom mirror, and started off for Janet's, smelling like an orange.

Nice day outside, warm, and redolent of the oncoming summer. Lilacs blooming; he stopped to sniff one, closing his eyes, remembered his mother. Okay, that wasn't good, but everything else was. A hot girlfriend, steady work, if not exactly the job of his dreams, money in the bank with the prospect of more. Maybe it was time to buy a boat. From Wheatfield, pulling a trailer, he could be at Lake Okoboji in an hour, and the Iowegians kept it stocked with walleye, pike, bass, and muskie.

Of course, as is the way of the world, and most of his dreams, it all went straight into the toilet when he got to Fischer's.

Janet Fischer lived in a tiny house that looked exactly like a big house only shrunken; it was roughly the size and shape of a boxcar. The roof was peaked, with a small window at its apex; the roofline couldn't have been more than twelve feet up; a narrow plank porch framed the front door.

The house had been built by the same man who'd built all the town windmills, sometime after World War II. It contained a compact kitchen that was separated from the living room by a breakfast bar; the living room contained a two-cushion couch and two easy chairs, separated by a coffee table. The single bathroom had only a sink, toilet, and shower, no tub. The single bedroom contained a queen-sized bed. The bed frame butted against the wall at the head end, with not more than a six-inch-wide clearance on one side and two feet on the other, and no more than four feet at the end of the bed. When the sex got intense, the bed knocked on the wall between the bedroom and the living room and shook the entire structure.

Van Den Berg crossed the porch and walked in without knocking, where he found both chairs at the coffee table occupied, one by Fischer and the other by Skinner. A laptop computer sat in the middle of the table.

"What's the kid doing here?" he asked.

Skinner shrugged, and Fischer said, "I went over to your house to clean it up a little bit and I got curious and I looked in your computer and you know what I found? Porn. All kinds of disgusting porn. You pig. We are no longer engaged."

She had her one-third carat diamond ring in her hand and she threw it at him. He tried to grab it, but it bounced off his chest and landed on the floor. She threw something again, this time a house key, and he managed to catch it. "I'll want my key," she said. "Right now."

Van Den Berg was taken aback, and some of his confidence leaked away. He thought he might be able to talk his way out of it, but it'd be tougher with the kid sitting there. "We can chat about it," he said, as he stooped to pick up the ring. To Skinner, he said, "Get lost, dickwad."

"We're waiting for Wardell," Skinner said. "He should be here in a minute or two."

"Oh? He wants to talk about the Virgin Mary, huh?"

"Not really," Skinner said. "I'm making a movie, and I'm hoping you three will give me some criticism, to make it better."

"You're making a fuckin' movie? Of what? The Virgin Mary?" Van Den Berg hee-hawed, and at that moment they heard the odd, unmatched footfalls of the mayor on the porch. Fischer shouted, "Come in," before Holland knocked and pushed through the door. He said, "Hey, Larry. Skinner. Jennie."

"Now that everybody's here, let's get the movie going," Skinner said.

Van Den Berg said to Fischer, "I'm not here for no movie. We gotta talk."

"Give me my key," she said.

"Everybody quiet down, the movie's started," Skinner said. "It's only a minute or two long."

The movie started on the laptop, a shaky video of a farmhouse. There was a voice-over, recognizable as Skinner. Van Den Berg, much to his surprise, was immediately engaged.

> *I'm at the farm of Ralph Van Den Berg, as you can see. Right here we're crossing the ditch and fence into Ralph's woodlot, but wait, what's this? A trailer from a tractor-trailer, back in the woods? Wonder what that's doing here? It's almost new. Still has this year's license plate.*

There was a close-up of the plate, and then a jump cut, and all the shadows shifted, as if a couple of hours had passed. A silver GMC pickup backed up to the trailer, and a man got out. A whispered voice said,

I believe that's Ralph. Wonder what he's doing?

That became clear when Ralph Van Den Berg took a padlock off the trailer, rolled the door up, and began loading boxes of Legos into the pickup.

Oh, my goodness. Look at all the Legos. L'eggo my Legos . . .

"What the fuck is this all about?" Van Den Berg demanded, as the movie rolled on and his brother unloaded more Legos into the bed of the pickup.

Holland cleared his throat. "Well, you called Jennie and said you thought she looked a lot like our Virgin Mary. She's not the Virgin Mary, but she does look a little like her. All you'd have to do to fuck up the town, Larry, is start talking it around. We can't have that."

"Bullshit. What you mean is, you and this fuckin' Skinner can't have it," Van Den Berg said.

"However you want to cut it," Holland said. "The Marian apparition is real. Jennie had nothing to do with it. But a few people think it was faked somehow, and if you start talking it around . . . well, you'll wreck the town. So, as mayor, I'll tell you what, Larry. You say one fuckin' word about Jennie being the Virgin, and we'll take this movie down to the Iowa cops. Me'n Skinner tried to figure out how much a trailer full of Legos was worth and we came up with a half million dollars minimum. And it could be a million, depending on which sets you got. That about right?"

"You motherfuckers," Van Den Berg said.

"We're the motherfuckers?" Holland asked, his voice rising to a dangerous growl. "You're threatening to wreck the town, and we're the motherfuckers? You stole a trailer full of Legos, and we're the motherfuckers? I'll tell you something else, Larry. We have a state cop in town, and I kinda casually asked how long somebody who stole a half million dollars' worth of merchandise would go to prison for. He said maybe two years, unless there were exacerbating circumstances. There's nothing like destroying a town's economy to qualify as an exacerbating circumstance, Larry. You go to trial in this county, and I believe you'd get five to ten. Of course, you'd have your brother in there to keep you company."

Skinner said, "We'd hate to see anybody from our town go to jail, Larry."

"You know what I want? Does anybody know what I want?" Fischer asked. "Nine years with an engagement ring but no wedding?"

Skinner said, "Uh, what do you want, Janet?"

Fischer looked at Van Den Berg. "I want a cut of those Legos, that's what I want, Larry."

"Oh, fuck you," Van Den Berg said. He stalked out, across the porch, across the yard. He ignored the line of sweet-smelling lilacs.

Fischer shouted after him, "I want my key."

They watched him go, and when he was out of sight, Holland said, "I think we're okay."

Fischer said, "I'm sitting here thinking about it, and you know what? I do want a cut of those Legos. Nine years. What am I supposed to do now?"

Skinner said, "Jennie, you're the prettiest girl in the county, and one of the smartest. You'll have all kinds of dating opportunities now that Larry won't be around. I'd bet you a hundred dollars that you'll have a husband and a kid in two years, and a whole happy life."

Fischer said, "Stick it up your ass, Skinner."

Skinner and Holland left, satisfied that they'd fended off the threat from Van Den Berg. Fischer sat on her two-cushion couch and thought about her nine lost years. She was now making great money down at Skinner & Holland, but who knew how long that would last? Van Den Berg was a man who liked his beer—make that beers, plural—and she'd bet that sooner or later he'd start talking about who the Virgin Mary resembled.

If those Legos were worth a half million, and if the Van Den Bergs were selling them for twenty-five percent of their retail value, like Skinner thought, they'd be getting a hundred and twenty-five thousand dollars, no tax. And if they were worth a million, they'd be getting two hundred and fifty thousand.

The longer she thought about it, the angrier she got—nine years!—until she finally put on her jacket and walked over to Van Den Berg's house. There, she pounded on the door until a still-angry Van Den Berg opened up, and demanded, "What do you want?"

"Nine years back, Larry, that's what I want. You have been fooling around on me the whole time. That gentleman's club out by Cheyenne, where you stop both coming and going, that's no better than a whorehouse. I want my key. And I want some of that Lego money."

Van Den Berg had a beer in his left hand, and it wasn't the first of the day. He glowered at her, then said, "There ain't no more money. The Legos are long gone."

She knew he was lying because Skinner had maneuvered

around the woodlot while Ralph Van Den Berg was hauling the Legos to his house for packing, and she could see from Skinner's video that the truck was still more than half-full.

"You're lying, Larry. We got photographic proof."

"That fuckin' . . ." He pushed the door open. "I'm not gonna stand here, arguing. You better come in."

She stepped inside as he stepped back, and she said, "All I want is my share."

"Tell you what I'll give you," he said. "How about this?"

He hit her right in the eye—hard—and she bounced off the door, and then he hit her in the mouth, and she fell down. "Now, get the fuck out of here," he said, kicking her hip. He was wearing steel-toed trucker boots, and she felt as though her hip had broken.

She tried to crawl away, and wailed, "Don't, don't, Larry . . . Don't, please . . ."

He kicked her again, and she cried out, and as she crawled back through the door, he kicked her in the butt, and said, "Come back, and I'll fuck you up. You tell your Skinner and Holland the same thing. They fuck with me, I'll fuck with them. Now, get the fuck out of my yard."

Fischer managed to get to her feet. Her hip burned like fire, and she hobbled back to her house, crying as she went. At her house, she looked at herself in the mirror and began to weep, for her nine years, for her hopes that she'd have two or three bouncing babies by now. Maybe she wept even a little for Larry.

12

Virgil woke early but lay in bed, thinking about Sherlock Holmes and that whole Holmes thing—that once you've eliminated the impossible, then whatever remains, must be the truth. What Holmes never admitted was that there is a vast universe of the possible, and sorting through all the possibilities is often impossible. Holmes would have been better off, Virgil thought, working with the Flowers Maxims:

If it's criminal, it's either stupid or crazy.

Stupid people usually have guns, crazy people always do.

In a choice between stupid and crazy, first investigate the stupid, because stupid is more common than crazy.

In many cases, stupid is also more dangerous than crazy. You could sometimes talk to crazy, but there's no dealing with stupid.

None of the above is always true.

Having established that the criminal was most likely dumb—with exceptions—the question became, how was he avoiding detection? A rifle shot actually makes two loud noises: the boom or bang caused by the exploding gunpowder and the loud crack when the bullet breaks the sound barrier.

When he was in the Army, in Serbia, Virgil had once spent some time in the pits below the targets on a rifle range. He was six hundred yards out from the shooting line and became familiar with the difference between a muzzle blast and a supersonic crack. The two sounds were separate and distinct. The passing bullet produced a crack—some people described it as *ZINGGGG!* or *WHIZZZZ!*—that was quite loud, followed by the hollow boom of the muzzle blast. On the other hand, the *ZINGGGG!* didn't sound like what most people thought of as a gunshot.

Other than Bram Smit, the old man with the shotgun, nobody had reported either one, and Smit had said the noise he heard sounded like a muffled thud—somebody dropping a shoe overhead. The muzzle blast would be attenuated by the suppressor, but it would still be loud. There must be other ways to muffle a shot, though—and that might be the thud that Smit had reported.

Maybe, Virgil thought, other witnesses actually had heard the shots but hadn't recognized them for what they were.

If they had heard them at all . . .

If the bullet was subsonic and didn't break the sound barrier, that would be far more interesting. There were a few commercial loaders of subsonic .223, but the energy levels of subsonic bullets were far lower than ordinary bullets, and the shooter would probably have to be much closer than they'd thought—likely not more than a hundred yards out, and possibly closer than that.

The arcing ballistics of the bullet might explain the two lower body shots. At a hundred yards, a subsonic bullet could drop a foot, so the shooter, not aware of that, might have been aiming at the victim's heart and hitting too low. And then by the Osborne murder, might have fully compensated for that.

A combination subsonic ammunition and suppressor would mean that the shot would be silent at the point of impact with the victim. As far as he knew, nobody had looked for the shooter at only fifty to a hundred yards out . . .

But all that subsonic stuff sounded crazy smart and didn't explain the two thuds heard by Smit. Nope. The shooter was probably using standard ammo, and the witnesses simply hadn't identified the sonic boom as a rifle shot. Sonic booms, as far as Virgil knew, might be reduced by the frontal area of the bullet, and .223s were small, sleek slugs.

But Smit . . . Smit created a problem. Was it possible that he hadn't heard the muzzle blast, the bang, but instead heard only the sonic boom, as the bullet passed close to his house?

Virgil was shaving when another thought occurred to him. He'd had an appointment the day before to meet Bud Dexter at Skinner & Holland at 4 o'clock. Virgil'd run a few minutes late, and they'd been talking for a while, but not too long, when Osborne got shot. She'd been shot, he'd bet, at 4:15, at almost exactly the time the other two were shot.

Why 4:15, or within a couple of minutes of 4:15? The obvious answer was that 4:15 was the time when you got the biggest crowds on the street corner across from the church. The first service was at 4:30, and if the Virgin Mary were planning to pop up, you'd want to be there a bit early to get a good seat.

But exactly 4:15? There'd be people on the corner at 4:10 and 4:25, as well. Maybe the shooter was coming from a job that ended at 3:30 or 4, and after going through whatever preparations he had to perform, it simply worked out to 4:15?

Nope. That wasn't right.

Another little mystery.

When he was cleaned up and dressed, Virgil thought about walking out to Mom's Cafe but decided he couldn't face a Mom's pancake. There wasn't much to eat at Skinner & Holland, either, but even a nuked chicken potpie would be better than Mom's.

Holland was hauling in more edible crap when Virgil walked into the store. The crowd was noticeably thinner than it had been the other times Virgil had been there, and he overheard two people who looked like townies complaining about the toll the shootings had taken on the tourist trade. "If I catch that rat, I'll pop his head like a fuckin' pimple," one guy said to the other, who replied, "Shhhh. That's the cop."

Virgil nodded, and said, "How ya doin', boys. If you catch the guy, let me know. I'll come over and shoot him for you all legal-like."

"Nice thought, but that's not what I heard about you," the pimple popper said.

Hung up deciding between a turkey potpie or a chicken, Virgil took a chicken, then put it back and took a turkey, then put that back, and one of the guys said, "Take the chicken. The turkey gives you bad gas."

Virgil took the chicken, walked it into the back room, and

shoved it in the microwave. Holland came through with a box full of blue corn chips, and said, "Hope I can sell this stuff."

"I ought to bust you for trying," Virgil said.

"That's how Communism got started," Holland said, as he disappeared through the curtain into the store. He was back a minute later, and said, "You know what goes with a chicken potpie?"

"A water glass full of Everclear?"

"Well, yeah, but I was thinking of Zingers. I got a gross of Zingers coming through in a minute."

Virgil waved off the Zingers, when they came through, and poked holes through the potpie cover with a plastic fork. Holland took the Zingers into the store. He was back a couple of minutes later, pushing through the door curtain with the empty box, when Virgil heard Skinner's voice call, "Wardell! Wardell!"

Wardell turned, halfway through the curtain. "Yeah?"

Virgil couldn't see Skinner but clearly heard him say, "That fuckin' Larry beat up Jennie, man, real bad. She's got—"

He suddenly stopped talking, and Virgil knew that Holland had cut him off and was making some finger gestures that meant "Flowers is in the back."

Virgil swallowed some potpie, and called, "Come on back and tell me about it, Skinner. Janet getting beat up and all."

Skinner poked his head past the curtain. "You don't know Janet."

"Come in here. I want to hear about it, and I want to know why Janet got beat up," Virgil said.

Holland came through with Skinner a step behind him, both obviously uneasy, shuffling their feet. Holland said, "This has nothing to do with the shootings. This is something else."

Virgil kept eating, and, between swallows of molten chicken grease, said, "Tell me about it anyway."

"Ah, man," Skinner said. Then, to Holland: "I think we ought to tell him. We can't let it go."

Holland bowed his head, gripped his skull with one hand, then said, "This fuckin' apparition is gonna be the end of us. We already got two dead and two wounded. It's like we're back in the 'Stan."

Skinner: "We don't even know that the apparition has anything to do with it. The guy's obviously a nutcase. He was gonna go off sooner or later. What does that have to do with Larry?"

"Maybe . . ."

"Fuck it, I'm gonna tell him," Skinner said.

"Go ahead," Holland said. "I've got more boxes to unload." He started toward the back door, stopped, turned, came back, and sank into a chair facing Virgil. "I'll tell it."

"I'm listening," Virgil said.

Holland told the story, folding in a few carefully selected lies. Larry Van Den Berg was a truck driver engaged to Skinner & Holland's afternoon cashier, Janet Fischer, who they called Jennie. Fischer had done some bragging on how well the store was doing, and Van Den Berg, after thinking it over, had decided he wanted a cut. He'd told Fischer that if he didn't get one, that he'd tell everybody that the apparition was faked by Skinner and Holland, and that Fischer had posed as the Virgin Mary.

"He made it all up. It's complete bullshit. But if he started talking it around—well, he could mess up the whole town. Jennie told us what he wanted, and we went over to her house to have a talk with him."

Skinner said, "Tell him the rest of it. Tell him about Ralph."

Virgil said, "Yeah, tell me about Ralph."

Holland said, "Well, we were desperate to keep Larry from

starting this kind of talk. Jennie had seen some . . . emails . . . on Larry's computer, about some Lego sales . . ."

"Lego sales?"

When it had all come out, Virgil said, "We had Iowa cops up here last year, looking around. They called me to let me know. Lot of Legos involved, I guess."

"Thirty-eight hundred cubic feet, worth between a half million and a million bucks, depending on what they were," Skinner said. "Looked to me like more than half of them were still in the trailer."

"I'll have to tell somebody about this," Virgil said. "If he beat up your cashier, I don't feel too bad about it."

Holland and Skinner looked at each other, and Skinner nodded.

"But what's the right thing to do?" Holland said. "I mean, I know what the legal thing is, but we've known Larry a long time, and he had a really awful, mean childhood. I went to school with him, so I know. We want him to go to prison? We could get a couple of Jennie's friends and have a chat with him."

Virgil asked, "Would that chat involve a pool cue?"

"I don't know where we'd get a pool cue," Holland said, "but something like that. Jennie has quite a few friends in town. Larry doesn't."

Virgil shook his head, and said, "I'll handle it, Wardell. You? Stay out of it."

At that moment, Fischer pushed through the door. She was wearing a pleated skirt, a white blouse, and a faded high school letter jacket with a Greek harp where the letter would normally go, the insignia of a marching band letter. She had a purple ring under one eye, and a badly swollen lip where her teeth had cut into it. She said, "Whoops!" and started to back out, but Virgil said, "Janet? Come in here."

She stepped inside.

Virgil asked, "Are you still engaged?"

She asked Skinner and Holland, "You tell him about it?"

Skinner said, "We couldn't let it go."

She said to Virgil, "The engagement's over. I thought about shooting him, and I would have, but I don't have a gun."

"I'll take care of it," Virgil said. "I'll put his ass in jail."

Fischer said, "Fuckin' A," and tears began rolling down her cheeks.

"You can't count on him being inside for long," Virgil told her. "When he makes bail, you gotta stay away from him. We'll get a court order that says he has to stay away from you, too."

"Be tough, in a town like this, with one store and one cafe," Skinner said.

"So what? You can't go around beating up women," Holland said.

"What a dummy," Skinner said.

Fischer put her fists on her hips. "You keep calling him that. He might not be as smart as you, but he's thinking all the time. About money, unfortunately . . ."

Skinner jumped in. "And porn."

Fischer continued. "Money. That's what that day-trading thing was all about. And remember when he was going to start that Jimmy John's? And when he was going to be a landscaper? All he thinks about is money. He's smart. I bet he knows more about money than anybody in town. Who's got it, who doesn't; how they got it, why they didn't."

"Then why's he driving a truck?" Virgil asked.

"Because that's what he can do," Fischer said. "His folks were pure white trash. Larry started from zero and worked like a dog, and now he owns his own house and truck."

"I don't like to hear you defending him," Skinner said. "Not after he beat you up, the way he did. Show them your hip. Go on."

"No, I'm not going to do that . . . I don't know . . ."

Skinner said to Virgil, "She looks like she's been in a car accident. I tried to get her to go to the hospital, but she won't do it. Now she's saying how smart he is and what a hard worker he is."

Fischer said, "It's a bad habit. I'll break it."

Virgil called the sheriff's office to get a deputy to stand by while he was busting Van Den Berg. Zimmer told him that because of the shootings, he'd kept at least two deputies in the immediate area and he could have one at Skinner & Holland in a few minutes. Virgil reheated what was left of the chicken potpie while he waited for the deputy, and told Skinner, Holland, and Fischer that he was struggling with the problem of why nobody had heard the supersonic crack of the rifle bullet and the apparently nonrelated question of the timing of the shootings.

"There's something important going on there," Virgil told the other three. "I can't figure out what it is."

They hadn't figured it out when the deputy arrived, a woman named Lucy Banning. She pushed through the curtain, saw Fischer, did a double take, and said, "Oh my God, Janet, it's you? Did Larry do that?"

Fischer started to cry. "Yeah."

The deputy looked at Virgil. "I'll take the complaint."

She did that, and when Fischer finished a short statement, with Banning taking notes, Banning tipped her head toward the door, and said to Virgil, "Let's go get him."

Outside, she said, "I want to do this. I'd appreciate backup, but I want to haul his ass in myself."

"You know him?"

"We all went to high school together," Banning said. "I could never figure out what Janet saw in him. He was a jerk then, he's a jerk now."

"But he's not the dumbest guy in the world . . . at least, that's what Janet thinks," Virgil said.

"Oh, he's not dumb. Did real good in math and accounting. I mean, I'll tell you, Larry had a rough time growing up. Everybody knows it. It's his folks who made him a jerk, but a jerk is still a jerk wherever it came from. And you don't go around beating up your fiancée."

"Ex-fiancée," Virgil said.

"I hope. I've seen a lot of them go back."

Nothing in Wheatfield was very far from anything else. Virgil followed Banning over to Van Den Berg's house. Van Den Berg was in his side yard when they pulled up, washing his tractor unit. When he saw them coming, he said, "What do you want, Lucy?"

"Janet Fischer said you beat her up last night. That right?"

"We had a fight, but she was into it, too."

"Not what she says," Banning said. "Doesn't look like she messed you up much."

"Look. Let me talk to her, we'll straighten it out," Van Den Berg said.

"Too late for that. I'm going to have to take you in," Banning said. She unhooked handcuffs from a belt case, and Virgil moved off to one side, where he'd have a clear run at Van Den Berg. The other man looked at him and then back at Banning. "You always wanted to do this, you bitch." He threw the hose he was holding on the ground, and it snaked around, pumping water.

But he didn't resist. Banning put on the cuffs and led him to the car. Virgil walked over to the house and turned off the faucet, and asked Banning, "You want me to follow you in?"

"Naw. He'll be okay in the back of the car. You getting anywhere on the shootings?"

"Trying to figure out why nobody can hear the gunshots. They were from a .223, so . . . they had to be loud. And we're wondering why they're all exactly at four-fifteen."

Banning scratched her ear, frowning, then shook her head, and said, "Beats me."

They loaded Van Den Berg into the backseat of the patrol car, Banning said, "See ya," and drove away. Virgil got in his truck and started back to Skinner & Holland. He was halfway there when the patrol car pulled up behind him, and the flashers came on.

Virgil pulled over, and Banning hopped out, and when Virgil rolled down his window she said, "Larry says he has something to tell you."

"Okay." Virgil followed her back to the patrol car, and Banning opened the back door, and Van Den Berg leaned out, and said, "I know why nobody heard the gunshots and why everybody got shot at four-fifteen. You let me go, and I'll tell you."

Virgil said, "Larry, if you know something, you have to tell us.

It's murder we're talking about now. You beating up Janet, that's a whole different thing."

"You're not going to let me go? Then you know what? You can go fuck yourself." He looked at Banning. "Shut the door."

Virgil said, "Larry . . ."

"Fuck you." He laughed. "Fuck you."

Van Den Berg sat in the center of the backseat, staring at the screen separating him from the front seat, and wouldn't say anything else. Virgil tried again, but Van Den Berg turned away.

Virgil said to Banning, "Take him."

She slammed the back door, and Virgil said, quietly, "See if he'll talk to you. Maybe he does know something."

"I will," Banning said. "Sorry about that language."

"Lot of people have been telling me to go fuck myself," Virgil said. "It's starting to wear on me."

At the store, Virgil found Skinner and Fischer still in the back room, and Fischer asked, anxiously, if they'd made the arrest.

"He's on his way to jail," Virgil said.

Holland came in and asked the same question as Fischer.

Virgil answered the same way, but added, "You know what? He says he knows why nobody heard those shots. And why all those people got shot at the same time. He said he'd tell me if I'd let him off the hook on the assault. I wouldn't do that. But he figured it out in five minutes, and I kinda believed him."

The other three looked at one another, all frowning, then Skinner said, "If that dumbass figured it out . . ."

Fischer said, "I keep telling you, he's not a dumbass. He

probably did figure it out. If he did, then I say let him out. That's more important than—"

Holland shook his head. "No. He's going down."

"What we gotta do here is crowdsource it. Ask around," Skinner said. "If he figured it out in five minutes, somebody else will even if we can't. We could get Danny Visser to put it up on the town blog."

Virgil said, "We can do that. We need to find that out. Our real problem is, right now we don't have anything to work with. We know where the killer got the gun and the suppressor and the ammunition, and none of that helps. The crime scene people aren't giving us any help, because they're like us—they got nothing to work with. If we knew why he was always shooting at four-fifteen, if we knew why we can't hear the shots . . . then we'd know something serious."

The priest, George Brice, stuck his head into the room, saw Virgil, and stepped inside. "I heard you were back here, and I wondered if you're getting anywhere? People are unhappy that we've closed the church. I won't reopen it until we have a handle on what's happening . . ."

Virgil: "We don't know enough yet."

He explained about the gunshot problem and the 4:15 shootings, and Brice looked from one to the other, and then said, "I can tell you why that is—though I didn't think of it until this second."

"What?" Virgil asked.

"We've got these big speakers up in the bell tower," Brice said. "Recordings of the bells of Notre-Dame. We start playing the bells at four-fifteen, for three minutes. The call for the four-thirty Mass."

They all stared at him, then Virgil slapped himself on the forehead, and said, "Duh."

Holland said, "We should have thought of it. But we've been playing the bells every day since Christmas. They're louder than heck, but I don't even hear them anymore."

"Same with me," Skinner said, and Fischer nodded.

"The bells would cover the gunshots for anyone near the church, and he wouldn't fire until he heard them. The bells determined the time. I thought I'd figured out something important, but I hadn't," Virgil said. "We really are back to square one."

13

Virgil, now seriously bummed, went out to his truck and called Frankie, asked her how she was feeling. Better, she said. The morning sickness had receded, at least temporarily. He told her what had happened with the bell recordings.

"Sounds like you were trying to avoid an actual investigation," she said. "Where would figuring out the boom and bang get you? You checked all the various directions and didn't get anywhere."

"Thanks."

"I speak only the truth," she said. "Go work harder."

"It's weird—I'm both frantic and bored. I gotta find this guy, but I'd rather be home with you."

"The harder you work, the sooner you'll get here."

He told her about arresting Van Den Berg and the circumstances surrounding it. "Good for you," she said. "You know what I think about that kind of thing."

She'd once been attacked by a couple of hired thugs outside a convenience store when they'd mistaken her for somebody else.

Retribution had been exacted, in the guise of several Armenians armed with baseball bats who thought they were doing Virgil a favor by beating up her attacker. Virgil disapproved, in theory, but Frankie admitted that the men had greatly lifted her spirits and she sent a thank-you note and a bottle of top-end Artsakh to the chief Armenian.

When he got off the phone, Virgil sat in his truck for a while, thinking about his next move. He couldn't think of anything relevant, so what he did next had nothing to do with the shootings. He called a friend named Bell Wood, a major crimes investigator with the Iowa Division of Criminal Investigation.

"Virgil fuckin' Flowers," Wood said when he picked up his phone. "The poor girl's answer to soft porn."

Virgil asked, "Did you guys lose a trailerload of Legos last year?"

"Not only that, we lost the trailer," Wood said. "You wouldn't know where they are, would you?"

"As a matter of fact, I do," Virgil said. "They might not be there long. One of your suspects is in jail up here for beating up his girlfriend. He'll probably get out tomorrow morning, and he'll probably be afraid that she or one of her friends will rat him out and he'll move everything."

"Give me the details," Wood said. "There's a ten-thousand-dollar reward from the insurance company, but since you're a law enforcement officer, you don't qualify."

"I was told this by the girlfriend, so maybe she would," Virgil said. "She could use the money."

"Probably. But since she'd be dealing with the weasels from an insurance company, I wouldn't hold your breath," Wood said. "In the meantime: details."

Virgil told him the whole story, and Wood said, "What? They're down here in Iowa?"

"Barely, I think. They're not actually in Armstrong; they're a few miles north of town. You don't have to go very far north before you're out of Iowa and into Minnesota. The guy who found them, who is fairly smart, says they're in Iowa."

"I've been in Armstrong," Wood said. "The high school's on the north side of town, right as you'd be coming in. You can't miss it. Why don't you come on down around ten o'clock, we'll meet in the parking lot?"

"That's good. The guy'll make bail between nine and ten, and if he's going to move the truck, he'll have to pick up his tractor unit. We can watch his brother's place until he shows and grab both of them. I'd sorta like to see this guy get some time."

"Ten o'clock, then," Wood said. "By the way, Jack Carey told me this morning that you'd been seen in Wheatfield and that shortly after you arrived a woman got murdered."

"You shouldn't draw any conclusions from that, about me being a curse, or anything, but yeah, that's basically what happened," Virgil said.

Virgil had pulled back onto Main Street when his phone buzzed again: Jenkins, another BCA investigator.

"Where are you?" Virgil asked. "Is Shrake with you?"

"He's about a hundred yards back," Jenkins said. "We thought two cars would be handy. We're on I-90, going past Blue Earth. See you in a half hour or so."

"Glad to have you. We've got some boring stuff to do today."

"That's great. I love boring stuff. So does Shrake. Any nice-looking women in Wheatfield?"

"Well, as you know, there's the Virgin Mary," Virgil said. "If she knows you're coming . . . But, of course, she would."

"Yeah, yeah, yeah. Where do you want to hook up?" Jenkins asked.

"About fifteen miles past Wheatfield," Virgil said. "You got your iPad?"

"Does the Tin Man have a sheet metal cock?"

"I assume that means yes," Virgil said. "Let me give you the address. It's out in the countryside."

Bea Sawyer, the crime scene specialist, had hidden the key to Glen Andorra's house, wrapped in a plastic baggie, beneath a brick by the mailbox. Virgil retrieved it, went into the house. The odor of death still lingered, but not with the choking virulence of Virgil's first visit; the Vicks wouldn't be necessary.

Sawyer's partner had duplicated the hard drive on Andorra's Dell laptop for further examination at BCA headquarters. The password had been "ppasswordd," and Virgil turned the computer on, entered it, and searched for "range."

He found a long series of emails and several WordPad documents, including one that was a list of range members, with their addresses, phone numbers, and emails. He printed out the list, which turned out to be twenty-four pages long, then scanned through the last hundred or so emails, where he found nothing of interest.

He remembered what Bud Dexter, Andorra's shooting friend,

had said about Andorra getting a new showerhead. He climbed the stairs to the main bathroom, where he found what looked like a new showerhead in the stall and, in the wastebasket, the package it had come in. Maybe Andorra never emptied the basket, but it seemed more likely that he'd been killed shortly after Dexter had spoken to him on the range.

As he was walking back down the stairs, a civilian Crown Vic that dated back to 2011 pulled into the driveway, followed by a Ford Explorer. Jenkins got out of the Crown Vic, waited for Shrake to catch up. They were both large men, somewhat battered, who wore too-sharp gray suits and high-polish steel-toed dress shoes.

Virgil went to the door and let them in, and Shrake wrinkled his nose, and asked, "You got something in the oven?"

"Guy was dead here for a couple of weeks," Virgil said. "Anyway, we need to interview a bunch of people. We're looking for a good marksman who knew Glen Andorra. Andorra was the dead guy here—"

Jenkins interrupted. "We got a briefing from Jon before we came down. He told us you'd screwed up the investigation, as usual, and were looking for a couple of pros to figure it out for you. We know about Andorra and Osborne and the two wounded victims, and that you can't figure out why nobody could hear the gunshots—"

"Figured that one out," Virgil said.

He brought them up to date, including the fact that they were back to square one. "We've got some legwork to do. I'd be willing to bet that the shooter was a regular out here and knew Andorra well enough to be invited to his house and allowed to walk around, out of sight, while Andorra sat in his easy chair. The range has something like a hundred and eighty members. I don't think we need to interview all of them; I think we can talk to a couple of dozen, at random, and get some pointers to the real possibilities."

He divided up the list of range members, taking eight pages himself and giving eight more each to Shrake and Jenkins, and added, "We'll want to spot these addresses on our mapping software so we can work through clusters of people instead of running all over the place."

"Good," Jenkins said. "Let me get my iPad. Does this place have WiFi?"

It did.

Shrake found Marlin Brown crawling around his freshly tilled garden plot, following a yellow string across the ground, his nose about two inches from the dirt. He was a compact man, wearing compact coveralls with plastic knee protectors. Shrake watched him, puzzled, then called, "Mr. Brown?"

Brown looked up. He had dirt on his nose. "Hi."

"I'm with the state Bureau of Criminal Apprehension. I'd like to speak to you for a moment."

Brown stepped carefully out of the garden plot, and Shrake asked, "What the heck are you doing?"

Brown said, "Planting radishes." He held out a cupped palm.

"Really." Shrake peered into Brown's hand, which contained perhaps a hundred reddish gray spheres smaller than BBs.

"Cherry Belle Organics," Brown said. "I'm a little late getting them in, but it's been cool."

"Those'll turn into radishes?"

"Not a gardener, huh?"

"I once grew a marigold," Shrake said. "It died and made me sad."

"That's life on the farm," Brown said. "Anyway, what can I do for you?"

Brown went to Andorra's range to shoot his shotgun and didn't know much about the rifle guys. He did have some names of people whom he'd seen shooting rifles, and Shrake made notes on his list. "This is shotgun country down here," Brown said. "Not much call for high-powered rifles."

Dick Howell was a rural route mail carrier. When Jenkins pulled into his driveway, he found Howell's girlfriend unloading groceries from her car. Jenkins was aware that country women, when alone, were nervous about large men in suits showing up unexpectedly, so when he climbed out of his car, he stood next to the car door, and called, "I'm an agent with the state Bureau of Criminal Apprehension. Is Mr. Howell here?"

"He's out carrying his route," she called back. Jenkins had seen her relax, so he took his ID out of his coat pocket and walked up to her, showed her the ID, and asked, "Do you know where he might be?"

"I can call him and ask," she said.

She did, and Jenkins caught Howell as he waited in a turnout by a bridge over a wide creek; he was sitting on the railing, looking down at the water.

Jenkins introduced himself, and asked, "Any fish in there?"

"Nothing you'd want to eat, I don't believe," Howell said. He was chewing tobacco, and he hocked a wad into the creek.

Jenkins thought, Not now anyway, but didn't say it. Instead, he said, "I'm looking for information about target shooters over at Glen Andorra's range."

"I heard about Glen," Howell said. "Sounded bad."

"Yeah. Anyway, we need to talk to people who were friends with Glen, who might've spent some time shooting with him."

"The only guy I saw him shooting with at all was a guy from town, Clay Ford. Don't go telling Clay I told you that . . ."

Virgil found Will Courtland working on a piece of farm machinery in the welding shop next to his house. The shop smelled of hot metal and welding rods, and Virgil got him out in the driveway and asked about Andorra's friends.

"The thing about Glen was, everybody liked him but he wasn't a hang-out kind of guy," Courtland said. "As far as I know, he mostly worked around his farm and at the range. Close friends . . . I'm not sure he had any. I can tell you the names of a couple of people I supposed would be his closest friends and maybe they could tell you more, but I can't say that they're superclose to him. I wasn't. But, you know, you don't have to be a close friend to go inside somebody's house. You get deliveries from UPS and boxes from the mailman; you maybe get plumbers or electricians for stuff you can't do on your own . . ."

He gestured to the machine in his shop, and said, "I'm working on this fellow's rake. When I take it back, I'll probably go sit at the kitchen table while he writes a check or gives me his VISA card. I mean, I'm friendly with him and all, but we're not close. But there I'll be, right in his house. Like the guy who shot Glen."

That's the way the day went.

They met at 5 o'clock at the Tarweveld Inn, where Jenkins and Shrake checked in. They left their luggage in their rooms, and Virgil took them down the street and introduced them to the back room at Skinner & Holland. Holland sat in with them.

Virgil summed up. "We got six consensus names and seven more random maybes," he said. "The problem being, not a single person thinks any of those guys would be the shooter, and only two of them live in Wheatfield."

"You think the shooter has to live here?" Jenkins asked.

"I think the shooter has to be somebody that people see regularly, so that he fits in, and they ignore him. Also, he's familiar enough with Wheatfield that he's got a spot to shoot from, and that he can get out of, without people noticing."

"How about this?" Shrake asked. "What if he's on a roof? And he doesn't get out? He stays there with his rifle maybe for hours and sneaks off after dark? Has anybody looked on a roof?"

"I looked on the Eagles Club roof, but only because you can jump off it," Virgil said. "Never occurred to me to look on the roof of the higher buildings. You know, where you might need a ladder or a rope to get off of it."

"I didn't think of that, either—that the guy would hide right where he was," Holland said. "He'd still need a way to get up there. Couldn't just put up a ladder with nobody noticing."

Virgil pointed at him. "What about those remodeling jobs? Was there anyplace where they opened up the roof, and you could get up on top from the inside? Where there was like a hole in the ceiling?"

Holland said, "I don't remember any—but I don't know."

"We have to go look," Virgil said. "If he was up there and left anything behind—anything—we could get DNA."

"And we got two guys we should interview, the ones who live here," Shrake said.

Jenkins sighed. "We gotta do all that, but you want to know something? The roofs ain't it. And neither one of those townie guys is the shooter. That's all too easy. This guy's doing something else."

"Mr. Bright Side," Holland said. To Virgil: "I was arguing with Father Brice about opening the church. I suggested we form a kind of militia to walk the streets before and during the Masses. I thought we could get Clay Ford to organize it. Brice said he'd think about, but I don't think he'll do it."

Virgil, Jenkins, and Shrake all trooped down to the business district. They could find no openings from the remodeled apartments that led to the roof, but one building at the near end of the downtown block did have access. The building housed what had been a dying hardware store that lately had been doing better. The owner opened what looked like a closet door on the second-floor storage area and led them up a dark, narrow staircase to the roof.

Up on top, they had a good view of the corner where the victims had been shot, and the building's parapet would have made an excellent rifle rest. They searched the area on hands and knees and came up with not one atom of evidence nor any indication that anyone had recently been up there.

"If the guy came up to the roof and put a sandbag on the wall here," Jenkins said, pointing at the two-foot-high parapet, "there'd be no sign. With this hard tar roof, there's no scuffing. There's nothing here."

"Possible sequence," Shrake said. "The guy has a key to the hardware store—don't ask me how. He comes up here at the crack of dawn, before the store opens. He has a rifle and a sleeping bag and maybe even one of those little tents like canoe guys use. Maybe a rope, for a possible emergency getaway. He bags out all day until the bell rings and he shoots. Then he takes a nap until dark and the excitement's over and he slides out the door."

Jenkins said, "I'm still back where I was: the roof ain't it. This guy is too smart to put himself where he could be trapped with no way out. The guy's doing something else."

They interviewed the two townies. Both had alibis for at least one of the shootings, and the alibis were convincing. One of the men, who claimed to be the best shot in town after Clay Ford, and possibly Roy Visser, said, "You tell us the guy didn't even have his own rifle. You don't even know how close he was when he fired it, so you don't know if he was a good shot or not. I gotta tell you, it doesn't sound to me like he's a big marksman if he had to steal a rifle and had to kill to get it, huh? Sounds to me like it could be anybody who's ever looked through a scope, which is everybody in town. No offense, but you need a whole new tree to bark up."

His wife poked Jenkins in the chest, and said, "Yeah."

14

Virgil went to bed discouraged. Every time he found something that looked like a lead, it turned out to be a dead end. God didn't show up that night, so he slipped off to sleep without conversation.

Bell Wood, the Iowa state investigator, called at 9 o'clock the next morning, and said, "We're going through Humboldt right now, so we're an hour out of Armstrong. We still on for ten o'clock?"

"Might as well be, I'm not solving any murders," Virgil said. "And who's 'we'?"

"Special Agent Easton, Special Agent Rivers, and myself," Wood said. "If this thing works out, I might take a day off and come up and solve your Wheatfield problem myself."

"I'd appreciate that," Virgil said. "See you in a bit."

Virgil called Jenkins and Shrake, who were at Mom's getting breakfast. "I'll be there in four minutes," he said. He drove to Mom's, parked, went inside, and saw Jenkins and Shrake picking at their pancakes.

When they saw Virgil, Shrake pointed at his plate, and asked, "What are these things?"

"I asked the same question," Virgil said. "Got a tip from Mom's son: stay away from the meat products."

"So what are we doing?" Jenkins asked, pushing the pancakes away.

"I'll pick up Skinner and drive down to Armstrong, where he'll take us to Ralph Van Den Berg's place. You two will hide in Jenkins's piece of shit and wait for Larry Van Den Berg to get back to his house. He'll be back on the street about now, and it'll take him twenty minutes to get here. If he heads south for Iowa, we want to know about it. If he doesn't for an hour or two, we'll raid Ralph's place anyway."

"We gotta find something to eat," Shrake said.

"Skinner and Holland have chicken potpies that aren't bad. I've had a couple of them," Virgil said.

Shrake looked at Jenkins, and said, "We gotta hurry."

Virgil picked up Skinner as Jenkins and Shrake ran into the store.

"They're in a hurry," Skinner said, looking after them.

"Breakfast," Virgil explained. "They were down at Mom's. They were uncertain about the food."

They walked by Jenkins's Crown Vic on the way to Virgil's Tahoe, and Skinner asked, "What kind of car is that?"

"Crown Victoria—they quit making them before you started driving, even if you started driving when you were twelve," Virgil said.

"Actually, I started when I was eight. I only started running into that cop when I was twelve." Skinner stooped to peer through the Crown Vic's side window. "Looks like a piece of shit."

"You have naturally good taste," Virgil said.

They headed south, and Skinner said, "I had a bad thought this morning. If the guy quits shooting right now, we'll probably never get him. If Father Brice left the church open, we might have another chance."

"What you mean is, if we let somebody else get murdered, we might be able to ambush him because we'd be waiting for the shooting."

"The way you say it, it sounds wrong," Skinner said.

"I apologize."

"See? Now you're giving me a hard time."

They engaged in more pointless speculation all the way to the Iowa line; and Skinner filled in some of his own background. His mother, he said, was a pleasant, intellectual woman who communed with the earth and Buddha, and sometimes went on earth- or Buddha-related trips, and other times on mind-expanding trips, depending on what was coming in from Colorado. "She's a positive enough person, but ambition to my mom is like kryptonite to Superman," Skinner said. "She wants nothing to do with it. With the money from the trust fund Grandpa set up for her, it's not a problem. We're not rich, but we're not poor, either."

He was not curious about the identity of his father. Virgil suggested the red hair might be a tip-off, but Skinner said his mother was tall, red-haired, and freckled, so appearance wouldn't help.

In Armstrong, Skinner pointed out the high school. "I played a basketball game there in junior high. I can't remember why."

A pickup truck with a camper back and a dusty black Mustang pulled into the parking lot ahead of them, moved to one side, and parked. Bell Wood got out of the Mustang, hitched up his pants, and looked around, and, a second later, a woman got out of the other side. Another man got out of the pickup, wearing overalls, a plaid shirt, and a ball cap. Skinner muttered, "Cops."

"Yeah, what'd you expect?"

"Cops. They look like cops. They dress like farmers and they still look like cops. The stink hangs on them. Even the chick," Skinner said.

"Careful with that 'chick.' She's probably armed."

"See, the thing you don't know is, lots of women cops want you to think of them as chicks," Skinner said "Because the alternative is, they're like Nazi prison guards, all waxy-faced and carrying billy clubs. You gotta think about their self-image, not some kind of artificial construct in your own head. And they think they're 'chicks.'"

Virgil couldn't think of an immediate rebuttal—"artificial construct"?—and let it go.

Bell Wood was a big, square man with a brush mustache and gold-rimmed glasses that made him look a little like Teddy Roosevelt, which he knew. He was a major in the Iowa National Guard and had done a tour in Iraq. His subordinates, relishing the double entendre, called him Major Wood behind his back and occasionally to his face.

The woman with him was slender and square-chinned, had pale brown hair and amber eyes—possibly the best-looking woman in Iowa and all adjacent states. The man who'd driven the pickup truck was narrow-faced, with shoulder-length brown hair and a three-day beard; he would have looked at home on a bench in a bus station. Skinner was right: despite the surface patina of a farmer, he was giving off a distinct law enforcement vibe.

Skinner, in the meantime, had introduced himself to the woman, whom he then introduced to Virgil as Katie Easton. Virgil shook her hand, and he shook hands with the bus bench guy, Joe Rivers, and Wood asked Skinner, "You're the kid who found the trailer?"

"Yeah. It's a couple of miles back north."

Virgil pulled an aerial view up on his iPad, and they gathered around the hood of his Tahoe and looked at it. "Can't see the trailer," Wood said.

"Can't see it from off the property, either," Skinner said. "It's right . . . here." He put his index finger on the center of the farmstead's woodlot.

"All right. Well, we've got a warrant on the basis of the video Virgil sent me, so we can go in. We'll move as soon as this Larry Van Den Berg shows up with his truck. If he doesn't show, we'll go in at noon, or thereabouts." Wood said. "You guys better hang back. We'll wave you in."

"If you run into trouble?"

"Then we'll wave you in faster," Wood said.

Virgil and Skinner waited while Wood, Easton, and Rivers armored up. They didn't look at Easton, because she was so pretty that they didn't want to be seen staring. When the Iowans were ready to go, Wood handed Virgil a police handset, and said, "You know how these work. Turn up the volume and leave it on your passenger seat."

Virgil took the radio, and, two seconds later, his cell phone beeped: Jenkins.

"Van Den Berg showed up, ran inside his house, came back out two minutes later, jumped in his truck, and he's headed your way. In a hurry."

"Excellent. Stay way back, don't let him spot you," Virgil advised.

"You mean, like experienced cops?"

"Exactly. You've got a half hour ride."

Virgil relayed the word to Wood, who said, "Then we gotta go. I want to cruise the place. I'll get off at a crossroad as far down as I can get and still see the truck coming in. And I want to take Mr. Skinner with me while we make the pass at the house. I'll drop him off before we go in, and you can pick him up while we wait."

Virgil nodded. "I'll follow from way back. There's not much time . . ."

Wood's Mustang, with Easton and Skinner riding along, was a black dot on the horizon when Virgil saw it take the left turn past Ralph Van Den Berg's place. Rivers, in the pickup, continued on the highway past Van Den Berg's and, before Virgil got to the turn, pulled into a field access track and parked, so conspicuous in the pickup that he was inconspicuous.

Virgil took the left past Van Den Berg's, following Wood. The house was a blue-painted rambler with faded white shutters, and sat a bit lower than the road, with a detached garage to one side and a red metal barn in back. A sprawling woodlot sat west of the house along a fence line. Virgil saw no hint of a trailer. Janet Fischer had referred to the place as "an acreage," and Virgil estimated there were six, surrounded by bean fields that didn't seem attached to Van Den Berg's place.

Access to the house was by a wide driveway across a culvert; the ditch along the front was four feet deep and steep-walled. There were four cars; and three men and a woman were standing in the driveway, talking, an air of tension or contention about them. They were dressed for work—canvas jackets, long-sleeved shirts, jeans, and boots. All four cars were pulling trailers.

The people in the yard looked toward Virgil as he went past. But dusty Tahoes were as common as pickups, and Virgil accelerated away and, a mile farther down the road, found Wood parked around a turn on a side road. Wood, Easton, and Skinner got out of the Mustang and walked back to Virgil as he pulled in behind them. Virgil got out, and Wood said, "More of a crowd than I expected."

"We should get my guys to fall in behind Joe and arrive all at once," Virgil said. "You guys can lead, but if there's trouble, we'll have six cops right on top of them. I'll come in last and put the Tahoe across the driveway—they won't make it across the front ditch pulling trailers if somebody decides to run for it."

"Sounds like a plan," Wood said. "Talk to your guys. They must be, what, ten minutes out?"

"Something like that," Virgil said.

He got on his phone to Jenkins and asked where he was. "Got a ways to go yet. Shrake's iPad says we're still ten miles north of the Iowa line. We're staying way back."

Virgil told them to look for Joe Rivers and follow him in. "There are a bunch of people there, at least four, and maybe more that I didn't see. We're all going in at once."

They waited. It was a clear, cool, damp day in northern Iowa, ankle-high beans and corn as far as they could see. Blue metal silos were sticking up here and there, marking farmsteads. A cock pheasant sprinted across the road a hundred yards down. Easton leaned her well-toned butt against the Mustang and thumb-typed on her cell phone while Skinner ambled back and forth between the vehicles, hands in his pockets, occasionally glancing at Easton. Waiting.

Easton asked nobody in particular, "Anybody take the train from Paris to London?"

"I haven't, but my old man has," Virgil said. "Goes through the Chunnel. I think he said it took two hours, or something."

"So you could make the round-trip in a day?"

"My dad did," Virgil said. "Took an early train, spent the whole day in London, rode back that night. Never had to change hotels."

"Cool," she said without looking up, still thumb-typing. "I'm going in June."

"Where in the fuck are they?" Wood asked.

"Been six minutes since you last asked," Skinner said.

"Shut up, punk," Wood said.

"Fuckin' cops," Skinner said.

Nerves.

Virgil's phone beeped. Shrake said, "We crossed the line ten seconds ago. We're three minutes out."

"Saddle up," Virgil said to the others. "Three minutes."

Wood called Rivers as he and Easton walked up to the corner, where they could look down the road toward Van Den Berg's acreage. Virgil pointed Skinner to the passenger seat of the Tahoe and then he got in himself and started the engine. Skinner said, "I can't believe Katie could stand there and text when we're going on a raid. I don't even know why they'd allow a woman to go on a raid."

"So here's something you don't know, Skinner," Virgil said. "You never say that about a woman cop. Never. Not unless you're ready to run for it, 'cause they will flat kick your ass."

Skinner considered, then said, "You're right. I was being stupid."

He really *was* smarter than he looked, Virgil thought. As he thought that, Wood and Easton turned and jogged back to the Mustang, and Easton called, "He's here," and, a moment later, they were all rolling.

Rivers's pickup turned the corner as Wood's Mustang approached Van Den Berg's driveway, and the pickup was right on Wood's tail as they pulled into the yard. Shrake and Jenkins were fifty feet behind the pickup and went down the driveway, and Virgil pulled into the entrance of the driveway and then turned so the Tahoe blocked it. He said to Skinner, "You sit tight."

Skinner said, "Bullshit, I want to see this," and he was out and walking to the middle of the yard, where Larry Van Den Berg's truck was pooping out diesel smoke, and the cops had surrounded Van Den Berg and the three men in work clothes. Virgil saw the woman running toward the woodlot, with Easton and Shrake close behind, and Virgil could hear Easton's soprano voice as she shouted, "Down on the ground. On the ground . . ."

Larry Van Den Berg saw Virgil and pointed his finger, and said, "You motherfucker. You motherfucker," and one of the other men asked, "For Christ's sakes, what the hell is going on? Why are the cops here?"

Shrake and Easton caught up with the woman, put her on the ground, cuffed her, Easton patting her down, and they brought her back. Shrake said, "Skinner nailed it. There's a trailer back there."

Rivers had cuffed Larry Van Den Berg, and Wood asked the woman, "Are you Jill Van Den Berg?"

"Who wants to know?"

"Iowa Division of Criminal Investigation," he said. "Where's Ralph?"

She said, "In the house." And, "This isn't fair."

"Does he have a gun in there?" Shrake asked.

"Yes, but he'd never shoot anyone," Jill Van Den Berg said. She said her daughter, Billie, was in the house with her father.

Wood made Larry Van Den Berg and Jill Van Den Berg sit on a trailer, told Rivers and Jenkins to keep an eye on them, told the other three men to sit, uncuffed, on another trailer, "Until we have a chance to talk." Then he, Easton, Virgil, and Shrake walked to the house, with Skinner trailing despite Virgil telling him repeatedly not to.

The screen door was closed but the inner door was open, and Wood pulled the screen open and shouted, "Ralph! Ralph, come on out here." A man's voice answered. "Don't scare my little girl."

"You're fine, Ralph. We'll give her to her mom."

Ralph Van Den Berg, a thin man with a scruffy dishwater-blond beard and shoulder-length hair, poked his head around a corner, and said, "We're coming. Don't do nothing."

He was leading a little girl by the hand. When they were outside, Easton told him to face the house while she cuffed him and patted him down. Wood took the little girl's hand, and said, "C'mon, Billie, we'll go see your mom."

The girl started to cry, but Wood had Rivers uncuff Jill Van Den Berg, and told her, "Why don't you take Billie back in the house. Don't do anything weird. We'll be in to talk to you in a while . . ."

The semitrailer was still stacked with Legos. The three men who'd been in the yard, with their trailers, told Wood that they'd been hired by Ralph Van Den Berg to unload the semi and haul the Legos to a self-storage unit in Emmetsburg. They said Van Den Berg told them the big trailer had to be returned to its owner. The Iowa cops got their names and addresses and, after recording their individual statements, sent them on their way.

A couple of sheriff's cars showed up and hauled away the male Van Den Bergs. Jill Van Den Berg was told that she might be charged in connection with the theft but, for the time being, would be left with her daughter.

By 4 o'clock, it was all done, and Wood said to Virgil, "I owe you one."

"At least one," Virgil said.

"No goddamn excitement at all," Jenkins said. "I expected more."

"This is Iowa," Shrake said. "Your expectations were grossly misplaced."

"We got a big meth bust coming in a day or two," Easton said. "The cookers have lots of guns, from what we hear."

Jenkins regarded her for a moment, then said, "Now you're teasing me."

She said, "I don't tease, pal. I deliver."

That killed conversation for a few seconds, then Jenkins asked, "You ever think of moving to the Cities and the big time?"

That made her laugh.

As the Minnesota cops and Skinner were packing up, Virgil quietly asked Wood, "So what exactly is your relationship with cupcakes?"

"Shhhh . . . Don't even ask that question, and for God's sakes don't use words like 'cupcakes.' Or 'peaches.' Or any small, round objects at all," Wood muttered.

Virgil said, "Or any members of the melon family?"

"Oh, Jesus, no," Wood said, glancing sideways at Easton, who was thirty feet away, talking with Skinner. "Tell you the truth, I'm almost afraid to work with her. She's an excellent cop, but she's too good-looking, and that ain't good, if you know what I mean. I don't joke with her. I don't walk too close. I won't even buy her a cup of fuckin' coffee. Or even non–fuckin' coffee."

"Very strange," Virgil said.

"It is, and she doesn't like it any more than us guys. But it's not up to her. Somebody else could say I was walking too close to her, and, the next thing you know, there'd be an inquiry and we could both have career problems," Wood said. "The world is getting goofier by the minute, Virgie."

"I will be talking to you," Virgil said. And to Skinner: "We're outta here."

Skinner was silent for the first ten minutes of the ride back, but shortly after they crossed the Minnesota line, heading north, he said, "I kinda liked that."

"What? Being a cop?"

"It's embarrassing," Skinner said. "All I ever knew about cops was that they'd hassle you for having a beer."

"When you were twelve," Virgil said.

"Minnesota and Wisconsin are to beer what wine is to France, and, in France, kids can drink a little wine," Skinner said.

"Okay. Now, let me tell you about cops," Virgil said. "There are a lot of good ones, but I couldn't claim that they're in the majority. Maybe a third of them are pretty good, another third are just getting through life, and the last third are bad. They're poorly trained or burned-out, not too bright, have problems handling their authority. You got cops who'll hassle women for sex, use drugs, steal stuff . . . basically, criminals. But you get a job like mine, it's interesting. And you're doing some good."

"I don't know if I could handle making people feel bad, like Jill and Billie," Skinner said. "Of course, there's the money thing. Cops don't make any."

"There are some downsides," Virgil said. "The money thing,

and, then, crooks are human. They cry. They get sad, they apologize. But you know what? All that comes after they fuck somebody over. You gotta keep that in mind. The money thing . . . I have a hard time worrying too much. I got enough."

"Stealin' Legos? Is that really fuckin' somebody over? Bet it all got covered by insurance."

"Probably. But people who steal and don't get caught, they don't stop until they do get caught. They do all kinds of damage along the way. If Van Den Berg hadn't gotten caught, and if he'd gotten rid of all those Legos, he'd be looking for another score," Virgil said.

They rode along in silence for a minute, then Virgil added, "A few weeks ago I busted a guy about five years older than you, over in Owatonna. He was burglarizing houses. He'd stalk housewives, who'd leave their house to pick up their kids at school. He knew when they'd be gone, and he knew what their husbands did and that they wouldn't be home. He'd ransack the house, looking for anything small and valuable. Wasn't all that much money involved, and most of it was covered by insurance, but some of those women? They didn't want to live in their houses anymore. There'd been a criminal inside, somebody had been watching them, and it scared them. That guy's going away for a while, but he did a hell of a lot of damage before I got him. The damage won't go away, because the damage was done to those women's heads."

Skinner said, "Huh."

Virgil said, "A smart guy like you, Skinner, you could do four years at the U and maybe get a graduate degree in something. From there, you could get a job with the cops, do two or three years on the street, which is fascinating in itself, and then move into investigations. It's an interesting life, if you're the kind of guy who likes to think."

"You know I do."

"That's why I said it," Virgil said.

Virgil, Jenkins, and Shrake rendezvoused in Skinner & Holland's back room to try to rekindle the investigation into the shootings. With the church still closed, there wasn't much movement around town.

Jenkins said to Virgil, "We can't operate on the theory that the shooter's a nut, because if he is, we can't do anything but wait until he gives himself away. If he quits now and throws that rifle into a river, we'll never get him. We've got to assume there's a motive."

"If he's got a motive, it'd almost have to involve Miz Osborne," Virgil said. "The other two victims weren't from here, didn't know each other, didn't have anything in common that we know of, other than they were both shot."

Skinner, who was sitting in, said, "What if the real target in this thing was Glen Andorra, and this guy's done these other shootings to divert attention away from Glen?"

They all thought about that for a while, then Shrake shook his head. "It's possible, but I don't think so. The three shootings here in town were too carefully thought out. He planned all this before he went after Andorra."

"We have to go back to Andorra, though—and Osborne, too," Virgil said. "We're getting late in the day. Let's think about it and pick it up tomorrow."

Jenkins and Shrake wanted to get something decent to eat, which meant going out to a larger town. They invited Virgil to go along, but he decided to drive back to Mankato and spend the night with Frankie.

"I'll be back by nine o'clock. We'll go back on Osborne and Andorra. Something has to be there, with one of them."

15

After Larry Van Den Berg and his brother were arrested, they were taken to the Lewis County Sheriff's Department and processed. Bell Wood came by later with Katie Easton, but Ralph Van Den Berg had called a local lawyer, who'd told them not to make any statement at all until he could talk to them the next morning, so they didn't.

The Van Den Bergs were put in separate cells at the county jail, far enough apart that they couldn't talk. There'd be a bond hearing the next morning, the lawyer told them, and they'd need to put up either cash or something of serious value if they wanted to get out. Ralph could put up his house; Larry could put up either his house or his truck, or, if he needed to, both.

The real problem was, cash to pay the lawyer.

Larry lay on his bunk and thought about that. They needed cash and they needed it in a hurry. He had four thousand dollars in his checking account, and something like another four in savings, but that wouldn't cut it. If he hadn't punched Fischer, she might have been a source of a few thousand more, but that was gone now. Couldn't sell the house, because he'd probably need it for bail; even if he did sell it, it'd go so cheap that he'd never find a comparable place that he could afford.

He was jammed up, due to that fuckin' Flowers.

The jail turned out to be a good place to think: there weren't many customers, and so the place was fairly quiet.

And as evening shaded into night, Van Den Berg began thinking about the Wheatfield shootings. As Fischer had said, he wasn't stupid. He knew more about Wheatfield money, and who had it, than anyone. There was only one good reason to kill somebody, he thought, and that was money. Shortly after midnight, having thought about several dozen possibilities of who the shooter might be, and with his mind going round and round, he thought he'd identified his man.

The guy was superficially mellow enough, but Van Den Berg had known him since he was a child and had always been wary of him. His own parents were heavy boozers and brawlers, and he'd been regularly whacked on the side of the head and occasionally beaten with a leather belt, but even as a child he'd recognized that the shooter was something a bit different. Not so much an active threat; but when he looked at you, he looked at you like you were a bug ready to be stepped on.

Since the Lego heist wasn't related, and wasn't even under Minnesota jurisdiction, giving the identity of the shooter to Flowers wouldn't raise a nickel or buy him a break. On the other hand, the shooter had a few bucks . . .

He thought about that for the rest of the night. When the sun came up, he was sixty-seven percent sure he was correct in his identification of the killer; and thirty-three percent possibly wrong.

The next morning was tedious, going back and forth from the cell like a trolley car, talking to the lawyer, signing papers for the cops and finally for his release. The local prosecutor stood in for the state at the bail hearing and agreed to release the brothers if they both wore GPS ankle monitors and put up their major assets—their houses—as bond for their later appearances in court.

In Larry Van Den Berg's case, the judge agreed that he could continue to drive his tractor-trailer cross-country if he agreed to sign a waiver of extradition processes from whatever state he tried to hide in, if he did that. "I don't want to deprive you of your source of income before you're found guilty of a crime, but if you abuse this agreement in any way, I can assure you that I'll put you in jail, and leave you there," the judge said.

Van Den Berg agreed, and after his attorney gave him a forceful nudge, thanked the judge for his consideration.

Outside, the lawyer was up-front. "If we go to trial, I'll need twenty thousand dollars. I'll need a down payment of ten thousand, to cover expenses and all, and I'll need it in the next couple of weeks. We can work out a schedule on the rest, but I'll need the ten right away. If there's no way you can get it, well, the public defender here is . . . okay."

"Oh, fuck that," Ralph Van Den Berg said. "I know that guy."

Larry Van Den Berg said, "I'll get the money. I got some of it now."

He had to get back to Wheatfield. He had eight thousand

dollars that he could get at, but it was hard-earned, and he was loathe to spend it if there was any alternative.

Which he now thought he had.

The Lewis County sheriff released his tractor unit, and Van Den Berg said good-bye to his brother and headed home, the GPS monitor already chafing his ankle. He had an hour on the road to indulge in fantasies in which he shot that fuckin' Flowers and that fuckin' Skinner, and even that fuckin' Janet, who, if she'd kept her fuckin' mouth shut after the accident—he was now thinking of the beating as an accident that was, basically, Fischer's fault—nothing would have happened, and he'd be a free man.

But mostly he thought about money and about the Wheatfield shooter. He might not be absolutely sure he had the right guy, but he was fairly sure. While the guy was definitely a psycho—he had to be to do what he'd done—he was also a weenie: Van Den Berg would put the guy up against the wall and squeeze him. How much? The lawyer had said he'd need twenty thousand through the course of the trial, and the shooter could get that much, for sure, with a new mortgage on his house.

Maybe. If he really was the shooter.

Back in Wheatfield, he parked his truck in the yard, and as he turned to get out he saw a curtain move in a side window.

What?

He got a tire iron out of a door pocket and carried it with him to the front door, used his key to get in, and pushed through . . . and found Janet Fischer, staring at him from the hallway. Her arms were full of clothes and a pillow. "I'm leaving right now. I came to get my stuff."

Van Den Berg's eyes narrowed. He tossed the tire iron aside, and asked, "How'd you get in? You gave back the key."

"The back door was open."

"Bullshit. I locked up tight before I left, and I got good locks." He stalked toward her, pushed the pile of clothing—hard—forced her back. Pushed her again, and again, until she was in the kitchen. He looked at the back door, which had little, diamond-shaped windows set at eye height, so he could see out to the porch. One of the diamonds had been broken in, and there was glass on the floor. "You fuckin' broke in."

"I wanted to get my stuff while you were away . . ."

Her black eye had started to turn purple, her lip was still swollen, but Van Den Berg didn't even think about that. What he did was, he hit her in the other eye, and she screamed and dropped the clothes and put her hands up, and he hit her again, high in the stomach, knocking the breath out of her, and she sagged against the kitchen counter, and pleaded, "Larry, don't . . . Larry, don't . . ."

He hit her in the mouth again, and she went down, and he kicked her in the thigh once, twice, and finally thought, now what? And, I'm out on bail . . .

He looked at her, cowering on the kitchen floor, and backed away and took his cell phone from his pocket and dialed 911. When the county officer answered, he said, "I found somebody broke into my house and I'm holding her until a cop gets here. She attacked me . . ."

Virgil had talked to Frankie the night before, and she'd said he better come out to the farm. "I'm kinda hung up here."

"By what?"

"You'll see when you get here," she said.

When he got there, he found a strange car, a new Chevrolet, parked in the driveway; and when he went inside, he found Frankie sitting in the kitchen with her sister, Sparkle, who was apparently the hang-up. Sparkle was a thin, pretty blonde of suspect morality with a freshly minted Ph.D. from the University of Minnesota.

She said to Virgil, "How ya doin', good-lookin'?"

"Sparkle was going by on her way back to the Cities. She dropped in to see how I was," Frankie said.

"So how are you?" Virgil asked, taking a chair.

"Today wasn't bad, until Sparkle got here," Frankie said. The sisters loved each other—maybe—but had a thorny relationship; Sparkle deliberately exacerbated the thorniness by flirting with Virgil.

Frankie asked him how the investigation was going, and Virgil said, "We might finally be seeing some movement," and then had to explain it to Sparkle, and Sparkle asked, "Listen, if you were to arrest me for some reason . . . would you put handcuffs on me?"

"Probably around your ankles," Frankie said. "Then you wouldn't be able to spread your legs apart."

Sparkle: "Says the woman who has five children with five different men and has a bat in the cave with a sixth guy."

"Maybe I ought to go home and mow the lawn," Virgil said.

Sparkle left a half hour later, after some further snarling and spitting, promising to return as soon as she could. Virgil and Frankie got Frankie's youngest kid off to bed—the others could take care of themselves—and then they sat in the farmhouse living room and talked about the case. Frankie suggested they get a pad of paper and think up and list all the possible reasons for the murders in Wheatfield.

"There's greed," she said. "Money—that's number one. Always is."

"Or a religious kink in a crazy guy," Virgil suggested.

"Outright love or hate," Frankie said.

"Does somebody benefit if the town is ruined? Or was somebody damaged when it started doing well?"

"That should be under 'Money,'" Frankie said.

"I'm not making that kind of a list, where there are subtopics," Virgil said. "Besides, the benefit or damage wouldn't have to be financial, it could be psychological."

Frankie was skeptical. "Somebody got hurt when the Virgin Mary showed up? How?"

"Don't know."

"Something else you have to rethink," she said. "You're stuck on the idea that this whole thing goes back to the church and the apparitions and the change in the town. Maybe it has nothing to do with the town or the church or the Virgin Mary. Maybe it's totally personal. Something completely off the wall."

"That's a thought," Virgil said. "Maybe those people got shot because, you know, they were standing where the shooter could see them."

No fooling around that night.

Virgil hadn't been gone long enough for reunion sex, and Frankie's stomach was still unsettled. Still, it was nice to be back in a familiar bed, and one that was long enough for him. The Vissers' bed was too short, and he couldn't stretch out his toes.

He was so comfortable that he wound up sleeping late, and then lingered over breakfast with Frankie, and it was 10 o'clock when he headed south again, Honus the yellow dog and the youngest kid, Sam, standing in the driveway to watch him go. When he crossed I-90, he called Jenkins, who said that he and Shrake had driven to Fairmont to get breakfast. "We can be back in twenty minutes, if there's a problem."

"Take your time," Virgil said. "I don't know what the fuck we're doing."

Five minutes later, Zimmer called.

"We got a situation," Zimmer said. "Are you in Wheatfield?"

"I'm a mile north, in my truck."

"I got a deputy heading your way, but she's ten minutes out."

"What happened?" Virgil asked, thinking, another one?

"It's that damned Van Den Berg. The way I understand it, Janet Fischer went over to his house to get some clothes, and other personal stuff, and he caught her. He says there was a fight. He beat her up again, but he's saying he caught her in the house, that she broke in, and that he wants her charged with breaking and entering."

"I'm on my way," Virgil said.

When he got to Van Den Berg's house, the front door was standing open, and Virgil stuck his head inside. He could see straight through to the kitchen, where Fischer was sitting on the floor with her knees pulled up to her chin, weeping, and Van Den Berg was hovering over her, his fists balled up.

Virgil knocked once and pushed inside. "Did you hit her again?" he asked.

Van Den Berg pointed off to his side. "Look at my door. She trashed my door, getting in, and was stealing stuff."

"It's my stuff," Fischer cried. "It's my clothes."

"She broke in!" Van Den Berg shouted.

Virgil, stepping into the kitchen, looked at the door and saw the broken glass. He asked, "Did she break it or did you break it so you could blame her?"

"She broke it! Of course she broke it," Van Den Berg screeched. "What the fuck?"

"He broke it," Fischer muttered, "so he could beat me up."

Virgil squatted to take a close look at her. Now her other eye was closed and going purple, and her lip was twice as large as it had been the last time he'd seen her.

Virgil stood up, and Van Den Berg barked, "Get the cuffs on her. I'm charging her with breaking and entering and . . . stealing stuff."

Virgil said, quietly, "I think what we have here is a standard he said, she said domestic. Without outside witnesses, I can't arrest her for breaking and entering."

"Bullshit," Van Den Berg said, pointing a finger at her. "She . . ."

"Larry, let me tell you something," Virgil said. "There's no way I'm going to arrest her. If you want to file charges, go down to the sheriff's office and do it. And she can go down and file assault charges against you. And since you weigh, what, two hundred pounds, and she weights a hundred and twenty, guess what's going to happen? They're gonna yank your assault bail, and you'll be sitting in jail until your trial. Then I'll call Bell Wood and tell him that you committed a crime up here, and they'll be waiting for you to get out of jail so they can hook you up in Iowa, and you'll be sitting down there without bail . . . What's it gonna be?"

Van Den Berg gave it ten seconds, then said, "Get her the fuck out of here."

Virgil stepped close to him, six inches away, and grabbed Van Den Berg's throat while pinning his hip with his own, and Van Den Berg's right arm with his left, and squeezed the man's throat until his eyes bulged out, and Virgil said, in a near whisper, "If you ever, ever touch her again, I'll arrest you for assault, and you *will* resist. Then I'll beat the hell out of you, and I'll charge you with resisting arrest with violence and attacking an officer of the law, and you will go to Stillwater prison. Do you understand what I'm saying?"

Van Den Berg made a gurgling sound that might have meant "Yes," and Virgil released him, brushed off the front of Van Den Berg's shirt—hard—and said, "I'm extremely pissed off. Don't give me a reason to beat the shit out of you now because I don't know if I could stop."

Van Den Berg held his throat with one hand and backed away, and Virgil reached down to take Fischer's hand and helped her to her feet. "Get your stuff. We need to get you to a doctor."

When they got out on the street, a sheriff's car was coming, fast. It was Banning again; she pulled up to the house and climbed out, and said, "Did that fucker do it again?"

"Yeah, but there's a complication this time," Virgil said. He told her about the break-in problem and the broken glass above the back door lock. "I've spoken to Van Den Berg about it and I don't think it will happen again."

"You sure?"

"Fairly sure," Virgil said. "It'd be nice if somebody could run

Janet to a doctor. And while you're there, take a few photos in case we need them later. "

"I can do that," Banning said. "I'll email them to you."

Van Den Berg came to the door, still holding his throat. He saw Banning, made a strangled sound, turned back inside, and slammed the door. Banning nodded at Virgil, and said, "Thank you," and, to Fischer, "Come on, honey, let's go see the doc and get you cleaned up."

Van Den Berg lay on his couch for a half hour, fantasizing about bringing assault charges against Flowers, but he wasn't a stupid man and he knew they wouldn't hold up, not with Fischer looking as though she'd fallen into a lawn mower. Everybody in town was against him . . .

His throat hurt bad, and he thought about finding a doctor, but as he lay on the couch the pain lessened, and he finally got up and got a can of Sanpellegrino Limonata from the refrigerator, and the bubbly water soothed his throat. He carried the can to the front window, and there, a half block away, and getting closer, came the shooter, eating an ice-cream cone.

Van Den Berg opened the door and stepped outside, and the shooter nodded at him, and said, "Larry, how you doing?"

Van Den Berg said, "You're gonna drip."

The shooter looked at the side of the cone, saw the liquid ice cream oozing down the far side, and said, "Thanks," and licked it off the cone.

"If you got a minute, I need to talk to you," Van Den Berg said. He looked up and down the short street. Nobody in sight. "It's important."

"Well, okay, I got a minute," the shooter said. They weren't friends. "What's up?"

"Come on in," Van Den Berg said.

"Well . . ."

Van Den Berg stepped back, and the shooter followed him inside.

I developed a major problem yesterday," Van Den Berg said, backing into his living room. "I'd . . . come into possession . . . of a trailer full of Legos that turned out were stolen."

"I saw it on 'Wheatfield Talk,'" the shooter said. "Wheatfield Talk" was Danielle Visser's town blog. "There was a story in the *Des Moines Register* this morning, and Danny put up a link."

"You know what happened, then," Van Den Berg said. "My problem is, I need about ten grand, up front, for the lawyer, and probably another ten later on. I was hoping you could help out, since I'm keeping my mouth shut about you being the Wheatfield shooter."

"What!"

"Yeah, I figured it out," Van Den Berg said. "I'm willing to keep my mouth shut. I'm taking a risk, because this might make me an accessory, but I gotta have that cash."

"I got no idea what you're talking about," the shooter blustered. "I don't know why you'd think . . ."

"Then let me explain," Van Den Berg said. He did, and when he was finished, the shooter said, "That's not right. You're making a horrible mistake. Did you tell anybody else about this? I'm completely innocent, and I don't need other people looking at me like . . . like . . . I'm some sort of maniac."

"If you didn't do it, why are you arguing instead of leaving?" Van Den Berg asked.

"I am leaving," the shooter said. He turned and headed for the door, still holding the remnants of the ice-cream cone.

"You better think about it," Van Den Berg called after him. "Because I know you're the one."

"You ever say anything like that to another person, I will sue you for every dime you've got," the shooter shouted back. "I can't even believe . . ."

"I'll give you until tomorrow morning, and then I'm going to Flowers. I need ten thousand now, and another ten . . ."

"You're insane!"

And the shooter walked away.

Van Den Berg had gotten little sleep the night before, in the Lewis County jail, so he made himself a peanut butter and onion sandwich, ate it, lowered the shades in the bedroom, and lay down on the bed. He thought about calling the dispatcher at the packing plant to see if he could get a load out of town in the next couple of days, thought briefly about whether he'd put the finger on the wrong man as the shooter . . . and then he passed out.

He woke at 6 o'clock, hungry again, made himself a fried egg sandwich with a side of link sausages, thought about what to do; there were a couple of hours of daylight left, but he couldn't think where he might want to go. He eventually went down into his man cave, got online, and went to Pornhub and spent three straight hours, with two five-minute recreational breaks, watching a variety of videos.

The shooter waited until well after dark before he left his house, which was four blocks down and one over from Van Den Berg's house. He was carrying the rifle. The rifle didn't have a sling, but he'd improvised with parachute cord, one loop around the narrowest part of the stock, at the grip, another loop around the barrel. He slung it over his shoulder, so that it hung straight down, and then pulled a hip-length coat over it.

No gloves yet. If anyone saw him, he wanted his bare hands visible . . . and empty.

Wheatfield mostly shut down at 8 o'clock, except when there was a service at St. Mary's, but the church had been closed. By 9:30, it was dark and cool, and there were TV shows to watch. The shooter moved slowly and easily down the dark streets, unseen.

There were lights on at Van Den Berg's. The shooter looked around, saw nothing moving, pulled on a pair of thin leather gloves, went to Van Den Berg's front door, unslung the rifle, held it low but aimed at heart height, and pressed the doorbell.

Down in the basement, Van Den Berg turned his head at the sound of the bell. Who could that be? The shooter? Not Flowers . . . unless he'd hurt Janet worse than he thought.

He stood up, walked across the room to a cupboard, and took out a .357 Magnum.

No point in taking a chance.

The shooter heard him coming up the steps. Checked around again. The front door had a small window in it, at head height. He expected Van Den Berg to look out to see who'd come to the door. He was correct. He saw Van Den Berg coming and he pressed the muzzle of the gun against the door. Van Den Berg turned on the porch light, put his face to the window, saw the shooter's face, unlocked the door, and pulled it open, and the muzzle of the gun was there, already aimed. He never had time even to flinch before the shooter pulled the trigger.

BANG!

The blast was fairly loud, if you were close to it, and sounded like nothing more than a gunshot. If you were more than a few dozen feet away and inside your own house, it would be hard to tell exactly what it was. There'd been no supersonic crack because the bullet had never traveled more than a few inches. The suppressor—the silencer—had taken care of the usual muzzle blast.

The shooter stepped inside, where Van Den Berg was sprawled on his back in the short entrance hall, a silver revolver by his side. The bullet had gone directly through his heart. The shooter turned off the porch light, closed the door, and waited for any sign that the gunshot had disturbed the town.

Nothing happened.

Satisfied that he was safe, he contemplated the body. He'd considered a variety of plans; the most appealing had involved Van Den Berg's disappearance. He checked Van Den Berg's pockets, found his car keys. He took a painter's semitransparent plastic drop cloth out of his own coat pocket, unfolded it, and rolled the body onto it and rolled it over until it was completely cocooned. Van Den Berg hadn't bled much, not like those bodies in the movies, and the shooter found some paper towels in the kitchen and cleaned up the small crimson puddle the dead man had left behind.

When everything was neat, he walked around to the windows

in the living room, looking carefully up and down the street. The town was either asleep or glued to video screens.

He dragged the body through the kitchen, past the side door, and down into the garage, where Van Den Berg's head went *BUMP-BUMP-BUMP!* down the three steps. He lifted the body into the back of Van Den Berg's Jeep, went into the house to get the rifle, turned off all the interior lights but the one in the kitchen.

Before he got in the Jeep, he ejected the spent shell from the rifle and put it in his coat pocket, jacked another shell in the chamber, checked the safety, and put the rifle on the floor of the backseat. If he ran into a cop . . .

But he didn't. He used the remote to open the garage door and then close it. He drove six miles out of town, to a cow pasture he was familiar with. The moon was high and three-quarters full. He lifted the body out of the back and carried it over his shoulder like a rolled carpet. Unexpectedly, he went ankle-deep in the mud in the roadside ditch. He crossed a nearly invisible barbed-wire fence, which hooked his coat; he had to struggle to get free. Finally, he carried the body up a hillside, where he dumped it behind a tree.

The police, he thought, would think that Van Den Berg had fled the theft charges in Iowa. The pasture wasn't visited often, other than by the farm family's two milk cows. Since there wasn't much grazing grass growing yet, it would be at least weeks before the body was found, and maybe a few months.

He made it back to the Jeep, stamping his feet to take off the worst of the mud and water, which smelled like sulfur, did a U-turn, drove back to Van Den Berg's, and parked in the garage. Inside, he turned off the kitchen light and then sat in the living room, waiting, and finally, at midnight, let himself out the side door and walked quietly to the street.

There was little electric light to be seen in Wheatfield at that time of night, and the stars looked close and only a little smudged by humidity. Nobody bothered him on the way home.

What a nice Minnesota night.

There'd be fireflies soon.

16

After choking the breath out of Van Den Berg, Virgil met with Jenkins and Shrake at Skinner & Holland. Skinner was in school, but Holland was working in the store, and Virgil told him about Fischer getting beaten up again.

"Somebody needs to have a word with Larry," Holland said. "As mayor, I'm exactly the right guy to do it."

"I already had a word with him," Virgil said.

Holland eye-checked him, then said, "I hope you didn't get yourself in trouble."

"I don't think there'll be a problem. Janet's a mess. Banning is taking her to see a doc, and she'll take some evidentiary photos in case we need them."

Jenkins and Shrake had been talking about the case, and when they got in the back room, Jenkins said, "I think we've got to look real close at this Barry Osborne. Son of Margery."

"I already talked to him. He was pretty screwed up," Virgil said.

"You might be screwed up, too, if you'd shot your own mother," Shrake said.

"Okay. I'll buy that," Virgil said. "Why did he shoot her?"

"Because he wanted to inherit?"

Virgil nodded, then shouted, "Hey, Wardell!"

Holland stuck his head through the curtain, and asked, "Yeah?"

"Did Margery Osborne have any money?"

Holland stepped into the room and shook his head. "Not as far as I know. She and her husband had a little farm down south of here, too small to be economic. Margery worked in town as a health care aide . . . you know, hospice care and Alzheimer's people. She and her husband retired, moved to town, and he died a couple of years later. That must've been . . . jeez, ten, twelve years ago."

"What about her house?"

"She lives with Barry. That's actually Barry's house, I think. I could make a call and find out."

"Could you?"

"Probably with the Blue Earth bank," Holland muttered. He took a phone out of his pocket, scrolled through a directory, pushed a button, and said, "Hey, this is Wardell . . . I know, I know, but I've been drop-dead busy. Listen, I'm calling for a state police officer. You know Barry Osborne? His mom was Margery Osborne, the lady who got shot? Okay, can you check something? I need to find out who owns the house. If he owns it, or if maybe his mom did . . . Okay?"

He smothered the phone against his shirt, and said, "I'm talking to a friend at the Blue Earth bank. They got links into the title company. She wants my body. Real bad."

"She gonna get it?" Shrake asked.

"She already has, on several occasions," Holland said. He went back to listening on the phone, and a moment later said, "Yeah, I'm here." He listened some more, and then said, "Thanks, Sara. I'll call you again when you get off work."

He hung up, and said, "Barry owns it. Bought it seven years ago, with a fifteen-year mortgage, minimum down payment, but it was cheap. Seller was a guy named Ole Birkstrum, no relation."

"Well, poop," Shrake said. "Nurse's aide, kid already owns the house. Not like she was a walking gold mine, huh?"

"Maybe he hated her," Jenkins said. "One of those bad mother–son things. He's a psycho, and he knocks her off."

Virgil said, "That's possible, but, like I said, when Zimmer and I talked to him, he'd been crying."

"Obviously faked," Shrake said.

Virgil said, "Yeah. What else you got?"

Holland said, "Since you're wondering about inheritances . . . I bet Glen Andorra's place was worth three or four mil."

Jenkins and Shrake looked at each other, and Shrake said, "Whoa! There's a motive."

"Where'd you get that number?" Virgil asked.

"Pulled it out of my ass," Holland said. "Except for that shooting range along the creek, he had a nice piece of property. I think he owned a whole section, and he inherited from his parents, so I doubt there's a mortgage on it. Good land around here sells for seven thousand dollars an acre, give or take. If he's got six hundred and forty acres, you take out a hundred acres for the range . . . you've still got property north of three million. And the range isn't worthless. Plus, the house and machinery."

Virgil to Holland: "Somebody said his kid lives in the Cities?"

"Yeah. Zimmer's talked to him, I think, and most likely he would have talked to the medical examiner and maybe a funeral home."

"We gotta talk to him," Jenkins said. "The Cities are two and a half hours from here, he could have gone back and forth easy enough, do these other shootings, take the spotlight off his old man."

Shrake was tapping on his phone, looked up: "Including the house, and if he's got average farm machinery, the place isn't three million, it's more than four. No tax."

"Did his kid grow up here?" Virgil asked Holland.

"Yeah, he was here through high school, a couple of years ahead of me," Holland said. "We both played basketball, but he wasn't good enough for college ball."

Virgil said to Jenkins and Shrake, "We need to track him down and push on him. Why don't you guys figure out where he is right now? He could be down here. Or if he's back in the Cities, go on back and find him."

"Good with me," Jenkins said. To Shrake: "We can get a decent pancake."

Shrake asked Virgil, "What are you going to do?"

"We haven't talked to any of the people who run the church, except Father Brice. I'll track down some of the church council and see if they have any ideas of what might be going on."

"Weak," Shrake said.

Jenkins and Shrake were out of town in twenty minutes, having spoken to Jared Andorra on the phone: he was in the Cities and could talk to them as soon as they got there.

Virgil had gotten Brice's cell phone number and called him to ask about the church council. Brice had gone back to the archdiocese headquarters in St. Paul; Virgil had gotten the impression that he worked there as a kind of troubleshooter. "There's almost always somebody from the council around the church in the afternoon," Brice said. "Go on across and knock on the door."

Virgil did that, and a Hispanic man opened the door and peered out. "You are the Virgil?"

"Yes. I need to talk to some members of the council."

"Come in," the man said, pushing the door open. Inside, Virgil found two more men and a woman mounting an elaborately framed, life-sized photograph of the Wheatfield Virgin Mary on the wall of the narthex. The photo had been taken by somebody with a decent camera rather than a cell phone. Thinking back to what Van Den Berg had said, threatening to blackmail Holland, Skinner, and Fischer, Virgil thought that the Virgin did resemble Fischer, except that the Virgin had dark hair, Fischer was a blonde. Looking closer, Virgil noticed that the Virgin had blondish eyebrows, which would be unusual for a brunette Israelite in the first century.

Something to think about.

As it turned out, all four people were members of the ten-person council. Virgil sat them down in the pews at the back of the church and interviewed them as a group. He learned nothing: nobody knew of anyone who was jealous of the church's sudden fame, or resented it, or who'd wish to slow the stream of worshippers.

"Only two churches in town, and the other church—the pastor was happy with this vision," one of the men said. "More people go to his church, too."

Virgil went back to Skinner & Holland. He'd had breakfast but no lunch, so he bought a chicken potpie and a Diet Coke and carried them to the back room. He tried to think about the case but found he didn't have anything of substance to think about. When he finished eating, he drove out to Glen Andorra's house, went in, and spent the afternoon looking for anything that might be relevant.

Anything.

He gave up at dinnertime, drove to Blue Earth, and ate at a Country Kitchen, then sat in his truck in the parking lot and talked to Frankie for a half hour. As he was talking to her, he saw Banning, the sheriff's deputy, and a man walk into the restaurant. He said good-bye to Frankie and followed them in. Banning saw him and waved from her booth, introduced the man as her boyfriend, Gabe, and said that Fischer would be in the hospital overnight.

"She had a headache, and they thought she might be concussed, though . . . not badly. They also want a specialist to take a look at her eye. He wasn't there today, so he'll look in the morning."

"Worse than I thought," Virgil said.

She shrugged, and said, "We did the only thing we could—we took her to the hospital. Next, we get all over Larry's ass. Sheriff Zimmer came by and took a look at Jennie, and said Larry's used up all his rope. If he drives twenty-six in a twenty-five zone, he'll regret it."

Virgil drove back to Wheatfield, parked next to the Vissers' house, lay on his bed for a while. An hour after dark, when everything was quiet, he went back out for a walk. Fischer's tiny house was set back from the street; he checked around for obvious eyes, saw not much, tried the screen door, which opened up. The blade of his butter knife slipped the old lock, and he was inside.

He had a simple excuse, if anybody asked: he'd been walking by the house when he noticed the screen door standing open, and, when he tried the door, it was unlocked. He knew Fischer was in the hospital, but, given her history with Van Den Berg, he thought he'd better check the house.

Not search it, simply check it. He turned on the lights—nothing attracts the eye like a flashlight in a dark house—and checked it thoroughly, made sure that nobody was hiding in her closet or her bureau drawers or even under her unmade bed.

There was nothing under her bed, but a stamp-sized patch of blue cloth was sticking out from between the mattress and the box springs. When he lifted the mattress, he found a thoroughly flattened garment. He shook it out, and thought, by golly, it looked a lot like the gown that the Virgin Mary had been wearing in the church photograph.

Holland, Skinner, and Fischer: the Wheatfield Trinity.

He put everything back, turned off the lights, locked the door, and ambled back to the Vissers' place. Danielle Visser knocked on the connecting door when she heard him stirring around and, when he opened it, asked, "Roy and I couldn't stand it anymore: did you find out anything interesting today?"

"Not a thing," he said. "This is a very opaque little town."

"I never thought that," she said. "I always thought that everybody knew everything about everybody."

"Then why doesn't anybody know who the killer is?"

"Now, that," she said, "is an interesting topic for a column. I'll start writing it up right now. I'll call it . . . mmm . . ."

"'Who did it?'"

She ticked a finger at him. "You oughta be a writer."

Virgil had a bad night, stressed by the sense that he was getting nowhere, until at 8 o'clock the next morning, as he was shaving, Bell Wood called from Iowa. Virgil put the phone on speaker, and asked, "What's up?"

"You know we put that ankle monitor on Van Den Berg?"

"Yeah. He cut it off?"

"We don't know what he did. What we do know is, the monitoring service called this morning and said that he spent all night in what appears to be a cow pasture about six miles outside of Wheatfield."

"A cow pasture?"

"That's what it looks like on a satellite photo. The monitoring service has a time line on him: he was home until around eleven o'clock, and then he drove out to the cow pasture and stayed there. He's still there."

"Kinda chilly last night."

"Not hunting season, so that's not it . . . I was hoping you might go out and take a look. If we keep getting a signal, and you don't find a body, we'll have to figure he cut the monitor off, threw it into the pasture, and now he's in the wind."

"Doesn't sound like Larry," Virgil said. "Email me directions on how to get out there."

"Five minutes. I'll send you a bunch of screen grabs of Google Maps."

Virgil couldn't look at another potpie, but he stopped at Skinner & Holland and bought a bag of potato chips. When he told

Holland about the ankle monitor and the cow pasture, Holland volunteered to come with him. As they drove out, Holland looked at Wood's maps on Virgil's iPad, and said, "If the monitor signal is accurate, looks like he's about halfway down the pasture and halfway up the hill."

"In other words, about dead center."

"Yup."

They left the car on the side of the road. Holland went prosthesis-deep in the roadside marsh, while Virgil managed to jump over the soggiest bit. They clambered over a sagging barbed-wire fence and walked slightly uphill, across a pasture spotted with last year's dried cow pies, and found Van Den Berg's body wrapped head to foot in semitransparent plastic. He looked like a luna moth's cocoon.

Holland said, "There's a lot of blood at the bottom of the plastic . . . Bet he was shot."

Virgil looked around the pasture, the sprouting corn in an adjacent field, the top of a red barn, an actual television aerial on the top of the house next to it, the blue skies, the puffy clouds, and said, "We can't catch a break. We can't."

17

Never actually found a dead body before," Holland said, "though I've seen a lot of them."

"I gotta know where you were last night, and where Skinner was," Virgil said. "I know where Janet was, in the hospital. But you three had big problems with this guy."

Holland wasn't surprised. He said, "I was on a date, actually. You heard me set it up with the bank girl. Sara McDonald. She came back to my trailer and left about midnight."

"What about Skinner?"

"I don't know where Skinner was. But sometimes I just sit in my trailer, shootin' flies with a pellet gun . . ."

"Shootin' flies?"

"Yeah, and Skinner doesn't like it because he feels sorry for the flies. The chances that he killed Larry are slim to none. Besides, whoever killed Larry"—Holland squatted and looked at the body again—"probably shot him with a small-caliber, high-powered bullet. There's no blood on his back, that I can see, but a lot on his chest. He was killed by the same guy who shot the other people, and we know Skinner didn't do that because he actually witnessed one of the shootings."

"Yeah . . . I pretty much knew all that," Virgil said. He pulled out his phone and called Zimmer.

Zimmer: "You're calling to tell me you found the shooter?"

"Well, I found somebody. Larry Van Den Berg. Lying dead in a cow pasture. Probably shot."

"What!"

"Yeah. Holland's with me, and we think it's the same guy who shot the others," Virgil said. "We need some of your people out here, and I'll get the crime scene crew moving again."

Virgil called Bell Wood in Des Moines and told him what had happened. "I had a bad feeling about it," Wood said. "Listen, I talked to the monitoring service, and they peg the time that he left his house at eleven-nineteen, and he got out to the pasture at eleven twenty-eight. He was probably killed right around eleven, unless he was shot at the pasture."

"Nah," Virgil said, looking down toward the fence. "The killer would have had to march him across a swampy ditch, and over a fence, in the dark. It would have been too awkward. Besides, he's got that Saran Wrap all over him. No point in doing that if he was killed here."

"Sorry about that, Virgil. I doubt that it has anything to do with Van Den Berg getting killed, but it probably kills our case against his brother, too. Ralph can claim he had no idea that the Legos were stolen. Since we'd have to prosecute Larry to nail down what happened with the Legos, where they came from, and he'd have to have a chance to respond, but he can't now . . . we're sorta out of luck. What I'm saying is . . ."

"You're saying Ralph has a motive."

"Or his wife. Or some associate that we don't know about."

Virgil thought about it, then said, "Nope. The two brothers were working on what was, basically, an impulse theft. I doubt there are any associates."

"I would tend to agree, but, uh, better to bring it up now than to find out later."

An hour later, a line of a dozen deputies was slow-walking the pasture and the roadside, looking for anything that might relate to the murder. Holland had called Skinner, who left school to drive out, and who told Virgil that nobody was going to find anything. "The killer drove him out here, threw him in the pasture, and drove back home. Period. What's to find?"

"Thanks for that."

Zimmer came by, said that he'd parked a deputy outside Van Den Berg's house. "You'll want to go in there, so I thought it'd be best to keep an eye on the place."

A deputy gave a loud whistle from the roadside ditch, and they all looked toward him, and he followed with a "come here" gesture. "There goes your genius badge," Virgil said to Skinner. "He found something."

The deputy had spotted a scuff mark in the dirt by the fence, and some fuzzy gray threads on one of the fence's barbs. "If he parked here, crossed the ditch, and went up the hill . . . it's almost a straight line," the deputy said. "And we've had enough rain that those threads shouldn't be all puffy like that. Unless you and Holland left them there."

"No, we crossed the fence down a ways," Virgil said. "You've found something. The guy was probably operating in the dark and got hooked on the fence. Leave it for the crime scene crew. Keep people away from here."

Holland and Skinner left, while Virgil waited for the deputies to finish their search. They did, without finding anything more, and Zimmer left four deputies to keep watch until the crime scene crew arrived from St. Paul. Virgil wanted to check the body for house keys but knew the crew investigators would have a fit if he did, so he drove back to Wheatfield, to Van Den Berg's house.

The front and back doors were locked, but Van Den Berg hadn't repaired the window that Fischer had knocked in the back's. Instead, he'd taped a piece of cardboard over the hole. Virgil put on a pair of vinyl gloves, pushed the cardboard in, unlocked the door, went inside, and walked through the house. A silver .357 was lying in the front hallway. He left it. He could see no sign of any disturbance; but when he went down the stairs, he saw LED power lights on Van Den Berg's computer and the computer speakers, and when he touched the "Return" key, a pornographic image popped up on the screen.

Would Van Den Berg have left that image on-screen when he left the house? Virgil doubted that he would but didn't know Van Den Berg well enough to be sure either way.

Van Den Berg: Fischer had insisted that the man wasn't stupid. He'd figured out why no gunshots were heard, before Virgil or anyone else. She said he knew more about who had what, in Wheatfield, than anyone else in town. He'd once tried to make a living as a day trader, which, even if unlikely, did require an interest in finance and some basic ability with numbers.

Had he figured out who the killer was? Had the killer found that out?

Virgil walked through the house one more time, and as he hesitated before going out the kitchen door into the garage, he saw a bullet hole in the steel hood over the gas range. Until he went over and checked, he wasn't absolutely sure it was a bullet—it could have been a rivet or the head of a screw—but when he looked closely, there was no question. The rim on the other side of the range was dented; the remnants of a bullet would be around somewhere, but probably so damaged they wouldn't get any good information from them. The hole had been made by a .22 caliber bullet—like the .223 everyone so far had been killed with.

From the two holes, he could tell where the shot had come from. He turned and looked down the hallway to the front door, where the .357 still lay, and a sequence of events offered itself: Van Den Berg had been in his man cave, looking at porn. Somebody had rung the doorbell. Van Den Berg, not expecting a late visitor—and 11 o'clock was very late in Wheatfield—took his .357 up the stairs with him, had looked out the front door, and had recognized the visitor, not knowing he was also the killer. When he opened the door, the killer had shot him in the heart.

Virgil went back outside and, from the yard, called the crime scene crew. Bea Sawyer picked up, and said, "We're still a half hour away. You gotta be patient."

"I am patient, but I've got a second place for you to check. I think I found the actual murder scene—he was dumped in the cow pasture, but he was murdered in town."

He got Van Den Berg's house number off the mailbox and walked a hundred feet down to the corner and read the street sign—Harley Street—and Sawyer said they'd stop there first.

"He was shot from the front door, I believe, with that same .223 he used in the other shootings. It's possible that the killer rang the bell."

"You've been messing around in my crime scene, haven't you?"

"I'll see you when you get here," Virgil answered. "I'll be talking to the neighbors."

The house to the left of Van Den Berg's was vacant. An elderly man answered the door of the house to the right, blinking through Coke-bottle glasses, and Virgil identified himself, and asked if the old man had noticed any activity around Van Den Berg's house the night before.

"What happened, somebody kill him? Or did he kill somebody else?"

"Why do you think that?"

"Because you're that cop who's been investigating the murders . . . So which is it?" the old man asked.

"Somebody killed him," Virgil said. "Stood at the front door and shot him in the heart. Did you hear a shot about eleven o'clock last night?"

"I don't know, but something woke me up. Don't know what it was. I don't sleep so good anymore, so I was pissed off about that. I was awake when he drove away, and I was still awake when he came back. His goddamn garage door sounds like a cement truck making a dump."

"You heard him go and then come back?"

"That's right. I sleep downstairs now, because, if I sleep upstairs, one of these days I'd come tumbling down ass over teakettle, and that'd be it for me. I'd lay there and suffer until I died of thirst, since nobody comes to visit me anymore. They're all dead, anybody who might come. Anyway"—he scratched his bald head—"what was I saying? Oh, yeah. I sleep downstairs, so I not only heard him but saw his headlights sweep across the walls."

"And that was about eleven o'clock?"

"Damned if I know. It was dark. I laid there for a long time awake, and it didn't get light, so it was sometime in the middle of the night."

"Think anybody else might have heard the shot?"

"Well, Louise Remington lives across the street. If anybody had her nose between the curtains, she'd be the one."

Louise Remington, who appeared to be as old as the old man, slept at the far end of her house, away from the street. Like the old man, she'd been awakened by a sound she couldn't exactly identify, but it was almost exactly 11 o'clock. "I looked at my clock when I woke up. Later on, I heard a car go out, and then come back not long after that, but I didn't look at my clock. I read my magazine for an hour or so, and the car came back while I was reading, so it wasn't gone long."

The houses on both sides of Remington were lived in, but nobody was home at either. Virgil thought, If the car both came and went sometime after 11 o'clock, then the killer was probably driving it.

He walked back across the street to Van Den Berg's, put on another set of vinyl gloves, lifted the garage door, lifted the back hatch of the Jeep, and immediately saw a small, thread-like line of blood that was feathered on one side, as if something had been dragged over it when it had already partially dried.

Something like a body. Maybe the crime scene crew would actually find something useful, Virgil thought.

If the shooter used Van Den Berg's Jeep, then he probably walked to the house. And he hadn't known Van Den Berg well enough to know about the ankle monitor. That was the first bare inkling of good news: a beginning picture of the killer. He closed the Jeep's hatch and the garage door, and called Sawyer again.

"Where are you?"

"Turning off I-90. We should be there in ten minutes," she said.

"Good. I've been talking to neighbors, and I have reason to believe that Van Den Berg's own car was used to move his body. We need to process the car, and the sooner, the better. This is the first thing we've got that I believe the killer touched, other than the body."

"You've been messing with my crime scene some more, haven't you?"

"Of course not," Virgil lied. "I've been too busy interviewing the neighbors, and they say they heard the garage door go up and down about the time Van Den Berg was killed and moved. When you get here . . ."

"We'll look first thing," she said.

Sawyer and her partner, Baldwin, got out and looked at the garage door, then Baldwin asked Virgil, "Tell the truth. Did you touch that door?"

"Yeah, but I was wearing gloves."

"Still, wouldn't have done a lot of good for any fingerprints on it," Baldwin said.

"You know how many times prints have helped me with a case? I can count the times on an imaginary finger," Virgil said.

"Be quiet, and get the door open," Sawyer said.

Inside the garage, the two crime scene specialists did a walk-around before touching the car, then Baldwin said, "Whoa!" and, "Bea, I think Virgil was telling the truth, for a change. He didn't mess with the crime scene."

"How so?"

"Because if he'd messed with the crime scene, he probably would have seen this .223 shell on the floor and picked it up."

Virgil said, "What?" and he and Sawyer walked around the car and looked where Baldwin was pointing: a brass .223 shell had rolled against the garage's outer wall. "Let me get my camera," Baldwin said.

Five minutes later, Sawyer had inserted a five-inch steel turkey lacer into the end of the shell to pick it up, and they examined the case under a bright beam of an LED flashlight. "Nothing I can see," she said.

Virgil said, "There's a partial."

"There's no partial."

"Yes, there is, and I'm going to put the word out that I've got a partial," Virgil said. "And that I bagged it, and that I'm carrying it around town with me."

Sawyer said, "That, mmm, could be dangerous if the killer . . ."

"I need something to happen," Virgil said.

"You might want to wear a vest under that T-shirt," Baldwin suggested. "This guy is supposedly a long-distance shooter."

Virgil ignored the advice. "Listen, you guys got your fuming wand with you?"

"Yes, but we don't have a print yet," Baldwin said.

"You will," Virgil said.

Virgil drove to Bob Martin's house, the elderly gunsmith. He was home. "I need an empty .223 cartridge, and I need you to keep your mouth shut about me needing it," Virgil said.

"The first is easy, the second is harder," Martin said.

"Yeah, well, if you don't keep it shut, you could hurt the town even worse than it already has been."

Martin agreed to keep his mouth shut, retrieved an empty shell from his workbench, and said, "Listen, Virgil, I think I know what you're planning to do and I don't like it."

"About keeping your mouth shut," Virgil said, "I wouldn't mind if you told your friends I came over and fingerprinted you and cleared you when I compared your print to a picture that I had on my cell phone . . . that I got off this shell . . . You gotta lie sincerely."

"I can do that . . . But, jeez, Virgil, you gotta be careful."

When Virgil got back to Van Den Berg's house, Sawyer and Baldwin were examining the streak of blood in the back of the Jeep.

"That nails down the Jeep transporting the body," Sawyer said.

"Good work," Virgil said, not mentioning that he'd already seen the blood and knew that the Jeep had been used to transport the body, and that none of that helped. He showed the .223 cartridge to Sawyer—she wouldn't have let him use the actual cartridge found in the garage—and rolled his thumb across it. "I need you to fume this and pull the print."

"I don't like this," she said. "You're going to get hurt."

"Nah, I'm gonna live forever."

"I'll only do it under protest," she said. "Then when I visit you in the hospital, or at the funeral home, I can tell you that I told you so."

"I'll take it any way you want to do it."

The fuming wand looked like a black, industrial-strength dildo but was actually a butane torch with a brass tip filled with Super Glue. The idea was to heat up the glue and then fume the .223 cartridge; the glue's fumes would stick to the fatty acids in Virgil's print and would then harden. When it was hardened, Sawyer dusted the print with a black powder, making it more visible. The process took only a few minutes, and, when it was done, Virgil took a photo of the print with his cell phone.

"And I need one of your tiny evidence bags. Plus, one of those fingerprint ink pads," Virgil said.

The pad looked like a woman's compact, except it was made of plastic and half as large. The pad inside was filled with purple ink that would make a nice, readable fingerprint on ordinary paper. The .223 cartridge went in a transparent four-inch ziplock bag.

"You think the shooter will believe you're walking around with evidence in your pocket?" Baldwin asked.

"I don't know. Maybe it'd be more believable if I let out the word that *you're* walking around with evidence in your pocket," Virgil said.

"Never mind," Baldwin said.

Virgil left them to process the house and drove down the street to Skinner & Holland. On the way, Shrake called to say that they'd located Andorra's son, heir to the farm, and he had good alibis for two of the shootings: he worked at a truck dispatching company and had signed out on time-stamped loads. "He's out," Shrake said.

"Okay. Look, I need you guys back here. Change cars—find some old crack-and-dent sedans that you can get comfortable in. We're talking surveillance mode."

"You got a suspect?"

"Not yet, but I hope to get one."

At Skinner & Holland, Skinner was behind the cash register, and Holland was in the back room, counting the daily take. When he saw Virgil, Skinner said, "Jennie's back. She's down at her house, and she's okay. Except she hurts."

"Good. I need to talk to you and Wardell."

"I can't leave the register."

"Then one at a time . . . But let me get a potpie."

Virgil carried the frozen potpie to the back—nasty, but he was starving, having had no real breakfast—and put it in the microwave. He told Holland what he was going to do and what Holland should say about it. "I need to explain it to Skinner as well, but I want to do the actual printing out in public."

"I dunno, man. Frankly, this sounds a little stupid . . ."

"Send Skinner back here."

When he'd told Skinner what he was planning, Virgil sent him back out front, then sat and ate the potpie. When he was finished, he went out the back door, around to his truck, got the fingerprint pad and a piece of white paper, and carried them into the store. He printed both Holland and Skinner, as three locals watched, then compared their prints to the print on his cell phone.

"I guess you guys are in the clear," he said. "Neither of you have that big of a whorl."

"You got it off a cartridge?" Holland asked. "Can I see it?"

"Not much to see," Virgil said. He took the evidence bag out of his jacket pocket and dangled it in front of Holland's nose. "The print's clear enough. Now, I just have to find a match."

He put the bag back in his pocket, turned to the locals—a fourth had joined the first three, and none were leaving—and asked, "Anybody else want to get cleared?"

Virgil's last stop was back at his room, where he knocked on the connecting door between his room and the main part of the house. Danielle popped it open, and asked, "What's up?"

"About the town blog . . . ?"

"Yes?"

"Could you put a news story up for me without saying where it came from?" Virgil asked.

"Depends on what it is."

Virgil explained about the cartridge shell and the fingerprint. "I'd like to get the word out that I'm going around printing suspects, without it coming from me."

"Hey, that's a good story. I'll put it at the top of my 'Heard Around Town' column."

When she'd gone to post the news, Virgil locked the door, went out to his truck, got his armored vest and his iPad, and started reading all the news he'd neglected over the past few days. He checked a few wildlife forums and "The Online Photographer."

He had nothing to do until news of the fingerprinting had percolated through the town and until Jenkins and Shrake got back.

How long would that take? In Wheatfield, everybody should have heard about it before nightfall, he thought. Jenkins and Shrake should be set up by then.

And finally he asked himself, how stupid is this?

18

Jenkins called from his car at 9 o'clock, and said, "We're in place. I'm down the block from the front of the house, and Shrake will set up on the street behind you. You got your radio?"

"Yes."

"Tac light?"

"Yes." Virgil had a LED flashlight.

Jenkins: "You got your vest?"

"Yes."

"He'll probably shoot you in the head," Jenkins said.

"Listen, you moron . . ."

"I'm not the moron, you're the moron for even thinking this up," Jenkins said. "If you're going to do it anyway, set your radio so we're all getting the same thing at the same time. Stay away from your fuckin' window. I'm looking over that way, and I saw the shadow of your head on the window shade. It looked like a gourd sitting on a fence."

"All right, I'll watch it. But I want him to see me moving around inside," Virgil said. "I'll walk out to the truck every fifteen minutes or so until midnight. He won't come after that because he'll figure I'm asleep."

"If he knows where your bed is, where it is in the room, he could try a blind shot," Shrake said.

"I don't think so. He has to wait until he sees me because shooting me won't be enough. He'll want to get that print and the cartridge. He's got to shoot, then he's got to watch what happens after that, to make sure he's alone, and then he's got to come in to get it. He'll have to be close. You should see him before he gets here."

"We will if he comes on the street," Jenkins said. "I'm a little worried if he sneaks down through the backyards. I'm looking down between the houses, and there are a lot of bushes in there, trees, fences; there's a swing set and a couple of sheds . . . We should be there in the backyards with night vision goggles."

"Too late for that." Virgil told them to watch for somebody cruising the streets, doing recon, as well as movement in the backyard. "We'll start at nine-thirty. It's about eighty percent that nothing'll happen, but we've got to give it a chance. Don't go dozing off."

"Talk to us," Shrake said. "Put your goddamn vest on. If you don't have your vest on, I'll shoot you myself."

Virgil had what was called a Level IIIA hybrid armored vest. The vest itself was made of Kevlar, and other composite fabrics, and would stop most pistol bullets. It also had two pockets, one in front, one in back, that held armor plates. The plates would stop rifle bullets up to a .30–06. The Level IIIA was thicker, heavier, and more uncomfortable than ordinary bulletproof police vests.

Highway patrolmen and street cops, who both make unpredictable stops, mostly need protection from concealed handguns. Their vests have to be comfortable enough to encourage the wearing of them for a full shift; that meant light vests made from soft, bullet-resistant materials.

Virgil didn't make traffic stops in the rural countryside, where he usually worked. When he was confronted with a weapon, which had happened a few times, it was a rifle or a shotgun as often as it was a pistol. An ordinary urban cop's vest, made to stop handgun rounds, wouldn't stop a bullet from a rifle heavier than a little .22.

He got to think about all of that as he took his vest out of the truck and felt its weight in his hands.

At 9:30, Virgil called Jenkins and Shrake on the radio, and asked, "Anything?"

Shrake said, "Nothing. Darker than a pig's asshole out here. Why doesn't this place have streetlights?"

"Can't afford them," Virgil said. "I'm coming out."

He pulled on the vest, slapped the Velcro tabs to keep it in place, and stretched a T-shirt over it. He wished, for a second, that he had a helmet, even though he knew it would be a dead giveaway. He tucked his Glock into the small of his back, picked up his radio, turned on the yellow bug light outside, and stepped out on the concrete-block stoop. Nothing happened.

He walked to the Tahoe, opened the door, fumbled around in the back, shut the door and locked it, walked back to the house and on inside. He could feel the pinch between his shoulder blades.

"Nothing moving here," Shrake said.

"I didn't see anything," Jenkins said. "But, man, you are some target in that doorway, with the lights behind you and all. You look like a silhouette on a rifle range."

Nothing happened at 9:45, and nothing happened at 10 o'clock.

"Starting to skizz out," Virgil said on the radio when he was back inside after the 10 o'clock walk. Each time he took the walk, his feeling of vulnerability increased. He was totally dependent on Jenkins or Shrake spotting the shooter coming in, and Wheatfield, without streetlights and with residents who tended to turn in early, was a very dark place.

"It is stupid," Shrake said. "We've all been telling you that all day."

"We'll quit at eleven," Virgil said.

And they would have, if he hadn't been shot at 10:15.

Virgil turned on the bug light and stepped out on the porch. A second later, he was hit with a hard thump—there was no sound whatsoever—and he looked down and saw an arrow sticking out of his chest.

He tumbled back inside, and shouted into the radio, "He shot me with an arrow. I'm shot with an arrow. He's out there . . . He's right here . . ."

Trap.

The shooter had moved silently across a dozen lawns to the back of the Vissers' house. The basic plan was simple enough: noise outside that back door—thrown stones—should bring Flowers outside. Simple . . . but frightening. If the arrow missed, the cop would be right there with a gun, and the shooter was twenty yards away. There'd been a couple of stories on the internet that hinted that Flowers was not the best pistol shot in the world, but he could hardly miss at twenty yards when a body hit anywhere would be sufficient . . .

Then the back porch light came on, a yellow bug light, and the shooter's arrow was already nocked. Flowers stepped out on the stoop and posed there like one of those range targets showing an ISIS terrorist staring at you with mad eyes . . .

The bow was up, the arrow on its way and flying true, and Flowers tumbled back into the house, and then the shooter stood up, and Flowers shouted, "He shot me with an arrow . . ."

Trap.

Virgil heard somebody shout "Going now," either Jenkins or Shrake, and the other one yelled, "Are you hurt?" Virgil wasn't registering which one, and he pulled the arrow out of his armor, sat up, looked out into the dark, and shouted, "I'm okay, I'm good. I'm coming."

He could see nothing at all, but he did hear car doors slamming and the thumping footfalls from somebody running, and then more, and then Shrake yelled, "There he goes, he's running west toward Sherburne . . . Jenkins . . . he's going across the fences in the backyards."

"You guys . . . be careful . . . You can't see him, you can't hear him . . . Be careful . . ." Virgil yelled into the radio. He rolled to his feet and ran out the door and saw Jenkins running in front of the light coming from a neighbor's window, and he ran that way, shouting, "Jenkins, I'm behind you. I'm back here, don't shoot me."

Jenkins shouted back, "Virgil, go out to Westfall. Shrake, get up on the corner of Sherburne, he has to cross the street. I'll push him out of these yards . . . I'm gonna put some light on him."

Jenkins, who was carrying a superbright tactical flashlight, turned it on and lit up the backyards, as Virgil jogged out to Westfall Road, crouched behind a tree, and turned on his own light. He could still see Jenkins, on his knees, gun up, playing his light over the area between the houses. A block away, Shrake was lighting up a cross street. Unless the shooter had been moving very fast, he should be boxed in in the backyards.

More lights began coming on in the neighborhood as they called back and forth. Jenkins shouted, "Moving up one. This yard is clear."

Jenkins was moving slowly back and forth across the wide backyards; the side yards, between houses, were mostly clear of bushes and didn't have good hiding places. The backyards, though, were a tangle of fences, grape arbors, decorative grasses, and last year's gardens, with their foot-high, now dead plants. The shooter, he thought, was wearing camo, and in the harsh shadows thrown by Jenkins's flashlight, and with the snarl of folliage and fence, could be hiding almost anywhere.

If he wanted to shoot his bow, though, he'd have to come up at least to kneeling height, unless he were concealed behind a tree or hedge; and Jenkins's light was designed to be blinding.

So Jenkins didn't hurry; he sent the light into every nook and cranny, his pistol tracking with the light.

The shooter crossed a lot of fences and shrubs in a hurry, had to get south, to the Wilsons' house. The Wilsons had a hedge that ran all the way out to the street. It would provide cover. And if the cops were out of sight for only ten seconds, then it would be possible to cross the street, and, once there, it should be possible to shake them free altogether.

The biggest threat would be if the neighborhood woke up, and it probably would, sooner or later. Once all the backyard lights and garage lights came on, getting lost would become impossible.

No time, no time, had to keep moving . . .

And a cop ran by in the street, carrying a flashlight that appeared to be as bright as any searchlight . . .

Shrake had run up to the first street corner and thought he'd gotten there in time to keep the shooter from crossing it. Not being absolutely certain of that, he lit up the spaces between the houses across the street as well.

A man called something to him, and he shouted back, "Police . . . Police . . . Go inside. Go inside, lock your doors."

Virgil had gotten back on his radio, and said, "He could live in one of these houses, and he's already inside."

"That would cut down the possibilities," Shrake said. "Basically, if he's inside, we'll get him."

"Unless he's inside somebody else's house and he just killed them," Virgil said.

Jenkins: "Virgil, keep moving up. I'm sweating like a motherfucker over here. We've got to be pushing him into a corner."

"We need to get some deputies down here, wrap up the entire neighborhood, and wait until it gets light," Shrake suggested.

"That's seven hours away, but it's not a bad idea," Virgil said. "I'll call Zimmer, get some guys started this way."

Shrake said, "Jenkins, if he's in there, he's gotta move. You're only a hundred feet out from me."

Jenkins had come up to a white board fence separating the backyards of two houses. "I'm going to stop at this fence. If he's not behind me, he's got to be close, and I don't think he got past me. Virgil, why don't you walk up the street and shine your light between the houses up ahead of me. If that doesn't flush him out, get between the houses and light up the two backyards ahead of me. Shrake, you stay where you are, watch both streets."

"Got it," Shrake said.

"Careful," Virgil said. "He's good with that bow—hit me right in the heart."

The cop was standing in the street, thirty yards away. He looked huge, and fat—a bulletproof vest. The shooter was both frightened and angry. The broadheads could rip through a four-hundred-pound elk. They wouldn't be slowed down by a man, but they wouldn't make it through that vest.

Not unless the cop turned and opened up with a shot from the side. The cop was moving this way and that as he shined his light down two interesting streets, first this one, then the other. The shooter nocked another arrow.

Virgil moved up the street, shining his lights between the houses on his side. A woman came out, and called, "Who are you? What are you doing? I've called the sheriff . . ."

"Police. We're looking for a man. Go inside and lock all your doors."

She disappeared, and he moved on.

He was coming to the last pair of houses before he got to the next street, where Shrake was, and could see the beam from Shrake's flashlight when its beam seemed to flip in the air, and Shrake screamed, "I'm hit . . . I'm hit."

There was more, but Virgil didn't hear the rest. He started running, and Jenkins shouted, "I'm coming." Virgil ran between the last two houses into one of the backyards and saw Jenkins clearing the fence, and, at the same time, he saw a dark figure dart into the street on the opposite side, and somebody in another house yelled, "There he goes!"

Virgil saw Jenkins running up to Shrake's light—he couldn't see Shrake—and he decided to go after the shooter, running between the two houses opposite, vaulting the board fence, tripping on the top rail and falling facedown onto the hard lawn, got to his feet, ran on; he was wearing the cowboy boots and wasn't as fast as he might have been, but he got his light and gun out in front of him and ran into the street, and a man on a porch, wearing a white T-shirt and white underpants, yelled, "He went there, by the gray house," and Virgil ran past the gray house and saw . . . nothing. Nothing moving.

He jogged first one way, then the other, desperately flashing his light around, looking for something, anything, but the shooter was essentially invisible, and the backyards on the new block were even more clogged with shrubs, hedges, and fences than the last one, and Shrake was down, and Virgil moaned, "Ah . . . fuck it!" and ran back toward Jenkins and Shrake.

Shrake had been wearing the same kind of vest as Virgil, and Jenkins was struggling to pull it over Shrake's head as Shrake groaned in pain, and Virgil saw that Jenkins's hands were already red with blood. Virgil grabbed Shrake's shoulders from the front and pulled him to a half-sitting position so Jenkins could get the vest free, and Shrake said, "My back . . . Got me from the side . . . Never saw him. Never saw him . . . Hurts . . ."

"You would have if he'd tried to cross the street without shooting you," Virgil said, and to Jenkins, "Roll him on his side."

They rolled him. Shrake was wearing a Patagonia jacket with a shirt beneath it; both were soaked with blood. When they tried to get the jacket off, Shrake said, "No, no . . . don't do that, I feel like I'm coming apart."

"We got to get it off in case there's a big artery," Jenkins said to Virgil. "We can't move him without knowing."

Shrake looked up at Virgil, and said, "Left pant pocket . . ."

Virgil went for his left pant pocket and pulled out a six-inch switchblade. He said to Jenkins, "Hold him up," and Jenkins propped him up, and Virgil cut the coat off and then the shirt and the undershirt with the razor-sharp knife, and Shrake groaned again, and then said, "I'm puttin' in for all the wrecked clothes," and Jenkins said to Virgil, "Hold the light. Put the light on him . . ."

Shrake: "How bad?"

"Cut the T-shirt all the way off," Jenkins said. "I need to sop up the blood."

Virgil did that, pulled the shirt free. Jenkins used the unbloody part of the shirt to wipe Shrake's upper back. The big man was bleeding profusely from a long, twisting cut across the middle of his back, at the level of his armpits. Jenkins said, "I don't see any big pulses, so we got that. Twiddle your fingers at me, Shrake."

Shrake twiddled, and Jenkins said, "Move your feet back and forth . . ."

Shrake did, and Jenkins said, "Looks like your spine's okay. Of course, if we don't get you to a hospital, you're going to bleed to death, and we'll have all that fuckin' paperwork. It's like you to do that to me, you inconsiderate fuck."

Virgil told Jenkins, "Use the T-shirt to pack the cut. I'm going to run get my Tahoe. Back in one minute."

"Go."

As he stood and ran, Shrake said, "Tell me how bad . . ."

Virgil didn't wait to hear Jenkins answer but instead sprinted for the truck. The back door of the house was standing open, and he thought about the shell inside—no fingerprint, but the shooter still didn't know that. He swerved to the door, yanked it shut, jumped in the Tahoe, and roared away.

They put Shrake in the front passenger seat; he was fully conscious, and Jenkins dropped the seat back as far as it would go, put him in, and said, "Lean on your back. Keep that shirt packed in the cut. You're gonna owe me big-time for taking care of your ass."

Virgil said to Jenkins, "Get in, get in . . ."

"Nothing I can do in the backseat," Jenkins said. "You go. I'm gonna run back in the neighborhood and talk to people and find this motherfucker and kill him."

"Jenkins . . ."

He was already jogging away, gun and flashlight in hand, when Shrake shouted, "Kill the motherfucker," and then groaned, and said, "All right, no more yelling."

Virgil shifted into gear, and they were gone.

The shooter was five blocks away, breathing hard, listening. Nobody out there. A siren started: they were moving the cop.

I'm okay . . . I'm safe.

19

There may have been faster runs between Wheatfield and Fairmont, but the driver would have been pushing a Porsche. The ten minutes to I-90 was done in six minutes, the fifteen minutes down I-90 to Fairmont was done in eleven. Virgil was steering with one hand and holding his phone, and shouting into it, with the other, and he almost lost it at the Wheatfield on-ramp to the Interstate. Shrake swayed in the seat, groaned, and said, "You're gonna kill me. I don't want to die in a car accident."

Virgil, with the front grille lights and the siren going, was met by a highway patrolman at the Fairmont exit, who rolled them through town to the medical center in what onlookers agreed was probably another land speed record.

Three nurses were waiting with a gurney at the emergency room entrance, and Shrake was out of the Tahoe and gone in thirty seconds.

The patrolman asked Virgil, "How bad?"

"If they can get some blood in him, he'll be okay, but it's like somebody dragged a straight razor across his back."

With nothing else to do, Virgil called Jenkins, who asked, "How's Shrake?"

"Docs are looking at him. It's the longest cut I've ever seen in my life. He's got some meat on him, though, and I don't think it hit his spine anywhere. He pumped a lot of blood. I'll call you soon as I hear anything."

"He's not gonna die?"

"Jenkins . . . what do I know? He was still talking when they took him in, so I can't believe . . . What happened with you?"

"We've got three deputies here now, we're going bush to bush in these backyards, we got everybody turning on their lights, but he's gone."

"This is my fault," Virgil said. "You all were right: it was stupid. I just thought . . ."

"It should have worked—though, you're right, it was stupid," Jenkins said. "Now we're gonna have to listen to that fuckin' Shrake bragging about getting shot with an arrow and how he gutted it out. Lunch is gonna be a total shitshow for the next six months."

"Could be worse."

"Yeah, it could be. By the way, we recovered both arrows. Maybe . . . Nah, there won't be anything on them, except blood."

An emergency room doc came out a half hour after Shrake was taken into an operating room and told Virgil that a surgeon had been called in to do the repairs. "There were no huge bleeders back there, and we zapped the bigger ones with a cautery. We've got some Ringer's ready but haven't had to hit him with it yet . . . Unless there's something going on that we don't know about, he'll be okay. Though, his back will itch like fire for a few weeks."

"I'll take that," Virgil said. "I need to call his best friend and tell him."

Virgil passed the word to Jenkins, who said, "I never was very worried."

And Virgil asked, "Then why'd you pee your pants?"

"I guess it'll be a long recovery?"

"A few weeks, is what I hear so far," Virgil said. "Cut into your golf season."

"Wouldn't you know it? Bright side is, he's got that loose swing with his driver, maybe this'll tighten him up."

"I'll give him the good news when I see him," Virgil said.

"Keep calling me. We'll wind things up here in the next little while, but I'll still be up until I hear from you."

A surgeon came out to talk to Virgil an hour later, and said, "He's all stitched up. A wicked kind of wound; I've never seen anything quite like it. The blade was rotating when it went through, a spiral wound, almost like what you see when somebody gets run over by an outboard motor. We've got to worry about infection, is the biggest thing now. Let's hope the shooter didn't punch that arrow through a deer before he shot your friend."

"How long will you keep him?" Virgil asked.

"Three days, four, depends on how it comes together. He's asleep now; he's gone for the night. You might as well take off."

Virgil squeezed a few more details out of the surgeon, then called Jenkins and filled him in. "I'm coming back. You might as well get some sleep. We'll run over here first thing tomorrow morning soon as we hear he's awake."

"About the motherfucker who shot him? I'm gonna kill him," Jenkins said.

"You already said that."

"I know. I'm reiterating. Don't tell Shrake."

On the way back to Wheatfield, Virgil thought about all the trips he'd made to hospitals, all the unhappiness he'd seen there. He'd been a few times himself and had the scars to show for it, but the worst trips were with cops he knew, or bad scenes he'd tumbled over when interviewing people in emergency rooms.

He'd once gone to a hospital to interview a woman who'd been shot by her boyfriend. She'd said it was an accident, and after Virgil checked the circumstances, he thought she was telling the truth. He was chatting with her doctor when a teenager was wheeled into the emergency room with an injured neck and no feeling in his limbs. His girlfriend was with him, and she told Virgil and the doc that the kid had jumped off a boat into the Minnesota River and apparently hit an underwater log with his head.

An X-ray was taken, and Virgil and the doc wandered back into the radiology department as the on-duty radiologist was bringing the images up on a video screen, and the first thing he said was, "Goddamnit . . . Goddamnit . . ."

He tapped the screen with a fingernail, and Virgil could see an abrupt shift in the narrow line of the kid's spinal cord.

Virgil: "Is he . . . ?"

"Yeah. He's a quad. He's done."

Virgil was leaving the emergency room when the kid's parents arrived, worried, and they spotted the girlfriend, and asked, "Is he okay?"

"I think he just hit his head a little," the girl said.

They didn't know yet, but Virgil did, and he felt like crying that night, and into the next week, every time he thought about it.

He got back to Wheatfield at 2 o'clock in the morning and managed to get to sleep by 3. At 8, Jenkins called, and said, "I didn't want to wake you up, but I'm heading over to Fairmont."

"Give me fifteen minutes. I'll pick you up," Virgil said. "You got the arrows?"

"No, the sheriff's got them. Carbon fiber, identical; three broadhead blades, sharp as razors. When we get the guy, maybe he'll have a few more to match."

When Virgil had bought his Tahoe, he'd negotiated to get premium seat covers thrown in the deal. They resembled the real leather seats beneath them but were actually a skillfully manufactured vinyl, because Virgil often transported untoward people and occasionally things like bait buckets. That had paid off, because when he went out to get in the truck, he found the passenger seat covered with dried blood.

He spent five minutes, and used most of a roll of paper towels and half a bottle of Formula 409, cleaning it up. When Jenkins got in the truck, he sniffed, and said, "Four-oh-nine . . . Original, not Lemon Fresh."

"The policeman's friend," Virgil said.

At the Fairmont medical center, they found Shrake awake and in a bad mood—but a groggy bad mood, more pissy than violent:

"They say I'm staying here for three or four days. If I keep running my mouth, they'll keep me for a week."

"Must have some smart people running the place to shut you up like that," Jenkins said. "So, you gonna live?"

"I don't feel like it right now, but they don't seem to be concerned about how I feel," Shrake grumbled.

"Still hurt?" Jenkins asked.

"It's more annoying, than anything, and I expect I'll be annoyed for several more weeks, from what they tell me."

"Any good-looking nurses?"

"Yes. They already worship me."

Jenkins suggested that the scar would tighten up Shrake's wild golf drive, and Shrake advised him to go fuck himself. "Attaboy," Virgil said. "You're on the way back."

Virgil apologized again for setting up the trap to catch the shooter, but Shrake waved him off. "We had nothing, and it coulda worked, shoulda worked. I don't know what the hell I was thinking, though, standing around in the night with a flashlight, looking for a guy in camo and carrying a bow. What'd I think was gonna happen if I found him?"

They talked for a few more minutes, said good-bye, and Virgil and Jenkins headed back to Wheatfield. When they got there, they found Zimmer and five deputies working the neighborhood where the shooter had been seen, going door-to-door. Virgil told Zimmer about Shrake's condition, and Zimmer nodded, and said, "This guy's local, and he's a bow hunter and a shooter. There are going to be several dozen guys in town who fit that description, and a few hundred around the county."

"What about Osborne?" Virgil asked. "Margery's son. Is he a bow hunter?"

"I don't know—I could ask. What're you thinking?"

"I'm thinking that he lives up in that corner of town, where we last saw the shooter. And he's directly connected to Margery."

Zimmer said, "I'm not doing anything. Why don't we go ask him?"

"I'll come along, in case I have to kill him," Jenkins said.

Zimmer looked at him strangely, then said, "If you do, don't hit me with the ricochet."

"It'll be one of those bare hands deals," Jenkins said. "If he's the guy, I plan to yank his lungs out."

"Okay, then," Zimmer said. "Meet you there."

At Osborne's house, Zimmer was leading the way to his front door when Virgil glanced at the van in the driveway, noted the logo on the side, hooked Zimmer's arm, and asked, "'Steam Punk'—that's a rug-cleaning company?"

"That's what it is."

"When we went into Andorra's house, there were two rolled-up rugs in the kitchen. You think he could have been waiting for . . . Osborne? Or maybe Osborne delivered them, and Andorra never had the chance to unroll them?"

They all looked at one another, and then Zimmer said, "Damn," and Jenkins said, "I'll rip his lungs out."

Virgil said, "Wait, wait, wait . . . it's not a sure thing. We need to look at Andorra's checkbook, or his bank records, or his credit cards, and see if he paid Osborne and when . . ."

Osborne's door popped open, and Osborne, dressed in jeans

and a "Steam Punk" T-shirt, looked out at them, and called, "Are you coming here?"

Virgil said, "Yeah . . . we're working our way through the neighborhood. We're trying to figure out who's a bow hunter and who isn't."

"Well, I'm not," Osborne said. "I don't hunt anything. Guns, bows, spears—nothing."

Virgil was momentarily nonplussed. "Really?"

"Yeah, really," Osborne said. "Bow hunting is barbaric. Bow hunters retrieve less than half the animals they shoot. The rest are left to die out in the woods and rot."

"All right," Virgil said. "I'm sorry we disturbed you. We're asking around. Another question: was Glen Andorra a rug-cleaning client of yours?"

"Nope. Never was. I did know him, but not well. Why do you ask?"

Virgil considered not answering the question but, after a few seconds, said, "He had a couple of rolled-up rugs in his kitchen when he got killed. Like he didn't have a chance to unroll them. Or maybe he was waiting for them to be picked up."

"Okay. Well, you have to understand, I don't haul rugs around with me. I steam them right in the client's house, and it's hardly ever rugs, it's wall-to-wall carpet. If somebody has good rugs, like Persians, they'd take them to a specialty house. If they're crappy rugs, they'll clean them by themselves, with cleaner they get at the hardware store. It's the wall-to-wall carpet they can't clean by themselves, because you gotta have the machinery that'll suck the cleaning fluid back up out of the rug. If you pour fluid on them and then try to soak it up with a mop or something, it'll stink to high heaven for weeks."

That was more than Virgil needed to know about the rug-cleaning business, and he thanked Osborne again, and said to Jenkins and Zimmer, "Time to move on."

They sort of trotted back to their vehicles, and, when they got there, Zimmer asked, "What do you think?"

"I think he sounded real," Virgil said, looking back at Osborne's house. "I can tell you, the guy last night knew what he was doing. He had the gear, too—the camo. He shot Shrake in the dark at, what, twenty-five yards? If that arrow had been three inches farther forward, it would have gone through Shrake's heart. And he hit me right in the heart."

Jenkins chipped in. "I'm with Virgil. He sounded real to me, too."

Zimmer asked, "Do you think he was right about recovering deer? I've been thinking about getting a bow."

"I bow-hunt, and I'm eight for ten, so . . . what's that? A twenty percent loss rate?" Virgil said. "I'm gonna have to think about it."

"You a good shot?" Zimmer asked.

"Yeah, I am," Virgil said. "Most bow hunters aren't. There's a tavern up where I hunt that has a shoot-out the night before the season opener. I've seen guys who couldn't get an arrow inside a full-sized paper plate at twenty yards. These were guys who actually entered an archery contest."

Jenkins: "So what we're looking for is a guy who probably isn't primarily a gun hunter, because he had to steal the gun he's using and he killed to do it. But he's probably an expert shot with a bow, which takes practice."

"Lots of practice," Virgil said. "Let's ask around."

Virgil and Jenkins drove back to Skinner & Holland, where the back room had become their unofficial headquarters. Neither one of them had eaten breakfast, so they got potpies out of the freezer, carried them back to the microwave, and nuked them.

"We still haven't figured out a motive," Jenkins said. "We could get the names of every bow hunter in the county, but if we can't figure out a motive, and we can't prove where he was at the time of the killings . . . we're toast."

"You're saying we need more information," Virgil said.

"Yeah. The best information we have is, Andorra was worth a lot of money, even if it wasn't visible to most people. You actually have to jump through some hoops to understand it. I mean, how many people driving past some old farmhouse, with a barn out back, a subsistence garden, and a goddamn clothesline, would reckon that the place might be worth four million bucks? I mean, why would you think somebody worth four million bucks would keep riding around backwoods Minnesota on a fuckin' tractor when he could take the cash and move to Miami and buy a fuckin' Ferrari?"

Virgil poked his fork at Jenkins. "Here's another thing. We think Larry Van Den Berg figured out who the killer was. What did he have to go on? Money. Janet Fischer said he knew more about money than anyone in town—who has it, who wants it. Has to be money, one way or another. But, Osborne didn't have any. So, why was she shot? Maybe she wasn't the primary target? Did she step in front of someone?"

"Or, maybe the shooter is a random sniper, and is nuts," Jenkins said. "I mean, they're out there. Something like this religious apparition thing might be the kind of spark you need to set somebody off."

"Which is completely backwards from what you were saying. You were saying we have to devote time to finding a motive; now you're saying that there might not be one."

"Being nuts is like a motive," Jenkins said. "Have you thought about asking around town about who might be nuts? If somebody was treated? In a town this size, people would know."

Virgil thought about that, then shouted, "Skinner!"

Skinner pushed through the curtain, and Virgil asked him if he had somebody to take over the cash register. "For a minute anyway," Skinner said.

"So, who in town is certifiably nuts?" Virgil asked. "Not a little eccentric, but, you know . . . insane."

Skinner shook his head. "Nobody I know of. There have been some . . . unsettled people here, but they usually get out. If people start avoiding you in a small town, all you get is silence all day long. So they move to Rochester, or up to the Cities."

"Can you think of a crazy person who might be carrying a grudge, resenting Wheatfield ever since things started getting better for the town, so they would come back and try to upset the apple cart?" Virgil asked.

"No . . . And if there were, we would have seen him around town," Skinner said. "Not much way you wouldn't get seen."

"Then the whole town is, mentally, above average?" Jenkins asked.

"I didn't say that. We've got some unusual people. Daria McCain is eighty years old now, and when she was in her seventies, she decided she'd spent her whole life as a man when, in fact, she was really a woman in a man's body. She got people to start calling her Daria—she used to be Darrell—and she wears a dress and everything. Other than that, though, she seems normal enough. Holland appointed her to the fire commission. I can promise you, Daria didn't go running through any backyards. After the big change of mind, she didn't bother to stay in shape. She's really . . . soft and willowy."

Jenkins said, "Did she . . ." He made a scissors-cutting motion with his fingers.

"No, she never got anything cut off, far as I know."

"And that would be the . . . oddest . . . of the Wheatfield residents?" Virgil asked.

"We've got the usual collection of old men shouting at clouds, but nobody who's obviously nuts," Skinner said. "If I had to pick a name, I would have picked Larry Van Den Berg. He always struck me as over-tense, but he got along okay for a long time . . . You know, before . . ."

Jenkins said to Virgil, "Motive."

"Gotta be money," Virgil said.

"Didn't I already say that about a hundred times?" Skinner asked.

Wardell Holland stepped through the curtain. He had a letter in his hand, and he said, "You guys won't believe this."

20

As Virgil was driving Shrake through the night to the hospital in Fairmont, the woman who had swastikas tattooed on her earlobes was sitting in Jim Button's Nazi kitchen with her hair pulled up over the top of her head in two horns, held in place by two fat, blue rubber bands. She said, "Ow! . . . Ow! . . . Ouch! . . . Goddamnit, ow! . . . Hey! . . . Ouch! . . ."

Another woman was working on her with a sewing machine needle and a puddle of black ballpoint pen ink, converting the two tiny swastikas to black squares. The Nazi earlobe woman, Marie York, had been offered a waitress job in an Albert Lea bowling alley. She'd worn big, gold-plated earrings to the job interview to hide the swastikas but knew the truth would come out sooner or later, so she was having them obliterated.

When Button accused her of anti–National Socialist treachery, she'd said, "I've got to eat. I'm not giving up this career opportunity."

When the tattoo lady had shown up, Button retreated to the dining area to sulk: the fact was, the wheels were coming off

Minnesota's National Socialist wagon. Nobody would hire them, and they didn't have a whole lot of salable skills, other than the ability to lift heavy weights and/or make methamphetamine out of Energizer lithium batteries, Sudafed, and farm fertilizer.

Recently, they couldn't afford either the batteries or the Sudafed, and when they'd tried to steal anhydrous ammonia from a farmer's wheeled fertilizer tank, they'd managed to break the handle off the spout, and the ammonia had run down the farmer's driveway and stunk up the whole neighborhood. Also, they'd damn near gassed themselves to death, suffered some spotty burns on their hands and arms, and, in the end, had only come away with one two-liter Pepsi bottle of the stuff.

At this point, they were living off their individual SNAP cards, which would not allow them to buy either alcohol or tobacco, and which, realistically, could have been a good thing, because if SNAP did allow it, that's probably all they'd buy. The cards also wouldn't allow them to buy any hot food or food that could be eaten at the store.

The only thing left was nutritious crap like hamburger and noodles that they had to cook themselves, and if they hadn't found a convenience store that would take their SNAP card in return for nothing, giving them half back in cash, they'd probably all be kicking the nicotine habit right now.

Button lit up one of his last five Marlboros and put on his thinking cap, and as the tattoo lady was finishing up with Marie, and he finished up a half sack of Cheez-Its, he went back in the kitchen, and said, "I've had my thinking cap on."

The tattoo lady said, "That can't be good."

"Listen, that state cop Flowers is still here, and he hasn't figured out a goddamn thing. There's three people dead and two more shot. They gotta be desperate. The other thing is, Skinner and Holland were making a fortune in that store until the priest closed the church, right? Am I right about that?"

The tattoo lady said to Marie, "Put that Neosporin on your lobes every two hours, and keep doing it until you run out. I'm gonna get out of here before Jim tells you his plan. I want nothing to do with it."

"You don't even know what it is," Button said.

"And I plan to keep it that way," the tattoo lady said. "I don't want to be no accomplice."

She left, and Marie asked, "You want Sylvia to hear this, whatever it is?"

"Yeah, because she knows how to write good. We'll have to tell Raleigh, too, because it could get complicated, and I might need his help. But it's gonna bail us out, babe. We'll be in tall fuckin' clover when we pull this off, and there's not a fuckin' thing illegal about it."

"That's a change," Marie said. "Am I right thinking that even if it's legal, it's still stupid?"

Button bared his teeth at her. "We don't need that kind of defeatist thinking."

"Ah, fuck it, I should've joined the SHARPs."

"Never! They're not even real skinheads . . ."

"They're better skinheads, Jim . . . You know, you're making me tired," Marie said.

Button took the chair vacated by the tattoo lady and leaned toward Marie, who was dabbing the ointment on her earlobes.

"You're not listening, Marie. If we pull this off, we could all move to Texas, where, you know, they'd treat us right."

"So tell me what you thought up," she said. And then: "Hey! Hey! Did you eat all the Cheez-Its? Goddamnit, those were mine. I was saving them . . ."

The sound of wheels coming off.

Twelve hours later, Wardell Holland pushed through the curtain into the back room at Skinner & Holland, where he found Virgil, Jenkins, and Skinner sitting around the card table, Virgil and Jenkins finishing off potpies.

He held up the letter, and said, "You guys won't believe this."

"I don't believe I ate another potpie, so that'll be two things I don't believe," Jenkins said.

Virgil: "What is it?"

"You might want to handle it carefully in case there are fingerprints," Holland said. He handed Virgil the envelope, and Virgil opened it, shook out a sheet of wide-lined notebook paper, and used a clean paper napkin to unfold it. A message was written in purple ink:

To who it may concern (Agent Flowers):

We know who the killer is. We were talking to Lawrance Van Den Berg about the killer before Lawrance (Larry) was killed and he told us who it was. We didn't believe him (because you would never think of that name), but when he got killed, that proved it. We are afraid but we will tell you who it is if you give us the reward (up front). Put $10,000 in a *secure envelope (not a letter envelope like this one) and wait for our phone call to tell you where to leave the money ($10,000 in Small Bills like 20s). We don't know how to call Agent Flowers, so we will call Wardell at the store and he can tell Agent Flowers. We will call soon.*

Virgil looked at the envelope, and said, "No stamp."

"Somebody left it in my mailbox last night," Holland said. "I heard a car stop outside, but then it drove away. Maybe . . . two o'clock? I didn't look at what time it was."

Jenkins and Skinner had read the letter over Virgil's shoulder, and Skinner said, "Sounds like the Nazis."

"That's what I thought," Holland said.

"Do they have anything to do with Van Den Berg?" Virgil asked.

"Not as far as I know," Holland said, and Skinner shook his head, and said, "Don't think so."

Virgil turned the letter over, but there was nothing else except a small yellow smudge at the bottom of the page. "Looks like whoever it is, they were eating Cheetos."

"Cheez-Its," Skinner said. "There's a subtle difference in the yellow grease, as you'd know if you worked in the store."

"What do you think?" Jenkins asked Virgil.

"I'll bag the letter, but they'd have to be dumber than the Nazis to have left any fingerprints on it," Virgil said. "I suppose we could drive out and ask them if they're the ones behind it, but I doubt they'd admit it."

"There's always the chance that they're not the guilty ones," Skinner said.

"There's that," Virgil said.

He carefully slipped the letter back into the envelope, and said to Wardell, "Let us know the minute they call. If they're on a cell phone, we can probably track the call."

Virgil and Jenkins went out to Virgil's Tahoe, and Jenkins said, "I'm going to suggest something you might not want to hear."

"Lay it on me. I'm hurting for help."

"Wardell Holland and J. J. Skinner. Holland's a combat vet. Probable history of killing people. Claims to have been in the store for one of the shootings, but do we know that for sure? He'd only have to sneak out for a minute."

"He was with a woman when Van Den Berg . . ."

Jenkins shook a finger at him. "He told you he was with the woman until about midnight. Van Den Berg was moving a little after eleven o'clock. Suppose he set his clock forward an hour, the woman thinks she left around midnight. It's hard to keep track of time when you're getting your brains banged loose."

Virgil: "Wardell was in the store talking to me when Osborne was shot."

"But where was Skinner?"

"Thin," Virgil said. "Very, very slender."

"Maybe, but consider this: they're huge beneficiaries of the apparitions."

"Which is where you lose the motive," Virgil said. "Why would he want to shut down the church?"

"Wait, let me finish. He's not closing down the church permanently, he's only closed it down temporarily," Jenkins said. "Suppose Margery Osborne was going to close it permanently?"

"Like . . . how?"

"From what everybody says, she went to church all the time. She was on the church council, came back from Florida after the apparitions, stayed all winter. Now, I gotta confess, I don't go for all this Virgin Mary magic show horse manure. I think it's a shuck. What if Holland, or Holland and Skinner together, set up the whole thing somehow?"

"I might have visited Janet Fischer's home when she wasn't there," Virgil said. "And . . . You'll keep this strictly confidential . . ."

"Of course. I'd never rat out a colleague on a righteous burglary," Jenkins said.

"I think I found the Virgin Mary costume under her mattress."

"Think?"

"Ninety-five percent anyway."

"So, there we are," Jenkins said. "She also works at the store, making the big bucks. Big bucks for this town. Skinner, Holland, and Fischer set up the shuck. Osborne finds out about it. Thinks she's figured out how it was done and lets it slip to one of those three. Holland knows where he can get the gun he needs and he kills to get it. He then shoots two innocent people to set up the real target, Margery Osborne. Then Van Den Berg gets some semblance of the truth out of Fischer and threatens to expose them. Holland kills him. Then he goes after you with a bow . . . wearing combat gear and showing some real nighttime combat mojo. Cold as ice, nails Shrake—who has a gun, for Christ's sakes."

After a moment, Virgil said, "That's well thought out, but I don't believe it."

"Why?"

"Because Wardell's a good guy, and I like him," Virgil said. "So's Skinner."

Jenkins nodded. "That's a problem, and that's why I said you might not want to hear it."

"Holland's working all day," Virgil said.

"True."

"His trailer's out on the edge of town . . . You could drop me," Virgil said.

"It's a risk. And you don't have a key."

"There's no trailer on the face of the earth that I can't get into with my butter knife," Virgil said. "Even if I got caught, if I explained it right, I don't think he'd turn me in."

"I could watch him, tell you if he's leaving the store."

They cruised the trailer once and decided on a diversion. Jenkins would drive and would stop close to the front of the trailer. Virgil would get out of the backseat on the same side. Jenkins would go to the front door while Virgil slipped around the side to the back door. There were no other houses looking at that side, or the back, either. Jenkins would get in the truck and drive away when there was no answer at the front door.

Should work.

Jenkins dropped him, and Virgil tried to stay in the shadows until he got around to the side. He didn't need his butter knife to get into the trailer because the back door wasn't locked. He was inside ten seconds after Jenkins drove off.

The trailer smelled like microwaved everything—tacos, burritos, pasta, pizza, oatmeal—anything you could jam in a microwave. Even a few potpies. Holland was not the neatest man, nor the messiest.

The good thing about a trailer was that it was a metal box: a capsule. There weren't a lot of innovative places to hide things. Virgil started with the bedroom, worked toward the kitchen, and took the place apart. He found a pellet gun in a closet, but Skinner had told him about Holland shooting flies. He glanced at a TV, apparently hooked to the satellite dish on the roof, and an old laptop computer.

The key find was in the bedroom, in a cardboard box; in it, a small Epson projector, the kind used for business presentations. Sitting on top of the projector, loosely wrapped to avoid wrinkles, he found a piece of fabric, the sheerest he'd ever seen—something that you might use to make nylon stockings.

The material was two feet wide and six and a half or seven feet long, with a thin Plexiglas rod glued to the top of it. Transparent nylon fishing line was attached to each end of the rod so that the material would dangle from the rod like a transparent banner. And finally, in the box itself, a CD.

He called Jenkins, "How are we doing?"

"I'm in the back room, with a Coke. Wardell's behind the counter. You done?"

"Come get me in ten."

He carried the CD to the MacBook, plugged the computer in, loaded the CD, and brought it up. There was only one thing on it: a two-minute movie of Janet Fischer—he was sure it was she—dressed as the Virgin Mary, lifting a hand to bless the crowd, and speaking—*"Bienaventurados los mansos, porque ellos heredaran la tierra"*—in her best Minnesota Spanish.

He put everything back, then did a six-minute review of the whole place, opening doors and drawers. No .223. rifle, no shells. If Holland had a .223, he could be hiding it somewhere off the premises, simply as a basic precaution.

But Virgil didn't believe it. Holland was too nice a guy.

One oddity, though: nowhere in the trailer did Virgil see anything to indicate that Holland had ever been in the military—no photos, no memorabilia, no letters from the Veterans Administration.

Jenkins was outside the door eleven minutes after they spoke on the phone. Virgil climbed into the truck, and they headed back downtown. "We were right about one thing—it was Holland and Fischer who pulled off the Virgin Mary thing. It's gotta be illegal, somehow, but hell if I know the exact statute."

Jenkins said, "How about Skinner?"

"I'm sure Skinner was in there, too. Anyway, all three of them now have anti-motives for shooting somebody. Shooting anybody. Right from the start, they've seemed sort of panic-stricken by the shootings. They'll lose their asses if the shootings continue . . . By the way, Holland doesn't have a bow. Neither does Fischer."

"Then what the fuck are we gonna do, man? We still got nothing."

Then Holland called on Virgil's cell, and Virgil took it on the truck's Bluetooth connection.

"I got the call," Holland said. "Woman's voice. I got instructions for the drop spot."

"How stupid is it?" Virgil asked.

"Surprisingly not stupid, if you're stupid enough to do this in the first place," Holland said. "There's this place west of town, called the East Chain . . ."

"I know it," Virgil said. "We'll be at the store in two minutes. We'll talk then."

On the way to the store, Virgil called the phone guy at BCA headquarters to tell him the call had come in on Holland's cell phone. The guy was ready for it, and he said he'd have the caller's number in five minutes.

"What's the East Chain?" Jenkins asked, when Virgil was off the phone.

The East Chain was a series of swamps, bogs, marshes, and shallow lakes west of Wheatfield, linked together by a creek. Years earlier, Virgil had done some wildlife photography in the area, hired by a painter who wanted authentic scenes of red foxes and their offspring as models for a painting for a wildlife stamp contest. As Virgil remembered it, East Chain was ten or twelve miles long from north to south, and would be an easy place to run and hide.

At Skinner & Holland, Virgil and Jenkins went straight to the back room, where Holland was waiting with a legal pad and Skinner's laptop.

"They want you to leave the money on the edge of a bridge abutment on Highway 18 . . . right here . . . at ten o'clock. Exactly ten o'clock. No earlier, no later."

Holland had a Google map up on the laptop and touched a pencil point to the screen. The satellite image showed an elongated lake coming down from the north, dwindling to a stream, which opened into another shallow lake, or marsh, a couple of hundred yards to the south. The bridge crossed the stream between the two lakes.

Jenkins: "Did they say if we didn't leave it, the chick is gonna get it?"

Holland frowned. "No, they . . . What?"

"Jenkins humor," Virgil said. "Ignore it."

Virgil's cell phone rang. He looked at it, answered. The phone guy in St. Paul said, "I got the number okay, but you won't like it. It's a pay phone at a bowling alley in Albert Lea."

"They got a pay phone?"

"Yeah, they're still out there. Sorry about that."

Virgil rang off, told the others about the phone. "So it looks like we've got a stakeout tonight."

"It's gonna be way dark out there," Holland said. "I suspect they'll get out there early, on foot, to watch for somebody doing surveillance. If they don't see anybody, they'll snatch the envelope and sneak off, up or down the creek, to somewhere else, where somebody will pick them up. If it is the Nazis, they've lived here all their lives, they probably know the area pretty well."

Virgil looked at the map for a minute, and Jenkins asked, "Well?" and Virgil said, "I'm gonna run home and get some stuff. Be back in three hours."

"What are you going to get?" Jenkins asked. "What am I doing?"

"I need my wildlife gear," Virgil said. "There's a sporting goods store at the mall in Albert Lea. You need to buy some camo or dark sweatpants and a dark sweatshirt and some cheap gym shoes. It'll be muddy out there, you could ruin a pair of good shoes."

"I'd like to help, if I can," Holland said.

"You can," Virgil said. "You'll make the drop. You're gonna be Virgil Flowers for an hour."

On the way home, Virgil called Sheriff Zimmer and told him about the letter. "What we'd like is, at ten o'clock, we'd like some patrol cars well out away from the site, maybe five miles and moving, so if these people see them it'll look like a routine patrol. I don't want them parked someplace unless they can hide. When they try to make the pickup, and if we don't get them, we might need your guys to run them down."

"We can do that," Zimmer said, after Virgil gave him the details. "Sounds like those Nazis."

"That's the general impression," Virgil said. "I thought about driving out there, but they'd just deny it. Grabbing them and squeezing them, is the thing to do."

When he was off the phone with Zimmer, he called Frankie and told her he was heading north. "I'll see you there," she said.

When he got home, she met him at the back door, and said, "I put all your stuff in your big duffel: your camo, the trail game camera, the thermonuclear flashlight, and those Nikes you were supposed to throw away. Plus, I added your mosquito nets. The mosquitoes were thick at the farm last night, and you're gonna need them."

"Great. This'll be a quick trip."

She grabbed the front of his shirt. "Not so fast, buster. It's been a while, and my stomach has finally settled down."

"I don't have time. We've got three dead . . . Okay, maybe I've got a little time, but no more than fifteen minutes. Okay, no more than half an hour. Forty minutes at the outside . . . There are people depending on me . . ."

"Yes. I'm one of them."

21

Virgil used his flashers going back to Wheatfield, not that there was much traffic, but he could run at ninety miles an hour without worrying about a sheriff's speed trap. Running that fast, he arrived back in Wheatfield almost exactly three hours after he left. Jenkins was waiting at Skinner & Holland, and said, "You look a little haggard."

"Anybody would be haggard, working this fuckin' disaster. Are we wasting our time?"

"I suspect we are, but we don't have a choice," Jenkins said. "If it turned out these idiots actually know something, and we didn't follow up, there'd be hell to pay. Besides, I already learned something very worthwhile."

"About the killings?"

"No, about clothing. I bought some black jeans and a long-sleeved black polo shirt. Black really is slimming. I give off this terrific artist vibe. When I get back to the Cities, I'm gonna head go over the Art Institute. Horny art women are stacked up like cordwood over there."

"What happens when they find out the truth, that you're nothing but a sexual predator?" Virgil asked.

"By that time, they'll have gotten a dose of Dr. Jenkins's female cure and they won't care."

"Yeah, they'll probably have gotten a dose of something," Virgil said.

"Hey! Is that kind? You gotta try harder to be kind, man. We're all trapped on this earth together."

Holland came in, and asked, "What are we doing?"

"You're delivering the envelope and a game-trail camera in my Tahoe, wearing my cowboy hat so they think it's me." The camera was sitting on the table, and Virgil turned it toward him. "The camera's got an infrared flash and a five-second delay. You'll get flashed a few times when you plant it, but, since it's IR, you won't see it. You need to set it up about fifteen feet from where you put the envelope. You don't want it facing anything that might move. You don't want any swaying tree branches, or anything. Point it at the bridge, if you can. You're gonna have to be fast so they don't get suspicious."

"I can handle that," Holland said. "While you were gone, I drove over the bridge. I can put it down in some weeds; it'll point right back to where he'll be coming down the bank."

"Hope you didn't spook anybody," Jenkins said.

"I borrowed my girlfriend's car. She dropped it out back. Nobody saw me."

Virgil said, "Good. I'll have the camera all set, all you have to do is turn it on and make sure there's no grass or weeds in front of the lens. When it senses movement, it'll start flashing, and it'll keep going until the movement stops. The flashes are five seconds apart."

"Cool," Holland said. "Where will you guys be?"

"We'll take Jenkins's car, head north to I-90, make sure nobody is following us. Then we'll cut south, around the west side of the East Chain, to a farmhouse—it's only about a half mile from the bridge, and we can walk through the farmer's fields all the way up to 18. If we do it right, we'll only be a couple of hundred feet from the bridge. From there, we ought to be able to ease down real close."

"Does the farmer know you're coming?"

"Not yet . . . just in case he might want to chat about it. We'll tell him when we get there."

"I have only one objection," Jenkins said.

Virgil: "Yeah?"

"The bow hunter tried to kill you last night. What if he set this up? What if he's going to try again? What if it's an ambush?"

"That hadn't occurred to me," Virgil said. He gave it a moment's thought, then said, "That's unlikely. First of all, Wardell said the caller was a woman. That'd mean there'd be two people involved in the murders, and I don't see that. This is a loner. Another thing: he would have had to think this up and deliver the letter to Wardell a couple of hours after we chased him all over the neighborhood."

"I'm with Virgil," Holland said. "I'm not worried about an ambush. I'm more worried about falling in that fuckin' creek."

"When you get killed, don't come complaining to me," Jenkins said.

Virgil checked the time. "We got a couple of hours. I didn't have a chance to eat, and I . . . Man, those potpies."

"Why don't we all run over to Fairmont and get something decent?" Holland said.

"Good. I made it down there in, like, eighteen minutes last night," Virgil said. "We'll take my truck, use the lights and siren, see if we can beat the time."

They spent ten minutes with Shrake at the hospital, ate, and made it back to Skinner & Holland, where Virgil parked the Tahoe out front. Sundown was about 8:40, and it was fully dark by 9:15. Virgil had worn his pale straw cowboy hat getting out of the truck, and Holland would wear it going back out.

As soon as it was dark enough, Virgil and Jenkins snuck out the back and down to Jenkins's rented Toyota and left for the East Chain. Virgil called Zimmer, who said his patrol cars were all set. "We hid them. Nobody's going to see them unless they go looking off-road."

"We'll call your nine-one-one line if we need help," Virgil told him.

The farm they'd targeted was owned by Don and Donna White. Zimmer knew them—not well, but well enough that they would recognize his voice. He would call them a few minutes before Virgil and Jenkins arrived at their farm to avoid scaring them and to vouch for the state cops. When they pulled into the farmyard, the Whites were waiting at the side door.

"The sheriff told us not to turn on the porch light," Don White said. "I got some stuff to show you."

They followed the couple inside, where Don had sketched a map of his farm buildings, the waterways behind them, and the best way through the fields.

When her husband finished, Donna White said, "We have to warn you, there might be one tiny problem with this idea."

Jenkins: "Uh-oh. What is it?"

"We don't have much traffic through here at night. A little while after dark . . . maybe ten after nine, a car went past while I was doing the dishes. I couldn't see it, but I could see its headlights on the trees, and it looked to me like it stopped a little way up the highway. Like it might have been dropping somebody off."

Virgil and Jenkins looked at each other, and Virgil said, "We might all be wandering around the same field?"

"I thought I should mention it," Donna White said.

They got the Whites to turn off all the lights on the north end of the house before they slipped outside. They were both wearing dark blue armored vests over their night clothing, and Virgil was carrying the thermonuclear flash. They both carried Glocks, and Jenkins had his shotgun. They'd memorized angles and distances on White's map, but Holland had been correct: it was dark.

The farm did have a bright pole light by the barn, and so they were able to barely see the line of a fence that separated the farm yard from a cornfield, and they crossed the fence without a problem. White had told them that if they walked toward the lights of the KFMC radio tower in Fairmont, they would come to Highway 81, but a couple of hundred yards farther down the road than they wanted.

They decided that was okay: they were walking less than half a mile total, before sneaking back toward the bridge. They should make it well before 10 o'clock.

The field was open enough, but walking was tough: it had been plowed that spring, and they were walking across the rows of furrows. One minute out, the mosquitoes showed up. They paused to pull the nets over their heads and gloves on their hands. The nets made it even harder to see, but they stumbled on. Ten minutes into the trek, Jenkins, who was a couple of yards behind Virgil, caught up, touched Virgil's arm, and, when Virgil stopped, he whispered, "Look at the stars."

Virgil said, "Shhhh," but looked: the stars were good, though he'd seen better in the desert Southwest, he thought. Still, they craned their necks upward for a minute, the Milky Way looking like a rainbow, only it was in black and white, before they moved again. They were about a hundred yards from the highway when a car went past, which helped. They no longer had to navigate by the radio tower lights, but turned straight toward the highway. There'd be another fence to cross when they got close to the road. They were nearly there when Jenkins caught up again, touched Virgil's arm, and whispered, "Look."

Virgil looked. He wasn't quite sure what he was seeing, but he thought it might be the flashlight beam from a cell phone, maybe a hundred yards away toward the bridge. Jenkins breathed, "I think the idiot's tangled up in the fence. You want to light him up?"

"Not until we're a lot closer," Virgil whispered back. "If he gets outside the flash coverage, we might not see him again. He could hide, and warn off the car picking him up . . ."

They continued on to the fence. There were three strands of

barbed wire, which they managed to cross without incident, but then Virgil went knee-deep in muck in the roadside ditch. Jenkins whispered, "What happened?" and stepped into the same muddy hole.

Virgil got out, but Jenkins said, "I think I'm losing my fuckin' shoe . . . Wait, wait . . ."

He had to reach, elbow-deep, into the sulfurous muck to get hold of the shoe and then managed to stagger out onto the dry ground of the roadside bank. "I lost my fuckin' sock," he said. He sat down on the highway and tried to clean out his shoe, to get it back on.

From not too far away, they heard somebody talking; couldn't make it out, but it sounded like somebody had said "Motherfucker."

"I think he fell in the ditch," Jenkins whispered.

Virgil wanted to laugh at both of them but stuffed his knuckles into his mouth and managed to smother the impulse.

As they waited on the highway, they saw the cell phone light again, blinking off and on, as the person ahead of them walked toward the bridge. Virgil turned to block the light of his own phone, and looked at the time. Eight minutes to 10. "Wardell's gotta be close," he whispered to Jenkins. "We gotta move."

Jenkins got on his feet, and they walked toward the bridge, Jenkins's foot squeaking in its wet shoe. It was dark enough that they could stay on the road, and the road was quieter than walking on the gravel shoulders. They were fifty yards away from the mystery walker when the cell phone flash came on, and they saw it move down into the ditch.

"He's hiding. Waiting for the drop."

The cell phone light came on again, and they could see the other man's arms windmilling in the night, and they could hear some more squealing.

"Mosquitoes," Jenkins said, and Virgil could hear him trying not to laugh.

"Sneak up another few steps and sit down," Virgil suggested.

They did that, and waited. The night was not quite silent: they could hear a bird, up in a tree, chirping like an old man muttering in the night; and also the sound of flowing water. The man up ahead coughed once, and then again.

A minute before 10 o'clock, a set of headlights turned onto Highway 18 from Highway 53, which was about a mile and a half away. Virgil nudged Jenkins, and they duckwalked onto the shoulder of the road. The headlights got closer, bright enough that Virgil couldn't see the truck behind them, but he was sure it was Holland in the Tahoe.

The truck stopped on the bridge, the driver hopped out, walked around the abutment, was out of sight for a minute, and then was back in the truck. When the Tahoe passed them, Holland's hand was pressed to the driver's-side window glass: he must've caught them in the headlights, crouched on the side of the road. Another minute, and the truck turned north and was out of sight.

Ten minutes, then the cell phone flash came up, moved across the bridge, down under the abutment. A moment later, it was back, and whoever was holding it was jogging toward them. Virgil whispered, "I'm going to light him up."

Frankie had referred to the flashlight as "thermonuclear." Virgil had been given it by a DEA agent and was fairly sure that it could be seen on the moon. The man coming toward them was in the middle of the highway, and when he was thirty feet away, Virgil hit him in the face with the light, and Jenkins yelled, "Stop! Stop there!"

The man—Virgil recognized him as Jim Button—screeched to a stop, looked wildly around, as if for a place to run, dropped the brown manila envelope full of magazine pages cut to dollar-bill size, and said, "Ah, shit. There's no money, is there?"

"How you doin', Jim?" Virgil asked. And, "My friend here has a twelve-gauge pointed at you. It'd cut a hole the size of a softball in your chest . . . if you have a gun or knife, or whatever."

"I don't," Button said. "Goddamnit."

"So who's the shooter?" Virgil asked.

Button stared at him for a few seconds, then said, "Well, it's gotta be Barry Osborne."

Jenkins asked, "Who is this guy?"

"One of the Nazis," Virgil said. To Button: "Barry Osborne, is what you've got? That's all? That's it? I hate to tell you this, pal, but we've already eliminated him as a suspect."

"Well, that's dumb," Button said.

Virgil said to Jenkins, "Get your Glock out and point it at his head. I'm gonna cuff him."

Button said, "Aw, we gotta do that?"

"Yeah, we do, Jim. You tried to defraud the state government out of ten thousand dollars."

Button refused to say where he would have been picked up, but Virgil suspected it would be the same place he was dropped off. He called Holland, who'd pulled off the highway a couple of miles away, and he came back to pick them up.

They retrieved the camera, though they didn't need the

pictures anymore. Virgil got Button's phone out of his jacket pocket, and they drove back to the Whites' farmyard, Jenkins and Button in the backseat. Button's hands were cuffed, and one ankle was locked to the steel ring in the floor of the Tahoe.

Fifteen minutes after they got to the Whites' place, Button's phone rang, and Virgil answered it.

"You got it?" Male voice.

Virgil whispered, "Got the envelope. But I'm in this field, I'm lost . . . Get me where you left me. Maybe ten minutes . . ."

"You okay?"

More whispering. "Yeah, but I can't talk. I think there might be some cops up on 18."

"I'm coming . . ."

Virgil hung up. "He's coming."

They brought in a sheriff's car, hidden on a side road, and when Raleigh Good rolled past the Whites' house and down the highway in Woody Garrett's black Camaro, the cop pulled out across the highway and turned on his flashers. Virgil pulled out in the Tahoe, behind the camera, and turned on his own flashers. Good pulled the Camaro over, and when Virgil walked up and shouted, "Get out of the car!" Good got out, and asked, "What are you guys doing here?"

"Collecting you, and Jim," Virgil said. "Jim's already in my truck."

"Was that you on the phone?"

"Yes, it was."

"That goddamn Button. I will never, ever . . ."

Jenkins patted him down. "Get in the truck," Virgil said.

They headed back to Wheatfield, trailed by Jenkins and the sheriff's patrol car. Holland, looking over the seat back, asked Button, "What the hell were you thinking? Or did you think at all?"

"You're the guys who're gonna look like stupes when it turns out we're right," Button said. "Running around like your asses are on fire, gettin' nowhere, and all you had to do was listen."

"Why'd you think it was Osborne? Shooting his own mom?"

"For the money," Button said.

Virgil said, "Aw, Jesus. Everybody keeps saying money, and there isn't any."

Button asked, "What?"

"There's no money, Jim," Holland said. "Barry owns the house. Margery was living there for free."

"Well, yeah," Button said. "But what about the Florida house?"

Virgil: "What Florida house?"

Button said to Good, "They don't know about the Florida house."

Good said, "What a bunch of stupes."

Virgil looked over the seat back. "What are you talking about?"

"Where are we on this fraud thing?" Button asked. And he said to Good, "Keep your mouth shut, Raleigh."

"We can talk," Virgil said. "What about the Florida house?"

"You know Rose? You met her at the house, you sicced her on Clay Ford? Chick with the rose tattoo?"

"I remember," Virgil said. "What about this house?"

"Rose cleaned house for Marge once a week when she was in Wheatfield. And she watched over Barry's house when he drove Marge down to Florida. Marge wouldn't fly," Button said. "When they were packing up last fall, she heard Barry telling Marge that she ought to sell the place and move back to Wheatfield, where her friends were. They had an argument about it."

Holland asked, "How much is it worth? The house?"

Button said, "I don't know. Rose might. Rose is a snoop. But I bet it's worth a lot."

"Is Rose still at your place?" Virgil asked.

Raleigh said, "When you told her that Clay Ford might be interested, she hotfooted it right over there, and they been fuckin' up a storm ever since. She's moved in with him."

"That didn't take long," Virgil said.

"She's the restless sort," Button said. "So . . . we got a deal? I solved your case. I wasn't trying to fraud you."

"This better not be Nazi bullshit," Virgil said.

"Cross my heart," Button said. "Go ask Rose."

22

The Tahoe's clock said 11:51 when they passed the "Wheatfield City Limits" sign, but Virgil drove over to Clay Ford's house anyway, Jenkins following behind. Ford's house was dark when they pulled up outside. They left the Nazis chained in the back of the Tahoe, and Virgil knocked on the door and rang the doorbell, and a light went on in the back of the house.

Ford, barefoot, wearing jeans and a T-shirt, and carrying a .45, came to the door, looking wide awake. "Virgil?"

"Is Rose here? Put the gun away."

Ford looked toward the back of the house, and said, "Yeah? What happened?" He put the gun behind his back, probably in a carry holster.

"We arrested the Nazis, and they told us a couple of things we need to check with Rose. We're not arresting her, or anything, but we need some information."

From the back of house, Rose called, "Give me a minute to put my pants on."

They gathered in Ford's living room, and Virgil told her what Button said about Margery Osborne's Florida house.

"Yeah, that's right," Rose said. "When Margery came back this winter, after the Virgin Mary thing, she told me that she might sell. She was excited about the Virgin Mary; she started going to church every day. When she asked me what I thought about the apparitions and I told her I smelled a rat, she got really upset. I thought she might fire me."

"What about this Florida house? You know anything else?" Virgil asked.

"The usual stuff . . . She and her husband sold their farm down south of here, which was small but worth quite a bit for land, and they moved into town. They rented a place; they were saving the money for their 'real' old age. Then, when her husband died, which was sort of unexpected, Margery started going to Florida with a friend. After a couple of years, she bought a place down there. This was a few years back, when the prices were lower and she figured it would be a good investment. I . . . mmm . . . I got the impression that it might be worth a million now. Maybe more."

Jenkins said to Virgil, "There you go."

"You know where the house is?" Virgil asked.

"Naples. I've got a phone number," Rose said.

"Jim told us that Barry thought she ought to move back here," Holland said.

"They talked about that," Rose said. "I heard them. She said it was too gloomy and cold in winter, but he hated driving her back and forth every year. After the apparitions, when she came back up here, she mentioned that she might be selling. Nothing definite, but she was thinking about it. If the Virgin came back, she was not going to miss it."

When Rose ran out of new information, Ford asked Virgil, "You think Barry killed his mom for the inheritance?"

"I don't know," Virgil said. "There are some reasons to think he didn't—but we've been looking for a motive, and a million dollars is a powerful motive."

Out in the street again, Jenkins asked, "What are we going to do? You want to go talk to him?"

"Not tonight. I need to do some research on this house, make some phone calls. See if she owns it, for one thing. See how much the farm sold for . . . I'd like to know what I'm talking about when we go back to Osborne."

"I can probably find out about the farm sale from my girlfriend, but that won't be until nine o'clock tomorrow," Holland said.

"Do that," Virgil said. "We'll meet in the back of the store at nine."

"It's already past midnight, so make it ten o'clock," Jenkins said. "We oughta drive over to Fairmont and check on Shrake again, and get a decent breakfast. I can't look at another one of those potpies."

"Okay," Virgil said. "Skinner and Holland at ten."

"What about Button and Good?" Jenkins asked.

Virgil asked, "What if we cut them loose?"

Jenkins nodded. "That's what I'd do. I mean, we could do a mountain of paperwork to get them on a bullshit charge, but they did give us something interesting. I think we at least broke even."

"Scare them and let them go," Virgil said.

They were on the move at 8:30 the next morning. Virgil called the BCA computer specialist and gave him Margery Osborne's name and Florida phone number and asked him to find out what he could about the house.

They stopped at a Subway on the way to the hospital to pick up a sandwich for Shrake, who they found in a much-mellowed mood—possibly because one of the nurses had a mouth that matched his and because she'd given him a back scratch and early-morning lotion rub. And, of course, because Jenkins had smuggled in the foot-long Italian BMT.

"Wish I'd been there," Shrake said about the chase the night before, as he gnawed through the sandwich. "I got a feeling we turned a corner. Has that feel."

"There is the bow hunter problem," Virgil said. "I believed Osborne when he said he didn't have a bow."

"If he's a psycho—and he'd have to be a psycho to kill his mom—he's probably an excellent liar," Jenkins said.

"Sure, but . . . would he lie if everybody in the neighborhood knew he used a bow and we were sure to find out?"

"Dunno, but my gut says we're onto something, and my gut doesn't lie," Shrake said.

"There was that time with that Rudolph chick," Jenkins suggested.

"That's because my dick overruled my gut, but my gut was telling me the truth," Shrake said. "What can I tell you?"

"Don't want to hear about it," Virgil said.

"Yeah, like you haven't been there," Shrake said. And, "Damn, that was a tasty sandwich."

Virgil and Jenkins got a pancake and link sausage breakfast and drove back to Wheatfield for the 10 o'clock meeting. Holland had talked to his banker girlfriend, who'd come through with details from the title agency.

"They sold the farm ten years ago," Holland said. "They got a million two hundred and eighty thousand for it. Nice piece of property, I guess. A hundred and eighty acres, good land, but not enough to be really economically feasible. It was right at the time when the speculators were buying up farmland, so they did all right. Sara doesn't think there was much if anything in the way of taxes, so after the real estate commission and some other deductions, she thinks they walked away with around a million-two."

"Whoa! Did she know anything about the Florida house?" Jenkins asked.

"She didn't know anything about that, but she took a peek at Margery's local bank accounts, and there was a little more than six thousand in them."

Virgil said to Jenkins, "Get on the phone, call Dave at the AG's office, get a subpoena for her bank records. I'll want to look at them this afternoon."

"Can do," Jenkins said, and he went out to the back alley to make the call.

While he was doing that, Virgil called the computer specialist at BCA headquarters, who said he was about to call him back. "I have an address for you, and I also found an old listing for the house. The former owner was asking $680,000 for it back when the real estate market was still falling apart, and Osborne did better than that. I called the listing dealer and asked what she thought it'd be worth now, and she said maybe a million. I had her look up her records on it, and she said Osborne's end of the deal was handled by a local lawyer named John Ryan. I've got a number for him, if you want it."

Virgil called Ryan, who not only remembered Osborne but said he was still her Florida attorney, although he hadn't heard that she'd been killed.

"That's awful—she was a nice lady. She was thinking about selling out here and moving back to Minnesota because of that miracle up there . . . She said it was a miracle, the Virgin Mary showing up at her church."

"She hadn't listed the house?"

"Not yet. Listen, I think you should talk to a banker down here. He's at Lost Coast State Bank, name is Bob Morgan. Margery was planning to use some of the house sale money to set up a charitable trust for that church."

Virgil thought, Uh-oh, and said, "Bob Morgan . . . You got a number?"

Morgan had gone to lunch, but Virgil wheedled the number of his personal cell phone from his secretary and caught him halfway through a bacon and sausage quiche.

"Margery has an investment account with us, not huge, but not insignificant, either. When she came down here, she spent half her money on her house, put the other half in the market, and lived on her Social Security. The stock market's gone wild since then, and the housing market's come back strong. I'd need a subpoena to give you the exact details of her accounts, but I can tell you that she was working on a plan that would move most of her appreciated assets to the church, which would mean that she could give them a bundle. Then she could sell her house and move back to Minnesota, where she could live free, and use the proceeds to get her through her old age, should she need nursing care later in life . . ."

There was more of that, but the bottom line, Virgil thought, was that if Margery did need late-life nursing care, there wouldn't be much left for Barry.

"If I supposed, just as a . . . conjecture, that she put half of the farm money into her house and half into her investments, the investments would have appreciated at least as much as the house, wouldn't they?" he asked Morgan.

Morgan said, "Speaking purely hypothetically, if someone had done that, actually, the investments would have outpaced the appreciation of her house."

"Thank you."

"Tell her son to get in touch—we have a lot to talk about," Morgan said.

Jenkins had come back in, and said, "Dave's gonna get the subpoena down to us . . . What's the deal with Florida?"

"If I understood everything the banker guy was hinting at, Margery was probably worth two million bucks, maybe more, and was about to give a big chunk to the church. And if she had a difficult late life, Barry could have been left with almost nothing."

"There you go," Jenkins said. "Let's jack him up."

"I dunno," Virgil said. "He still seems like a weak possibility."

"Better than no possibility," Jenkins said.

Virgil couldn't argue with that, so they drove over to Osborne's house. The rug-cleaning truck was gone, and there was no answer when Virgil knocked. "Call him," Jenkins said.

"I'd rather jump him face-to-face," Virgil said. "Why don't we . . . Wait, here he comes."

The Steam Punk van turned the corner, slowed when the driver saw Virgil, then pulled into the driveway. Osborne got out, carrying a grocery sack, and asked, "What's up?"

"We need to talk," Virgil said. "Can we go inside?"

"Sure. If it won't take too long. I've got an appointment to make arrangements for Mom. I've got to buy a coffin. Can you believe that?" His voice pitched up; stress leading to a crying jag. "The medical examiner is done. God knows what they did to her. I don't want to know . . ."

"It's tough," Virgil said, as they walked to the door. "I've seen enough of it to know. We can't tell you anything but that we're sorry."

Osborne unlocked the door, led them inside, put a couple of packages in the freezer section above the refrigerator, opened the main compartment and got a bottle of Dasani water, and offered bottles to Virgil and Jenkins. They both accepted because it established a friendlier mood, even only a fake one. In the living room, they all sat, and Virgil said, "I talked to some people in Florida today, and they said that you'd be inheriting from your mother."

Osborne nodded. "Yeah, probably, although I think she gave some money to the church."

"She was going to give money to the church? Do you have any idea how much?"

Osborne shook his head. "No, not exactly. I don't think she was planning to give them all of it . . . I'd get something."

Virgil and Jenkins glanced at each other: the interview wasn't going exactly as they'd foreseen. "So . . . did that bother you? That a good bit of it was going to the church?"

"No, not especially. I don't worry much about money—what's

gonna happen is gonna happen," Osborne said. "I miss Mom, though. That didn't have to happen. The guy who killed her . . . If I knew who it was, I'd think about killing him myself."

"Not what you usually want to tell a couple of cops," Jenkins said. "Now if he gets run over by a car, people are going to be looking at your front bumper."

"Okay, so I'll back over him," Osborne said.

Virgil said, "Listen, Barry, the reason we're asking is, we're looking for a motive. You could get a couple of million, from what we hear. That's a motive."

"C'mon," Osborne said. "How many people do you know who'd kill their mom for money?"

"A few," Virgil said.

"But it's rare, I bet."

"But it happens," Virgil said.

"You know where I was for some of those shootings," Osborne said. "I couldn't have done it, you know that."

"You wouldn't necessarily have pulled the trigger yourself," Jenkins said.

Osborne rolled his eyes. "Of course not. I could have hired the Wheatfield hit man to do the job for me. Then I wouldn't even have had to watch a bullet blow her heart out."

"Barry . . ." Virgil began. He stopped, and took another direction. "Let me run out to the truck for a minute. I'll be back."

He was back in a minute, bringing the fingerprint kit with him. "This will probably clear you for good," he told Osborne. "You might have heard that we got a print off a cartridge shell. We might normally need a warrant, but if you're innocent . . ."

"Everybody in town heard," Osborne said. "I'm innocent. Bring it on."

After that comment, they didn't have to, but Virgil printed him anyway, rolling all ten of Osborne's fingers on a blank white piece of dress shirt cardboard. He compared Osborne's prints to one of his own, taken from the cartridge Virgil had gotten from Martin, the gunsmith. After inspecting the prints, he said to Jenkins, "Nothing here."

"Worth a look, though," Jenkins said.

Osborne: "So I'm clear?"

"At this point," Virgil said.

They tried jerking him around for a while longer but he didn't jerk easily because, Virgil thought, he was innocent. Back on the sidewalk, Jenkins said, "What was that whole fingerprint thing about?"

"As far as the killer knows, we're still printing people. The print's still out there. If Osborne spreads the word around, maybe the killer will come back."

"Real fuckin' smart," Jenkins said. "Next time, he'll shoot you in the fuckin' head."

"You got any better ideas?" Virgil snapped.

"Yeah, I do. What we've got is a wonderful, classic, free-floating motive: two million bucks. That apparently didn't inspire anybody to kill her? I don't believe it. It's involved, somehow," Jenkins said. "We got that subpoena; let's go look at her bank accounts. See if there's something we haven't thought of. Maybe somebody else wanted to get money out of her."

"That's a possibility," Virgil said. "I wonder if there's anything in Florida? If maybe she committed to something down there that wasn't going to happen . . . But, nah. That's weak. How's a Florida guy gonna fit in up here? With a gun? How would he know about Andorra?"

"It's weak, but it's something," Jenkins said. "We need to think about Florida and go look at her accounts."

When Virgil and Jenkins had gone, Osborne went upstairs to his bathroom and took a shower, to get the rug-cleaning odor out of his hair, changed out of his Steam Punk coveralls into jeans and a flannel shirt, went down to the kitchen and took one of the Skinner & Holland potpie boxes out of the freezer. He'd removed the pie from the box and was reading the cooking instructions when he heard a knock at the back door. He wasn't expecting anyone, and when he looked out, found his backyard neighbor, Davy Apel, on the steps.

He opened the door, said, "Hey, Davy."

Apel asked, "How are things? You okay?"

"All things considering. Come on in. You want a chicken potpie?"

"No, I ate fifteen minutes ago," Apel said. He sat in a kitchen chair. "I was driving back home from the store when I saw that Flowers's car parked out front of your place. I thought maybe he had some news."

"Not really. They thought I had a motive for the shootings. You know, inheriting from Mom. I told them they were crazy, thinking that I'd kill Mom for . . . financial reasons. I guess they believed me. Then they fingerprinted me 'cause of that thing with the cartridge case they found at Larry Van Den Berg's."

"So at least they know you're innocent," Apel said.

"I guess. Kind of a kick in the butt, though. I was up in St. Paul, signing papers at the medical examiner's to get the arrangements started on Mom . . ." Osborne went back to the potpie, stuck it in the microwave, and took a chair across from Apel.

"So bizarre," Apel said. "I was talking to her last week. I can't believe she's gone."

A tear trickled down Osborne's cheek. "I can't, either . . . Somehow, you think your mom is going to last forever, even if you know she won't. One thing about it, I guess, is I'll be able to pay you the money back."

Then his eyes closed down a fraction of an inch and cut sideways to Apel.

Apel said, "I guess you'll have the service at the church, huh?"

"Yeah, I already talked to Father Brice about it . . . So how have you been, Davy? How's business been?"

"Fine. It's been fine. I've been working that new hog factory down in Iowa, the one that's got everybody pissed. And Ann's got an overdue ditching job that'll keep her busy for two more weeks. So it's been good." Apel stood up, and said, "You know, all this talk reminds me of something. About Marge. I gotta go get something. I'll be right back."

"What is it?"

"A surprise," Apel said.

Apel walked through the gate in the fence between his house and Osborne's, went down the basement and took the .223 out from behind the workbench, carefully pulled a cartridge out of the magazine, washed it with soap and water. He dried it with a paper towel, used the towel to press it back into the magazine, and jacked it into the chamber.

He hesitated to do this, but he'd seen something in Osborne's face: Osborne had realized that Apel had a motive. And if Flowers was asking about Osborne's finances, then, sooner or later, he'd find out about the Mad Hatter Brew Pub and what had happened with that.

He'd learn that Apel held a two-hundred-thousand-dollar note from Osborne that wouldn't get paid if Margery had been so goddamn dumb as to leave her money to the church. Barry would never make enough with his rug-cleaning business to pay it; the money had to come from Margery.

Eventually, when Margery's estate was settled, and then Barry's estate was settled, he'd have to submit the note to the executor to get paid. All the legal work, with the two deaths, and two separate estates, could take a year, according to what he'd read on the internet. Even if Flowers found out about the debt, a year from now all the details of the killings, all the weapons used, all the momentum, all the witness memories, would be obscured or gone. Flowers, if he found out about the note, might suspect, but he'd never convict.

He slung the rifle over his shoulder and pulled on a raincoat to cover it.

Two minutes later, he'd recrossed the two yards and walked up Osborne's back steps, called, "It's me again."

Osborne said, "Come on in."

When Apel got inside, he found Osborne bent over a plate, his back to the door. No point in waiting; no point in talking about it.

He pushed the door shut, lifted the rifle, pointed it at the middle of Osborne's back, two feet away.

BANG!

Loud, but not deafening. Osborne jerked upright, pushed one hand on the table, then toppled over, facedown, into his lunch. The steaming hot potpie, Apel thought, would definitely leave a mark.

He could see no blood, nothing but a dimple in the back of Osborne's shirt.

A minute later, he was out the door, back across the yard. Time to do nothing at all, he thought. Time to be a good citizen who knows nothing about nothing.

If it weren't for that damned fingerprint, he'd be all clear. He could ditch the rifle, and that would be the end of it. He wasn't convinced that there was a fingerprint, though the fact that Flowers had printed Osborne was evidence of something.

One thing: the rifle had to go, and soon. Everything else could be finessed, but not that.

23

Virgil and Jenkins spent an hour at the Blue Earth bank. The bank president came out to talk with them about Margery Osborne: "Most of her money was in Florida. I don't know why—I guess they sweet-talk a little better than we do. Anyway, most years, we'd get two checks to cover her local expenses. She'd draw each one down to nothing before we'd get the next one. Right now"—he looked at a piece of paper he'd brought out with him—"she has $6,142.74 in her account. Or had."

But that year a third check had come in, for twenty-five thousand dollars, he said. All of that had gone almost immediately to St. Anne's, handled through the Diocese of Winona-Rochester.

"So she was already donating large chunks to the church," Virgil said.

"Yep. I talked to her about it, and there was more to come. I'm not Catholic myself, but I have to say I was impressed by her charity and devotion. Her whole face lit up when she talked about the church and the Virgin."

Other than the big check to the church, there wasn't much

interesting about her account—they looked for names going back three years, and while Osborne had made small donations to several local charities, the largest check was for a hundred and twenty-five dollars for a Coats for Kids charity.

"She wasn't exactly throwing it down ratholes," Jenkins said, as they walked across the parking lot back to Virgil's Tahoe. "I don't see anybody hustling her. Not here anyway. Probably oughta get her Florida checks, too."

"The shooter's local," Virgil said.

"Yeah . . . I know . . . You wanna go see Shrake?"

"You go. I'll drop you at your car . . . I'm going to walk around and talk to people," Virgil said.

"Don't get shot in the head."

On the way back to Wheatfield, they took a call from Holland on the Tahoe's speaker: "Did you arrest Osborne?"

"No . . . we talked to him. I think he's okay. Why?"

"I was wondering. I got a call from Jacoby and Sons . . ."

"Who's that?"

"The funeral home in Fairmont. He had an appointment to pick out a casket and didn't show up. They can't get in touch with him. Doesn't answer his phone. I know Don Lee Jacoby, and he thought maybe I'd seen him. I thought maybe you had."

"Not since this morning," Virgil said.

"With everything that's happened . . ."

Holland rang off, and they drove along for a while, then Virgil said, "Goddamnit."

"That's what I was thinking," Jenkins said. "Hit the lights."

They drove the rest of the way to Wheatfield at thirty miles an hour over the speed limit, pulled up outside Osborne's house, and saw the Steam Punk van in the driveway. "He parked a little crooked this morning," Jenkins said. "Still crooked. He hasn't been out of the house."

They went to the back door—the one Osborne used—and knocked, then pounded on it. Jenkins tried the knob, but the door was locked.

They could hear a lawn mower going in the yard and they went that way, around the house; but it wasn't Osborne, it was the man in the house behind Osborne's. He didn't see them coming. He was wearing headphones and riding away from them, and Virgil had to shout "Hey!" four times before he paused and looked around and saw them at the hedge separating the yards.

Virgil waved to him over, and he killed the noisy engine and walked over, pulling off the headphones. "What can I do for you?"

"Have you seen Barry in the last couple of hours?"

"No. I was working this morning. I got home a half hour ago and started mowing, but I haven't seen him since I got here. Something wrong?"

"He's missed an appointment," Virgil said.

The man shrugged. "He's been distracted ever since his mother got killed. Not his normal self at all."

Jenkins: "You don't think he'd hurt himself?"

"Jeez . . . I don't know. But, I know Lou Simpson has a key to his house. She lives there . . ." He pointed at the house to the left of Osborne's. "She checks the place when he's out of town . . . You know, makes sure the heat's still on and so on. She could probably let you in."

Virgil said, "Thanks, Mr. . . ."

"Apel." He reached out, and they shook hands. "Davy Apel. We almost met—I was the one who yelled at you when you were chasing that guy through the backyards. I was the guy on the porch in the white undershorts."

"Oh, yeah. Thanks for the help."

"Too bad you didn't catch him. Looked like a big guy to me, and he was really moving."

They walked over to the Simpson house. Simpson was another old lady, heavily stocked. with red tabby cats that curled around her ankles and meowed at Virgil. "I haven't seen him today. I was more friendly with his mother than with Barry, but we're still friends."

"We're worried," Virgil said. He explained about the casket, and the old woman frowned. "Well, that's not Barry. He's been very sad, but he wouldn't miss that appointment unless . . . I hope he hasn't hurt himself. Let me get the key."

She let them in Osborne's. Virgil took a step inside, opened a door to the kitchen, turned to her, and said, "You'll have to go back out."

Jenkins knew what he was talking about, took the old lady's arm, and backed her down the stoop. "You can help. Could you go back to your house and call the sheriff and tell him we need some deputies here immediately?"

"I can." She knew what was happening and hustled back to her house to make the call. Virgil was already on his cell phone to Zimmer: "Barry Osborne's been killed. At his house. A woman named Lou Simpson's going to call nine-one-one in a minute and ask you to send some deputies. She let us in Osborne's house, and we're getting her out of the way, but we do need some deputies over here."

"I'll get them moving," Zimmer said. "I'll be there as soon as I can."

Virgil hung up and looked down at the body slumped in the chair. He could see a hole in Osborne's back surrounded by a spot of blood the size of a large strawberry.

Jenkins had moved around Virgil to look at Osborne from the side, and said, "You're not going to believe this. He's facedown in a potpie."

"Ah, for Christ's sakes." Virgil moved to Osborne's side to look. He hadn't slipped off the chair, because his chest and head were resting on the tabletop. "He knew the guy who killed him. The guy came through two doors, and Barry must have heard him, but he didn't even turn around to see who it was. They must've been talking."

"Maybe I should go back and talk to the lawn mower guy," Jenkins suggested.

"Do that. I'm going to stand here and look at things for a while.

Jenkins went out the door, and Virgil looked around the kitchen, staying away from the body and the puddle of blood beneath the chair. The puddle wasn't large: most of the blood would be on Osborne's lap and legs.

A chicken potpie carton sat on the countertop. Virgil checked the freezer compartment of the refrigerator and saw a second, identical potpie carton. Virgil had seen Osborne put the cartons in the freezer when they interviewed him that morning. Osborne had said he didn't have a lot of time to talk because he had an appointment to buy a coffin for his mother. He'd changed clothes; he was no longer wearing the Steam Punk coveralls he'd been wearing when they interviewed him.

That meant that after Virgil and Jenkins left him, he must've changed clothes—maybe he'd taken a shower—and then come down and heated up the potpie. That took six minutes in the microwave, and he'd eaten only a few bites of it, from what Virgil could see.

He'd probably been killed, Virgil thought, within twenty minutes of when he and Jenkins had left the house.

Had somebody seen them there?

He backed out of the scene, closed both doors, and walked back into the side yard between Osborne's and Simpson's houses. A sheriff's car pulled up in the street, and a deputy got out, someone that Virgil hadn't yet met. Virgil walked out to the street, and said, "Barry Osborne's been murdered. We need to keep the site as tight as we can. Don't let anybody near the doors. Not even other deputies."

"The sheriff's on his way," the deputy said. He was wearing a name tag that said "Logan."

"Okay. I'll be right in the neighborhood. When he gets here, tell him to find me. He shouldn't go inside."

Virgil saw Simpson peering out a window. Her back door was on the other side of the house, and Virgil gestured to her, then walked around back. Jenkins was talking to the lawn guy, who'd quit mowing but was still sitting on the machine.

Virgil knocked on Simpson's door.

"He's dead, isn't he?" she asked, as he stepped inside. The layout of her house was identical to that of Osborne's: a mudroom inside the back door, with another door leading into the kitchen.

"He was murdered," Virgil said. "Did you hear a gunshot between about eleven-thirty and noon?"

"No, nothing like that; but I had the TV on, and my hearing's not so good, so it's always turned up."

"You saw nobody in his yard, walking up to the house?"

"No, his house is on the wrong side for me to see much. I'm mostly in the kitchen, or the TV room, and they're both on this side. You could talk to Marvel Jackson across the street. She's got a better view."

He asked about the man on the lawn mower.

"Davy Apel? I don't know, he's . . ." She put her fingers to her lips.

"You started to say something else," Virgil said.

"Oh, Davy and I don't get along," she said. "I have that big maple tree out back, and the leaves used to fall on his yard. There was nothing I could do about it—leaves fall off trees, that's what they do. Anyway, he got all angry about it—every year—and used to call me up and want to know what I was going to do about it. Well, what could I do? So, back in the fall of 2007, I was gone one day, and he came into my yard and cut some limbs off the tree. That's why it's all lopsided like that . . . I called the sheriff on him, but nothing happened. Anyway, Davy and Barry were friends."

"Did Davy ever say anything that made you think he might get violent with you?"

"Oh, no, no, nothing like that. No."

Virgil walked across the street to Marvel Jackson's house and found it unoccupied. So was the house to its left, but a woman named Casey Young lived in the house to the right. She hadn't seen anyone around Osborne's house. "Why are the deputies there? Did something happen to Barry?"

Virgil said, "Yes. Somebody shot and killed him. If you could talk to your neighbors, ask them if anyone saw any activity around Osborne's house."

"You don't think . . . Maybe I should go someplace else for a while. If that killer thought I might have seen him . . ."

Jenkins was standing in the side yard, talking to two sheriff's deputies, when Virgil got back to Osborne's. He met Virgil in the front yard, and said, "The lawn mower guy . . ."

"Davy something or other . . ."

"Apel. He's kinda hinky. He says he didn't see anybody over there at the house, but I had the feeling that he knew something that he wasn't telling me. Also, he shoots a bow, but he says not very well. Doesn't own a gun, he says. I asked if you'd fingerprinted him yet, and he said not yet, but he was happy to do it, so . . . there's that. I believe it'd be worthwhile asking around about him."

Virgil nodded. "We can do that. Maybe Holland or Clay Ford would know something. I couldn't find anyone who saw any activity around Osborne's house . . . I can't think . . . Did the killer walk in? There's enough shrubbery around that he could almost make it in from the side street, but if anyone had seen him, he'd have been toast. He's gotta be local; they would have recognized him, would have known that he didn't exactly belong in those yards."

"Apel says the two houses on the end are occupied by Mexicans who work at the packing plant. There's nobody home during the day. If he's local, he might've known that. He could have come in from that side, but that would have taken some serious balls."

"We know he's got balls . . ." Virgil pushed a hand up his forehead. "I gotta tell you, I'm kinda feeling disoriented here. How could this happen? Did we set it off when we came to talk to Osborne? I wonder . . . We gotta check his cell phone, see who he talked to, see if he talked to anyone after we left. We need to know where he was this morning, too. Did he tell somebody something that triggered the killer? We gotta get on this . . ."

"Whoa! Whoa! Slow down, man. You're freakin' out," Jenkins said. "This ain't our fault, it's the killer's fault. We'll have the guy in the next day or two . . . He's gotta be plugged in tight to what's going on in town, him always being one step ahead of us."

"One step ahead of me, you mean," Virgil said.

Virgil got on his phone. Calling the crime scene crew back to town was a waste of time, but it was a part of the routine—and, after all, they had spotted the .223 shell at the Van Den Berg crime scene. That hadn't amounted to anything, except fingerprint bait, but it might have.

The sheriff showed up, took a peek at the body, shook his head, and said, "Where are you?"

"Same place we've always been. There's something going on that we don't see, Karl. The guy is taking risks, but there's a reason for it. It's not just some crazy guy. I would bet that he's finished killing because he's achieved what he set out to do, whatever that is. He'll get rid of that gun now, and that'll make it a lot harder to get him into court."

"No suspects at all?"

"Well . . . there's the guy who lived behind him: Davy . . . Apel? He's close enough to have snuck over, and he admits that he's got a bow. Says he doesn't have a gun, though . . . We have no motive."

"Maybe some kind of feud?"

"Apel does have feuds . . . but Osborne let the killer in his house, and turned his back on him at the dinner table. That doesn't sound like an enemy. That sounds like a friend."

They talked for a few more minutes, then Zimmer left. Virgil went back into the house with Jenkins, eased past the body, and the two of them spent a half hour looking for anything that might give them a hint of who the killer might be—or even a hint that Osborne was worried.

Osborne's cell phone was on the kitchen counter. It was password-protected but also had Touch ID. Jenkins said, "You once told me how you used a dead guy's finger to open up a phone. I mean, we got a dead guy. And a finger . . ."

Virgil looked at the phone, the body, and Jenkins—in that order. "Bea would have a spontaneous hysterectomy if she found out."

"I ain't telling her . . ."

"We could handle both the finger and the phone with paper towels . . ."

They did that. Because of his prior experience, Virgil began with Osborne's right index finger. Nothing happened. He tried the right thumb, and the phone opened up. He and Jenkins hovered over the "Recents" list, which had three calls that morning, and a half dozen the day before. Virgil wrote them down, then they shut off the phone and placed it back on the kitchen counter.

"What Bea doesn't know won't hurt us," Jenkins said.

In the next few minutes, they learned that Osborne had called the Fairmont funeral home twice that morning, and there was a third call, earlier, at 8 o'clock, to a rug-cleaning client out in the countryside.

"If the client was involved, he'd have killed Osborne out there and dumped the body in the weeds somewhere instead of sneaking into the house and killing him here," Virgil said.

"True. But you know what people have been saying all along? It's money. Somehow, it's money," Jenkins said. "What if it wasn't his mother's money but Barry's?"

They were in the kitchen, and they both looked at the body, facedown in a four-dollar potpie, and Virgil said, "I don't think he has any."

"But we don't know that," Jenkins said. "To look at where she lived up here, you wouldn't think his mother would, either. But she does."

"So let's go look at Barry's bank accounts," Virgil said. "I'll call for another subpoena."

An hour later, they were back at the bank in Blue Earth. The bank president, who they'd dealt with in the morning, was astonished by the turn of events and told them so. "Honest to God, what is the world coming to? I don't think there'd been a murder in Wheatfield in the last century, and now there are, what, three in a week? An entire family wiped out?"

When they got him calmed down, he sat them in front of a computer, where they could look at images for the checks Osborne had written in the last four years. "Back further than that, we'd have to go to another cloud, and that would take a while," the bank president told them.

They didn't have to do that. They found an anomaly in Osborne's accounts. On the first of September, every year for the past four, he'd written a check for $6,550 to David D. Apel.

"Every year," Virgil said. "Wonder what it is? Rent? He owns the house."

They asked the bank president for an opinion. He pulled on his lower lip for a minute, then said, "Since he's dead, you could probably check his income tax records on this, but, if I had to guess, I'd say it's a loan payment."

They asked him to start the process of getting further records from the cloud, and when he went away to do that, Virgil said to Jenkins, "Try this: it's a loan payment, and Apel needs the money—the principal. But Osborne doesn't have any money. Apel counts on getting it when Margery dies, but then he hears that the old lady is giving her money to the church. He kills Margery Osborne so that Barry will inherit. Then Barry's talking to him over the hedge, mentions that we're looking at his mother's money and trying to figure out who might benefit from her death . . ."

"And that freaks him out," said Jenkins, "and he doesn't want Barry to tell us that he owes Apel a bundle. In the meantime, that greed head Van Den Berg figures it out, because he knows more about who has what than anybody else in town. He needs money himself and tries to blackmail Apel . . ."

"Who walks over and kills him," Virgil said.

"Whew! Glad that's settled," Jenkins said. "I'm heading home; you go over and bust Apel."

"We're not there yet."

"No kiddin'. But if we're right . . . we can figure something out."

The bank president came back after a while, and said, "You can come look at the checks, if you want, but I can tell you that Barry was paying Mr. Apel exactly the same amount since September of 2009. Rent, or anything else, would have gone up since then—I bet it's a fixed interest loan."

Virgil called a researcher/hacker at the BCA, with whom he'd had a hasty romance a few years before and was still on tenuous terms with. "Sandy, do you remember when you once found a way to look at state income tax returns?"

"I remember nothing of the kind. That's would be illegal," she said.

"Listen, babe, we've had four murders now, and three people hurt bad, including Shrake. All we need to know is whether this guy is getting interest on a loan and how much . . ."

Long silence. Then, "I heard about Shrake. And I'm not your babe. Or sweetheart. Or honeybun."

"So . . . Shrake . . ."

More silence. Then, "Give me a name."

She called back a half hour later, as Virgil and Jenkins were driving back to Wheatfield. "It's an interest-only loan. I can tell that because he's paying tax on all of it, so none of it is return of principal. I looked up loan rates on the internet. In 2009, the normal interest rate was probably between four and five percent, because the big recession had started, but if it was a loan between friends, it could have been as low as three percent. At five percent, the loan would be for $130,000 or so. At three percent, it would have been more, something around $225,000."

"Thank you."

When they were off their call, Jenkins said, "Even if he kills both Margery and Barry, he still gets the money. He'll have to wait a while, but if he has a signed note, he can make a claim against the estates. That all goes on in private. If we hadn't figured this out, we might not ever hear about it."

"Yes."

"Of course, if we looked further down the line, there might be more Osborne relatives who'd inherit with Barry dead."

"That would be a stretch. Apel has the motive, he had the opportunity—at least with Barry—and we know he shoots a bow. Now we need to put together the rest of the case. We don't know if he's got alibis for any of the shootings. I want to look at what he does and where he does it."

"He's a heavy-equipment operator and contractor," Jenkins said. "I asked, when I was talking to him."

Jenkins didn't know where Apel's business was, but Virgil made a call to Holland, swore him to secrecy, and asked. "He's got an old Quonset on Second Street," Holland said.

"Is that anywhere near Bram Smit's house?"

"Well, yeah. Down a ways, but not far. Fifty or sixty yards. Not far from the Vissers', either. Look over your shoulder when you go to your room tonight and you'll see it right there, down the street."

Virgil rang off, and said to Jenkins, "We need to check his business. This looks promising."

"If he's the guy, we still need something else. Something physical. At this point, I don't see a conviction. I don't even see a search warrant. If he did it for the money, he's gone as far as he can go, he doesn't need to shoot anyone else, which means he's probably thrown the gun in a river somewhere. Or he's getting ready to."

"He still had it this morning," Virgil said. "I doubt he'd risk moving around with it when the next yard's full of cops. Maybe get rid of it tonight."

"He could have gotten rid of it right after he shot Osborne. Be a priority, I'd think," Jenkins said.

"Let's hope he didn't—that's all we can do. And don't forget that we have that .223 shell, and he still believes we have a fingerprint," Virgil said.

"He offered to let us print him . . ."

"Calling our bluff. We should check this Quonset, see if it works as the place he might have been shooting from. If it does, we need to maneuver him."

"By doing what?"

"You'll think of something," Virgil said.

Apel's Quonset was a seventy-year-old, post–Korean War two-story steel shed meant to cover heavy equipment and its associated appurtenances, and nothing else. Access was through twelve-foot, outward-swinging doors at one end of the hut.

The Quonset had a half dozen two-foot-square windows on each side, through which they could see a Bob-Cat and some attachments, an older Caterpillar excavator, and space for a couple of more pieces of equipment. A long wooden workbench on one wall held cans that they couldn't identify, along with what appeared to be spare or damaged parts, some tools, shovels, and miscellaneous operating gear.

Standing at the end of the Quonset that faced the church, Virgil said, "Guess what? You couldn't see the targets from here." They couldn't because there was a low wooden hut in the way, with signs on all three sides that said "Pet Parlor—Pet Bathing and Grooming." The signs were old, and the hut appeared to be vacant.

Jenkins stepped back from the Quonset, looked up, and asked, "How about from up there?"

Virgil stepped back and looked up. The roof of the Quonset overhung the vertical wall, under which, right at the top of the wall, was what looked like a ventilation grille. They walked back along the side of the hut, trying to see the grille through the windows, but they couldn't because of the way the windows were pushed out from the rounded sides, each under its own small gable.

They walked around to the swinging doors, which were locked with a hinge and a padlock; but there was a half-inch space between the doors, near the bottom, and when Virgil got down on his knees and looked through the crack, he could see light coming through the grille at the other end.

"What?" Jenkins asked.

Virgil stood, brushed off his knees, looked up at the Quonset's overhanging roof. "That's, what do you think, sixteen to eighteen feet up there? Something like that?"

"Probably."

"It's clear, open space inside, and I don't see any ladder."

"He could bring one . . . A construction guy's probably got to have one," Jenkins said.

"Let's go back to the scene of the shooting, see if we can see the top of the Quonset from there."

They got in the truck, drove past Bram Smit's house on the way out to Main Street, and down to the church. On the way, Virgil said, “You know what? I bet you could raise that excavator bucket up high enough that he could crawl up there.”

Jenkins said, “I bet you’re right.”

Across the street from the church, where the three victims had been shot, Virgil got out of the truck, got his Nikon and longest lens, and looked down the street toward the Quonset. It would have to be three hundred yards away, he thought; and while he couldn’t see much of the building, he could see the peak of its roof and the ventilation grille. He took a picture.

“Time to call the sheriff,” he said.

24

Zimmer was accompanied by Lucy Banning, the deputy who'd taken Larry Van Den Berg to jail. They gathered in Skinner & Holland's back room to talk about Apel. Skinner was in school, but Holland was at the store and wanted to hear about what Virgil had found. When Zimmer asked if Virgil thought it was appropriate to include a civilian in a police discussion, Virgil shrugged, and said, "Sometimes. And this is one of those times. Nobody knows more about the locals than the locals."

"And I *am* the mayor," Holland said. "By a landslide."

Virgil told them what they'd learned about Apel. All of it was suggestion, but the fact that Apel lived in what amounted to Osborne's backyard and had easy and rapid access to the house was convincing.

"Plus," Jenkins added, "when the guy shot Virgil, and Shrake was running, we almost had him cornered. But when he disappeared, he was running that way—toward his house and Osborne's."

"You know what? When I talked to Apel, he reminded me that I'd seen him standing on his porch and that he'd pointed out where the guy had run to," Virgil said. "No way he had time to change into a white T-shirt and shorts. We're talking about a couple of seconds."

Jenkins said, "Huh." And, "We'll figure that out later."

Holland thought he knew what the loan to Osborne involved. "Years ago, back when I was in college, Barry and Davy started a brew pub out on the Interstate in that old Burton Ford dealership. The rumor at the time was, Davy's wife had come into an inheritance, they put up the money, and Barry operated the place—Davy and Ann had their own business to run; they make good money running their heavy equipment."

"What I remember about it is," Zimmer said, "the brew pub went down like the *Titanic*."

"Wasn't there some kind of . . . disease that they caught out of there?" Banning asked.

"Wasn't a disease. I heard that tanks were contaminated with soap of some kind, and, at the grand opening, everybody who'd had a beer got the runs something fierce," Zimmer said. "They'd named the place the Mad Hatter, and after the grand opening, everybody started calling it the Mud Butter."

"That's not good," Jenkins said.

"It was a bad location anyway," Zimmer said. "There's nothing out there. If you go in and have three or four beers, you're automatically driving drunk when you leave. Took the highway patrol about one second to figure that out. You got to drinking at the

Mud Butter, and there was about a fifty-fifty chance the bears would be all over your ass when you left."

"That's not good," Jenkins said.

"So the place goes down, and Barry winds up getting stuck with a piece of the original investment," Virgil said. "His mother was their backstop. He'd keep paying interest on the loan, and when she finally died, he'd come into a bundle, and Apel would get the principal back."

Jenkins asked Zimmer, "You think it's enough for a warrant? You know the judges around here."

"I got a guy I can talk to," Zimmer said. "What do you want to do?"

"First we hit that Quonset hut," Virgil said, "see if there's any sign that somebody's been shooting through the vent. There's a big padlock on the door, so Apel couldn't hardly say somebody else got in there. Then, if there's anything, we go to the house and hope to hell he hasn't ditched the rifle. And we check to see if there's arrows matching the ones that hit me and Shrake."

"Goddamnit, I think we're rolling," Holland said. "Though, I gotta tell you, if you'd said Davy Apel last week, I would have said you were full of it."

"That's not good," Jenkins said. He added, "I'd be happier if you'd said he's a psychotic asshole you hadn't thought of."

"Money does weird things to people," Zimmer said. He looked at his watch. "You all go get some of those potpies. I'll make a call, get the warrant over here. Probably take an hour, if old Hartley's out on the golf course, which he probably is."

Holland said to Virgil and Jenkins, "Hartley's the judge."

"Been a bad spring for golf," Jenkins said. "The greens are always wet; you see the balls throwing off that spray, so you can't judge how hard to hit a putt. And then there are footprint indentations around the cup . . ."

Virgil jumped in before it became a conversation. "Let's get the judge going. Let's get the potpies going." And to Jenkins: "Fuck golf anyway. Stupid goddamn game, chasing a ball around a perfectly good cow pasture."

"I've lost all respect for you," Jenkins said.

"Can we get the warrant without all these histrionics?" Holland asked. Everybody looked at him, and he said, "I know, it's a big word, I apologize, but I couldn't think of anything else on the spur of the moment. So, we should stop dicking around and get the warrant. Okay?"

"There you go," Jenkins said.

Hartley, indeed, was on the golf course. The deputy drove up and down twelve fairways before he found the judge's foursome, and Hartley was so pissed off, Zimmer said, that he almost refused to consider the warrant. Reminded about the killings—and the voters—he reconsidered.

"We're good to go," Zimmer said. "Lucy's got a bolt cutter in her car, but don't we need a ladder?"

They did, for the inside of the Quonset hut. The town had one, in the municipal equipment shed, and Holland went to get it with the store's pickup truck. They then met at the Quonset, Banning used her cutters to take the padlock off, and they were in.

The hut was on the back side of the Main Street stores, so they had no audience for their entry. A tired-looking Bob-Cat sat in one corner of the hut, but the large excavator was gone. Zimmer looked around, and said, "You know what? This is one of those

Korean War surplus huts, so it's insulated. See how thick the walls are? Gotta be a foot thick. Probably full of asbestos . . . But it would sure cut down the sound of a gunshot."

"Smit's only about, what, fifty yards from here?" Virgil said, looking down the street. "Man, this looks almost too good."

Getting the ladder up was harder than expected—they couldn't figure out how the extension worked and, when they did, it turned out to be somewhat broken, but Jenkins hammered the relevant stopper in place, and Virgil climbed up to the grille. It was eighteen inches high and a foot wide, with eight rotating metal louvers that could be moved from completely open to fully closed. They now were almost closed.

Zimmer called, "What do you see?"

"We need to get our crime scene people here to look for fingerprints," Virgil called down, "because this is where the shooter was. There are . . . let me see . . . eight slats, and six of them are covered with dust and two are clean. I'm going to use a pencil to push this open . . ."

He did.

"And, yeah, I'm looking through a maple tree, but I can see right down there where everybody was shot . . . I'm coming down."

Zimmer climbed up to look, and then Banning, and they agreed that behind the grille was probably where Apel had been perched. "Probably in the excavator bucket, like you thought," Zimmer said. "You could get it adjusted just right and have the perfect sniper's nest."

"I believe we got him. Thank God for this," Holland said.

"Let's go hit the house," Jenkins said.

"We got two machines missing here," Holland said. "Davy and

Ann are likely out on jobs somewhere. There won't be anybody at the house."

"Not a problem," Virgil said. "That's even better, in some ways. We get what we need . . . We'll bust him as soon as he shows up."

Banning had another padlock, which they put on the door. "That'll tip them off when they get back," Holland said, "unless they've got a bigger job and leave the equipment overnight."

"I'll have a couple of guys look around," Zimmer said. "Somebody'll have seen them."

Apel's house was like a reverse image of Osborne's—a front door giving onto a porch, both appearing to be little used; a door halfway down the side of the house; and a back door, with a stone walkway that led to a detached garage. Virgil forced open the back door, which led into the mudroom, which was hung with winter coats. The house smelled old, from musty plaster, like most houses in Wheatfield.

Virgil and Jenkins cleared the place to make sure there was nobody inside and then headed down to the basement. The basement had an ancient wood-and-coal-burning furnace, bigger than a Volkswagen, no longer in use, with a modern, forced-air gas furnace beside it. A dozen fluorescent fixtures had been wired into the low ceiling, and when they were all on, the place was as brightly lit as a television studio.

What probably had once been a coalbin, with heavy walls made of four-by-four timbers, had been converted into an archery workspace. Apel owned seven bows, including four compounds and two recurves, all hung on wooden pegs, along with several sets of arrows and a couple of dozen miscellaneous arrows. Four different suits of camo clothing were on hooks on one wall, hanging over four different targets.

Jenkins checked the arrows, and said, "You know what? No matches."

"They got rid of them," Virgil said, peering around the basement. "Find the gun."

They couldn't find the gun, either. Zimmer brought in two more deputies, and they searched the place from top to bottom, poking into every possible nook and cranny. As they worked, neighbors stopped by to ask what was going on. They were brushed off, but Virgil thought one of them might tip Apel.

"If he shows up . . . be careful," Virgil said.

"If he shows, we need to look in his car; and, if he runs, we need to get on him right away," Jenkins said, "though I suspect he's thrown the gun in a lake since he doesn't need to kill anyone else."

"I wonder if Ann knows about this," Zimmer said. "I wonder if both of them are in on it."

"This kind of craziness . . . I kinda doubt it. But keep them separated when they show up," Virgil said.

Banning came in from the garage, covered with dust. "Nothing," she said. "I did everything but dig up the floor."

They were in the kitchen, talking about further possibilities, when a deputy stepped in the back door and called, "Apel's back. He's in the driveway; he sees us."

Virgil said, "Get on top of him. Don't give him a chance to fight." The deputy went out the door again, with Jenkins and Banning right behind him. When Virgil got outside, two deputies had

Apel pinned to the side of his truck and were patting him down. Apel spotted Virgil, and shouted, "What the hell are you doing? What is this?"

Virgil stepped around the nose of the truck, and said, "We have reason to believe that you may know about the shootings in town."

"What! Are you nuts?"

"We found the sniper's nest in your Quonset downtown," Zimmer said.

"Sniper's nest? What are you talking about? There's no sniper's nest . . ." He started struggling against the deputies. "You can't see out of the place; you can't even open the windows . . ."

"Through the grille up at the top of the building. Perfect view from up there," Jenkins said. He added, "Man, you might as well give it up. We've got you. Period."

Virgil: "We know all about your loan to Barry Osborne. We know he's paying interest only on the loan. And we know you must've been worried about getting your money back when you heard that Margery was going to give a lot of money to the church . . ."

Apel looked at the faces surrounding him, seemed to pull himself together, and asked, "You got a search warrant for my house? I see you've been all over it."

"We do," Virgil said.

"Didn't find anything, did you? You know why?" He shouted his answer into Virgil's face: "BECAUSE I DIDN'T DO IT!"

Virgil took a step back. "Does anyone else have a key to the padlock on your Quonset?"

Apel scratched behind his ear. "Well, yeah. Everybody who plows in the winter."

"How many people is that?" Virgil asked.

"Well . . . five, I guess. But we've used different guys in different winters, so there might be more keys out there . . . I never kept a close count because there's nothing in there worth stealing except our equipment, our machines, and you couldn't hardly steal those without twenty people seeing you."

Virgil said, "Are any of those guys bow hunters? Because I'm sure you heard . . ."

Apel shouted, "Hey! Hey! Why don't you ask me if I've got an alibi for the shootings?"

All the cops looked at one another, then Jenkins asked, "Well . . . do you?"

Apel pointed a finger at Virgil, and said, "Yeah, I do. You know where I was when Margery was shot? I was sitting in Danny Visser's beauty parlor, getting my hair cut. Somebody ran in and told us about it . . . Kathy Meijer . . . and we ran outside and saw you running down the street like your hair was on fire . . ."

Virgil said, "What?"

Dead silence. Then Jenkins said, "There's something going on here that we don't know about. We've got too much . . ." He looked at Apel and shook his head.

Virgil: "Goddamnit, I'm going to go talk to Danny. You all stay right here, I'll be back in one minute. If he's telling the truth, we'll know it."

"Unless he's got something going with Danny," Jenkins said.

All the locals groaned, and Banning said, "No . . . No, that's not right."

Zimmer said, "I'll tell you something that's worried me right from the start. We don't know who was in bed with Glen Andorra. We know she'd been with him right before he was killed, right? And she apparently never went back after that, because she'd have found him dead."

"We don't know that," Virgil said, "'cause we don't know exactly when Glen died. Probably ten days to two weeks ago. We don't even know there was a woman. All we know is, he had a little . . . mmm . . . semen in his underwear."

Banning said, "Yug," and, "Doesn't have to be a woman, though. There's more than one way for that to happen."

Zimmer said, "I think we're all aware of the possibilities, Lucy. We don't really have to explore them any further."

Jenkins said, "Condoms."

"We know," Zimmer said. "We know that, too."

Virgil said to Apel, "We'll keep you here for a while; I'm going to find Danny. Don't make me do this if you're lying."

Apel said, "Go . . . Go!"

Virgil went.

And because he drove, and because the Apel house was only four blocks from Visser's, it took one minute. He knocked on the beauty shop door and pushed in and found Danny Visser wrapping a woman's hair with what looked like strips of tinfoil.

She turned to look at him, and said, "Virgil?"

"Danny, this is important. Could you step outside for a minute?"

"Sure."

"Can I listen?" asked the woman with the tinfoil in her hair.

"Mmm . . . no," Virgil said.

When they were outside, with the door shut, Virgil asked, "What were you doing at the precise time that Margery Osborne was shot?"

"Why?"

"Just . . ." He made a rolling motion with his index finger: tell me.

"I was right here, cutting hair. Davy Apel was here, and Kathy Meijer had an appointment after his. She came running in and said there was another shooting. We went out in the street and looked toward the church and saw all those people on the sidewalk outside it. We saw you, too, running around the corner. I said, 'There goes Virgil, it must be bad.'"

Virgil went back to Apel's place. Two deputies in the driveway were tossing Apel's truck; everybody else was still waiting in the kitchen. Virgil went inside and looked at Jenkins, and said, "You're right. We know something's going on here, but we don't know what it is."

25

After more talk, which veered into argument and a bit of shouting, Virgil closed down the search of Apel's house, and he and Jenkins retreated to the Skinner & Holland back room to try to figure out where they had gone wrong.

Jenkins insisted that they'd done everything right. "Apel's in this. I don't care if he's got an alibi. I honestly think we've got to take a close look at the Visser chick."

"It's not only Visser—remember, there's another witness who saw him in the barbershop when Margery Osborne was shot. Besides, Danny's like Holland: too nice. Nope, she's not involved."

"Then what's next?"

"Apel says at least a half dozen other people have keys to the Quonset, and he knows at least one of them bow-hunts," Virgil said. "I guess we take a look at him."

"Gonna be a waste of time unless maybe Apel talked somebody into shooting those people," Jenkins said. "Apel's in this somewhere, with that loan, that payback. We had a solid case on him. Still solid, except for Visser."

"And the Kathy woman."

"Yeah, well . . ."

While they were raking over the possibilities, Apel was in his basement, putting his archery collection back together after the search. The cops had not been tidy. They'd not exactly thrown things on the floor, but they'd moved everything around and stacked it helter-skelter, broadheads on top of field points, compound parts on top of stickbow tools. They'd dumped a pack of bowstring peep sights, and the tiny black plastic circles were scattered all over the worktable.

He was still at it when Ann came home. The cops had moved everything in the living room, looking behind curtains, under couches, and beneath rugs, and, as he ran up the stairs, he heard her go off. "What happened! What happened? David! Where are you?"

Apel crossed the top of the stairs and saw her looking around, aghast. She'd been using one of the Bob-Cats to clean ditches for a farmer down on the Iowa line and was wearing jeans that were wet to the knee; she'd left her shoes on the back stoop and was barefoot. Apel blurted, "That fuckin' Flowers, the state cop, got a search warrant, and every cop in the county was in here . . ."

"What!"

"All kinds of weird shit is going on," Apel said. "We maybe need to get a lawyer. I'm freaked out. Freaked out!"

"We gotta talk," she said.

Davy Apel told Ann everything that Flowers had told him about the evidence, and that he'd told Flowers about getting his hair cut while Margery Osborne was getting killed. Then he asked, "What do you think about an attorney?"

"Well, they went away . . . I think it's too early for a lawyer, and it'd cost a fortune."

They talked some more, and when the conversation finally ran down, Ann said, "I'm going to take a shower, and an Aleve, and lie down and put a wet washcloth on my eyes. I didn't need this."

When she got out of the shower, they both lay on their beds and worked through it, slowly, going back and forth over the details. Finally, Apel said, "You good with this?"

"I guess so."

Apel left the house and drove downtown to Trudy's Hi-Life Consignment and went inside, where the owner was sitting in a high-backed, broken-down chair, looking at her laptop screen.

She jumped when he came in—not many people came in—he having banged the door open in his haste. She said, "Davy," and he said, "Trudy." He walked over to her, put his hands on the back of the chair, imprisoning her, put his face six inches from hers, and said, "I'm going to ask you an important question and you better tell me the truth or, honest to God, I'll stomp a major mudhole in your ass. You understand what I'm saying?"

"Davy . . ." She shrank back in the chair.

"Was Ann fuckin' Glen Andorra?"

"Davy, I'm-a . . . I'm-a . . . I'm-a . . ."

"Stop the 'I'm-a' shit. Was she fuckin' Glen?"

She tried to shrink back even farther, which was impossible, and he leaned even farther into her, and she finally muttered, "Maybe . . ."

"Maybe? Maybe? WAS SHE FUCKIN' GLEN?"

She stared at him, and then said, "I don't want . . ."

"WAS SHE?"

Trudy was pale as a winter sky now, and she said, in a voice that was barely audible, "I think so . . ."

"THINK?"

"Yes . . . Yes, she was . . . For a while . . . I'm so sorry, Davy. I didn't know your marriage was so troubled. When she told me that you were going to divorce, I could hardly believe it . . ."

"I can hardly believe it myself," Apel said, "since this is the first I've heard about it."

"That's impossible," Trudy said. "She said you haven't been sleeping together for a year."

Apel twisted away from her, rubbed his forehead. "Oh, horseshit, we're still doing it all the time."

"That's not what she . . ."

Apel: "Okay, not all the time. But a couple of times a month anyway."

"She said . . . Never mind."

"WHAT?"

"Oh, God, please don't tell her you talked to me. She's my best friend—ever," Trudy said. "She said thank God you weren't doing it anymore because she didn't think she could keep two men happy."

Apel turned away. "Then it *was* Glen. For sure."

"I think so . . . You're not going to hurt me, are you?"

He turned back, his forehead wrinkled. "Hurt you? Of course not. Who do you think you're talking to? I've known you since we were in kindergarten."

"She told me that she thought you might have found out about Glen, and she thought that maybe . . . you know . . ."

He didn't catch on for a moment, then said, "She thought I killed him?"

"That's what she hinted at."

"That witch," Apel said. He walked a couple of circles around the shop, picked up a well-worn sweater, looked at all the fuzzballs put it back, said, "Listen, you can't call her and tell her anything about me coming here, okay? No matter how good a friend you are. You know why?"

"Maybe."

"That's right," Apel said. "If you do, she might kill you. Like she might have done to Glen, who she was fuckin'. And maybe how she killed Barry and Margery and Larry Van Den Berg, and shot that cop and those other people . . ."

"Oh my God," Trudy said. "Oh, God."

Virgil, Jenkins, Skinner, and Holland were all sitting in the back room, eating chicken potpies, when Apel pushed through the curtain that separated the back from the front of the store. They all stopped eating to look at him, and he said, "I might know who the killer is."

Virgil: "Okay, who is it?"

"Let me start by saying this. All that evidence you had against me? You were right about it," Apel said. "It all points to me, but I didn't do any of it. You know where I was when Margery got shot . . . But you were right about the money. Margery Osborne probably had enough money for me to get paid off. That's the only way I'd get it back."

Holland: "So, you shot her, Davy?"

"Not me," Apel said.

A few seconds passed before the penny dropped.

Virgil: "Are you telling us your wife . . ."

"I don't know. I really don't, but . . . maybe. Maybe. I'm a little scared right now because I'm the last guy standing between her and all that money, and I believe she knows I'm thinking about her."

"But you have no proof, other than what you believe?"

"I know somebody who'll tell you that Ann was sleeping with Glen Andorra, not that there was much sleep involved." He explained about Trudy at Trudy's Hi-Life Consignment.

"Your wife bow-hunts?" Jenkins asked.

"Damn right, she does. She's good at it, too. She goes after turkeys and gets one most every year."

"All right, that's interesting," Virgil said. "You think . . . she might shoot you?"

"Well, is it possible that she killed Glen for his gun? Glen wouldn't have been crazy enough to go through with what she was planning, so she got rid of him? But I don't really know. She hasn't said anything. I didn't see any signs . . . But Ann and I haven't been in the best shape the last few years, so maybe I wouldn't see it. I don't think it'd bother her much if I went away. But—" He put his hands together, his fingers under his chin, as though he were praying, and finally said, "I don't know. I might be wrong. I might be wrong about all of it."

I'm too young to be such a sexist pig," Skinner said. To Virgil: "You kept asking me who the crazies in town might be, and all I ever thought about were male crazies. If I'd included women, I might have put Ann in there."

"She's not totally crazy," Apel said. "She can be, you know, really nice . . ."

Holland said, "Davy, if you're right, she's killed four people in cold blood and hurt three more."

Davy sat down, looked around, and asked, "You got a beer?"

Virgil ignored the request. "Do you have any idea of what she might have done with the gun?"

Apel shook his head. "She's not slow. Since the place got raided, and you didn't find anything, I'd think she got rid of it. Or, she's innocent and never had it. There's no one in line to get shot after Barry, and I think I probably caused that . . ."

He told them about his conversation with Osborne shortly before Osborne was killed. "I went back to the house and told Ann about it . . . about how Barry kind of thought I might have been involved somehow. That probably set her off. She was still home when I left to go back to work."

Virgil asked the key question: "Will you help us get her, arrest her?"

"That's why I came here to talk," Apel said. "I don't think I can trust her. If she figures out that I knew she was the killer, she might stick a knife in me. Or we'd have a hunting accident or something. She's smart, but she's rough. And, like Skinner says, maybe a little crazy. She goes out there with the excavator and holds her own with construction crews. So . . . if you can think of a way to do it, I'd help out."

Virgil looked around the room. "Well, we have the brain trust right here. Let's figure something out."

"She thinks I'm on my way to the supermarket in Fairmont, so I gotta go," Apel said. "I'll call her from there and then I'll stop here on my way back. You can tell me what I should do."

"Go, then," Virgil said. "We'll see you back here in an hour or so."

He left, with Virgil staring after him, checking out his hair. Nicely trimmed, Virgil thought. He said to the others, "Give me twenty minutes. I'll be back."

"Where're you going?"

"Up the street. Be right back."

Virgil drove up Main, took a left, and pulled into the Vissers' house. Danny and Roy were watching television, and when he knocked on the door connecting his room with the house, Roy opened it, and asked, "Trouble?"

"I need to talk to Danny about a haircut," Virgil said.

They all met in the front parlor, which was used as the beauty shop. Danielle Visser got her appointment book, tracing her finger down the list for the day that Margery Osborne was shot, and said to Virgil, "He was on for four-thirty. But he was here a few minutes early."

"How early? Exactly."

She squinted at the ceiling, thinking. "Let me see . . . I'd already finished Carol Cook and I was getting money from her. She came in for a blow-dry at three forty-five, and I would bet that I finished her up in a half hour. She was paying with a check and so she had to write it out . . . Davy probably got here at four-twenty, or maybe a couple of minutes either way. I try to time things with my male clients so they don't overlap with the women; I want them to feel like they're in a barbershop and not a beauty salon. He would have sat down in the chair at between maybe four-eighteen to four twenty-five."

"You told me that when you heard about the shooting and ran outside, you saw me turning the corner . . ."

"Yes. You know, right down there."

"Remember that, where you saw me, but don't tell anyone else," Virgil said.

Roy: "Is that a clue? That they saw you?"

"Right now, I don't have a clue," Virgil said.

Virgil went outside and peered down the street. He was looking at the back side of Apel's Quonset hut. He checked his watch, walked over to the Quonset, then back to his truck.

From there, he drove a block over to Trudy's Hi-Life Consignment. When he walked in the door, she was standing next to a pile of used blue jeans and was picking them up one at a time, folding them, and putting them on a sales table. When she saw Virgil, she said, "Oh, no . . . Oh my God . . ."

"Did you just talk to Davy Apel?" Virgil asked.

"Yes, but I can't believe . . . Ann is my best friend." She was still folding jeans, but faster now.

"And was she having an affair with Glen Andorra? She told you that?"

"Yes. When she found out Glen had been killed, I went over to her house, she was crying, she thought—well, I think she thought—that Davy might have done it."

"She thought Davy might have done it?"

Still folding, even faster now—bending over, picking up a pair of jeans, folding them, stacking them, bending over again. "She hinted at it. She said she was worried . . . I don't know."

She started to cry.

Back at Skinner & Holland, Virgil took his chair again, looked at Jenkins, and said, "Davy Apel's alibi got a flat tire."

"Yeah?"

"Yeah. When he told me he was getting his hair cut when Margery Osborne got shot, he even told me that he saw me running down the street. Remember that?"

Jenkins nodded. "Yeah."

"That's one of the reasons I bought his alibi, that detail. When I talked to Danny Visser just now, she told me that when they ran out in the street to look down toward the church after the shooting, they saw me running around a corner. I was thinking they saw me down by the church—but the corner where they saw me, that's gotta be five hundred yards from the church. Before I got there, I was looking in backyards, checking out people I saw, running around like a chicken with my head cut off. But I didn't dash right down there. That must have been ten minutes after the shooting."

Holland: "Visser's place is a two-minute walk from the Quonset hut. A *slow* two-minute walk."

Virgil nodded. "Doesn't take that long. I walked it. Slowly. A minute, or a little more."

"Takes some major balls to pull that off," Skinner said.

"Whoever's doing this has got some major balls—we already know that," Holland said. "So Apel's back in play. You guys scared him this afternoon, and he decided to throw his old lady under the bus."

"Could be," Virgil said. "On the other hand, he is the guy I saw standing on his porch when I was chasing the bow hunter." And to Jenkins: "That creates a problem. You see it?"

Jenkins said, "If it's the same one you see."

Holland: "What's the problem?"

Assuming that everything Apel said about his wife is true but he no longer has a solid alibi himself, how do we take her to trial?" Virgil asked. "Every single piece of evidence that we have against her also applies to him. No jury is going to find her guilty beyond a reasonable doubt if she testifies that he must have done it, because the evidence points in both directions. To him and to her."

"Not only that, his alibi may have a flat tire but it's not completely flat," Jenkins said. "A good defense attorney would get that time all confused: get you up the street faster, get him in the shop earlier. Nobody could say it's not possible."

"He's still taking an awful chance," Holland said.

"Maybe he saw what was about to happen—that we had all of this circumstantial evidence—and he decided to move first and to blame her," Virgil said. "I mean, the marriage is apparently on the rocks."

"Plus, she was the one sleeping with Glen," Holland said. "She's the one who'd know about Andorra's guns, and she could walk right up to him . . ."

"Try it the other way: Davy follows Ann out to Andorra's place. She goes inside. The light comes on in the bedroom window, bedsprings can be heard squeaking a half mile away, Ann drives off with a smile on her face. Apel goes over to Andorra's the next day on some pretext and kills Andorra for screwing his old lady," Jenkins said. "What's more likely—what will a jury think is more likely? That a woman cold-bloodedly killed her lover so she could steal a gun? Or that a guy killed his wife's lover out of jealousy?"

"And then he decides to take a gun and collect on the debt. Kill one person, why not two? Some dimwitted idea of making it look like a crazy person was sniping people. But it gets away from him," Skinner said. "Wow. That's a neat problem. You know what? I like it."

Holland mimed a backhand to Skinner's head. "How is this neat, in any way, shape, or form, genius?"

"Because thinking about it is neat," Skinner said. "Let me make a suggestion. We tell Davy to go home and maybe open a window a little bit so Virgil and Jenkins can sneak over there and listen in. Then, he starts an argument with Ann—accuses her of sleeping with Glen. Then, when they're screaming at each other, he accuses her of killing all those people. Like he just thought of it. Killing Glen and Margery and Barry and Larry—shooting those other people, using a bow . . . See what she says to him. Maybe she admits it, but maybe she accuses him of doing it. All without knowing you're listening."

"Is he that good an actor, do you think?" Holland asked.

Virgil said, "I don't know, but it could work. We wouldn't listen in, though, we'd put a wire on him. I got a kit in my truck. We could record the whole thing."

"What if he won't do it?" Holland asked.

"Then we go back to thinking he might be the one," Jenkins said.

They all sat, staring into space, mulling it over, for several seconds, and Skinner finally said, "Wow."

26

Virgil kicked Skinner and Holland out of the back room. "You can't be here when Apel comes back. Gotta be cops only. Gotta be totally official. If this goes to a trial, we don't want to look like amateur night at the grocery store, with a bunch of yokels wandering around."

"Yeah, we yokels," Skinner said to Holland.

"Give Virgie the finger when we leave," Holland said. "I would, but I'm a cripple, and he might beat me up."

Apel was back an hour after he left, and Virgil had the body wire on the back room table. He pointed at it—a thin, black box, two inches by two inches, and a half inch thick, with the microphone wire trailing out of one corner—and said, "We've worked this out. We want you to confront Ann. First of all, we want you to ask about Glen . . ."

Apel was wearing a loose, button-front Carhartt work shirt. They taped the box to his back, above his belt, and trailed the wire around his body and pinned the dime-sized microphone under his shirt next to a buttonhole. Virgil checked the receiver/recorder to make sure it worked, rechecked the battery, and finally rehearsed Apel on the confrontation.

"I can do it," Apel said. "This thing with Glen: I thought something might be going on, but not with him. I thought maybe she had something with one of the guys she'd met on a worksite. I knew we were coming apart . . ."

He went on for a while, and Virgil and Jenkins heard him out, then sent him on his way.

As he was going out the door, Jenkins said, "On your way home, think about Ann and Andorra gettin' it on. Think about the details of it. It'll be hard, but you ought to be majorly pissed by the time you arrive. You want to have a real head of steam when you get there . . ."

Virgil and Jenkins would set up in Jenkins's rental car, parked on the street around the corner from the Apels' house. The receiver/recorder worked best within a hundred feet of the microphone and transmitter. On the way over, Jenkins said, "You're plotting something. Is there more going on than I know about?"

"Yeah, but I'm not going to talk about it because I'm probably wrong, and then you and Shrake would make fun of me until I got something even worse on you guys."

Jenkins thought about that. "What if you're not as clever as you think you are?"

"Then, uh, we go home without solving this case."

When they left Skinner & Holland, they told Apel to wait five minutes before he followed them. Five minutes after they parked,

Apel turned into his driveway and parked in front of the garage.

"Here we go," Jenkins said.

As he walked up to the house, carrying a grocery sack, Apel said, "I hope you can hear me."

"We can," Virgil said, though Apel couldn't hear him.

They heard the door opening, and Ann Apel said, "Took you long enough. Where've you been?"

"I got a story about that. Let me put the frozen stuff away."

Refrigerator door opening, paper and plastic rustling, then Ann: "What's going on?"

After a lengthy pause, Apel asked, "How long were you fuckin' Glen? Huh? How long was that going on?"

"What! I don't know what . . ."

Apel was shouting. "I just wrung it out of Trudy. When that fuckin' Flowers was here, he said Glen was fuckin' somebody, but he didn't know who, but I figured it out. It was you. I knew something was going on . . . Were you fuckin' him and me on the same day or did you trade us off?"

Ann Apel screamed at him: "I wouldn't have been fuckin' him at all if you could still get it up . . ."

"Oh, yeah, if I could still get it up? I could get it up if you weren't colder than a frozen fish stick . . ."

They went on.

Jenkins asked, "I wonder where they heard that 'fuckin' Flowers' thing? I thought it was only us cops who said that."

"Everybody says that, even Frankie. Now, shut up and listen."

Apel: ". . . brushed your fuckin' teeth when you got home anyway. But now I'm wondering, what else was going on? Did you have to get rid of him?"

"What the fuck is that supposed to mean?"

"You shot him, bitch. I know that, and if you get real unlucky, that fuckin' Flowers knows it, too. He's gonna figure out who was there with Glen; he got some DNA stuff off the sheets . . ."

"You think I shot him? I didn't shoot him. I thought maybe you did, you asshole, but I kept my mouth shut about it . . . Hey! What do you mean, brush my teeth . . ."

Sound of glass breaking.

Guy's not bad," Jenkins said. "They're rockin' out."

I'm not the one who wanted the money from Margery," Apel shouted. "Who was the one who was always going Margery, Margery, Margery: Margery's gotta go. When's Margery going to die? What I want to know is, why'd you kill Barry? You didn't have to do that. The money was already on the way . . ."

Ann's voice stayed loud but went cold, "Davy, you gotta know I didn't kill anybody. I had no idea what happened to Glen, and it scared me. I was worried that it might be you, that I'd be next. Then when those people got shot at the church, and the word got around that it was Glen's gun, I thought it was some crazy person. I was like everybody else in town: I had no idea. And why would anyone kill Larry Van Den Berg? What did that have to do with anything? Then Margery and Barry, I thought . . . That's when I started worrying that you'd gone nuts or something. About the money. I almost moved out then."

"You thought I'd gone nuts? You knew it wasn't me who killed Margery. I told you about being in the barbershop. It couldn't have been me."

"I didn't know you were telling the truth about that," Ann shouted. "It's not like I could go and ask Danny if you had an alibi. Then people would start wondering why we were trying to set up alibis."

"You could've figured out a way."

"Why don't we talk about me for a while," Ann shouted. "You know where I was when that lady got shot, and when that man got shot. The same fuckin' place, down in Hargrove's fuckin' ditch with the Bob-Cat. Clayton Hargrove wouldn't let me off the site one fuckin' minute early, so you know I was down there until four-thirty and later . . ."

Virgil was getting discouraged. "Hasn't given him an inch."

"I'll tell you something else—if we do find something and get them to trial, and Apel tells them about the wire, the defense is going to want to hear this recording. Then we will be truly fucked."

Ann was back to screaming. "You fuck, you goddamn . . . You motherfucker . . . I don't want you here tonight. I want you out of the house and I want a divorce. I want a divorce right now. And I'm going to talk to that fuckin' Flowers about this tomorrow, we gotta lot of shit to get straight."

More shouting, footsteps running up the stairs, screaming

apparently from below. And Apel: "I'm getting my underwear. I'm getting my socks . . ."

Five minutes later, he was out of the house, carrying an oversized gym bag.

"His clothes," Jenkins said. "Man, that Ann's gotta mouth on her, huh?"

They'd arranged to meet Apel at Skinner & Holland after whatever happened at his house, and he pulled up behind the store a few seconds after they got there.

"Well, that was a waste," he said, as they went inside. "That bitch wouldn't budge. You know what she did when I went out the door? Do you want to know?"

"I don't know, do I want to?" Jenkins asked, as they peeled the wire off Apel's back.

"She stuck her thumb in her mouth and sucked it," Apel said. Virgil checked: he wasn't faking the anger. "Can you believe that? That fuckin' Andorra, if he was still alive, I'd go over there and shoot him."

"Where are you going now?" Virgil asked. "We want to stay in touch."

"There's a motel I can go to, over in Albert Lea; I got a friend there who's the night manager, he'll give me a rate. But I'll tell you what, I ain't giving up that house. I ain't moving out. I'm going back after work tomorrow, I'm gonna put my bed in the office, and I'm gonna live there until the divorce. Say, can I borrow your recording for the divorce? I'm going to tell my lawyer about it. The bitch admits she was fuckin' Glen . . ."

"We'll have to let your lawyers work that out," Virgil said. "In the meantime, not a word about the wire to anyone, you understand?"

Apel felt the threat. "Yeah, yeah, don't worry."

When he was gone, Virgil ushered Jenkins out of the store. They looked after Apel's disappearing taillights and then followed him, in Jenkins's car, until he made the right turn onto the Interstate ramp toward Albert Lea.

"Follow?" Jenkins asked.

"No, back to town. To Apel's place."

"You're gonna talk to Ann tonight?"

"Why not? We know she's up."

"What do you think you'll get out of her?"

"Maybe nothing. I'm not counting on anything."

"Then why . . . ?"

"'Cause I'm going to wire her up," Virgil said.

"Say what?"

Ann Apel came to the door with a frown on her face but no sign of tears or even a flushed face. She was an attractive woman, in a fortyish, small gymnast pork 'n' beans way. When she turned on the porch light and saw who was standing there, she yanked open the door and shouted, "You ruined my marriage!"

Jenkins said, "Actually, you ruined your own marriage when you started playing house with Glen Andorra."

Virgil winced, and Apel tried to slam the door, but Jenkins got his foot in the door before it closed. He pushed it farther open, and said, "Stand back. Our search warrant is good until midnight, and I don't think I got a real good look at your undies."

All right, Virgil thought, good cop/bad cop.

Jesus, take it easy, Jenkins," Virgil said. To Apel: "I apologize for this, but we're tired. We were following your husband tonight, and we tracked him out to the Interstate. We need to talk to you."

She let them in, reluctantly, and gave the stink eye to Jenkins every time he said a word, but Virgil put her on a couch, and said, "Listen, I know this may come as a shock, but we think there's a very good chance that your husband is behind these killings in town. In some way or another. And he's behind the murder of Glen Andorra. We believe you may have had a relationship with Mr. Andorra . . ."

She began to talk after Virgil outlined the evidence they'd accumulated on the brew pub loan. "We think Mr. Apel might have been worried about the payback prospects if Mrs. Osborne gave all her money to the church . . ."

Apel told them about her own fears. That Davy had been acting odd, that he'd told her that he had an alibi for the shooting of Margery Osborne but that he had been worried Danny Visser would lie about the time he was there.

"He was acting strange enough that I started to worry myself. I woke up one night, and I could feel that he was awake. When I opened one eye, I could see in the moonlight that he was staring at me. I started to think he might hurt me."

"During the search today, I mentioned that Mr. Andorra may have had a girlfriend," Virgil said. "Is there any possibility that he knew about Mr. Andorra before I mentioned it?"

She hesitated, then said, "I used to go out to Glen's to shoot my bow. So did Davy, but we usually went separately, after work. That's how me and Glen got together. He'd laid out this 3D range along the creek, and I'd walk up the creek toward his house. I was coming back one day when Davy rolled in and he saw me coming down the creek. I told him I'd been shooting on the 3D range, and he said, 'Then how come you're on this side of the creek?'—I was on the wrong side for shooting—and I told him something. But, I don't know, he might have suspected."

"If your husband shot these people, you could be in danger yourself," Virgil said. "Somebody murdered four people in cold blood, and there's a lot of evidence against Davy. We were hoping you might help us out by wearing a wire . . . A wire is . . ."

"I know what a wire is," Apel said. "It seems like I'd be a traitor. We're still married."

"It's for your own safety," Jenkins said.

She gave him the stink eye again and turned back to Virgil. "But if he's innocent, it could help get him off the hook, right? I mean, other people do have the keys to the Quonset."

"If he's innocent, he's innocent," Virgil said. "We don't want to send an innocent man to jail."

She looked at Virgil and nibbled on her lower lip, then said, "Okay. I'll do it . . . When?"

"When do you think he'll be back?"

"I imagine sometime tomorrow. He took work clothes with him only for tomorrow, and he's too cheap to buy new."

"Then when he gets home, make an excuse to leave, call us, and we'll wire you up. It takes two minutes."

"We can meet at Trudy's Hi-Life," Apel said. "I've got a few things I want to say to Trudy anyway."

Though the afternoon was shading into evening, Virgil got on the phone to his nominal boss, Jon Duncan, at home. "I need some more support. I need another warrant and I need another guy," he said. "Get them to me, and we could finish this tomorrow."

He explained further, and Duncan said, "I'll have him down there by noon, no later than. He'll bring the warrant with him."

Virgil hung up and smiled. "All right," he said. "We're operating."

Virgil slept late the next morning, and he and Jenkins went over to Fairmont to check on Shrake and deliver another Subway. Shrake was healing, with no sign of infection, and he was anxious to get out. "They say maybe tomorrow," he said, as he munched through the BMT. "What have you guys been up to? I know you're handicapped with me being in here . . ."

"We can barely function," Virgil said.

"He's lying," Jenkins said. "We could wrap this up today. You want to know why?"

Shrake paused in his chewing, looked from Jenkins to Virgil and back to Jenkins, and said, "Because Flowers is a sneaky little shit?"

"Exactly," Jenkins said. He looked at his cell phone, and said, "Couldn't have said it better myself. It's almost noon. Let's go check on Ann."

The night before, Ann Apel told them that she'd be working all day on the farm ditch job. They'd had Zimmer's patrol deputies looking for the site, and Zimmer had called before they left for

Fairmont and told them where she was working. They drove cross-country to a hilltop a half mile away, and Virgil took a pair of binoculars up on top of the road cut and looked down at her. She was on her Bob-Cat but clearly visible.

He watched her working, then went back to the Tahoe, got on the phone, and said, "Harry?"

"Yo."

"Go."

They took the afternoon off. At Jenkins's suggestion, they drove over to Albert Lea and played nine holes at the Green Lea Golf Course; Jenkins traveled with his clubs as religiously as Virgil traveled with his boat and so had them in the trunk of his car. They had to share the clubs, Jenkins shot a 37 and Virgil shot a 51, but Virgil had insisted on an 18-stroke handicap—"A course I've never played, and playing with your clubs? And you with a two handicap? Are you kidding? I ought to get twenty-four strokes"—and won four dollars. As the winner, he had to pay for drinks, which cost him eight dollars and change, so Jenkins walked away happy.

They'd been waiting in Wheatfield for two hours when Ann Apel called. "He pulled in a minute ago," she stage-whispered. "I'm going to start a fight. I'll be down to Trudy's in ten minutes."

"See you there," Virgil said.

They waited a block from Apel's house, saw Davy Apel's car in the street, saw Ann back out of the garage. They waited a couple of more minutes to see if Davy would follow, but he didn't move, and then they drove over to Trudy's.

Ann was already inside, shouting at Trudy, who cowered behind a used-brassieres table.

Jenkins said, "All right, ladies, time out, you can have your fight later. We've got business to conduct."

"We're not done," Ann told Trudy.

As they'd done with Davy, they taped the transmitter to Ann's back, above the waist of her skirt. She was wearing a loosely woven peasant blouse that completely concealed the transmitter and the microphone.

Virgil rehearsed her, as he had Davy Apel, and said, "If you see a weapon, yell for help. If he gets physical in any way, yell for help. We want him angry, but if he goes over the top . . ."

"I know: yell for help."

"We'll be one minute away," Virgil said. "Leave the side door unlocked when you go in."

They slid into position a few seconds before Ann Apel drove into the driveway and parked outside the garage. She inserted her key in the side door's lock, opened the door, and disappeared inside. On the receiver/recorder, they heard the door close, then heard her walk up a couple of steps and shout, "I'm not talking to you!"

Davy Apel: "We gotta talk. No matter what happens between us, we're in deep trouble with Flowers. I don't think he believes us."

"I don't care. I've got my alibi, people who saw me when those people were shot—I was miles away, unlike you. You were, like, next door."

Davy Apel: "I had nothing to do with it. Nothing to do with it."

"I think you knew I had a relationship with Glen. I think you knew that . . ."

"Not until that fuckin' Flowers said something."

Jenkins laughed, said, "That fuckin' Flowers," and Virgil said, "Quiet."

"Well anyway, we're done," Ann Apel told her husband. "I don't want you in this house. You scare me."

"I'm not going anywhere," Davy Apel said. "I pushed my bed into the office, and I'm staying."

"Davy . . ."

Davy Apel went to pleading. "Listen . . . babe . . . you know I wouldn't hurt a fly. I mean, maybe a fly, but not a person. I never hurt anybody. Have I ever raised a hand to you, even when we had those bad fights? I'm a lover, honey, I'm not a fighter . . ."

That went on for a while, and finally Ann Apel said, "You can stay, but I'm NOT going to get in your bed. I'm not going to feed you, either; you can get your own goddamn food. Tomorrow, I'm going to talk to Phil and get going on the divorce."

"You fuckin' Phil now? Is that what . . ."

"Fuck you!" Ann Apel shouted. "Fuck you . . ."

Phil must be an attorney," Virgil said, as they listened to the fight escalate. Ten minutes later, Ann Apel burst out of the house, got in her car, backed into the street, and sped away.

"Skinner and Holland," Jenkins said. "If worse comes to worst, we can always get a potpie."

At Skinner & Holland, Jenkins peeled the wire off Apel's back, and she said, "I'm going to Fairmont to eat dinner. But I'm not leaving that house. I'll be back there at eight."

"I'll give you a direct phone number—you can put it on your

speed dial—in case there's a problem," Virgil said. "Maybe . . . it sounds like he's innocent. We should go look at those guys with the extra Quonset keys."

When she was gone, Jenkins said, "She has a nice ass. She could crack a walnut between those cheeks."

"You were supposed to be peeling the wire off her back," Virgil said.

"Yeah, right." Jenkins looked at the time on his cell phone. "I hate waiting."

27

They waited. Holland and Skinner came back, and, a while later, Janet Fischer turned up, her face still showing blue and yellow bruises despite heavy makeup. Again, Virgil warned them that he would have to kick them out. "When my guy gets here, it's cops only."

They got around to talking about the Marian apparitions. Virgil wondered if they could expect more of them, but Skinner shook his head.

"I've read up on them, and the Virgin usually only appears once or twice. There were several apparitions at Lourdes—sixteen or eighteen, I think—but only to one girl. There's never been anything like Wheatfield, where people actually had cell phones and actually got pictures."

"It's a miracle," Jenkins said.

"So, there probably won't be any more," Virgil said.

"Well, we hope there might be," Holland said. "You can never tell."

"Probably won't be any until the pilgrim traffic starts to thin out," Jenkins said.

Fischer said, "Hey! If you're going to think bad thoughts about the Blessed Virgin Mary, keep them to yourself, fathead. My ex-boyfriend disrespected her and he wound up dead."

"You think there's a connection?" Virgil asked.

"I hope not," Fischer said. "I hope it's something else. I hope the Virgin didn't set something off."

A few minutes after 11 o'clock, they'd been playing poker for an hour, using a box of washers for chips. Holland lost most of his washers on the first hand and started to take off his shirt, and Fischer said, "Oh, no. Oh, no way."

Skinner was the big winner and he gloated; he was becoming seriously offensive when a man knocked on the back door. Before anyone could get up, the man pulled it open and stuck his head inside.

He was tall, thin, balding, and dressed in dark gray coveralls. There was a red-bordered oval patch on the front of the coveralls, inside which was a name: "Bob."

"Hey, Harry, come on in," Virgil said. To the others, "Sorry, guys, but you'll have to go."

Holland led Skinner and Fischer out through the drapes that separated the back room from the store, but Virgil didn't hear the front door close. They were all listening from the other side of the curtain, but he didn't care as long as he could testify that nobody but himself, Jenkins, and Harry Scorese were in the room, should anybody ask.

Virgil asked Scorese, "So . . . what?"

"I put them to bed. I guess they're early to rise. Anyway, it's interesting listening," Scorese said. "We do have to get in there tomorrow and retrieve my mics."

"Bottom line?" Jenkins said.

"You got them, cold," Scorese said. "They were both involved."

"You were right," Jenkins said to Virgil.

Virgil said, "I hope you got the good stuff."

"I did," Scorese said.

He set his recorder on the table, along with a hand-sized speaker, and started pushing buttons.

Davy Apel: "What do you think?"

Ann Apel: "We're okay, any way they cut it. No way they're going to charge us, with our alibis stacked up like that. If they did charge us, they'd never convict. I'd like to move the rifle, but they could be watching. We should wait a few days."

Davy Apel: "I'm still worried about the cartridge. I can't figure out why they didn't print us. They had that warrant."

Ann Apel: "You know what I think? I think they were playing us. I don't think they've got a fingerprint. We were awful careful."

Davy Apel: "I thought about that, too. But they better not have a print, because I don't know how we'd beat that."

Here's another good one," Scorese said, looking at a digital counter on the recorder. More buttons.

Ann Apel: "How long before we can get our money?"

Davy Apel: "If Margery's will is read in Florida, I don't know how long that'll take. But I think we submit our loan papers up here—I think the money has to be passed from Margery's estate to Barry's estate, and we submit to Barry's estate. We need to get a lawyer involved, but I'm thinking six months, even a year?"

Ann Apel: "Stupid loan. I don't know what the heck we were thinking."

Davy Apel: "We were flush with the money from your mom, and it sounded like a great idea . . . lots of traffic and all. Shoulda worked."

And another," Scorese said.

Ann Apel: "I'm not sure it was necessary to kill Barry. That could be our biggest problem."

Davy Apel: "Maybe I panicked. But he was looking at me weird, and . . . I don't know . . . I think he would have said something to Flowers. If he had, then Flowers could have snuck up on us, somehow. Could have used Barry against us."

Ann Apel: "But if not for Barry, the cops would never have talked to us."

Davy Apel: "They would have, sooner or later. When they spotted the interest payments. You know what we could have done is, we could have gone to Margery, and said, 'Look, Barry owes us almost a quarter million, and we need the money. Help us out.' I think she might have. Then . . . I feel kinda bad about Glen. Not too bad, since you were fuckin' him."

Ann Apel: "I don't wanna hear—"

Davy Apel: "I'll tell you one thing. We're gonna have an amicable divorce, split fifty-fifty. I won't take a penny less. And I don't want to hear you sneaking around the house at night or you could get shot as a burglar."

Ann Apel: "Fuck you, David. You better stay away from my end of the house or you'll get the same thing that Glen did. I've still got that old Woodsman under the bed, and I'm carrying it during the day."

Davy Apel: "Well, fuck you back, bitch . . ."

One more," Scorese said.

Davy Apel: "I hope to hell you didn't touch that grille with your bare hands. Flowers said something about bringing a DNA guy down."

Ann Apel: "I had Tom Benson's old work gloves on, when I climbed up and down, and I didn't touch anything with my bare hands except the rifle. I hope you didn't—you're as clumsy as a circus clown. But, both our DNA is all over the machine, since we work with it every day. I don't think that's a problem."

There are some more bits and pieces, but those are the best ones," Scorese said. He looked pleased with himself.

It's more than enough," Jenkins said. "It sounded like they were all over the house. How many bugs did you stick in there anyway?"

"Eighteen. We could have recorded a rock 'n' roll record,"

Scorese said. "I got one in the bathroom, Ann Apel took a leak that must have gone on for five minutes."

"Can't wait to hear that one," Virgil said. And, "I'll call Zimmer."

"Take them tonight?" Jenkins asked.

"Why not," Virgil said. "They'll be tired and disoriented. We'll separate them, see if we can get them talking about who did what."

Scorese traveled in a van full of electronic equipment and didn't like to leave it where somebody might break into it. "The recordings are digital. I'll ship everything back to the office tonight and leave a thumb drive copy for you guys, and a copy of the warrant, and I'll keep the originals. If we can get this done early enough, I might pull my mics and drive back tonight."

"Don't run off the highway and kill yourself," Virgil said. "We'll need your testimony."

"From your lips to God's ears," Scorese said.

Virgil had been looking past Scorese's head, and he saw the curtain between the store and the back room twitch. To Scorese he said, "Listen, one more question. Suppose somebody made a recording of a person speaking but nobody knew whether it was an actual person speaking or another recording. Could a guy like you tell which it was? A recording or a natural voice?"

Scorese said, "Maybe. If the original voice recording was good enough and there wasn't much ambient noise between the second recorder and the first one . . . and if the acoustics were good."

"What if none of that was good? Bad acoustics, recordings done with iPhones, people screaming?"

"Not a chance," Scorese said.

Holland stuck his head through the curtain, and said, "We were out here working on inventory, but I couldn't help overhearing some of that."

"There's a surprise," Jenkins said.

"So, what are we doing?" Skinner edged through the drapes, behind Holland, and Fischer poked her head out behind Skinner.

"Who are these people?" Scorese asked.

"Store owners. All three of them. Potpie pushers," Jenkins said.

"At the very most, you're going to spectate," Virgil said to Holland, Skinner, and Fischer. "We'll get some deputies down here to help with the arrests. I don't want you around before we actually go into the house and grab them. When we've got them, you could stand out on the lawn and watch."

"How'd you figure this out?" Skinner asked.

"Jenkins kept saying the circumstantial evidence against them was too good, and he was right," Virgil said.

"Of course I was," Jenkins said.

"There was a case in California last year that failed because there were two possible suspects, both claimed to be innocent, both blamed the other guy, and the juries couldn't manage to convict either one. Once they were acquitted, they couldn't be tried again. This one felt like that. I bet they read that story when they were working this out. Anyway, if both the Apels had separate alibis and they did it, then it had to be both of them. When you look at their alibis, they never both had an alibi for the same shooting. One was always available to shoot."

"That's one of the coolest things I ever heard," Holland said. "Let's call the cops."

Zimmer was in bed but said he'd be in Wheatfield in half an hour. "Hot dog! It's about time. How many deputies do you want? I got five on the road right now."

"Five would be good," Virgil said.

The group sat around and told one another a few truths, but mostly exaggerations and lies, about other crimes they'd heard of, while waiting for Zimmer. The deputies began rolling in fifteen minutes after Virgil called the sheriff. They included Lucy Banning, who went into conference with Fischer about her injuries, and Darren Bakker, the deputy who'd been with Virgil on his visit with the Nazis. Bakker came in carrying a combat pump twelve-gauge and a box of shells and started loading up, which made Virgil and Jenkins nervous.

"This will be smooth. Smooth, uncomplicated arrests," Virgil said.

"Of course it will be," Bakker said. He jacked a shell into the chamber and clicked on the safety. To Holland: "I didn't have a chance to eat tonight; you got any of them potpies?"

So they cranked up the microwave, and when Zimmer arrived, Virgil had propped open the back door to disperse the odor of hot chicken and turkey. "You can smell that all the way down the block," Zimmer said. "Smells good."

"If I ever see another potpie, I'm gonna kill myself," Jenkins said. "Or maybe Skinner."

Virgil laid out the plan. One group of deputies, led by Jenkins, would drive over to Osborne's house and park on the street, then walk around Osborne's and spread out in the Apels' backyard "in case one of the Apels is a runner."

The other group, led by Zimmer and Virgil, would arrive in front of the Apels' house and cover the front and side lawns, while Virgil, Zimmer, and Banning would go to the front door and ring the bell and pound until they got an answer, and, if they didn't, they'd kick in the door.

"Best to have a woman with us because we're arresting a woman," Virgil said.

"And we need to have a sheriff there so he can claim credit for the arrest the next time he runs for reelection," Zimmer said.

"No shooting," Virgil said. "It's better that they get away than we get in a shoot-out. We can always pick them up later."

"They killed four people," one of the deputies said. "They hurt a cop and two more people. I don't have any sympathy for them."

Zimmer said, "Ronnie, if you shoot somebody, I'll fire your ass."

Virgil said, "Yeah, and most of the time, when somebody gets shot, it's because they think another deputy is the runner and they shoot him. Or her. We know the Apels have access to a gun, and some other weapons, and that makes me unhappy. If you see somebody with a gun or a bow, you get on your stomach and yell for help and point them out to us. Now, everybody have a flashlight that works?"

A layer of clouds had rolled through during the afternoon but had cleared out, and the sky was burning with Van Gogh stars when they loaded into their cars and headed for the Apels' house. For no other reason than the random arrangement of parking spots, Virgil's group got out first. And because they didn't have to go around a block, they arrived at the Apels' house before Jenkins's group got to Osborne's.

Ann Apel was lying on her bed with a laptop, reading a *Cosmopolitan* article about "7 Things to Know Before You Start Dating a Friend," when she heard too many cars in the street. She was still dressed but barefoot. She put the laptop down and looked out her bedroom window and saw the line of cars pulling to the side of the street.

She froze for two seconds, watching, then panicked.

"David! The cops are here, the cops are here . . ."

She grabbed her shoes and ran for the stairs.

Davy Apel was sleeping in the home office, where he'd dragged his bed. He heard Ann scream and he rolled over. He heard her scream again; this time, he sat up, still not comprehending, heard her thundering down the stairs, heard her, clearly this third time, yell, "David! David! The cops are here, a whole bunch of them. They must be coming to get us . . ."

He heard her running through the house, and as he got his feet on the floor, the back door slammed. Still confused, he pulled on his jeans and hurried through the house to the front room to look out the window at the street. As he got there, he saw Flowers, Zimmer, and a woman deputy walking up the porch steps.

Then he heard some shouting, from the yard, and Flowers ran back down the steps, leaving Zimmer and the deputy standing there.

Run, hide, or . . . what?

Running and hiding would be pointless. The cops were all over the place. If he resisted, they might shoot him—you heard about that all the time, on the TV news, and Apel made a snap decision: he didn't want to die that night. He walked to the front door, unlocked it, and looked out at Zimmer. "Karl? What's going on?"

Zimmer said, "Davy—Mr. Apel—you're under arrest. Step out here, and keep your hands where I can see them."

Apel heard more shouting from behind the house, and asked, "Under arrest? What for? And what's going on back there?"

But he thought he knew: Ann had panicked. They'd talked about what to do if the cops, looking at the accumulated circumstantial evidence, had come for them. They'd keep their mouths shut, get a lawyer.

But Ann had panicked. Was she going for the gun?

When the shouting started, Virgil ran down the porch steps and around the side of the house to the back, trailed by Bakker, with his shotgun. In the backyard, one of the deputies—Ronnie?—shouted, "The woman ran for it. She went that way."

He pointed to the house next to the Apels', which was dark.

The deputy had a pistol in his hand, and Virgil shouted, "Put the gun away," and then Jenkins ran around from the other side of the house, and called, "She must be inside the house; she didn't run past it."

Virgil ran to the front of the house and up the steps and banged on the door. No response. Skinner and Holland had arrived in Holland's pickup, and Skinner shouted, "Nobody lives there. It's empty."

The door was locked, and Virgil shouted, "Check the doors, she must be inside," and he ran back down to the side lawn.

"This one's locked," a deputy called from the back.

"Yeah, so's this one," another deputy called from the side of the house.

"Then where did she go?" Virgil asked Jenkins. "You sure she didn't get past you?"

"Positive. I saw her running across the yard and I cut around the house the other way, thinking I'd catch her, but I never saw her."

Virgil was looking at the house, and said, "I bet she went under the porch."

Jenkins looked at the porch: its floor was four feet off the ground, with a railing around it; the lattice that skirted it to the ground looked shaky, at best.

"That'd tell us why she disappeared so quick," Jenkins said. "We need more flashlights here. You got your thermonuclear?"

Virgil said, "Yeah, but . . . that could be where she stashed the rifle. Out of the house but right there, if she needed it."

Banning and Zimmer were on the street with Davy Apel, who had his hands cuffed behind him. Apel said, "I'd be careful. Ann can be violent. I wouldn't be surprised if she's the one who killed those people . . ."

"Ah, shut up," Virgil said. "Your house is wired for sound: we've heard everything you've said to each other since noon, you're toast. But if Ann's got a gun, and if she shoots somebody . . . whatever bad is going to happen to you will get a lot worse. So you better tell me: does she have a gun?"

Apel put his head down, muttering to himself, looked sideways at Banning, then looked at Virgil, and said, "Maybe. I mean, it's her gun, she said Glen Andorra gave it to her. I told her I didn't want it in the house, and I think she might have put it over there, under the porch."

"We got eight cops here. If she starts shooting, we'll kill her. You want to go over to the porch and tell her that?"

He would, Apel said. "This whole thing, start to finish, was her idea. I have alibis, man. I mean, I didn't know what she was doing until this morning . . ."

"Bull," Virgil said. "C'mon, we're gonna talk to her."

They went to the far side of the porch, and Apel pointed to a section of the lattice skirt, and said, "I noticed one time that the skirt is loose there . . ."

Virgil said, "Then talk to her."

Jenkins, Zimmer, and the deputies all had high-powered flashlights illuminating the latticework. Virgil and Apel approached from the side of the house, and Virgil said, "Stay behind the house . . . Call her."

Apel called, "Honey? Babe? You better come out of there. Flowers is saying they'll kill you if you shoot the gun that Glen gave you."

Silence. "Sweetie, come out of there. They know you're in there . . . Just say something. They won't hurt you if you come out."

Even deeper silence.

"Listen, Annie, honeybun, Flowers says they put bugs in the house and heard us talking today. It's over with. Please come out."

Nothing, not even a rat rustling under the porch.

Virgil said, "Goddamnit, let's back up." He led Apel away from the side of the house and circled around until they were behind the cop cars in the street, where he passed Apel to Zimmer, who passed Apel to Banning, and said, "Put him in your car."

Virgil looked at his watch: 12:30.

Jenkins came up. "What are we doing?"

"Need to talk to the mayor." Virgil, Jenkins, and Zimmer walked over to Holland's pickup. Skinner and Holland were standing behind it, and Virgil asked, "You know anything about the house?"

"Belongs to the county; they took it for taxes," Holland said.

"I suppose the electricity's been turned off?"

"Long ago. All the utilities are shut down," Holland said. "Some Mexican folks took a look at it, but it wasn't well maintained when the Boks lived there—they let it go to seed—so the Mexicans went somewhere else. The place is a wreck, from what I hear."

Virgil looked at his watch again, and said to Zimmer, "It starts getting light around five o'clock, the sun's up at five-thirty. Since we're pretty sure that she's either under the porch, or in the house, I think we ought to wait until daylight. Trying to the clear the house in the dark, with flashlights, is a good way to get shot, if she's inclined to shoot."

"Four and a half hours," Zimmer said. "If it keeps somebody from getting hurt, I'd say the wait is worth it. Hope she's in there."

28

They walked Davy Apel to the house twice during the night, thinking that as time passed, and Ann had more time to think, she might call it quits. She never answered him. Quite a few of the deputies thought she'd gotten past Jenkins's group and they started poking around the neighborhood.

Another deputy came out of the Apels' house with a piece of white typing paper that had been crunched into a ball and thrown in the wastebasket. He'd flattened it out and showed it to Virgil. Virgil read "I'm wearing a wire," written with something like a broad Sharpie pen.

He showed it to Apel. "Were you tipping Ann or was she tipping you?" Virgil asked.

Apel shook his head.

Later, outside the house again: "She told me once that she'd never go to prison," Apel told Virgil. "She's an outdoor girl. The idea of being locked up scares her to death."

"She should have thought longer about killing people," Virgil said.

"When I began to suspect she was doing that, I told her . . ."

"Don't even start," Virgil said. "You were in this up to your neck."

Dawn finally arrived an hour after people began asking "Is it getting lighter in the east?" which it hadn't been, but by 5 o'clock it had. A crowd of Wheatfieldians had gathered across the street, and an ambulance from Fairmont had joined the cop cars, as a precaution.

"We'll wait until the sun's up," Virgil said. "Jenkins and I will clear the place . . . and"—he looked at Bakker, who was leaning against the fender of his patrol car, the combat shotgun resting behind him—"we'll take Darren as backup."

"Ooo. Gives me a hard-on," Bakker said.

Banning: "'Bout time something did."

"Hey . . ."

At 5:45, Jenkins kicked the side door.

He, Virgil, and Bakker were armored up, Jenkins and Bakker both wearing helmets and leading the way in, Virgil trailing. They first went down to the basement, Bakker now leading the way with the muzzle of his shotgun. The basement had wall-top, dirt-grimed windows on all four sides, and they could see that one of the windows under the porch was hanging open. The basement floor was dusty and crisscrossed by woman-sized footprints, which finally went up the stairs.

It appeared that she'd gone up and down several times—"maybe when Apel was talking to her," Jenkins said. The basement was empty of anything useful. There were no lightbulbs in the sockets;

an old workbench stood against one wall, not worth salvaging; and built-in shelves had been stripped of whatever they'd been holding, except for a pile of decades-old *Tarweveld Advertisers*. A hot-water tank was tilted on one rusty, broken foot. The center-piece was a huge old coal-burning furnace, like the abandoned one in the Apels' house, its heavy metal door hanging open; to one side was a coalbin. Virgil checked the bin, thinking that Apel might have gone out its door, but it had been nailed shut.

"Gotta be upstairs," Jenkins said.

They turned toward the stairs. Virgil said, "Take it slow. Darren, if you want to lead . . . What?"

Bakker was looking at the furnace, then put a finger to his lips, and said, quietly, to Virgil, "Remember that hotfoot at the Nazis' place?"

Jenkins said, "What?"

Bakker stepped over to the pile of old newspapers, said, aloud, "If we gotta search the house, there's no point in freezing our asses off while we're doing it. Help me get some wood in the furnace."

He pointed at the ducts coming out of the ancient furnace; one of them was two feet in diameter.

Virgil said, "Yeah, you're probably right." He wrenched one of the rotting shelves off the wall and banged the side of the furnace.

Bakker took a cigarette lighter out of his pocket, muttered, "I'm probably gonna feel like an asshole," lit the newspaper, got a smoky fire going on the crumpling newsprint, stuck it in the furnace, and waved it around.

Ann Apel cried, "Don't do that."

Virgil stuck his head in the furnace. "Ann! Come out of there." She was in the largest of the ducts.

Her voice wavered. "I'm going to kill myself."

Virgil: "Don't do that. Ann, c'mon . . ."

"Go away!"

"We can't go away, Ann. Listen, you've still got all your rights to a—"

BANG!

They all jumped, and Jenkins said, "Oh, no."

There was a metallic rattling in the furnace, and a rifle stock fell partway out of the duct where Apel had been hiding. From upstairs, Zimmer shouted, "We're coming in!"

Bakker reached into the furnace, grabbed the rifle stock, and pulled it out.

Virgil was the thinnest of the cops, and he managed to crawl into the furnace up to his waist. Behind him, up the stairs, Zimmer was shouting, "What happened? What happened?"

Virgil could see one of Apel's lower legs. He grabbed her foot and pulled, and she slid slowly out of the duct and into the main chamber of the furnace. She was covered with soot and blood, and Virgil twisted her into a semifetal position, her feet toward the furnace door.

"Help me," he said to Bakker. Virgil's hands were now slick with blood, and he and Bakker eased Apel out of the furnace. She was trying to speak but failing, making an *ug-ug-ug* sound, maybe swallowing blood or bits of her tongue.

Zimmer looked over Virgil's shoulder as they lowered her to the basement floor and he turned and shouted up the stairs, "Get those ambulance guys down here. Get them. Bring a stretcher."

Jenkins was looking at Apel with an experienced eye. "Put the muzzle under her chin and pulled the trigger. Kinda fucked it up, huh?"

To Virgil's somewhat less experienced eye, it appeared that she'd managed to shoot off the end of her jaw, chunks of her lips, and the end of her tongue and the end of her nose. Blood was bubbling from her mouth. Her eyes were open and aware but dimming with shock.

Virgil shouted, "Hurry it up. Goddamnit!"

After that, it was all medical and forensics—getting Apel up the stairs, bagging the rifle, calling for the crime scene team again; the process of taking statements from the witnesses would start later in the day. Virgil and Bakker went next door to wash off Apel's blood and some of the soot, and Virgil said, "You did good, Darren. I never would have thought of that, that she might be hiding in the duct."

"My dad's an HVAC guy, I saw him rip out a lot of those old furnaces when I was young," Bakker said. "I knew you could get somebody inside one of those ducts because, when I was a kid, I made a fort out of them and I got inside myself."

Banning took Davy Apel to the lockup, and Jenkins called Shrake to tell him what had happened.

Shrake said, "Wait, she shot herself? If she shot herself, man, that doesn't count."

Virgil called his boss, who wasn't yet at work, and left a message, telling him about the arrests. When he was done with the immediate routine, the sun was starting its climb up from the horizon, still orange but now tending toward yellow-white. The old house had lilacs growing down one side, and he wandered over to give them a sniff.

The flowers' perfume was heavy, and redolent of simpler times.

Jenkins came over, and said, "You are a sneaky little shit. I gotta say, I admire that in a cop."

29

Zimmer's deputies took care of most of the paperwork, although Virgil's share took three hours the next morning.

Jenkins said, "Didn't I hear you say a couple of times—and I quote—'It's a guy, and he's a loner. There aren't two people involved'—unquote?"

"I never said anything remotely like that," Virgil said. "You gotta stop messing with the weed, Jenkins. It's a lot stronger than the stuff you smoked in school. It's ruining your memory."

"That must be it," Jenkins said.

They were crouched over laptops in the back room of Skinner & Holland when Shrake wandered in. He was eating a Zinger, and said, "Hey, guys, I hurt too much to do paperwork."

"Fuck you, then," Jenkins said.

"Where's my car?" Shrake asked.

"Back in the alley," Virgil said. "I got your keys in my Tahoe. I'll get them."

Shrake stepped toward the back door. He was wearing a beige cotton golf jacket and a pale yellow golf shirt. Virgil stepped up behind him, to follow him out, frowned, and said, "Hey, Shrake, take off your jacket."

"What?"

"Take the jacket off. Here, let me help."

Shrake shook his head, said, "Stiff," and let Virgil help him with the jacket. "What're you doing?"

Virgil pivoted him toward Jenkins, who stood up, and said, "Goddamnit."

Shrake: "What?"

"You popped a stitch or two. Or eight. You're bleeding through your shirt," Virgil said. He looked at Jenkins. "You want to take him?"

Shrake: "I'm not . . ."

Jenkins: "Yes, you are. Don't fight it; don't be a jackass. C'mon."

The two big men went out the door, and Shrake spent another two days in a Fairmont hospital bed.

Later in the summer, he told Virgil that Jenkins had been right: the scar tightened up his golf swing and took three strokes off his handicap.

The plastic surgeons at the Mayo were fascinated by Ann Apel's injuries, and she became something like a lab case. They could do a lot to help her because she hadn't totally destroyed anything on her face, though she'd injured much of it. She would always speak with a severe impediment because of the damage to her tongue, which was impossible to completely fix. The combination of missing tissue and scarring, and the lack of suitable transplant tissue, meant it would be permanently twisted and rigid.

Bone grafts repaired her jaw and made it nearly as good as new. Her lips had been ample, and after several surgeries, the bullet damage had been diminished to the point that strangers couldn't see it at all. Skin and cartilage from her ears re-formed her nose.

Not that it mattered too much. Disfiguration in a person is easily adjusted to by friends and coworkers, who become familiar with the situation. Since Apel would be in the same penitentiary until she was in her seventies, her friends and coworkers would have plenty of time to adjust.

Davy Apel was tried simultaneously with his wife. They were both convicted and got identical sentences. Their lawyers submitted bills to the Osbornes' estates and got all the money due to the Apels. Even that wasn't quite enough: their house and heavy equipment was auctioned off, and the lawyers got that, too.

The main evidence against them were the recordings picked up by Harry's bugs, but the rifle, and the threads of fabric taken off a barbed-wire fence and matched to the fabric of Davy Apel's coat, were the nails in the coffin.

The Wheatfield pilgrims came back when the church reopened, and the numbers even bumped up after the History Channel did a documentary, *The Mystery of Mary*, in which Wardell Holland, J. J. Skinner, and Wheatfield played starring roles. One shot showed Holland sitting in an office chair with a photo on the wall behind him, the platoon he commanded before he was wounded, all the members looking fit, tough, and happy. After Virgil saw the movie, he recalled searching Holland's trailer, finding not a sign of his having been in the Army. Passing through Wheatfield several months later, he asked Holland about the shot, and Holland said the movie people got it from a squad leader. "I don't do memorabilia. Too many people wound up dead. When I start feeling nostalgic, I look at my foot."

Virgil had been passing through Wheatfield, mainly to get a haircut and shoulder rub from Danielle Visser. She said she'd been involved in a tiff with Holland because she'd exposed his price gouging on "Wheatfield Talk." "He and Skinner were going over to Walmart and buying potpies for a dollar ninety-five and selling them here for four dollars each."

"So, you're, like, an investigative hairdresser?"

"Hadn't thought of it that way, but, yes, that's right," she said.

Roy Visser had been waiting in a customer's chair, reading the *Faribault County Register*, and he said, casually, "Get your tit out of his ear, Danny."

Pat, the dog, who was sitting by his feet, panted in agreement, and Visser reached down and gave him a scratch.

Margery Osborne hadn't changed her will to benefit the church, so St. Mary's got nothing from her. Barry Osborne didn't have a will. The total of Barry's estate, which included his mother's, after everything was shaken out, amounted to a little over two million dollars. The lawyers got a third of it, and the rest went to some impecunious Arkansas cousins who hadn't seen or spoken to the Osbornes in decades. For them, the money was Manna from Minnesota. They spent it all in four years and were broke again, though they still had four nice cars.

Janet Fischer met a divorced instructor in wind generator repair at the local community college. She got pregnant and married, in that order. The baby had her yellow-blond hair and blue eyes, and she and her friends all sighed in relief, as did Skinner, then a student at the University of Minnesota. Fischer made a claim for an insurance company reward for turning in the Van Den Bergs on the Lego theft. After some threatened litigation in both directions, she collected seventy-five hundred dollars of the pledged ten-thousand-dollar reward, reduced because a portion of the Legos were not recovered. Of the seventy-five hundred, a lawyer got a third. With the remaining five thousand, Fischer bought herself a new, and larger, engagement ring, and a new clarinet for her then fiancé.

Rose and Clay Ford did well in his business. He was not one for paperwork or bill collecting, but she was. Rose also pushed Ford into pistol competitions, which he hadn't been much interested in since he was primarily a rifleman. She liked handguns, though, and by cross-training each other, they came to dominate their respective divisions of the Midwestern competitions of the International Practical Shooting Confederation. Rose might even have been a tad better with the lighter calibers.

Father Brice couldn't root the last vestiges of skepticism from his heart, but the archbishop of St. Paul and Minneapolis took him aside, and said, "George, accept what is. A poor parish has been revived, a town is given new life, and coreligionists from all over North America come here to celebrate the Virgin."

"You're ordering me to believe?"

The bishop shook his head. "No, I'm asking you to relax."

As Virgil was packing up to leave Wheatfield after finishing the investigative paperwork, Skinner wandered into the back room, and asked, "You want a free Zinger?"

"No, thanks. How about you? What are you going to do? You gonna grow up and be a cop?"

"I don't think so," Skinner said. "You know what? What you do would make me feel sad. I know you're doing good, and that there's a satisfaction and a thrill involved, but it would mostly make me feel sad. I don't want to go through life feeling sad."

"You can't work in this store your whole life," Virgil said. "Man, you just can't do that."

"I won't. I'm stashing away the money, and I'll figure something out. I can't sing or play music, I can't draw or dance, I'm not interested in architecture, but I'm a good writer. I might write books."

"Not exactly the fastest road to riches," Virgil said. He looked around. "Where'd I put that Glock?"

"I think I saw it on the radiator."

"Oh, yeah." Virgil stepped across the room, picked up the pistol, and stuck it in his duffel bag. "So you have ideas for a book?"

"Not yet. My biggest problem is, ignorance," Skinner said. "I know all about this town and a little bit about women, but not nearly enough about women. Nothing about children, except from having been one. I need to go to college; I need some street time. Maybe even some Army time, like you and Holland. I need to get out in the world."

"You're a smart kid," Virgil said. "Do all of that. When I told my father that I wasn't going to be a minister of any kind, he said that I should never take cover in life, that I should stand out in the wind. Feel it. I'm trying to do that."

"Standing out in the wind," Skinner said. "I like it. I'll do that."

The next week, driving into Mankato for the much-anticipated ultrasound, Frankie said, "Listen, Virgie, I know what I've said . . . how I've been talking . . . I didn't mean it . . . but I know what I've said about having a daughter, and it sounds like that's all I want, but that's not true. If it's another boy, I think that's wonderful. You'd be a boy's greatest father. My boys think you're a great dad. Sam worships you."

"Hey, I don't care," Virgil said. "Either one is absolutely great with me. I'm so looking forward to this—it's an adventure. I'm praying that the kid's healthy, that's all. Boy, girl, I don't care."

The doc, whose name was Karel, came out to meet them. They'd both known him socially for years. He was a jolly fat man with a Czech accent, and he called them Virgie and Frankie. He took Frankie away and made Virgie sit on a couch.

Frankie was out of the lab in a half hour, looking concerned. "I could see the images of the video screen, but I've got no idea of what they were. They looked like potato salad," she said.

Virgil was instantly on guard. "There's nothing wrong?"

"I . . . don't know. He said everything was okay, but he was acting a little odd, said he wanted to look at the printouts."

Karel came out five minutes later, carrying a piece of paper.

Virgil: "Everything okay?"

Karel: "Everything is fine. Everything is coming up tulips, as we say in my country."

Frankie: "Oh, thank God." She leaned across and kissed Virgil on the lips and then turned back to Karel, and asked, "So . . . boy or girl?"

Karel smiled. "Well, folks . . . it looks like we've got one of each."

Frankie was jubilant.

She was on the phone all the way back to the house, calling everybody she knew. Sam, her youngest son, a nine-year-old, met them in the driveway, and asked, "Well, do I get another brother?"

"You get a brother and a sister," Virgil said, still stunned. "We got twins."

"Holy shit," Sam said.

Later, Virgil, Sam, and Honus the yellow dog were doing baseball fielding drills in the side yard, under the apple trees, Virgil with the bat, Sam at second, Honus in the outfield.

Virgil hit what might have been a Texas Leaguer, and the dog and the kid ran into each other going after it, tumbled into a pile, and Sam started laughing, and the dog ran around him, licking his face, and Virgil felt a surge of happiness so strong that he had to turn away.

At that moment, Frankie wandered out of the house, looking terrific in a loose hippie dress with flowers on it. She came over, stood up on tiptoe, nipped him on the ear, said, "I love you."